The Return of Panggau Warriors
The Curse of the Weaver Goddess

Oktavia Nurtjahja

ISBN-13: 978-1791354404

Cover by William Munan Albert & Clement anak Jimel

As always
For my rocks,
Keling and Sampurai

Glossary of the Iban Words

General guideline on pronouncing the Iban words found in the story:

The consonants are pronounced the same as the English consonants.
Note: the consonant 'k' at the end of a word such as 'Akik' is pronounced as glottal stop (silent sound)

The vowels, however, are pronounced consistently as the followings:

a	/ä/	like in f<u>a</u>ther, m<u>o</u>ther
e	/ə/	like in b<u>a</u>lloon, c<u>u</u>rb, k<u>e</u>bab
i	/ē/	like in p<u>ee</u>l, s<u>ea</u>m
o	/ō/	like in <u>o</u>zone
u	/ŭ/	like in m<u>oo</u>n

The diphthongs are also pronounced consistently as the followings:

au	/àu/	like c<u>ow</u>
ai	/i/	like <u>I</u>, m<u>y</u>

Akik	Grandfather
Antu	spiritual beings that disturb humans Each type of antu disturbs a different aspect of human life.
Antu gerasi /Gerasi	giants; spiritual beings that feed on human souls. They take the physical form of humans.
Antu raya	spiritual beings that have power over lightning
Apai	father; is usually used to call someone who has a child/children Apai Keling = father of Keling, with Keling being his first born
Apak	a more modern word for father
Argus	A species of pheasant birds from South East Asia
Batang Kapuas	Batang = river Kapuas = the longest river in Borneo island
Batu Besapak	Internal Twin Rock; a pair of charmed rocks that enables its bearer to call each other and transport the receiver of the call to the place of the caller
Batu Pengerabun	Invisible Rock; a charmed rock that enables its bearer to transform into any form he wishes

Bejalai	Iban rite of passage for a young male to become an adult. He is expected to travel alone to far away land to make something of himself.
Bilik	a family apartment in a longhouse
Bukit Bangkai	Bukit = Hill Bangkai = Corpse The Hill of the Corpses is one of the 7 shape-shifter longhouses
Bunsu	master of
Bunsu api	master of fire; shape-shifters who have the power to manipulate fire
Bunsu ai	master of water; shape-shifters who have the power to manipulate water
Bunsu baya	master of crocodile; shape-shifters who live their lives as crocodiles during day time and turn into humans at night time.
Bunsu tanah	master of earth; shape-shifters who have the power to manipulate earth
Bunsu kayu	master of wood; shape-shifters who have the power to manipulate wood
Fence-eats-the-crops plant	A local wisdom sayings which means those who are expected to protect you, end up to be the ones who harm you.
Gelong	one of the 7 shape-shifter longhouses; the next longhouse neighbor of Panggau Libau
Indai	mother; is usually used to call someone who has a child/children. Indai Sindun = mother of Sindun, with Sindun being the first born
Indai Tuai	aunty; an older sister of one's parent or, in general, a woman considered older than one's parent.
Inik	grandmother; is usually used to call an elderly woman
Lubok Naga	Lubok = the deepest part of the river, believed to be where all creatures unknown to humans exist, such as Naga = dragon The Dragon's Lair is one of the 7 shape-shifter longhouses.
Manang	shaman; a medicine man/woman.
Mensia	human beings
Miring	The ceremony of giving offerings to the spiritual beings of the forest
Nanga Langit	Nanga= river mouth Langit= sky The River Mouth of the Sky is one of the 7 shape-shifter longhouses.

Ngar	The ritual ceremony that start the weaving of pua kumbu
Ngayap	the act of courting a female
Nipah	A species of palm native to the coastlines and the estuarine habitats of the Indian and Pacific Oceans.
Panggau	The common area of a longhouse, next to the front doors of the longhouse. It is where the men usually gather.
Panggau Libau	the home of the Panggau warriors; one of the 7 shape-shifter longhouses; the next longhouse neighbor of Gelong
Parang nyabor	war sabre
Petara	shape-shifters who have the power to manipulate the five elements of nature: fire, water, metal, earth, and wood
Pintu Kayau	the doors of war. They are not physical doors. They represent the entry points of a territory where enemies can come and attack a settlement.
Pintu Langit	the sky door; the door in the sky that gives access from the realm of the sky to the realm of the land.
Pua kumbu	literally means 'woven blanket'. It is a traditional patterned multicolored ceremonial cotton cloth used by the Iban people in Sarawak, Malaysia.
Remaung	a spiritual creature that takes the physical form of a clouded leopard with wings.
Ruai	the common corridor of a longhouse, next to the doors of family apartment. It is where the women usually gather.
Sebayan	the underworld; the world of the dead where all departed souls reside
Sepatu/Spata	Sepatu is Malaysian word for shoes. In Iban language, the word is 'spata'.
Tanjuk	The outdoor verandah of a longhouse.
Tansang Kenyalang	Tansang = Nest Kenyalang = Hornbill The Hornbill's Nest is the longhouse of the Singalang Burong, the coordinator of the world.
Terabai	Iban war shield
Tuak	Iban traditional rice wine – made of fermented rice.
Ulu Tinting	Ulu = Interior Tinting = a narrow suspended wooden bridge Ulu Tinting is one of the 7 shape-shifter longhouses.

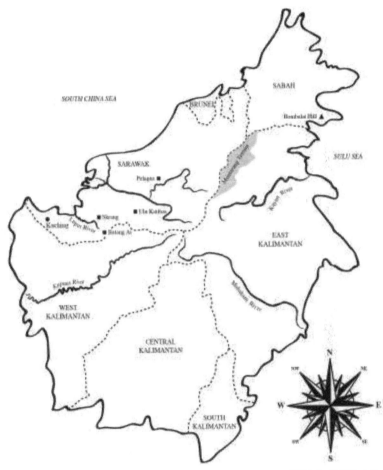

SOUTH CHINA SEA

SABAH

BRUNEI

Bondukit Hill ▲

SULU SEA

SARAWAK

Pelagus ■

■ Sibu

Ula Kubus ■

■ Kuching

Rejang River

■ Batang Ai

Kapuas River

EAST
KALIMANTAN

Mahakam River

WEST
KALIMANTAN

CENTRAL
KALIMANTAN

SOUTH
KALIMANTAN

N
NW   NE
W   E
SW   SE
S

LATITUDE   LONGITUDE
05° 00' S   110° 30' E
06° 00' N   118° 70' E

THE DEADLY CURSE

This extraordinary story began on one ordinary day inside the ancient forest of Borneo island, where hardly any man who considered himself modern entered.

Tenang daughter of Tinggi sat upright to appraise the artwork that she had just finished. She admitted that it was beyond magnificent, even if propriety dictated that she could not boast about her own accomplishment. No Master Weaver had ever created a better piece than this one. And no Master Weaver would ever produce a better piece after this. She was confident about her own prediction. Her smile was filled with pride. This called for a celebration. She nodded. It was definitely the time for a celebration.

She almost ran to the kitchen at the back of her *bilik*. She opened the door of the crooked kitchen cabinet on her left. It was filled with bottles of *tuak*. She closed it almost immediately. No, this was not the right time to drink the homemade rice wine. She deserved something better – stronger – much more satisfying. After all, this was a celebration. She opened every cabinet in her kitchen until she found an opened bottle of vodka at a dusty corner of one drawer. It was still three and a quarter full. She smiled blissfully. Her hand grabbed an empty glass from her rusty sink. Then, she went back to her artwork. She was half-dancing with happiness.

Once again her eyes inspected the *pua kumbu* she had just finished weaving. It was still attached to the backstrap loom of her weaving machine. Her name would surely go down in history for this. Smiling, she poured the vodka into the glass. It would bury that malicious woman's name deep under – so deep that nobody could find it even if someone tried to dig it up. She raised her glass in the air to salute her future fame and emptied the glass in one go. That pretentious woman would be forced to admit that she, Tenang daughter of Tinggi, was the true Master Weaver on the island. She gulped down another glass of vodka. And the husband of *the-fence-eats-the-crops* woman would drop her like a hot cake to crawl back to her, Tenang, the real love of his life. She threw the glass carelessly to the wooden floor. She did not need it anymore. The bottle could satisfy her cravings much better. Slowly but surely, she found herself kneeling in front of her artwork while she was chanting a poem of victory they always sang to their warriors for winning their wars. Giggling, she kept reminding herself not to be too loud. The artwork was a secret. Nobody was supposed to know about it for now. Her Spiritual Guide had specifically instructed her to reveal it at a specific time to a specific group of people. She giggled more when she imagined their faces when the time to see her work came. She took another gulp of vodka from the bottle and sang her heart out. By the time the last drop of vodka was transferred into her stomach, the only sound she could produce was a snore that was loud enough to shake the wooden walls of her *bilik*.

From a dark and full of cobwebs corner of Tenang's *bilik*, her Spiritual Guide watched her slip into the state of stupor with a sense of disgust. What a hopeless female! She had been born with a special gift to be a Master Weaver although she did not come from a long line of Master Weavers. For that reason and that reason only, one would expect that she would have dedicated her life to produce the best artworks the worlds – under, above, and beyond - had ever seen. And what had she done with a talent so generously bestowed upon her? She had wasted it – had completely wasted it by becoming a useless drunkard. Why? Simply because one worthless male, whom she decided to be the sole reason of her existence, had left her to marry her apprentice from the neighboring water tributary.

As if humiliating herself by clinging to his leg while he walked out of the longhouse with all his belongings was not enough, she buried her sorrow in bottles and more bottles of *tuak*. Instead of working hard with discipline to produce exquisite artworks to outshine the other woman, who in fact did not have half of her talent, she chose to spend her time losing her consciousness.

The residents of Batu Terkura longhouse erased Tenang's previous accomplishments after they had realized that her condition was not temporary. It was permanent. The status of Master Weaver that she had spent decades to build was stripped off her. Nobody wanted to call a humiliating drunkard Master Weaver when she was no longer able to work on the simplest design that a female adolescence was subjected to learn. The work of weaving a *pua*

10

kumbu was long, arduous, and meticulous. It required a lot of discipline and concentration that she no longer had.

It pained the Spiritual Guide that after decades of mentoring, what had seemed to be a promising future ended in vain. What pained her even more was that in the absence of the fallen-from-grace Master Weaver, a new Master Weaver emerged - a Master Weaver who never received a single visit from any Spiritual Guide simply because she did not have the gift to be one even though she came from a long line of Master Weavers, a Master Weaver who sold her works to the highest bidders, who handed over the sacred works to those who only knew how to defile them, who accepted personal adoration for her works instead of directing them to the higher beings her works were supposed to be dedicated to. It had gone too far until it could not be more insulting than what it had become. Therefore, the Spiritual Guide was resolute that she had to take matters into her own hands. All of them had to be punished. What was wrong had to be set right again.

On the same day the Spiritual Guide made that decision, she started contacting Tenang in her dreams. Actually she had distanced herself from Tenang ever since *tuak* became her new best friend. Unfortunately it had to be Tenang because she was the only one who had the required talent to create the complicated piece. Therefore, the Spiritual Guide took the degrading steps to restart their acquaintance. She filled Tenang's sleep with a dream, the same dream night after night. She implanted the suggestion in Tenang's subconscious mind that this was the best way to get her revenge towards the woman she hated to the core of her being. It took her a long time to penetrate Tenang's muddled mind for the barricade of alcohol was too strong. Her persistence bore the result she wanted when the message finally infiltrated Tenang's mind.

It took the Spiritual Guide even longer to wait for Tenang to have the ability to work. First, Tenang had to stop drinking for at least a year to work on this complicated piece. She failed over and over again. With patience that she did not know she had, the Spiritual Guide relentlessly reminded Tenang in her sleep about the dream she needed to weave in her *pua kumbu*. She continuously injected the message of how sweet revenge would taste – much sweeter than all the *tuak* Tenang had ever drunk combined. Until one day, Tenang found just the right amount of determination that she wanted her revenge more than she wanted her *tuak*. She set out to work.

11

Even then, the challenging process was far from over. Weaving a piece of *pua kumbu* was meant to be a community work, from the initial stage of preparing the cotton threads to absorb the natural dyes harvested from the forest to the arduous work of tying raffia strings over the white threads to protect them from absorbing the dyes. As such, Tenang had to work with the other weavers in her longhouse through these delicate stages. The biggest hurdle for her was to accept that she was no longer considered suited to lead the sacred process, being a drunkard that she was. The other weavers allowed her to participate in the process, but they made it clear to her that she was expected to be no more than a silent participant, and she had to do exactly as she was told. Their decision did not go well with Tenang's ego. She flat out refused their generous offer to begin with. Thus, more persuasion from the Spiritual Guide was needed for Tenang to swallow her pride and agree to the terms and conditions given by the other weavers. After that, she almost walked out of the rituals a few times due to injured dignity. The only thing that could be used to keep her going through the humiliation until the end was the constant reminder of how sweet revenge would be. Thankfully, like everything else in this world, the painful process finally reached its end.

The last stage of weaving allowed Tenang to work in her own *bilik*, away from the prying eyes of curious longhouse residents who wondered what kind of piece a drunkard could produce. Therefore, it was only Tenang and the Spiritual Guide, who guided her on every step of the design, as she wove - thread by thread - a story that was so horrific it would frighten even the bravest warriors of their worlds.

The Spiritual Guide chanted imprecations upon every layer of Tenang's threads so that her words blended in with the woven pattern that was slowly emerging. The moment Tenang tied the last threads to finish her artwork, a deadly curse was completely cast.

The creaking sound of a wooden door being opened brought the Spiritual Guide's attention back to the unconscious Tenang inside the *bilik*. A movement from the half-opened door caused her to step back to the corner where she became one with the dark shadow. From there she saw a young woman peep in timidly from the door.

The young woman stepped in carefully into the *bilik*. She went directly to check

12

on Tenang, who was snoring peacefully on the floor. She shook her head and bent down to pick up the empty vodka bottle. As she stood up with the bottle in her hand, she spotted Tenang's artwork on the backstrap loom. She took her time to stare at it as if she did not comprehend what she saw. Then, she looked down at Tenang. She kicked her gently with the tip of her right foot several times. When she did not get any response, she put the bottle on the floor and left the *bilik* as quietly as a mouse.

The Spiritual Guide waited patiently for what was about to transpire right in front of her. *Mensia* would not disappoint her. They were so predictable.

Her wish was granted soon. The young woman came back to the *bilik* bringing something under her shirt. She took it out and unfolded it on the floor, next to the unconscious Tenang. Her hands trembled slightly as she dismantled Tenang's artwork from the wooden backstrap loom and replaced it with a *pua kumbu* she brought from her own *bilik*. After she had completed the exchange, she looked around nervously as if she could sense that someone was watching her steal Tenang's artwork.

The Spiritual Guide whispered in the air. *Hurry up! Get on with it before someone else realizes that Tenang is drunk and comes to this bilik to 'borrow' her things as always! Don't worry, not a soul will say anything about what you've done here.*

After giving one last look at the peaceful Tenang on the floor, the young woman folded Tenang's artwork swiftly, put it under her shirt, and stealthily left the *bilik*. She did not come back afterwards.

The Spiritual Guide did not expect her to. All her painful efforts and patience were paid off. Her smile was that of serenity. Her deadly curse was spreading.

She walked closer to Tenang. *All of you will be punished*, she thought solemnly as she looked down at her apprentice. *What is wrong will be set right.*

THE RECURRING NIGHTMARES

Daniel sat up abruptly, panting for breath. As soon as he had regulated his breathing, he realized that he was bathed in cold sweat. He just had another nightmare – one that he never could recall what it was about. His eyes searched for the alarm clock beside his bed. It showed him the time was 3 a.m. He turned his head to his right where his wife was sleeping soundly.

He did not want to continue sleeping in sweat, so he got out of bed and headed to the shower. Unfortunately, the cold water only served to refresh him. It did not manage to shake off the dreadful feeling he had every time he got the recurring nightmares. It was pointless to try sleeping when he was worried about something he did not even know. The last six months had taught him that. He might as well do some work. He crossed the spacious bedroom to enter his study room. He took out a thick file from the glass cabinet on the right wall and went to sit behind the desk. In a matter of seconds, he lost himself in his work.

"Another nightmare?"

Daniel looked up from the scattered papers on his desk to see his wife leaning on the door of the study room.

"Oh, did the lights wake you? Sorry, dear." He got up to switch off the main lights on the wall next to his desk.

Matthea stopped his hand. "You need the lights. You don't want to weaken your eyesight even more, do you?" She touched the rim of his spectacles affectionately.

He smiled as he held his wife's warm hand. "Go back to sleep, Thea."

"You haven't answered my question," she reminded him gently.

"What question?"

"Did you have another nightmare? Is that why you are here working at this hour?"

He sank back to his chair.

She sat herself comfortably on his lap and locked her arms around his neck. "You really ought to see Doctor Sim."

He hated to see the worry lines on her forehead. "It's just a dream. And having a dream is normal, by the way."

"People don't have nightmare every night. That is not normal. There must be an explanation for this. And you told me you did not have dreams before."

"Certainly not like this."

"See? Let Doctor Sim have a look at you."

"What can he do? Scan my head to see what's inside? He won't see my nightmare in here." He pointed at his temple.

"Maybe you should see a psychiatrist," she continued. "The dreams could be your subconscious mind trying to tell you something."

"And what will I tell this psychiatrist? I don't even remember what my dream is about. What am I going to say?"

She bit her lip. "Would you prefer to search for an alternative treatment?" she sounded reluctant.

"You mean I should see a *manang*?" He smiled. "I thought you don't believe in this shaman thing."

She let go of him. "I don't. I just want an explanation for what is disturbing you. I want to help, but I can't. It's frustrating me."

"Hey." He pulled her closer. "It is nothing to worry about. It could be because I'm anxious about the exhibition. That is all."

She eyed him with distrust. "This is not your first exhibition. You did not have recurring nightmares before."

15

"This exhibition is different from the ones I have organized before. I am collaborating with scholars from a university who are specialized in graphic designs. They created an application on smartphones so that our visitors can use their smartphones to scan the symbols on a piece of *pua kumbu*, transform them into concrete images, and describe their meanings. It's brilliant! It's the use of technology at its best! They have finished working on the *pua kumbu* collection we have had. They want to start working on the new master piece, and they're pressuring me to hand it to them. I fully understand that they want to have enough time to work on the symbols, drawing new images, and so on. The problem is I don't have it with me. I have never seen it with my own eyes to be precise. From the way the weaver avoids my questions about the *pua kumbu*, I am beginning to think that it might not be in her possession."

"Why did you agree to give her the spotlight?"

"I've worked with her on a few occasions. She always showed me her works before the exhibition date."

"You mean you had to beg her to show you her works," she commented lightly.

"You must understand that it is against their belief to show off their works to the public. Their works are meant for private eyes only, designed for specific purposes and for specific group of people. It took me a long time to convince her that everyone deserves to enjoy the beauty of her work, that she deserves to receive the acknowledgment that is due for her talent."

"I don't understand the fuss she is making. Almost every shop in Merdeka Street sells *pua kumbu* for the tourists."

"No, the ones sold for the tourists are the commercial types. The symbols are just basic symbols, nothing more. And the patterns were printed on the textiles, not the result of weaving. The exquisite patterns, like the ones she produces, have stories to tell. Let me show you ..." Daniel moved the cluttered papers on his desk recklessly to search for something. "Ah, here is an example ... you see?" He lifted a photograph for her to see. "This one tells a story of ..."

"So why can't she show you her latest work this time around?" She cut him off. She did not even bother to look at the photograph.

"Huh?" Ah, he forgot. His wife was not interested in any of these things. "I don't know really."

"Is it a risk worth taking? What if the piece does not exist," she cautioned him. "It is your reputation at stake."

"I've seen a photo of it. Wait …where is it?" He rampaged the desk one more time to look for the photograph. "Her husband gave it to me. It is the most exquisite design I have ever seen by far. Some symbols are totally new to me. Come now….where is it?"

"I thought you know everything there is to know about Iban symbols." Her smile contained a hint of pride.

"I thought so, too. That's why I want to show you this piece. It has to be ancient symbols. There's no reference of them in any of the research compiled until now. It's like trying to solve a puzzle." He failed to hide the excitement in his voice.

"Why can't you just ask her about those symbols?"

"She refused to answer my questions, which I found odd. She showed reluctance towards showing her works to the public in the past, but she was always very helpful when it came to explaining her work to someone who came to ask her in private. Anyhow, I will get hold of the *pua kumbu* in the next couple of days. I should be able to examine the symbols more closely. But for now, I must be content with its photograph." His hands went back to the scattered papers on the desk. "Eh, why can't I find it?" He was annoyed with the missing photograph.

"It's all right. I can see it some other day." She caressed his shoulder.

He looked up to her. "You'd better continue your sleep."

Her eyes found the clock on the wall. "It's already five o'clock. I'd rather not. I must get ready for the board meeting today."

"It won't be until nine!"

"I need to go through some papers. I must get the figures right if I want to shoot Ezra's idea down. Only then, I can show Aunty Elsa how ridiculous her son's idea is. "

"Your Mother and Uncle Jo will definitely support you, won't they?"

17

"Always. But Elle always supports her brother. Aunty Elsa is the same. She always agrees with what her son says. They don't like the idea that I, a mere niece, have a say about how Uncle Chambai's business is run. Oh, why can't he come out of his coma? I miss him terribly! Now, he is a man who has excellent business sense. The rest of his family is useless. Aunty Elsa is just a house-wife. She never bothered to come to the board meeting before Uncle Chambai had his accident. Elle and Ezra are no different. They only know how to spend Uncle Chambai's hard-earned money!"

"They are his immediate family, dear. He worked so hard to build his business empire. Who else are supposed to spend his money if it is not his own family members? And that includes you, by the way."

"He can't earn money now, can he? He's been in a vegetative state for years. They shouldn't waste what he has worked so hard to collect. Proposing to open the biggest animal sanctuary in Borneo? Please!!!"

"You don't need to be so upset over an idea!"

"Yes, I do. Uncle Jo is actually willing to consider it! What rubbish is that? Animal sanctuary can't make money! That's throwing money down the drain. Uncle Jo should know better!"

"I'm sure he knows, but as you said, the company is Uncle Chambai's. It is only right to respect what his family members want in his absence. It doesn't mean he will agree in the end."

She pouted. "You always take his side."

"I like the guy, what can I say?" Before she could reply, he added quickly, "He is a decent man, Thea, you know he is."

"He is. I just wish he didn't marry Mother."

"She loves him. She wants to be with him, and she gets what she wants."

"But he doesn't love her, does he?"

"I believe he is fond of her."

"Mother deserves more! She deserves to be with a man who loves her back as much...after what my late father put her through..." She heaved heavily. "...

18

she decided to marry a man almost a decade younger! Sometimes I believe all the beatings she got from Father damaged her brain."

"The man makes her happy. Isn't that what matters the most?" He eyed her with concern. "You said he doesn't love her. So what? He gives her all the respect that she deserves. He takes good care of her. And it's not like he's looking for love in some other woman. You know he is not. He doesn't do that."

"Of course not! He's in love with a dead woman! No woman in the world of the living can measure up to his dead wife. How insulting is that! I don't understand how Mother could degrade herself so low."

"He told Mother about his first wife right from the start. She knew what she got herself into. If she can accept it and be happy, you'd better do the same. At least, learn to – for Mother's sake."

She stood abruptly.

"Thea, dear ... don't be angry ...."

She ignored him. She walked out of the study room and closed the door a little bit too forcefully.

Daniel took off his glasses to massage the bridge of his nose. His wife always ended up sulking every time they discussed the subject of her mother's marriage to her second husband. His eyes were dragged to the desk for no apparent reason. He raised one eyebrow. He quickly put on his glasses. Why couldn't he find the photograph when he wanted to show it to his wife? Now after his wife had left, it just popped up. His hand reached out to pick it up from underneath the scattered papers. He held it with both hands. It really was an exquisite design – far superior that any he had seen before. He adjusted the rim of his spectacles as he slowly scanned the pattern of the *pua kumbu* in the photograph, trying to recognize the symbols within. Without knowing what was happening, he was lost in the path of an untold story that made him have unexplainable goose bumps all over his body.

A CALL FOR HELP

Kumang of Panggau Libau stared at the calm surface of the water. No matter how hard she tried, her eyes could not penetrate its fluid shield. Therefore, the best way to find who she was looking for was to get underneath the surface. She was aware that it was unwise. However, what other option did she have?

She lifted her eyes to scan the forest lining on the river bank all the way to the distant hill on her right. She could see smokes puffing to the sky. A group of *mensia* settled there. Her mind quickly went to the memory of a meeting with a descendant of her human apprentice a few nights back. As usual, most encounters between a human being and a spiritual creature like herself happened in a dream for it was a meeting of souls.

"It is a curse. I am sure of it. The *pua* is cursed." The old woman shuddered in fear.

Kumang knew it was not the dark and void surroundings that scared her.

"Please help us," the old woman begged.

Kumang raised an eyebrow. "If you have done something wrong to someone, apologize accordingly. We have rules and regulations in place to settle it. It helps to naturalize the curse. Let your *manang* deal with the rest of it. You do not need me to interfere in the quarrels among longhouse residents."

"Our *manang* cannot help us with this. This curse was not given by one of our longhouse residents. I know better not to disturb you with petty matters."

Kumang frowned slightly. "Given by someone from another water tributary?" It could be a seed of war. Still, this old woman should not have come to her for help. As a spiritual creature – a shape-shifter to be exact - she possessed a much greater power than this frail human in front of her, but she was not the

Goddess of War.

The woman shook her head vigorously. "Given by a spiritual creature," she almost whispered in giving the information.

Kumang's frown deepened. "That is a serious accusation." She took a closer look at the old woman's soul. She wondered why she did not notice right away that the old woman's soul was withering away. Her old age could be the deceiving factor, but the soul of the woman kneeling in front of her was obviously not healthy. "What have you done to offend this spiritual creature?"

"I looked at the *pua* design." The old woman's voice shook.

"You don't get a curse by looking at a *pua kumbu*!" Kumang rejected the idea immediately.

"It is when the design is cursed."

"In other words, you are accusing one of the Spiritual Guides of the weavers purposely put a curse on a design she gave to her own apprentice?"

The old woman nodded weakly. "It must be the design. It must be. Everyone who has seen it got the curse. We've got nightmares night after night. Nightmares that we can't even remember after we wake up. We live in constant fear of the unknown. Everything frightens us. We are losing our minds." She bit her lip. "Please help us. Please! I know we are going to die!"

"What offense did you commit?" First and foremost, what was wrong had to be made right.

"I only looked at the design!" the old woman wailed. "I only looked at the design. Nothing else. I swear."

Kumang understood the implied statement. "What offense did the weaver of this *pua kumbu* commit against her own Spiritual Guide?" It had to be a grave offense for a curse to be cast. Every Spiritual Guide formed affectionate bonds with her apprentices just like she had formed the bond with this old woman's grandmother. But that was a long time ago. She had stopped having apprentices on the land for a long time. This old woman's grandmother was her last apprentice.

21

The old woman only shook her head. Kumang noticed that her hands trembled slightly.

"Who wove the *pua*? One of your rivals from across the river?" Kumang asked gently to calm the old woman's nerves.

"My grandson's wife," she mumbled.

Kumang could hardly hear her. "Who? Speak up!"

The old woman shook her head in dismay before she said in a louder but shaky voice, "My grandson's wife. She lives in my longhouse."

Kumang tilted her head. Did the weaver come from the new generation of weavers? Which Spiritual Guide still had apprentices on the land these days? Some still did, she admitted with a little envy. "Who did she offend?"

Only silence was offered.

"Who is your granddaughter-in-law's Spiritual Guide?" Kumang clarified the question.

All she received was more shaking of the head.

"It's all right. You can tell me. This Spiritual Guide has put a curse on you anyway. You can't make matters worse by saying her name."

However, the old woman only continued shaking her head.

Kumang became impatient. "I can't help you if I don't know who cast the curse. Only the Spiritual Guide who put it there can lift it. Do you want my help or not?"

This time she received a verbal answer. "I do, please, I do. You are my only hope because you are the only one I know whose power almost matches …"

"*Almost?*" Kumang asked sharply.

The old woman trembled from head to toe. She dropped her forehead to the floor. "Please forgive me. Please don't be angry with me. It was not my intention to undermine your weaving skills. Please, that was not what I meant. I beg you to believe me. I know I should not have come to you for help. But I don't know who else to turn to. The Spiritual Guide is very powerful."

"More powerful than I?" Kumang's voice became sharper.

The old woman folded her body into the form of a small ball. "Please forgive me. Have mercy. I am old. I do not mind dying. I am begging you to have mercy on my grandson. He is our only surviving bloodline. Who will inherit our *bilik* if we lose him? Everything our family has worked for until today rests on his shoulders. His wife can't give him a child."

"You do not like her." Kumang picked it up right away. "Why?"

"I have warned him not to marry her, but he would not listen. That good for nothing woman! First, she cannot give him a child. Now, she brings this curse upon our family."

The mention of the young woman's barren state stroke a chord with Kumang's heart.

"I'm begging you, please save him." The old woman started sobbing.

"You do not beg for the life of his wife?" Kumang asked coldly. Just because a woman failed to produce a child, did that mean her life was not worth saving?

The old woman swallowed hard. "If I were in the position of making a request, I would ask for all lives to be spared, including mine. Unfortunately, I can only beg for mercy. And his life is the only thing I dare to beg."

Kumang inhaled deep. "I don't think the Spiritual Guide will spare his wife since she was the one who committed the offense." Feeling betrayed was a strong feeling she could relate to.

The old woman did not give any comment.

"I'll talk her into lifting the curse," Kumang promised.

"Thank you, thank you. Our family is forever in your debt. I know I am asking too much of a favor."

"Give me the name of the Spiritual Guide," Kumang asked gently.

"I don't know …"

23

"Then how do you know this Spiritual Guide is more powerful than I am?" Kumang's snappiness came back.

"I saw the design."

Kumang squinted. "Are you telling me that your grandmother couldn't have woven that design?" She hardly believed it. This old woman's grandmother was her most talented apprentice.

The shaking of the head restarted. "She did not have that much talent," she said weakly.

"Even with my guidance?" Kumang insisted.

"She did not have such talent," her voice was barely heard. The hands covering her face could be the main reason.

Kumang understood what she meant, nevertheless. Every Spiritual Guide chose apprentices with weaving talents that matched her own weaving skills. And she, Kumang of Panggau Libau, was no ordinary Master Weaver. She was the best Master Weaver of all the shape-shifters in the whole dome of the sky. She was not the best Master Weaver of their worlds, she noted with humility. Only very few Master Weavers – less than a handful -- well actually, only one Master Weaver was better than she in their worlds. Her jaw tightened as soon as she remembered the identity of the one and only Master Weaver who was known for beating her in weaving. She was also famous for casting curses here and there.

"Never mind, I think I know who she is." Kumang's voice was void from any emotion, just like her face.

The old woman was frightened, nonetheless. "But I didn't say …"

"You don't need to. Don't worry. I will help you." Kumang did not need time to consider her decision.

"You will?" The old woman crouched on the floor one more time. "Thank you, oh, thank you so much. I do not know how I can repay your kindness." Her hands trembled again due to gratitude.

"For her to lift the curse, she might demand some kind of compensation to

24

atone for the offense your granddaughter-in-law committed," Kumang cautioned her.

"She can take anything she wants – anything, including my own life, as long as she spares my grandson's life. I am aware that I am asking too much as it is."

Kumang could not agree with her more. She should not interfere in a rift between a Spiritual Guide and her apprentice. The Spiritual Guide would tell her that it was none of her business, and she would be right. However, a Spiritual Guide should not punish innocent bystanders for a crime her apprentice committed. That was not right. That was downright bullying. She could make *that* her business.

DEALING WITH BETRAYAL

Kapuas River, the Land

The presence of another shape-shifter brought Kumang back to the present. It had to be her sister, Lulong. Her timing could not be more perfect. It was time to confront the Spiritual Guide who cast the curse.

Without looking back, Kumang addressed the shape-shifter, "Lu, I think we should …"

She stopped as soon as she detected the power level of the shape-shifter. Lulong was a fifth grade shape-shifter. This shape-shifter was a *petara*.

"What are you doing here?" She fixed her eyes to the irregular line up of natural rocks that served as a fence along the bank across the river. She refused to see the *petara*.

"I am here to take you home." His voice was very gentle.

"I don't want to go home!" Her voice was harsher than she intended.

"Mao …" He hesitated. "I am truly sorry for what I have done. I …"

"Stop saying you're sorry. I've heard enough of it!" Her breath became as uneven as a sudden surge of emotion flooded her heart.

"Then tell me what else should I say so that you are willing to go home with me?"

Kumang turned back to face her husband, Keling. "I've told you I don't want to go home. I have an important errand I want to do here."

"Such as what? Helping *mensia*? They can't be helped, Mao. They are hopeless." He paused. "Can we be honest with each other? We are husband and wife, after all. You left our home in the sky to come down to the land because you are angry with me. That is the truth. It has nothing to do with helping *mensia* and

26

their problems."

"It's funny that you feel like I am the one who forgets we are husband and wife! That we should be honest with each other!"

"When did I lie to you, Mao?"

"Hiding the truth is another form of a lie!"

"I did not mean to keep things from you. I just did not know how to tell you what happened without hurting you."

"So you think it would hurt me less if I heard from someone other than my own husband that he had another wife on the land? How very considerate of you! I thought you were dying down here. I truly believed you were badly wounded because of your battle with Apai Ribai. I was worried sick about you. It turned out that I worried about something completely unnecessary. You did not suffer at all. You were living happily with your new wife!"

"I lost my memory because I was severely wounded as the result of the battle. I did not remember anything about my past – where I came from, my family, you … I owed her father my life. He took me out the river, barely alive. They nursed me for many cycles of moon until I regained consciousness. When he asked me if I would not mind marrying his daughter to save her from the embarrassment from not being able to find a husband because of her deformity, I couldn't refuse. I myself was deformed at the time because of my wounds. I knew how it felt to see the flicker of disgust in people's eyes whenever they saw my hideous face. I pitied her. She was a kind-hearted soul. But had I remembered that I was already married …"

"You did not lose your memory because of the wounds you got from your battle! You lost your memory because you willingly gave it to that female water spirit!" She clenched her hands into fists, so tight that she could feel her own nails digging into her palms.

"I did not know she would really take my memory. I did not plan to lose the battle. I planned to go back home to you after I had avenged Apai's death. When she asked for my past memory, I didn't think she had the chance, or even the ability, to take it away."

"You promised her she could! What did you expect she would do with your

27

permission? You know that female knows a lot of nasty charms!"

"I only said those words to ease her pain. I left her to marry you. I hurt her deeply. I just wanted to …"

"Ah, the truth finally comes out. You only wanted to make her happy again. She is the one creature that you care most in this whole wide world. You will give her anything she wants."

"You are wrong. You are the one that I care most in this whole dome of the sky, above, beyond, and under. I will give *you* anything you want."

Kumang's face darkened. "I want to have a child with you. You never give me one, and yet you gave your new wife a child!"

"I didn't …"

"Didn't you? Are you saying that the child she carried was not yours?"

"It is not my decision not to give you a child! I don't know why the two of us don't have children until now."

"You're right. It is not your fault. It is mine. It's not that you can't give me what I want. It is me who can't give you what you want."

"Don't say that!"

"Why not? It is the truth. That *mensia* wife of yours could have your child. I can't."

"Mao, I …"

"You'd better find yourself another wife, have lots of children with her. That's what you have always wanted from this life anyway – having children. You will live happily ever after with her."

"Mao, please, can we …"

"Go away, Watt. Leave me alone. I don't want to go home. I don't want to go home to you." She continued as soon as he opened his mouth to reply, "Nothing you say can change my mind. I am staying on the land to help my apprentice's granddaughter solve her problem. Go back to Panggau Libau,

Watt. You are free to find happiness in this world in any way you see fit. Just do it without me."

Her last sentence could be the reason Keling did not say anything anymore. Not only that, he did not follow her entering the forest.

Kumang turned around and skipped with ease from one slippery rock to another until she reached the low hill where her sister was waiting for her.

Lulong stood up from the buttress tree root she was sitting on the moment she saw Kumang come towards her. "Mao," she greeted her. "I was about to meet you by the river as we have agreed, but then Watt was with you when I got near. I couldn't help overhearing your conversation. I thought I should not listen to the rest of it, so I waited for you here."

Kumang did not want to talk about what Lulong had overheard, therefore, she pretended to be busy pushing the outstretched forest leaves away from her body. The spot did not provide enough space for them to stand undisturbed by the residents of the forest. "I think we should go now. It's time to settle this problem."

Lulong knitted her forehead. "Are you sure you want to confront her?"

"How else can we break the curse if we do not confront her?" Kumang could not believe Lulong had to ask the question.

"We don't know for sure that it is she. Your apprentice's granddaughter never mentioned her name, did she?"

"She wouldn't dare. You did not see her. She was scared to death. And I know for sure it *is* she." Kumang's face became almost as gloomy as the shady forest. She eyed her sister. "And no, I don't want you to come with me. I can handle that female myself."

"I know you can, Mao." Lulong's hand absentmindedly caressed the leaf that touched her left arm. "I wasn't trying to tell you that you cannot. I was merely cautioning you that the culprit might not be her."

"Who else is there? She's the only Master Weaver who has better skills than I."

29

Kumang tried her best to say it without bitterness. She was not successful. "Or do you know some other creature who can weave better than I?" She hated how her voice sounded so emotional, but she could not help it.

Lulong shook her head. "You are the best Master Weaver I know, Mao. She beat you once in weaving – once! It did not make her a better Master Weaver than you."

Kumang laughed softly despite her annoyance. "That's what a sister's for. She will always be your loyal supporter."

"There's something else a sister is for," Lulong sounded cautious. "To remind her sister not to do something foolish."

"Do you think I am foolish to confront her in her own territory? You don't think I should? You're worried she'll hurt me?"

"My concern is not about you confronting her. I am worried that you confront her for the wrong reason. I am afraid that you'll hurt her for nothing."

"Helping another creature can never be a wrong reason! If she gets hurt, it is definitely not because of nothing."

"Are you sure helping *mensia* is the real reason you want to confront her?"

"What other reasons do I have?" Kumang's voice rose slightly. "Surely you're not suggesting that I want to confront her because I'm jealous of her?"

"Mao, you are the most beautiful female in the whole dome of the sky. Not a single living creature can dispute that. You are also the most talented, kindest and caring creature alive. You have no reason to be jealous of her."

"Then what is the foolish reason you think I have for confronting her?"

"She is his past, Mao, no more than that. It's not his fault and it's not hers either. It happened before our parents arranged your marriage with him. It's just how things were. You can't blame her for what had happened between them before he married you."

"I am not looking for her because of what happened between them long ago, although what happened between them lately is a totally different issue. She took away his memory when he was on the brink of death! Hoping that she could steal him from me - from all of us!"

"I know what she tried to do. Look Mao, he left her to marry you. That's what happened long ago. And as to what happened lately, he left her one more time to come back to you as soon as he had his memory back. He jilted her twice - for you. You don't need to look for a way to punish her anymore. She's got the worst possible punishment when it comes to him."

"The only reason I want to confront her is because she is cursing innocent people!" Kumang said forcefully. "It has nothing to do with her relationship with my husband - the past and the present. Do you think I care if the two of them want to spend the rest of their lives happily ever after from now on? You are wrong. I don't care. I don't!"

"All right ... all right ... as long as you are sure it is she who put the curse on *mensia*."

"I am!"

Lulong nodded. "Okay. Let's do it."

Kumang could not help looking back to where Batang Kapuas was.

"He's gone. I can't detect his presence by the river anymore." Lulong's voice sounded gentle.

"It is for the best." Kumang hardened her heart. "We'd better go. The sooner we find her, the sooner the curse can be lifted."

Upon Lulong's second nod, Kumang turned around and walked back to the river bank where she had left Keling. She stood on a mound of rocks to scan the whole length of the river as far as her eyes could reach. Although she did not detect his presence, she could not shake the feeling that he would suddenly materialize himself in front of her in a blink of an eye. With the travelling speed he had, there was no doubt in her mind that he could. She narrowed her eyes. So what if he decided that he wanted to come and interfere? She lifted her chin. She would fight him if he dared to defend that female water spirit.

"You gave me your word that you won't get involved," Kumang reminded Lulong. "I want you to stay on the land."

31

"I wish you would change your mind. It is not a good idea to confront a water spirit in her own territory. You never know what lurks underneath the water." Lulong pointed at the murky river. "At the very least, I can watch your back down there."

"I need you to watch my back from here. We've agreed on this. You know what to do if something goes wrong down there."

"If I stay here, I can't see what's happening inside the river. How do I know you are in trouble? I really don't think …"

"I need to do this alone, Lu. Please. Stay out of this. You promised me you'd let me do this my way. You gave me your word."

Lulong heaved. "All right. Be careful, will you? Be very careful."

"I will. Don't worry. I know what I'm getting myself into. I am fully prepared to face her."

CONFRONTING A WATER SPIRIT

Kapuas River, the Land

Kumang did not wait for more objections from Lulong. She dived inside the river and headed to the river bed. As a shape-shifter, she had the ability to transform herself to survive under the water.

All shape-shifters had the ability to transform themselves into other creatures. Apart from that power, each shape-shifter was born with different abilities in manipulating elements of nature. Those who were born to be *bunsu kayu*, or master of wood, had the power to manipulate wood. A *bunsu api*, or master of fire, could manipulate fire. A *bunsu ai*, or master of water, had power over water. A *bunsu tanah*, or master of earth, was able to manipulate earth with ease. And a *bunsu besi*, or master of metal, possessed the power to manipulate metal. Kumang, along with other blessings that Mother Nature gave her, was bestowed with the power of a *petara*, which meant she could manipulate all the five elements of nature. That being the case, breathing underwater was not a problem for her because she could transform the water into air once it went inside her *mensia* body. She did not need to transform herself into a water creature – a choice most shape-shifters would take in this situation. All she needed to do was to cover her *mensia* skin with a kind of slime a fish had on its body so that her *mensia*'s body survived the deep water pressure inside Kapuas river.

Kapuas River was the longest river on the island. Due to the warm climate and abundance of food supplies, the water was buzzing with living creatures that swam about, minding their own business. Only a handful pairs of eyes caught the unusual sight of a human body heading fast to the bottom of the river.

Thus, Kumang reached the muddy river bed unobstructed. She could not see who she wanted to find, but she knew the female water spirit resided somewhere in the river. Unfortunately, as a water spirit, she could blend in perfectly with water. The female water spirit could be standing next to her for all she knew. Then again, she could be somewhere else in the big river.

33

Kumang decided that she needed to create attention to herself. She blew air out of her mouth. Because of her power over natural elements, it turned into the shape of a water bubble that she carefully blew bigger and bigger. After the size had reached her own body height, she quickly whispered the water spirit's name inside the bubble before she let it float slowly upward. When it reached the middle of the river depth, she sent a powerful water force to burst it. The water bubble exploded instantly, creating an illuminating light that blinded all the creatures around it for an intake of breath. And the name she whispered inside it was freed to call out in magnitude: "ENNIE!"

The sound only lasted in a blink of an eye, but by the time its resonance was completely unheard, Kumang was left alone standing on the river bed with the very creature she wanted to see. The rest of the living creatures had fled the scene in haste as if they feared doomsday was coming for them today.

"That was very subtle," Ennie commented dryly. "You could've awoken the dead dragon down in the forbidden dungeon with your call. Worse still, you could've irritated my Queen with your call. Now you *don't want* that."

Kumang eyed the female water spirit in front of her. The light she created out of the burst bubble had disappeared, leaving the river bed as dark as ever. However, she could see Ennie clearly in front of her. She was aware it was because Ennie chose to illuminate her presence for her to see. The female water spirit still looked like part of the water. Kumang hated to acknowledge that the female was truly a master in using light to accentuate her beauty. She was forced to admit that her husband had an exceedingly high standard of beauty when it came to the females he fell for. Her heart contracted at the thought.

"This is a matter of extreme importance. I don't want to take any chances. I had to make sure you heard me," Kumang answered coldly.

"A matter of extreme importance, huh?" Ennie echoed her words. "How is it extremely important? It's not like I changed anything. I'm sorry, let me correct myself. I admit that I changed a thing or two, but now everything is just the way it was before, isn't it? Why are you still upset with me?"

"How can you claim that everything is just the way it was before? You have no right to do what you did in the first place!"

"Oh, please! I'm sure you would've done the same thing, had the situation presented itself."

"I would never do what you did. It's cruel. But you have always had it in you, Ennie. You can be heartless."

"Heartless? You can call me a lot of names, Kumang, but whatever I did only proved that I have a heart. I care so much, maybe too much, unfortunately for me."

"Care too much? Don't hide under the pretext of caring. What you did is despicable! Undo it!"

Ennie frowned. "I have."

"You haven't done anything to repair the damage you've caused."

"What else do you want from me? An apology? You won't get it. My conscience is clear." She turned away. "Go away, Kumang. You came here for nothing."

"Don't you dare walk away from me! Our talk is not finished yet!" Kumang yelled at Ennie.

Ennie did not turn back to speak to Kumang, "Yes, it is. I don't want to waste my time talking to a deranged female."

"This deranged female will not leave until she gets what she wants. And you will give me what I want!"

Using her hands, Kumang created a strong wave that rippled through the water towards Ennie. Before it could hit her, Ennie switched off the light that engulfed her, so Kumang could no longer see her. She could only feel a similar force travelling through towards her. Both waves collided half way, spreading vibrations to its surroundings. Only after the water had regained its calm state again did Ennie show herself to her.

Kumang looked at Ennie steadily. "I see. This is how you wish to settle the issue."

"No, Kumang, this is your wish. This is how you have always wished to settle this with me. You have always wanted to beat me."

"Don't talk as if I hold some kind of begrudge towards you. I'm sorry to tell

35

you that you are not that great until I should envy you."

"Yes, you do. I am not great, far from it, but you do begrudge me. Because he loves me, not you."

"He came back to me, didn't he? He didn't choose to stay with you. That shows how much he really loves you." Although Kumang knew Ennie was only taunting her, she could not resist taking the bait.

"Ah, he takes his responsibility more seriously than his heart's desire. And that's what you are to him – a responsibility. Nothing more. Oh, don't look so worried, dear, he will never walk out on you and every other responsibility that all of you thrust upon him: the well-being of the world, Panggau Libau longhouse, his mother, his brother, his sisters. He doesn't want to be responsible for any of them, but all of you brainwash him to think that he must live his life fulfilling what everybody wants – everybody, except him."

"He's been complaining to you about us, hasn't he?"

"He doesn't need to say a word. I know him too well. No other creature in this whole wide world, above and beyond, understands him better than I."

Ennie's smile incensed Kumang even more. "Is that a fact?" she said acidly.

"Talking about fact, I understand you, too. Why you are doing what you are doing now."

"Then, let us see if you can understand this." Kumang raised her arms to send Ennie a strike with all the power she had.

Her intention was stopped by a bright light that forced her to cover her eyes with her arms. By the time she put them down, she saw a male standing between her and Ennie. Just like Ennie, he glowed inside the water. She wondered if this male was another water spirit who came to rescue Ennie.

"What is going on here! Explain yourselves!" The male said with authority. He sounded as if he was used to giving out orders and having them obeyed without being questioned. He turned his head to his right and saw Ennie. He squinted. "Aren't you a water spirit? If my memory serves me correctly, I saw you a couple of times accompanying your Queen. You had better come up with a perfectly acceptable explanation for what you are doing here! I respect our agreement that we all share these water sheds, but I have specifically asked permission from your Queen – a permission that she granted, to use this part of the river to nurse my father. I do not mind that you pass through it, but to use this space to fight -- shattering the grounds and the river walls with all the explosions you made! What were you thinking? If my father's condition gets worse because of your fight, I will make you rue the day you were created." He added forcefully when he saw Ennie shake her head vigorously, "No, not even your Queen can protect the two of you from me!"

Ennie hurriedly apologized, "I'm sorry, King Ribai. I didn't mean to disturb your father's resting place. I was …"

Ribai cut in fiercely, "My father is still alive!"

"Yes, of course. Pardon my bad communication skill. I never meant to disturb the healing process of your father, the King of Baya. I was merely defending myself from an attack that female sent me. She tried to …"

"I am not interested in finding out why two female water spirits are fighting! I don't care if the two of you end up killing each other. Just do it somewhere else!" Ribai snapped.

"That female is not a water spirit, King Ribai." Ennie pointed at Kumang.

"As if it makes a difference to me if this fight is between a water spirit and a …" he turned half-way to Kumang. He paused immediately. Then, he turned fully to stare at her. He took a few steps closer to bring his light over to Kumang. "And what are you?" he asked. He probably wondered why she did not glow in the water like him and Ennie.

"You just said that it doesn't matter to you what I am," Kumang brushed off his curiosity. It was easy to be rude to an offensive male, especially when he looked like he was ready to scold every creature he came in contact with.

"It doesn't," Ribai quickly replied. "But what are you anyway?" He continued when Kumang did not answer his question, "Not a water spirit according to her - definitely not a *bunsu baya* - although you do look familiar somehow." He scrutinized Kumang some more. "Where have we met?"

"How can you tell that I'm not from the crocodile kingdom? I could be a *bunsu baya* for all you know," Kumang challenged him.

Ribai finally cracked a smile. "No way! You can't be a *bunsu baya*! I would remember you if you were."

Kumang failed to respond. It was more to the effect of his smile. She was mesmerized to see how his whole appearance was completely transformed because of a single smile. The glow that surrounded his body seemed to have brightened up. He suddenly looked agreeable although without a doubt his charm was nowhere near Keling's. Her jaw tightened at the thought of her husband. Had she not learned her lesson? How agreeable a male looked like did not automatically correspond to how agreeable his behaviors were.

"So? What are you?" Ribai would not let it go. He took another step closer. "*Bunsu penyu*? No? Not from the turtle kingdom then? Hmm…" Another step forward. "*Bunsu ikan*? Not from the fish kingdom either?" One more step. "Err… let's see … *Bunsu* …"

"She's a shape-shifter." Ennie stopped Ribai's guess from dragging on and on.

Ribai's smile faltered a bit. "A shape-shifter?" He eyed Kumang with curiosity. "What is a shape-shifter doing in Batang Kapuas? Fighting with a water spirit …" He turned back to stare at Ennie. Then, he looked at Kumang again. "Ah!" His face showed some sort of understanding that Kumang felt she was being slapped across the cheek. His eyes travelled up and down Kumang's stature one more time. "You are the wife," he said slowly.

Before Kumang could say something offensive, he continued, "Kumang. That is your name, isn't it?"

"I am Kumang of Panggau Libau," Kumang said haughtily. She threw a hateful stare at Ennie. "How kind of you to introduce me! You're afraid to fight me yourself, aren't you? You have to ask him to do it for you."

Ennie was quick to reply, "Why, I was only telling the truth. Surely you would not recommend that I lie to the King of Baya just so …"

Ribai cut Ennie off, "What makes you think I want to fight you? I don't fight a female. You …"

"Good," Kumang did not want to waste time talking. "Then, kindly move aside. This is between me and her."

Ribai did not comply. "I can't let you fight here." He was very firm.

"I'll fight you too if you get in the way," Kumang warned him.

Ribai's smile was full of amusement. "Will you? Is that pride speaking or just plain foolishness?"

Kumang inhaled. He really had a smile that warmed the cool water around Kapuas riverbed. She was severely tempted to smile back at him, but instead, she steeled herself to answer stiffly, "It is confidence."

"No, that's jealousy," Ennie chipped in from behind Ribai.

And just like that, the water temperature dropped lower than normal. "I am not jealous of you!" Kumang's voice was icy cold. "Stop saying that I am!"

"I will keep on saying it until you accept the fact that you are jealous of me. Now repeat after me, 'I am jealous of Ennie! I am jealous that my husband loves her more ...'"

Kumang could not stand it anymore. "Move aside!" she barked at Ribai, who did nothing but rising his eyebrows at her for giving him an order in such a rude manner.

She swept her arm swiftly to send a powerful wave to hit Ennie. It had to travel through Ribai first.

He did not seem to worry about the attack. Without even raising his arms, he flicked his fingers. As a result, the wave hit an invisible wall in front of him. Not only did the wall stop the wave from striking him, but it also bounced back towards Kumang with twice the speed it originally travelled and three times in size.

Whether or not Kumang could have survived Ribai's backlash she could never tell because she was not given the chance to react.

A swirling motion of water appeared in front of her and sucked the big wave inside. Then the tube went to the other side and vomited the wave backward. A loud commotion was heard in a distant, however, Ribai and Ennie only had their attention on the figure standing next to Kumang.

"Keling!" Ennie called out in delight. "How nice of you to drop by and visit

39

me!"

Keling ignored her. "You do not have qualms about fighting a female, do you?" he addressed Ribai coldly.

Ribai answered him with equal coldness, "Do you expect me to defend myself from a *petara* with only half of the power I have? I don't care which gender it takes form, a *petara* is a *petara*. I don't have a death wish."

"Watt, I could have handled it myself!" Kumang hissed.

Keling did not reply his wife either. "Is that how you want to avenge your father? By hurting my wife? Don't bother. I'm here. You can take your revenge on me."

"My father is not dead. You failed to kill him." Ribai laughed to see Keling's face. "You think you did, didn't you? Did you brag to everyone in Panggau Libau longhouse about something that you did not do? I'm sorry to tell you that my father is still alive. Correction, I am not sorry at all. It's quite the exact opposite. That being the case, you and I have nothing to fight about. Although if you wish to fight out of nothing, I'd gladly answer your challenge. I'm sure I can handle a *petara* ..." his eyes fleetingly went to Kumang, "or two. I only have one request. Can we do this somewhere else? Name the place, I'll be there. You have my word. Just not here."

"I do not wish to fight you," Keling answered. "As you have correctly put it, you and I have nothing to fight about."

"That's a wise decision." Ribai narrowed his eyes. "Now would the two of you be so equally wise to leave as soon as possible?"

"I am not leaving before I get what I want!" Kumang's answer was firm.

"What is it that you want?" Ribai was irritated. He glanced at Ennie. "Ah, you want to see her dead because your husband loves her more?" He nodded to Kumang. "I can give you what you want if it means you'll leave this place as soon as possible."

"Now hang on..." Keling protested at the same time Kumang replied, "No! I am not here because I'm jealous of her! I want her to lift the curse!"

"Curse?" Ribai turned to Ennie again. "Which poor creature has fallen into your enchantment now?"

"I didn't make enchantment over anyone," Ennie quickly responded. She took a glimpse of Keling. "All right, I took away his memory, but I gave it back to him. He's free now. Everything is back to normal. I don't know why she can't move on from it."

"This is not about him! I'm talking about the *pua kumbu* you cursed. *Mensia* are dying. I don't care what your apprentice has done to offend you, but more and more innocent people will die if you don't lift your curse on the *pua*."

Ennie grew defensive under the intense gaze of Ribai and Keling. "I didn't put a curse on *mensia*."

"Nie, if you did, lift it. Please," Keling said quietly.

"But I didn't, Keling. I really didn't."

Keling held Kumang's arm. "Mao, she didn't do it. Let's go."

Kumang was appalled. "How can you believe what she said?"

"He always believes what I say," Ennie said smugly.

"You…" Kumang's hand rose to strike, only to be stopped by Keling. "Mao, that's enough! No more fighting. We must go."

She wrenched her hand free from his grip. "You can go if you want, but I won't go until she gives me what I want. If you take her side, I'll fight you too."

"Nobody is going to fight here!" Ribai exclaimed. "How many times do I have to repeat myself! You!" He barked at Ennie. "Give me your word that you did not do what she accuses you of. And don't you dare lie to me. You know what will happen to you if I tell your Queen that you lie to me, the King of Baya."

"I did not put a curse on *mensia*, King Ribai," Ennie said steadily. "Upon my life and everything I hold dear." Her eyes went to Keling's handsome face before they went back to stare at Ribai boldly. "I swear to you."

Ribai said to Kumang, "Did you hear that? She did not do it. You got the wrong creature. Sorry. Now go somewhere else to find the creature who did it."

"She could lie for all you know!" Kumang refused to believe Ennie.

"She could, but I don't think she did. She wouldn't dare. The consequence of being found lying to one of the Kings or Queens of the Water Kingdoms is far more horrible than death. That's how it works around here ... Mao," he smiled as he said her family nickname as if he found the sound amusing.

Keling touched Kumang's shoulder. "She did not do it. There's nothing more for you and me to do here. Let's go."

She shrugged her shoulder to free it from his hand. "Fine, I'll go. If I ever find out that you lie," she pointed at Ennie. "I'll come ..."

"You will come to me and tell me all about her lie," Ribai finished her sentence. "I will reserve a special spot for you to watch how the Water Kingdoms punish her. I can assure you that you will be completely satisfied with our arrangements." Ribai did not take his eyes off Ennie when he said the last sentence.

Ennie held Ribai's eyes. "She will never get that satisfaction. I never lie to you, King Ribai."

Ribai turned to Kumang and lifted his hands. "Is there anything else that keeps you here?"

Keling answered him, "No, we're leaving now." He nodded his goodbye. Without missing a beat, he took hold of Kumang's elbow and pulled her with him.

With the speed they had, they reached the dry land in a blink of an eye. If there had been a *mensia* around, he would have testified that two people magically appeared out of nowhere on the river bank.

"Let go off me!" Kumang pulled her arm away from Keling. "Why did you interfere? You embarrassed me in front of them!"

"You were in danger. You can't expect me to wait and see what the result would have been."

"I could have survived."

"I was not going to take that chance."

"Didn't you hear him? I am a *petara*!"

"Being a *petara* means you can manipulate all elements of nature. It doesn't make you invincible! You were fighting in his element – water. It may be the only element he can control, but he has more power over it than you. I underestimated their powers in my last battle with them. It was a mistake. Look where I ended. I nearly went to Sebayan."

"I know what happened the last time you fought with them! It seems that the whole water kingdoms know what happened the last time you fought with them."

Keling's patience was limitless. "My battle happened inside the water kingdoms. Naturally, its residents bore witness of that incident. And they talk. It can't be avoided. They like talking to each other, just like we do in the *ruai* of our longhouse."

"Yes, they talk. The whole water kingdoms and beyond talk about you and her, the star cross lovers – how she is the one that got away."

Keling sighed. "Why do we keep coming back to this topic? That is not what matters now."

"What matters now is that I have told you to leave me alone, and you don't seem to get the message."

"I understand that you are upset …"

"Upset? Then, you do not understand. I can't accept what happened to you. I can't accept what you did. No matter how you explain yourself that you did not mean to hurt me, I can't accept it! Every time I see you, I feel like a dozen of knives piercing my heart. It hurts every time I think of you. I don't want to feel like this. I don't! I want this pain to stop." Kumang bit her lip to stop her shaking voice from turning into sobs.

"I am sorry I put you though it."

"If you are truly sorry, please be kind and leave me alone. I can't bear to see you. It hurts too much."

After a suffocating silence, Keling said quietly, "If my absence can make you happy again, that is what you will have, Mao. All I ever want is to see you happy." He nodded his goodbye and turned away.

Kumang almost shed tears to see him walk away with his shoulders slump like a beaten warrior. She hardened her heart to stop herself from calling out his name to apologize.

"Mao? How did it go?"

Kumang dragged her thoughts away from Keling. She took her time to calm herself before she turned around to Lulong. "It seems like I have made a mistake. It is not she." She was bitter that she had to admit it.

"Oh?" Lulong threw her eyes nervously to the direction where Keling went away. "If it is not she, then who?"

"You were right when you cautioned me. My apprentice's granddaughter never mentioned any name." Kumang squinted at the river. Her resentment towards Ennie was fully channeled towards the *mensia* now.

"You said it yourself, she's scared," Lulong reminded her.

"I don't care if she's scared. She must give me the name of the Spiritual Guide! How else can I help?"

"You'd better visit her again in her dream."

Kumang gritted her teeth. "That is exactly what I will do tonight. Let's see if she dares to hide things from me this time. She would rather choose death because of the curse than face my wrath."

THE LAST BATTLE

"I'm afraid I don't quite follow your story." Sitting on a flat rock on a cliff by a waterfall, Lulong folded her arms. The barren cliff allowed the morning sun to shine on her directly. "You're saying that her granddaughter-in-law does not have a Spiritual Guide?"

Standing across from her, Kumang nodded. "That's what she said to me last night."

Lulong gave Kumang a bewildered look. "Yet she is a Master Weaver?"

"She is widely acknowledged as one. Even people from across the shores regard her as one."

"How come a Master Weaver does not have a Spiritual Guide? Where does she receive the inspirations for the designs she is supposed to weave?"

"She comes from a long line of Master Weavers. Apparently, she learned all the designs that her ancestors made and reproduced them."

"No way! She can't have done it. She does not have a Spiritual Guide."

"Apparently she can because she has done it. I tell you, these *mensia* never cease to surprise me with what they are capable of."

"But … no… if she doesn't have a Spiritual Guide, where does the curse come from? Is there really a cursed *pua kumbu*? Or did your apprentice's granddaughter make the story up?"

"Oh, there is a cursed *pua*."

"Cursed by a Spiritual Guide?"

"Naturally."

"But not the weaver's Spiritual Guide? It can't be. She doesn't have one."

"My apprentice's granddaughter can't explain the existence of that particular *pua* as to who wove it. Because of that we don't know who cast the curse. But she has seen the *pua*. She is convinced that it is cursed."

"Based on what she's seen?"

Kumang nodded.

"What did she see?"

"She thinks the *pua* narrates a battle."

"Which battle is cursed?" The shape-shifters had experienced so many battles in which none of the females was involved. Recounting battles was not female shifters' favorite pastime.

"We don't have a cursed battle that we know of."

"So she is wrong. There is no curse."

"I don't think she is wrong. I believe the *pua* depicts a battle that has not happened. That's why whoever sees it is cursed."

Apart from the sound of the waterfall that cascaded down to the small stream below them, Kumang did not hear any sound around her.

"The *pua* is a premonition, Lu!" Kumang clarified. "It contains a secret of our world that we are not allowed to know just yet."

"A premonition about a future battle? What is so secretive about this battle such that innocent creatures must die for knowing that it is about to happen?"

"Don't you remember the battle at the end the world?"

Lulong continued giving Kumang a blank expression.

"You know ... the one that involves the boy who will destroy the world."

"Oh! The boy ..." Lulong's hand went to her mouth.

"You do know what I'm talking about?"

"I think so. There was a prophecy made about him, wasn't there?"

"That's the one."

"What was it about anyway? Err... it said that a boy would be born into our world to destroy it." Lulong frowned as she recollected the story. "If I'm not mistaken the prophecy was made not long before we were born. Why, it was centuries ago. It was suspected that the boy would come from our generation. I still remember my late Apai and Indai talked about it in our *bilik* when I was young."

Lulong was actually Kumang's sister by birth, but she was adopted by another family in Gelong longhouse who did not have a child of their own. It was long after Dilang and Idah had become known as Apai and Indai Lulong that Idah gave birth to a son they called Unjah.

Kumang walked to the edge of the wet cliff. Her eyes followed where the waterfall ended up, down in the stream. "Not only inside the *bilik*, but also in the *ruai*, the identity of the boy was a regular topic of discussion. Everyone wondered who he was. Every time a male youngster in our longhouse showed some kind of aggressive behavior, our *ruai* would be buzzing with speculations if he was the boy who would destroy the world. Fingers would be pointed at him. The poor boy would be subjected to prejudice until another boy did something worse and the cold hostility would be transferred to him. And it went on and on." She turned around to face Lulong. "It was really awful."

"I still remember." Lulong stood up to approach her. "Dom Unjah was suspected once because he accidentally hurt one of his friends when they were playing in the field outside. My parents were worried about his safety for weeks. They were scared someone would take law into his own hand and hurt him. I still remember that I felt glad I was a female, so nobody would think I was the supreme evil who needed to be exterminated just because I made a mistake." Her face changed into a dreamy look as she recalled the past. The mist that fell on her face from the waterfall brought her back to the present. "But the prophecy did not happen, did it? Nobody destroyed our world." She turned her face to Kumang.

47

"No, it did not happen. It has not happened, to be precise." Kumang stared back at her.

Lulong's frown came back. "Are you saying that it is going to happen soon?"

"I believe so."

Lulong was speechless for a while. "No, no, wait. We have known about this battle long ago, even *mensia* knew about it. Why is it suddenly a curse that we find out it is coming soon?" she argued further.

"Yes, we have always known it is coming. But we don't know when, or how, or who will cause it."

Lulong's eyes widened. "Are you saying this particular *pua kumbu* can answer these questions?"

Kumang nodded solemnly.

"It can't be! That's a secret that only the People of Tansang Kenyalang know."

"That is why *mensia* who have seen it must die."

"Is that what your apprentice's granddaughter told you last night?"

"That's my conclusion based on what she told me."

"Do you think she is telling you the truth?"

"I don't think she dares lie to me. As to whether my suspicion is correct, I can't say until I see the *pua kumbu*."

"Are we going to her longhouse to see the *pua kumbu*?"

Kumang shook her head. "It is no longer there."

"Where is it now?"

"It was taken away by *mensia* to a woman called Siti. I asked her how I could find this woman. She explained, but I do not understand what she meant. The only gist I could catch was this woman seems to have a lot of cats."

Lulong's eyes widened. "Cats?"

Kumang shrugged. "I really don't understand what she was talking about."

"What do we do now?"

"Honestly, I don't know."

The sound of the waterfall was magnified as they stared at each other in hopeless silence, until Lulong said with hesitation, "I suppose ... we can find Endu ..."

"Who?" Kumang was startled. *Endu* was one of the many generic terms to call a girl in a longhouse, as with *Wai, Dara,* or *Mao.* As a result, in one longhouse alone, there were countless females called Endu. She did not know which Endu suddenly entered the conversation.

"Endu Rikok ... your sister-in-law." Lulong hesitated as if she did not want to remind Kumang of her husband. "She has lived on the land with *mensia* for centuries. I am sure she can give us useful information about this woman... what is her name again?"

"Siti. But I don't see how she can help," Kumang expressed her objection right away. She was not eager to see a sister of Keling. Despite his shortcomings, her husband was the perfect brother for all his siblings. He was fiercely protective of them. He always put their welfare and safety before his. They reciprocated by looking up to him to the point of worship. She was sure Rikok had heard about her being on the land, avoiding her husband. And as always, she would take her brother's side no matter what the circumstances were.

"I just thought that ... since we don't have any idea about what to do next ... we could see her. She knows a lot about *mensia.* She has knowledge of who is who. Besides, she can tell us about ..." Lulong blushed out of the blue.

Kumang blinked a few times before she figured out why Lulong's cheeks changed color. "Ah...you want to ask her about Jang?" she said quietly.

Jang was one of the most popular generic terms to call a boy in a longhouse, apart from *Watt, Dom,* and *Igat.* As a result, in one longhouse alone, there were countless males called Jang. However, Kumang was certain that Lulong knew exactly which Jang she was talking about. There was only one particular Jang who could make Lulong blush: Sampurai, Keling's brother.

"No … not necessarily … but if we are going to see her, why not …" Lulong's cheeks were visibly rosy. "Oh, all right, we don't need to ask her about … him … but I really do think she can help us … to find this Siti your apprentice's granddaughter was talking about, for example…and also …"

Kumang did not have the heart to let Lulong continue struggling to find an excuse to see Rikok. She relented. "You might be right. It is something worth trying since we don't know what else to do."

"So, are we going to see her?"

Kumang had to smile to see Lulong's excited face. "We're going now to see her."

AN ADDITIONAL ALLY

Batang Ai, the Land

"A woman called Siti? Who has a lot of cats?" Those questions were out of Rikok's mouth as soon as Kumang had finished telling the story. Her eyebrows formed an arch that looked similar to the branches of the trees on both sides of the stream nearby.

Kumang nodded. "Do you know anyone fitting that description?" She highly doubted that Rikok did. They went to see her for a completely different reason anyway.

"Without extra information, I don't."

It was as Kumang had expected.

"Why don't you let me talk to your apprentice's granddaughter," Rikok suggested. "I know what questions to ask."

The rough surface of the dead tree trunk where Kumang was sitting on suddenly pricked her skin. "She doesn't know you. I doubt she will respond with truth." She shifted her buttocks to feel more comfortable.

"You're right." Rikok agreed. "Let's see. Do you know where she lives?"

"Yes, I know where her longhouse is. Do you think we should pay her a visit?" Kumang stood up when her sitting spot could not give her comfort anymore. Rikok was not supposed to take an interest in this. Unfortunately, by standing up the pebbles on the bank replaced the tree trunk in giving her annoying pricks.

"You need to visit her in her dream tonight and tell her that you will send someone to see her the next day. Tell her that she must answer all the questions the woman asks her to the best of her knowledge. That's the only way you can help her," Rikok gave her instructions.

"Someone? You mean you?" This was not good. Kumang did not want to involve her sister-in-law further. Rikok's face was a female version of Keling's. She really did not need a constant reminder of a husband she wished to forget.

51

Rikok tilted her head. "Of course. I thought we've established that only I know how to ask the right questions."

"But I want to be there to hear what she has to say. I may have some questions of my own." Kumang did not want to lose ownership of the mission.

"Fine. Tell her the two of us will come and visit her tomorrow."

Kumang wondered why Rikok talked about physical visitation when they could easily visit the *mensia* in her dream that very night. Had Rikok lived as *mensia* too long that she forgot how to behave like a shape-shifter? She was about to point it out when she realized that she did not want Rikok to visit her apprentice's granddaughter in her dream tonight, so she bit her lip to stop herself from saying anything.

"You mean three of us, not two." Lulong's remark put a stop to Kumang's wandering thoughts.

"You also want to come along?" Rikok looked at Lulong from the corner of her eyes.

"Of course she must come with us. I wouldn't dream of leaving her behind." Kumang was not comfortable going alone with Rikok.

"Fine, fine, we all go. Is there anybody else you want to bring along?"

See? This was the kind of behavior she had to put up with. "No, just the three of us." Kumang tried to calm her nerves.

"All right, I'll come back again tomorrow morning. We'll set off to see your apprentice's granddaughter right away." Rikok sighed. "I will have to find more excuses to leave home. I've been telling my adopted parents all sorts of stories so that I could check up on Jang. I'm running out of excuses to tell you the truth. They'll be suspicious soon enough."

"Oh!" Kumang looked at Lulong, expecting her to ask follow-up questions after the topic of Sampurai was introduced. Curiously, Lulong kept her mouth shut.

"If there's nothing else, I'd better …" Rikok moved to stand up from the tree trunk she had been sitting on.

"How is Jang?" Kumang decided to ask the question on Lulong's behalf.

Rikok stopped moving. "He's better. He's still a long way from fully recovered, but he'll survive. We know it for certain now."

52

"What does that mean? He almost didn't make it?" Lulong could not pretend not to care anymore.

Kumang noticed the calculative stare Rikok gave Lulong. She wondered why.

"He had internal bleeding because Watt stabbed him with a *parang* to begin with. Didn't Watt tell you? When he lost his memory, he did not recognize Jang as his own brother, so he thought Jang meant him harm. To top that, the *gerasi* beat him up pretty badly. If he had assumed a *mensia* form, we would have lost him to Sebayan for sure. Luckily, he is a shape-shifter, and he took the form of a *gerasi* at that time. He had a chance to fight to stay with us. And he did fight. Ah, you know what he is like when it comes to fighting." Rikok shook her head and smiled.

"That's good to hear." Lulong's voice was full of relief.

"And I really have to thank Gerinching for that. He wouldn't have survived without the right medication," Rikok added.

"Oh? I thought you were the one who supplied him with medication? At least that's what ... your brother told me," Kumang asked since Lulong shut her mouth again as soon as the topic of Sampurai's female companion was mentioned.

Rikok squinted at Kumang for failing to mention Keling's name. However, she let it pass unmentioned when she answered, "I did. I made him medicine based on what my adopted father taught me. He is a *manang*, remember? But G – that's how I call the Nanga female," she explained quickly, "she can converse with the trees so ..."

"Can she really?" Kumang was astonished. Although she had heard about it, she found it hard to believe. All shape-shifters could converse to every other creature of the forest, be it physical or spiritual beings. The trees, however, were the only exception to the case. They could understand what was said to them, but they never answered back. That was because they had very limited skills of conversing. At least that was what the shape-shifters believed all this while. That this Nanga female could actually have two ways conversations with the trees was amazing, even if she was a *bunsu kayu* who had control over wood.

Rikok sat down again. "Uh-uh. And the trees told her the best medicine our forest had to offer. She told me what they were and where to find them. My shape-shifter power level is higher than hers, so I can travel much faster than she. The trees were right, of course. What do you expect? Jang had the best medication the forest could provide. Much better than what I had prepared for him. It helped him survive."

"So, he is all right now?" Kumang asked for the reassurance that she knew Lulong wanted to hear.

"He is." Rikok nodded firmly.

"Then, why do you still need to see him every so often?" Kumang wanted to double-check.

"Because he is family and that's what we do with family. We see each other." Rikok looked at Kumang straight in the eye.

Kumang knew Rikok was hinting about her refusal to see Keling. Because she did not want to pursue that topic further, she turned the topic to a different path. "Does that mean we can see him on our way to my apprentice's granddaughter's longhouse tomorrow?"

Rikok was startled. "You want to see Jang?"

"Why not? As far as I know we should pass through his place on our way to the longhouse. Or has he moved?"

Rikok shook her head. "He's still there. We did not dare to move him when he was still in critical condition. Then, after he was healthy enough to be moved, they had made themselves comfortable with the place, they didn't want to relocate. So, yeah, he's still there. But I thought you want to help your apprentice's granddaughter as soon as possible."

"We will not stay long. We just want to see how he is doing." Kumang could sense that Rikok hesitated. "Why? Is there a particular reason why we can't see him?"

Unexpectedly, Rikok's eyes went to Lulong.

"Is there a particular reason why *she* can't see him?" Kumang had to ask. What did Rikok have against Lulong?

Rikok hesitated some more. "I know it is not my business ..."

"What is?"

Rikok shrugged. "I don't think she should see him. That's all."

"Why not?"

"It can complicate things."

"Things? What things?"

Rikok opened her mouth a couple of times without saying a word.

"Endu, you can speak your mind with us," Kumang urged her gently. She was beyond curious.

Rikok stared at her in silence for a while before she nodded. "All right, then." She turned to Lulong. "I don't think you should see him until you have made up your mind about which one of them you want: Jang or Igat. If you choose Igat, then, leave Jang alone. Why do you need to see him? To give him empty hopes? That's cruel. If you choose Jang, then, tell Igat to stop visiting you for *ngayap*. It is not right to give him false hope either! That is equally cruel."

"Endu!" Kumang was shocked. She did not expect the accusation was given so bluntly. She could see that Lulong was embarrassed. "You're right in the first place. It is none of your business," she exclaimed.

"Maybe not," Rikok mumbled. She eyed Lulong sulkily for a while before she raised her voice. "But maybe it is! Jang is my brother, Igat is my cousin. I don't want them to fight over a fickle female who can't make up her mind!"

Kumang dismissed her worry. "Oh please, don't make a drama out of it. Jang and Igat are very close. They're like brothers. The two of them will not fight because..."

"I am not making a drama out of it. You did not see what they were like when Jang found out that Igat has been visiting her for *ngayap*!" Rikok pointed at Lulong, who immediately gasped. "And don't talk to me about creating a drama when ..."

"Jang knows about the *ngayap*?" Lulong's eyes were as round as the pebbles on the river bank.

"He does now," Rikok replied sharply.

"And he minds?" Lulong's voice was a mere whisper.

"He minds very much from the looks of it." Rikok's jaw tightened to see the expression on Lulong's face. "And if you dare to say that you purposely welcomed Igat for a series of *ngayap* sessions just to find out if Jang would be jealous or not, I swear I'll..."

"No! That's not it … it's not … I swear it is not…" Lulong was clearly in a dilemma. "I … I only wanted to help him …Igat, I mean." She gulped. "I gave him my word I wouldn't tell anyone …"

"Tell anyone about what?" Kumang frowned. She was not aware that Lulong was keeping something from her.

Lulong bit her lower lip so hard that her dimples appeared. "It is not my secret to tell."

"Secret? Igat's secret? Are you talking about his visions?" Rikok asked.

Lulong's face told them the answer even when she did not say a word.

"What visions does Igat have?" Kumang asked Rikok.

Rikok ignored Kumang's question. She was more interested in Lulong. "He told you about his ability to see the future?" Now she was in awe.

"Igat can see the future?" Kumang did not believe what she heard. "How come I never heard of this?" she demanded to Rikok.

"He has stopped talking about it long ago. I always thought he has made up his mind to ignore his visions for good. He begged us not to discuss it anymore. We respect his wish, so we never do anymore," Rikok explained. "How come all of a sudden he told you?" she asked Lulong.

Lulong shook her head. "He did not tell me. I sort of figured it out. He had a vision right in front of me. And he saved Dom Unjah's life because of it. That's the reason for his first *ngayap*. He came to beg me not to tell anyone else about it. *Ngayap* is the only chance we can talk in private without anyone else around. You know how it is with our norms."

Rikok snorted. "One *ngayap* is enough for that. What? You forced him come to see you several times for *ngayap* before you agreed to keep his secret?"

"No, no, one *ngayap* is enough," Lulong assured her. "It's just that, he started to have visions about his late father's murderer."

"About Apai Ribai?" Rikok guessed.

"Yes, that's the one," Lulong confirmed. "He was troubled. He needed to talk to someone. He was not sure if he should do something about it. He said he had made a lot of mistakes whenever he tried to interpret his visions in the past. He had promised himself he would ignore all of them, like you said. But that particular one was about his father's murderer. He couldn't ignore it. He didn't

56

know what to do. I owe him my brother's life. How could I turn him away when he needed help? After all, he only needed someone to listen to him. I did not even give him any advice. And then, you know what happened after he decided to do something about that particular vision …"

Rikok pursed her lips. "Yeah, I heard. Watt told me. He killed Apai Ribai's daughter by mistake."

"I believe a piece of his soul died because of that mistake." Lulong looked sad. "I couldn't turn him away … I mean… really … I'm not heartless…you should have seen the state he was in …"

Rikok threw her eyes to the green forest on her right. When she finally turned to Lulong again, she said, "All right. I can accept your explanation. I apologize for what I have accused you of."

"Thank you," Lulong sounded grateful.

"Now, are you sure you want to see Jang?"

Lulong blushed because she understood the real question Rikok was asking her.

"Well?" Rikok insisted.

Lulong finally nodded.

"And will you give me your word that you will not welcome Igat for *ngayap* anymore?" Rikok was relentless. She widened her eyes to see Lulong hesitate. "And why not?"

"Because if he comes to me for help …" Lulong started.

"You will tell him to find help from someone else. You will tell him you cannot help him," Rikok stated firmly. "Why is it so difficult?"

"Because …"

"Because you do not want to say 'no' to him," Rikok made her own conclusion. "I don't believe you cannot put a stop to his visits. All of us have been trained since young by our mothers to reject unsuitable suitors when it comes to *ngayap*. If he still comes to see you, that's because you do not want him to stop."

"It is difficult to turn down someone's request for help, especially if you are in debt with that person. I've told you I owe him my brother's life. Why can't you understand?"

"I understand that you can't say 'no' to Igat."

57

"I really …"

Rikok did not give her a chance to finish. "That's okay. I have no problem with it. If that is your decision, leave Jang alone! Give him a chance to be happy with Gerinching."

Lulong blinked her eyes rapidly.

"Why can't you do that either? You can't or you won't?"

"Let it go, Endu." Kumang did not like how Rikok kept pushing Lulong. "It is not up to you whom Lulong wants to see. Or whom Jang should be happy with."

"She has to make up her mind! I know she is your sister and all, but what she is doing is wrong."

"She will make up her mind when she is ready, not when you tell her to. It doesn't work that way."

"I don't care. She is playing with my brother and my cousin. I won't have it!" Rikok stood up. "And I can't believe you support her behavior. You should know how it feels when you find out you are not the only one who matters in his life."

Kumang also stood up. "Don't you dare pass judgement about what happens between me and your brother …"

"Oh, yes, you bet I dare." Rikok glared at her. "You can't accept what Watt did to you. That's why you left him. You refuse to hear his side of the story. You know what? He is my brother, but as a female, I can understand your sentiment even if he doesn't. Now I can see for myself that you support what your sister is doing to Jang and Igat. So what is the meaning of all the fuss you've made after you found out you share his affections with some other females?"

"They are not even remotely close! How can you compare what your brother did with Lulong's situation?" Although Kumang was prepared to find that Rikok took Keling's side, she was still aghast.

"Because they are one and the same! You just don't want to admit it. You only want to see what you want to see!"

"They're not the same!" Kumang shouted. She fought to regain her composure. "Look, I don't need to explain myself to you."

58

"And I don't need to hear your explanation. Just because I am the youngest in the family, do not take me as a fool. I understand what is going on between you and him. And by the way, I did not look for you. You looked for me. If I had not considered Watt's feelings, I wouldn't have agreed to see you after what you've done to him."

"What I have done *to him*? He was the one ..." Kumang gritted her teeth. She forced herself to calm down. It was no use trying to point out Keling's fault to his siblings. They would never be able to see it. "If that is how you choose to see it ..."

"It is!"

"Fine! We'll find this Siti woman without you."

"Fine! I wish you the best of luck!"

"I will not welcome Igat for *ngayap* anymore." Lulong's voice sounded quiet in the midst of the heated exchange of words.

"I beg your pardon?" Rikok clearly had forgotten about the source of their argument.

"Lu!" Kumang hissed. "You don't need to promise her anything you don't want to do. We can find a way to help my apprentice's granddaughter without her."

"I will not welcome Igat for *ngayap* anymore," Lulong said firmly to Rikok. Then, she turned to Kumang, "I want to see Jang."

"We can see him without her consent! She doesn't own this forest." Kumang threw a challenging look at Rikok. "I want to see you try stopping us from visiting him."

Lulong placed a hand on Kumang's arm. "Mao, it's all right. I want to see him. I really do." She asked Rikok, "Can we visit him tomorrow? The three of us?"

Rikok took her time in replying. "Sure, if that's what you still want to do." She eyed Kumang cautiously.

Kumang understood that Lulong did not want her to burn bridges with her sister-in-law. As much as she did not like asking Rikok for help, she admitted that Lulong had a point. She nodded stiffly. "Sure, why not."

"I'll see you two tomorrow morning." Rikok nodded her goodbye. She was about to turn away when she stopped to say, "And Lulong ..."

59

"Yes?"

"Thank you."

After giving the last salutation, Rikok disappeared from their sight in a blink of an eye.

A SHORT VISIT

"We are nearly there," Kumang commented as soon as she detected the power levels of two fifth-grade shifters and a third-grade shifter behind the curtain of creepers ahead of them. Was it her imagination or did the trees suddenly overcrowd the area in front of her as if they wanted to hide something precious they did not want her to find? She felt foolish for thinking like that. The trees of the forest were the most indifferent spectators of the physical world. They did not actively take side. All they ever did was watching what was happening around them and keeping the secrets within their tightly knitted community.

Rikok smiled. "They must be wondering who is coming. I'm sure they can also detect our presence."

As if responding to Rikok's statement, the thick curtain of creepers in front of them was lifted. Kumang saw a man she detected as a fifth grader come out.

"Dom!" Rikok called out to the man. "Look who are here!"

Kumang recognized the male shifter whose lank hair was hanging loose over his shoulders. Pungga, whom Rikok called 'Dom', was Keling's second cousin. Instinctively, she was on guard. She did not know how Pungga would treat her because of what had happened between his cousin and her. She might have to bear his long speech on how she could have and should have been more forgiving towards her husband to save their marriage. She had all the answers lining up for each and every one of his reproves.

Pungga grinned at them. "Hello! How are you?" he addressed Kumang and Lulong. "Come, come, do come in! It is so nice of you to come and visit us." He parted the curtain wider to make way for them. "Welcome to our humble abode. I am sorry we cannot receive you with a more appropriate dwelling."

Kumang was grateful that Pungga acted as if nothing had happened. She should have known. Pungga might not have Keling's extraordinary good looks and irresistible charms, nor did he possess Sampurai's adorable boyish appeal, nor Laja's level-headed coolness, but he possessed flawless tact. He could easily win a female's heart simply by the way he treated them.

She smiled back at him. She bent down below the opening of the curtain. The moment she stepped forward, she was instantly in awe of her surroundings. For a moment, she was disoriented. She felt like she just entered a *bilik* inside a longhouse. How was it possible when she did not even enter a longhouse? A closer look around assured her that she was still inside the forest. The neat rows of poles standing around them were living trees, and the green walls were the creepers plants of the forest. She looked up, expecting to see a roof. There was a cover over her head all right, it was created by the giant trees that generously extended their branches to form a net of leaves. She looked at the ground beneath her feet. It looked like she was stepping on flat rows of woods, just like in a longhouse. She shifted her eyes up to find Pungga's smiling face.

"Do you approve?" he asked the question as if he could read her mind.

"Don't tell me you did all these." Kumang's eyes wandered around one more time. She still could not get over the fact that the forest could be transformed in such a way that she felt like she was inside a longhouse *bilik*.

"I most definitely did not. I am a *bunsu tanah*, remember? I can only manipulate the earth, not wood."

"You did this." Kumang pointed to the forest ground that appeared like the floor of a longhouse.

Pungga's smile widened. "Guilty as charged. But that is all I did. The rest is the work of wood manipulation."

"This is not a manipulation of wood forms," Lulong argued from behind Kumang. She stepped a few steps forward. "I am a *bunsu kayu*, and I cannot do this. This is …" she struggled to find the right word as she rotated her head around, "… I mean, they are living creatures. How can a *bunsu kayu* manipulate living beings to change their shapes? Don't they have minds of their own?"

Pungga chuckled. "That is a question you must ask the Mistress of the Forest. Ah, here she comes." He pointed his right thumb to his right.

Kumang turned to her left to see the 'Mistress of the Forest'. She was startled to see her. The first thing she noticed was that the female's lanky body was covered with clothing similar to those of Pungga's – a shirt and long pants. The other striking appearance that she failed to ignore was her hair. It was cut much shorter than Pungga's. It was so short that her hair only enclosed the shape of her head. The end of her hair nested neatly just below her ears. It's not only the shortness of it that was new to her sight, but also the way it was cut. Her hair was parted on the left side of her scalp, causing the front part to curve sweetly to cover the right side of her forehead, while the hair on the left side was tucked in neatly behind her ear. She had never seen a female shifter took a physical form on the land the way this third grader did. Was this how a woman of the land looked like these days? Her eyes went quickly to Rikok, who was standing next to Pungga. No, even Rikok who had been living on the land for the last few centuries kept her hair long to her waist.

Kumang recalled that she had met this third grader in her spiritual form in Panggau Libau longhouse, but she did not remember this female had looked anything similar to this. To be honest, she did not really remember how this female had looked like back then. She had not found anything particularly striking about her looks. She registered her in memory as another pretty female, just like any other regular female shifters. Her appearance had not created a strong impression on her – unlike now. She still would not consider her exceptionally beautiful, but there was something about her looks that captured the eyes. She wondered if the big difference came from the physical form this female chose on the land.

All shape-shifters enjoyed the power of transforming themselves into various forms. As spiritual beings, they took their spiritual forms at home, in the sky. When they went down to the land, they had to assume physical forms. This was when the fun happened. They could choose what forms they wanted to be seen by the rest of the physical creatures of the forest although the scope of their ability correlated directly to the power level given to them from birth. A *petara* like her and Keling enjoyed the full extent of changing their appearances to their every wish while at the other extreme, the first graders, who were bestowed with limited power, only had few choices when it came to the forms they could transform themselves into, mostly only forms that were more or less similar to their spiritual appearance. This female was a third grader, that meant her power level was somewhere in between the two extremes. Kumang did not know for sure how much transformation power this female had until she could look this different from her spiritual form.

Naturally, she had heard stories about how this female loved to transform herself into a man whenever she roamed the forest outside her longhouse territory - an idea that her father forced on her for the sake of her own safety. That could be the reason for the choice of men clothes and hairstyle. She also knew that the first time this female met Sampurai she was assuming the form of a man. Thus, he thought of her as a male shifter, and continued to regard her as one long after he had found out that she was, in fact, a female. Looking at her now, Kumang did not understand how anybody could have mistaken her as a male because even with the present clothing and hairstyle, there was nothing manly about the way she carried herself. But then again, all of them had long accepted that Sampurai was – well, to put it nicely – *different* from the rest of them.

Pungga's voice brought her to where they were. "This is Gerinching. We call her G. G, this is Kumang of Panggau Libau."

Gerinching smiled at Kumang. "Yes, of course. We've met before in Panggau Libau." She extended her hand to her.

Kumang accepted Gerinching's hand without knowing why it was offered to her. "Did he say they call you Jie?"

"Yes, G." Rikok ran her hand through the thick volume of her silky wavy hair. "G is the first letter of her name, Gerinching." She touched Kumang's shoulder gently. "You can let go of her hand. It is a handshake. That's how *mensia* greet each other nowadays."

Kumang had no idea what Rikok was talking about. She was certain that Lulong did not too.

"Can we just call you Gerinching?" Kumang asked the owner of the name.

"Sure you can." Gerinching smiled sweetly.

"Just make sure you don't do it in front of Jang," Rikok leaned forward to whisper.

"Why?" Kumang shifted her eyes from Rikok to Gerinching.

Gerinching pouted. "He thinks the name gives me bad luck."

"Oh? Well, if that is the case we'll call you …"

"Puyu! You will call her Puyu!" A male voice boomed from behind Gerinching.

Kumang did not need to see the male to know whose voice it was, especially when she saw how Gerinching roll her eyes without saying anything.

Kumang laughed gently as she patted Gerinching's hand. "I think I'll call you Jie." For that reply, she received a bright smile. Then, she caught where Gerinching's eyes went to. "Ah, I am sorry. I forgot to introduce my sister. This is Lulong of Gelong."

Kumang thought she saw an instant flicker of recognition on Gerinching's eyes upon hearing Lulong's name. As far as she knew the two of them had never met. So how did Gerinching know about Lulong?

"Hello, how do you do?" Gerinching extended her hand to Lulong, who accepted it with hesitation.

"Can we see Jang?" Kumang asked when Lulong did not say anything but smiled at Gerinching.

"Sure. I gather that's the reason you came all the way here. This way, please." Gerinching turned around to lead the way.

Walking behind her, Kumang wondered where Gerinching got the idea. Had she heard about Lulong and Sampurai? And Laja?

They passed another curtain of creepers that lifted itself the moment Gerinching walked by. Kumang began to understand why Pungga called Gerinching 'Mistress of the Forest'.

Apparently, they went inside a different 'room' behind the curtain. The first thing she noticed about the interior of this room was the giant tree that was located right in the middle of it. Kumang had seen thousands of trees in the forest all her life, but she had never seen one whose buttress roots were shaped almost to the point of symmetrical all around its main trunk as if a *bunsu kayu* had carved and positioned them according to his heart's desire.

Gerinching rushed to the extremely tall male resident in the room, "What are you doing standing up? You need to rest."

Sampurai grumbled in response. "I have been doing too much of it. I need to do something else to exercise my body. It's getting weaker by the day." He flexed his full of black tattoos muscular body to prove his point.

"That's because you are not healthy enough to work out. Rest is what you need right now." Gerinching pushed him to sit against the nearest buttressed tree root. "Stay here! Don't move too much."

To Kumang's surprise, Sampurai did not argue. Did his wound make him that weak? The Sampurai she knew would not listen to an order given by a female.

Gerinching turned to the rest of them. "Oh dear, where are my manners? Come, come, do sit down." She spread her arms all around the giant tree. "You can use any of the flat surfaces on the roots to sit down. I am terribly sorry you need to sit on the tree roots. Unfortunately, this is the best I can do, I hope they are good enough."

Kumang sat herself on top of a flat root that surprisingly accommodated her buttocks perfectly. "This is better than good," she pacified the worried female shifter. "We are in the forest anyway. I have never stayed in the forest and make myself comfortable like this. You do not need to stress yourself out to make us more comfortable than it is possible."

Gerinching only sat down when everyone else had chosen a flat surface to sit on. Instantly, she sat up straight. "Oh, would you like to have something to drink? Or eat, perhaps?"

"It's all right. Don't trouble yourself. We're only here for a while." Kumang let her eyes wander. She was astonished to find that all of them ended up sitting on a circle, facing each other, in the midst of the winding shapes of buttress roots.

"Oh? You can't stay long?" Gerinching adjusted her sitting position to face her better.

"We thought we stopped by to see how Jang is doing since your dwelling is on our way," Kumang explained.

"On your way?" This Gerinching seemed to like asking questions. "Where are you going?"

Kumang was not sure she wanted to share her story with them. While she was thinking about the best answer to give, her attention went to Sampurai, who fidgeted a lot. He did that frequently whenever he stayed on one particular spot, so she did not think much of it at the first glance. Nevertheless, she soon caught him quickly averted his eyes from hers as if it was not proper for him to do. Why? When did he start caring about propriety? Therefore, she purposely fixed her eyes at him hoping he would look at her. He did after a while, but once again, he diverted his eyes so quickly that she had no chance to smile at him. Kumang was convinced he did it on purpose. After that, he was determined not to look at her direction at all. They were sitting in a circle, and he was right in front of her, yet he refused to look straight ahead. He stubbornly stared at Gerinching, which was odd because she did not do any talking at the moment.

Although Kumang had accepted that this brother-in-law of hers was always peculiar, the way he was behaving now was so unlike him. Sampurai did not do avoidance. He did not possess Pungga's tact. Thus, direct confrontation was always his choice. He had to disapprove of her decision to leave Keling. She knew Sampurai would stand by Keling no matter what. Even if his brother committed the most heinous crime right in front of him, he would still be able to find an excuse to defend him. For that, she expected him to scold her for having the nerve to blame Keling for anything. Yet she received none. She could not believe the reason for his silence was because he actually took her side. It was even harder to believe that he had finally learned how to be tactful in matters as delicate as this.

The moment Kumang gave up trying to guess the reason behind Sampurai's odd behaviour, she found that Rikok, who sat on her left, had filled the silence by recounting the story she had told her the other day. Kumang was a little bit annoyed with her for doing that. However, it was too late to stop her now. She turned to Lulong on her right, wondering if she felt as annoyed as she did. It turned out that Lulong did not pay attention to Rikok. She was busy conversing with Pungga, who was sitting on her right about their life on the land, practically living without a longhouse. She listened to their conversation for a while before she stole another glance at Sampurai, who sat on Pungga's right, wondering if he would rather be involved in this neutral conversation with Pungga and Lulong. No, he was not interested in that topic either. He continued staring at Gerinching as if his eyes were glued to her face.

Kumang's eyes shifted to Gerinching. All right, she admitted that this female's appearance was strikingly appealing although she did not fit into the conventional standard of beauty they held. She still could not accept that was the real reason Sampurai could not take his eyes off her. If he was attracted to faces that please the eyes, he should fix his eyes to Lulong's sweet face too. Kumang could not shake the feeling that Sampurai was doing his best to avoid looking at her. She wondered why.

Her attention was suddenly caught by the canopies above them. She thought she detected a first grader up on a tree. Who could be up there? Ah, she remembered Keling's story about a first grader from Nanga Langit that Gerinching's father sent down to protect her on the land. And this first grader liked to assume the form of an orangutan. It had to be him up there on the tree.

"Mao?"

Kumang felt Rikok's hand on her arm.

"Eh?" She was startled.

"G asked if your apprentice's granddaughter's granddaughter-in-law is Tenang daughter of Tinggi."

Kumang blinked a few times to recollect her thoughts. "I have never heard of that name. The woman we are about to meet is Ramih of Lubok Sawo longhouse. I do not know her granddaughter-in-law's name."

"Lubok Sawo longhouse? Then it cannot be Tenang. She is from Batu Terkura longhouse." Gerinching made a face.

"Who is Tenang? What makes you think of her?" Kumang asked.

"It's just that when you mentioned a talented Master Weaver from Skrang tributary. There's only one name to mention: Tenang daughter of Tinggi."

"I'm sure there are many Master Weavers in Skrang," Kumang refuted the idea.

"Nara is the acknowledged Master Weaver from Lubok Sawo longhouse, recognized even by people from across the sea," Rikok offered more information.

"In other words, you are saying that she is the most talented Master Weaver? Not this Tenang?" Kumang clarified.

"Not necessarily. She is acknowledged worldwide mostly because she is the one being exposed. It doesn't mean she is the most talented," Rikok explained.

"But if she is not the best, why is she the one being exposed? Why not the others who are more talented? I thought that's how it has always been done. We recognize the talent and the art works produced," Kumang stated the norms they upheld.

"It is more to do with her family. She comes from a long line of famous Master Weavers. Here's the thing, a lot of *mensia* today don't know much about the art of weaving *pua kumbu*. The handful few who are interested in learning it usually find a family such as Nara's, an established family of Master Weavers who can and are willing to tell them the history and show them how it is done. This family has a lot of things to tell and show people what they have done. Also, I think luck also played a part in this. Out of the many families of Master Weavers, how come Nara's family was singled out? But there it is. Her family was chosen and Nara is, at the moment, the Master Weaver of the family."

"Why do you think Tenang, and not Nara, was the weaver of this cursed *pua kumbu*?" Kumang asked Gerinching.

She replied quickly, "I do not know much about how the people across the sea and their knowledge about the art of weaving. Endu Rikok is your trusted informant on the subject. However, if you are talking about local talent, I mean, if this woman really wove the battle that you described, it has to be Tenang. There's nobody else who has her talent in that area. You can ask anyone living in Skrang, you'll get the same answer."

"Does Tenang have a Spiritual Guide?" Kumang asked.

"I am most certain that she has. I have seen one of her works during my stay in one of *mensia* longhouses. Almost every longhouse in Skrang tributary has one or two of her works. They are sought after. Her works are like heirlooms to them."

Kumang turned to Lulong, who now had stopped talking to Pungga.

"I don't think Tenang is the granddaughter-in-law. This particular woman does not have a Spiritual Guide in weaving," Kumang explained.

"If that is the case, who cursed the *pua kumbu*?" Gerinching asked.

"That's what we are hoping to find out from this meeting with my apprentice's granddaughter," Kumang answered.

"I am really keen to know the answer," Gerinching said wishfully.

"Would you like to go with the three of us?" Rikok offered.

Kumang was instantly irritated. This was her mission, not Rikok's. She had no right to ask Gerinching to tag along without consulting her first. Thus, she was glad when Sampurai answered abruptly, "No!"

"Jang! I'm sure you can spare her for a few days. She needs a break. Pungga can stay here and take care of you for a while." Rikok giggled to see Pungga's face. "Surely you can take care of Jang for a while, Dom."

Sampurai scowled. "Don't get involved!" he said sharply to Gerinching.

"But I …," Gerinching tried to explain herself, which he did not allow.

"It's none of our business! Let them sort it out," he barked out the orders. "Stay out of it!"

Gerinching looked like she still wanted to argue, but his fierce glare kept her quiet.

"You don't need to obey his every command!" Rikok exclaimed. "If you really want to go with us, let's go," she urged Gerinching. "What is he going to do anyway? Tie you to a tree?" She grinned at Sampurai. "Fight all of us who will set you free? He can't. He is still wounded." She went over to give her brother an affectionate hug. "I'm sorry. That was mean of me. I didn't mean to rub it in." She squeezed herself in between him and Gerinching. "But you shouldn't be mean to G either. Let her go for a few days."

"No, I can't do that! I promised ..." Sampurai's jaw tightened.

"Yeah, yeah, yeah, I know you promised her Apai that no harm will come to her while she is on the land. Don't worry, I'll personally take care of her. We're only going to see *mensi*a. They're harmless. I'll return her back to you in perfect condition, she won't even have a scratch on her body. Her Apai won't have a reason to send all Nanga warriors to go after your head. I give you my word," Rikok tried to convince him.

Sampurai squinted. "No!" was all he said.

"Dom! Help me talk some sense into him!" Rikok pleaded to Pungga.

"I don't think she should go with you, Endu," Pungga offered his opinion in an instant.

"Dom! Not you too!" Rikok was disappointed.

Pungga smiled. "I am sorry. You ask me for an opinion, and there it is."

"You males are really too much!" Rikok grumbled.

"Err ... I actually cannot go with you," Gerinching said carefully.

"Cannot?" Rikok was exasperated. "G, don't let them tell you what to do."

"I don't." Gerinching patted Rikok's hand. "I can't go, and it's not because of the two of them."

"Really?" Rikok clearly did not believe her. "Well, I am going and you can't stop me," she challenged Sampurai.

"You don't need to remind me," Sampurai grumbled. "I don't want you to go either, but I know you won't listen to me. Yes, I would tie you to a tree if I were not wounded. Annoyingly I am, so there's nothing I can do to stop you. I just hope Watt ..." he let it go unfinished.

"Watt?" Kumang was instantly suspicious.

"He meant he hopes *what* you are looking for can be found in Skrang," Pungga finished Sampurai's sentence.

Kumang stared at Pungga, who returned her gaze with equal steadiness. She was certain Sampurai was talking about Keling just now. She turned to Sampurai, who had restarted his fixation on Gerinching's face. Oh yes, he was definitely talking about Keling. Had he been here visiting his wounded brother? But of course he had. Silly her. She would have been surprised if he had not. Her gaze went back to Pungga's face. There was something there that cautioned her not to pursue this line of questioning.

"If Watt were here, he also could not stop me." Rikok smiled lazily. She was the only one who did not seem to care that Kumang might not like to talk about Keling. "I am an adult. I have my own mind. He respects *that*, even if you don't. Stop wishing for his presence here." She hit Sampurai's arm playfully.

Apart from glowering, Sampurai did not say anything.

"Well, if there's nothing else, we'd better start our journey before it's too late. We've got to travel using *mensia*'s speed," Rikok reminded Kumang.

Kumang turned to Lulong, wondering if she was ready to leave. After all, she was the one who wanted to see Sampurai. When Lulong did not say anything, she nodded. "I agree. It is time to go."

She called out to Sampurai, "Bye, Jang. It is good to see that you are all right." She stood up without taking her eyes off him, waiting for a response. He did look at her briefly because of the goodbye note. And that was just about it. He did not do or say anything else.

Knowing him well, Kumang did not take offense. She smiled at Gerinching. "Thank you for your hospitality, Jie. I hope we'll meet again in the near future."

"We will meet again," Pungga said confidently as he stood up. "I'll escort you out."

"Thank you, Dom." Kumang directed her smile at him. "You don't need to send us off," she said hurriedly to Gerinching, who scrambled to get up. "We've troubled you too much already."

"It's no trouble at all." Gerinching dismissed her concern. "It's just a short walk out of here."

Pungga took the lead in opening the multiple layers of curtains they had to go through to get out of the spacious den.

After Kumang had said goodbye to Pungga, she looked for Lulong. She found her talking to Gerinching. She could not hear what they were talking about from where she was at. She could only see Gerinching nod her head repeatedly to whatever it was Lulong said to her. She waited patiently until Lulong came to stand next to her.

"Are you ready to go?" Kumang asked.

"I'm ready if you are," Lulong replied.

"Let's go," Rikok told them. "I need to give you a long briefing about the journey we are about to take."

The three of them walked away from Pungga and Gerinching. Before they disappeared around the forest bend, Kumang took one last look at the fellow shifters she left behind. She saw Pungga, Gerinching, and Sampurai standing in front of their den and watching them go. She wondered if that was how their warriors saw the family members they left behind at home whenever they went away for war. She could not explain why she felt that way.

THE SIGNIFICANCE OF SPATA

Skrang, the Land

"Ah, we are almost there. The longhouse is just across from this forest border." Rikok looked up to search for a glimpse of the sky. "It's already dark, but it might as well. By right we should take a speed boat from Sibu, a major town at the delta of Batang Rajang to Kapit, a small town in Rajang basin. And then we need to take another speed boat to the junction of Kain River. From there, we should take a longboat because some areas of the river are too shallow. We can paddle the longboat mostly, but when the river becomes too shallow, we must push it to move forward. Depending on the speed of paddling, we should reach the longhouse in about six hours. That's how *mensia* reach this longhouse. It takes the whole day. It is normal to reach the longhouse late in the day." Rikok stopped walking at the forest border. "Do you still have questions to ask before we face these *mensia?*"

"No, I've got everything covered." Kumang answered firmly even though she did not understand most of the things Rikok had explained to her. For one, it was an extremely long description on how *mensia* lived their lives nowadays. On top of that, Rikok used too many terms that she had never heard of. After asking a few clarification questions that only ended up making her more confused instead of understanding what Rikok meant, Kumang nodded and smiled her incomprehension with confidence to speed up the explanation. Come now, it could not be that difficult. A longhouse was a longhouse, how different could it be? She was sure it worked the same way as it had always been. If there were changes – she could accept it after a few centuries had passed, the lifestyle had to have evolved - she was sure it was minimal. Rikok only wanted to patronize her and Lulong, just because she had lived with *mensia* on the land for the last few centuries.

Although she resented the doubtful look Rikok gave her, she kept her smile. She did not like pretending, so she quickly diverted her smile to Lulong, who appeared to be busy with her feet.

"Don't worry, they're fine." Kumang touched Lulong's arm.

Lulong gave her a helpless smile. "I don't really mind the new type of clothing I must wear as a woman of the land. But I'm afraid I can't get use to this kind of

73

footwear in such a short time. It feels strange to wear them, not to mention moving around in them. Must we wear them?" she asked Rikok.

"Absolutely. You can't be roaming around the forest bare-footed as *mensia*. Your feet can't survive." Rikok eyed Lulong with amusement. "Those are the most comfortable footwear to use outdoor."

"But we are used to roaming the forest bare-footed. Our feet always survive the whole ordeal," Lulong argued. "And I came down to the land a few cycles of harvest ago. I did not wear any of these to cover my feet. They were fine."

"As long as you stay in the forest without meeting *mensia*, you can dress up in any way you like. The point is now we are about to meet them. It is best that we look like them. We don't want to stir suspicions that we are not human beings like they are."

"My apprentice's granddaughter knows that we are not," Kumang reminded Rikok. "Is it really necessary to pretend that we are one of them when they know that we are not?"

How Kumang resented Rikok's condescending sigh.

The tone of Rikok's voice also reflected superiority when she explained, "Your apprentice's granddaughter might be prepared to meet spiritual creatures of the forest, but we are about to meet the rest of the longhouse residents; many of whom might not believe in our existence."

"They do not believe we exist?" Lulong's jaw dropped. "After all this time we have been a part of their lives, they do not believe we are real?"

"You have not been in their lives for so long. Come now, admit it. Ever since you moved up to the sky, you severed your connections with them. They have learned to live without you. Don't look so surprise now that the new generation of *mensia* might not have heard of you."

Kumang noted the shift from 'we' to 'you' when Rikok spoke of the shape-shifters' migration to the sky. At that time, Rikok refused to follow the rest of her family because she wanted to marry a man of the land. She had not gone to the sky to visit her family ever since.

"When we lived on the land with *mensia*, they also did not roam the forest using foot protection," Lulong pointed it out to Rikok.

"Those days were not the same as today. *Mensia*'s life is free from a lot of hardship these days."

"Is that how you remember our life on the land back then? Full of hardship?" Kumang did not feel the same way. It was still more or less their life in the sky now. Surely Rikok did not think they lived a hard life? Was that the real reason she did not want to go home to the sky? She was afraid of hardship?

Rikok smiled. "*Mensia* of today would not have survived our life back then. They are too pampered now, if you ask me. Over the centuries, they have invented a lot of tools to ease their lives. The pair of footwear you have on are one of their inventions. The people here called them *sepatu*. They are supposed to protect your feet from the elements of the forest."

Kumang just blinked her eyes. She did not want to start asking why *mensia* needed protection from the elements of the forest as if the forest was a dangerous creature. She had the feeling that she could not accept the explanation. The forest was their home! It gave them shelter, it provided them food, water, and most of all, it was the source of their power.

"Trust me. You must wear them. It is for your own good," Rikok insisted.

Kumang finally relented. "All right, we'll wear these ...err... what do you call them?"

"*Sepatu.*"

"*Spata?*" Kumang smiled ruefully. "How in the world did they come up with a name like that?"

"Not '*spa-ta*'. It's '*se-pa-tu*'. The word was brought by men who came from far away shores. The people of this land did not have any word for them."

"Of course not, they had no need for them," Kumang agreed wholeheartedly. "Okay, okay, I will wear them. Don't worry," she cut in when she saw Rikok was about to argue further about the importance of wearing the footwear. "But I don't like this pair. Can I wear my own?"

Rikok eyebrows rose. "Your own? Ah, you mean ... you want to design your own *sepatu?*"

Kumang nodded firmly. "Since I must wear them, and I don't like this pair. I might as well ..."

Rikok grinned. "Sure, why not. Let's see what you have in mind."

Kumang beamed. She did not waste time in using her power of transformation to change the shape of the foot cover. "What do you think?" She twisted her right foot left and right.

"Let me see. Can you sit down on the rock behind you so that I can have a closer look?" Rikok pointed at the ground behind Kumang.

As soon as Kumang did what she asked, Rikok squatted in front of Kumang to see her footwear. "Oh, I see. You chose a pair of slip on. Good choice. They are comfortable and more importantly suitable for outdoor activities. And you use woven material to cover your feet. Hmm…what's this pattern on the *pua*? Ah, they're the plants of the forest."

"They are the ones that protect our feet when we travel around the forest. They should be acknowledged as such," Kumang built her case. She observed how Rikok inspected her foot. "Are they acceptable?"

"I can't believe that you actually made a pair of footwear that are acceptable to modern day living." Rikok looked and sounded amused. "You only need to make a minor adjustment."

"Which is?"

"You need to use rubber as the sole of your footwear. Other than that, everything else is good."

Kumang clasped her hands. "Considered it done!" She wiggled her latest form of feet in front of Rikok's face. "Like these?"

"Exactly like those." Rikok nodded her approval. She looked up to Lulong. "You can imitate her footwear if you wish."

Lulong transformed her feet to resemble Kumang's. She flexed her ankles to get comfortable with her new footwear. "They do feel much more comfortable than the ones before." Her eyes went fleetingly to Rikok's feet. "Aren't you going to change yours?"

Rikok laughed softly. "I'm perfectly comfortable in my sneakers, thank you for the offer. Let me see yours."

"I don't think there's a problem with them." Lulong showed her feet to Rikok, who squat in front of her to inspect her feet. "They're similar to Mao's."

"You use more green than red in your design. Ah, and you use different plants symbols." Rikok patted Lulong's calf. "Yup! They are all right. We are good to go now." She stood up. "Are you ready?"

"Yes," Kumang answered promptly.

Lulong nodded gently and stood up.

Kumang's eyes went to Lulong's feet covers one more time and then to hers. "These pairs of *spata* are quite acceptable," she whispered to Lulong. She flexed her foot to find the feeling of comfort. "Although I still don't get what the fuss is about."

"Just give in to her this time, Mao," Lulong whispered back. "Our *spata* are all right anyway. They fit perfectly to our feet." She looked down at her own footwear.

"What are you waiting for?" Rikok grew impatient to see the two of them did not make a move. "Let's go!"

THE RECIPIENTS OF THE CURSE

Kumang stopped to stare at the construction in front of her. For the second time that day, she felt disoriented. She did not register the building in front of her as a longhouse although Rikok insisted that they had arrived at their destination.

Lubok Sawo longhouse was not made of wood and it did not stand on tall stilts. It was erected on a solid ground. The roof was not made of dried *nipah* leaves. She gave it one last look of discomfort before she rushed to follow Rikok, who had climbed up the low slope towards the longhouse which seemed to glow from the inside. Its radiance made the moonlight pale in comparison. She did not know how a longhouse could emit light the way this one did. Panggau Libau and Gelong longhouses certainly did not have this big amount of light. She took another good look at the construction. At least, it was still long as a longhouse should have been.

The feeling of discomfort lingered as she walked through what she thought had to be the *tanjuk* of the longhouse because it was located right before the rows of doors. The solid ground she walked on was bathed with bright light. She looked up to see tall metal sticks were erected all around the compound. On top of each stick, an oblong glass shone so bright she had to narrow her eyes to protect them from the strong intrusion of light.

"Do you know which *bilik* she is in?" Rikok asked.

Kumang nodded. "The sixth from the right."

"Do you want to go inside using *mensia* way or do you want to go straight to her room?" Rikok continued asking her more questions.

"Does it make a difference?"

"Yes, a big one. If we use *mensia* way, we need to face the longhouse residents in the *ruai*. They'll ask many questions about who we are, where we come from, and why we are here. Hey, don't worry about it. I can handle them and their questions. You don't need to say anything. Just smile and look pretty." Rikok grinned at them.

"I think we should go straight to her *bilik* and skip all the unnecessary and difficult questions the longhouse residents would ask," Lulong suggested.

"Then, that's what we should do." Kumang did not like the idea that she was only expected to keep quiet, smile and appear pretty.

"If that is what we are going to do, there is no need to look too much like *mensia*." Rikok sounded disappointed.

"What do you mean?" Kumang asked.

"We had better look like our real selves – the shape-shifters. You'd better let that charming aura of yours shines to the fullest, Kumang of Panggau Libau. Let her know she is facing powerful spiritual creatures."

"Whatever you think is best, Endu." Kumang was relieved that she could be herself.

Because of that decision, apart from a strong gust of wind that forcefully opened the three front doors of the longhouse and knocked a *bilik*'s door opened, the residents who were hanging about inside the *ruai* did not see anything out of the ordinary. And since within a second the door of the *bilik* was closed again without any follow-up sound coming out from it, the residents were more preoccupied with trying to fix the three front doors whose hinges turned out to be pulled out from the door leaves.

The old woman, who was weaving a mat on the floor, gawked as three human figures suddenly materialized in front of her. It was not clear if it was their beauties that transcended human appearances or the celestial auras they brought into the room that made her drop the unfinished mat to the floor next to her as she assumed a kneeling position in front of her guests. She bowed deep.

She did not look up when she addressed them, "Thank you for coming to my humble abode, Priestesses. I did not expect you to come this early. Dinner is not ready."

Now that Kumang met her apprentice's granddaughter in her physical form, she acknowledged that Ramih was unusually pale. Her paleness was different from the shade of skin that lacked the exposure to sunlight. She looked like a living corpse.

"Let me offer you the best *tuak* our longhouse has ever produced while you wait," Ramih offered. She stood up. "Please have a seat." She made a gesture to welcome her guests to sit on the floor mat. "Excuse me for a few seconds." She fled to the back of her *bilik*, where the kitchen was located.

Kumang sat down and could not help touching the floor mat. "What is it made of?" she asked Rikok, who was sitting next to Lulong.

"This?" Rikok also touched the mat. "This is synthetic fibers. *Mensia* calls it raffia. Originally raffia is made of palm tree leaves, but nowadays they use synthetic fibers."

"I beg your pardon?" Kumang was perplexed. Her hand stopped rubbing the mat.

"Synthetic fiber is the imitation of the real fiber. It is the latest fashion to make floor mats. It is very popular."

"They don't weave mats using rattan anymore?" Lulong asked.

"They do sometimes. But they also use other materials. This one happens to be the one highly on demand lately."

Kumang eyes were busy scrutinizing the solid walls that was filled with images covered in glittering glasses. The glaring white lights made the room odd. She felt like she was being overexposed under a spotlight.

She vaguely heard Lulong make comment about the mat. "The pattern is not bad, though the colors are too striking for my taste."

Kumang's attention was immediately shifted to Ramih, who rushed towards them with a bottle of *tuak* and small glasses. Now she was eyeing the shape of the glass the old woman offered in front of them. They looked so thin they could break at her slightest touch. She picked one up, nonetheless. And it was truly light. She frowned as she inspected the curious thing in her hand.

The old woman's voice shook. "I am terribly sorry if what we offer is not good enough. We did not have time to prepare a better feast for honorable guests such as you. And as you can see, I am not well. I can't ..."

Kumang lifted the palm of her right hand to stop Ramih from rumbling further. "We do not come here to feast. We are here to talk to your granddaughter-in-law, Nara, about the cursed *pua kumbu*." She put down the glass without drinking the content.

The old woman blinked rapidly. "You know her name?" She quickly regained her composure. "Of course, you do. I am sorry I even questioned ..."

"Can we talk to her? Is she here?" Kumang did not feel like wasting time with empty pleasantries.

"Yes, yes ... I'll get her right away." Ramih was half running further down the *bilik* to open a door without knocking. In no time, she came back with a young woman behind her.

"Sit down," Ramih gave the order rather harshly to the young woman.

Kumang detected dislike in Ramih's voice.

The young woman sat down obediently in front of them. Although she was not as pale as Ramih, she definitely looked ill. She eyed her guests with much interest.

Kumang understood now why Ramih insisted that a curse had befallen on them. "Nara," she addressed the young woman kinder that she had intended. "We are here to ask you about your work."

Nara's interest turned into guarded suspicion. Her eyes moved from Kumang to Lulong, and then to Rikok. "My work? Are you art collectors?"

Ramih hissed fiercely. "Why, you ignorant girl!" Her hand went to slap the back of Nara's head. "Don't you know who they are? Show some respect!" She would have said more rebukes if she did not catch Kumang's warning look.

The young woman's ignorant question prompted Rikok to take over the questioning, "We want to see the last *pua kumbu* you wove, Wai."

Nara's eyes narrowed. "How do you know about it? I am not allowed to talk about its existence. I gave him my word."

Rikok quickly calmed her down. "We are not asking you to break a promise, Wai. You don't need to talk about it. We just want to see it. As we understand it, it is no longer in your possession. Can you tell us where it is now?"

Nara shook her head. "Why do you want to know? Who are you really? Are you reporters? I am not allowed to talk to any of you."

"Who does not allow you to talk to us?" Kumang asked.

"Daniel."

"Who is …?" Kumang failed to repeat the name.

"Daniel …" Rikok filled in the silence, "… he knows about your last work, doesn't he?"

"He knows all my works. He promotes them in his exhibitions. He finds them buyers."

"What do you mean …" Kumang started.

Rikok cut her off, "He wants to show your last piece of work in his exhibition. That's the reason he forbids you to talk about it to anyone. Does he have it with him now?"

Kumang stared at Nara's face. "I don't understand the need of secrecy."

Nara shrugged. "He said he wants it to be a surprise. The story should not leak before the opening of the exhibition."

"And what story is that, Wai?" Rikok asked.

Nara blinked. "I can't tell you," she said slowly. She diverted her eyes to the wall on her right side.

"Why not?" Rikok asked again.

"She does not know what the story is," Ramih answered on Nara's behalf.

"Inik, please," Nara protested.

"Because she did not weave that *pua*," Ramih continued.

"Inik!"

"You never wove that *pua kumbu*. Do you think you can weave the final stage of a *pua kumbu* in this *bilik* – *my bilik* – without me seeing the pattern? Oh, I've seen its pattern with my own eyes all right. Huh! Don't take me as a fool. You did not weave that *pua kumbu*!"

"I have never shown you my latest work. You could not have possibly seen it," Nara refuted Ramih's statement.

"But I have seen it! I asked Sibat to show it to me."

"He wouldn't dare!"

"He had no choice. I gave him none."

"Inik! How could you?"

"How could you bring a cursed *pua* into our longhouse? You subject all of us to its curse!"

Nara closed her eyes. "The *pua* is not cursed, Inik. There is no such thing as a curse. Daniel said so."

"Daniel? What does Daniel know about our belief! He is not even one of us! But you are, unfortunately for us. And you do not want to listen to those who know, you insolent girl!" Ramih glared viciously at her granddaughter-in-law.

"Stop calling my wife names, Inik." A man's voice made Kumang lifted her eyes to look for the source.

Ramih was instantly on her feet. "Why did you leave your room? You should stay there and rest!" She helped the frail man walk towards them. "This is my grandson, Sibat," she introduced him to the guests.

"Why do you want to know about the last piece of work she did?" Sibat sounded as if he was breathing his last breath.

83

"They are here to help you, Sibat. They will make you well again." Ramih patted his hand affectionately.

Sibat's eyes quickly scanned the faces of the strangers in his *bilik*. "Can you? Make us well, again?"

"We can try," Kumang answered.

Sibat observed the three of them closely.

"But you have to answer our questions truthfully," Kumang continued.

Sibat licked his dry lips. "Are you *manang*?"

"What makes you say that?" Kumang shifted her eyes to Ramih. Had she not told her family about their visit?

"You mentioned that the *pua* is cursed. Only our *manang* talk like that. I just never met a *manang* who look like the three of you. They are usually old people, not young and beautiful." Sibat narrowed his eyes to the three visitors in his *bilik*. "So, are you?"

"Does it matter whether or not we are?" Lulong asked.

Sibat smirked. "No. I just want to get well again. Can you make it happen?"

"We need to know what the problem is before we can offer you a solution," Rikok answered.

"You said the *pua* is cursed. That means you have identified the problem. Now tell me, what is the solution to that?" Sibat wiped his nose with his finger. He squirmed when he saw a tint of blood there.

Ramih quickly offered him a piece of cloth to wipe it off his finger. Then, she proceeded to inspect his nose for a sign of more blood.

Nara watched what Ramih was doing to Sibat with displeasure. "Sibat, the *pua* is not cursed! Daniel said …"

Sibat pushed his grandmother's hand from his face. "I don't care what Daniel said! I just want us to get well again. All the doctors we went to did not know what is wrong with us. I can feel whatever it is I am having is making me weaker

84

and weaker!" He directed his stare to Kumang. "I am willing to consider …" he cleared his throat, "… alternative solutions. Tell me, what ceremony do you think we should perform to lift the curse?"

"Not just yet," Kumang said. "Before we know how to lift the curse, we need to know why the curse was given." She turned to Nara. "Who did you offend?"

"Eh?" Nara gave her a blank look.

"Which Spiritual Guide did you offend?" Lulong clarified.

Nara's face was still blank.

"She doesn't know any Spiritual Guide," Ramih answered on Nara's behalf.

"Let me get this straight. You were never given a dream of a pattern to weave?" Kumang asked Nara.

"No," Sibat answered. "She doesn't have that kind of dreams."

"Then how did you weave your last piece of work? Where did you get the inspiration for the pattern?"

Nara did not utter a single word.

"She did not weave it!" Ramih said almost with glee.

"If she did not, who did?" Kumang asked Ramih.

This time nobody replied.

"How did you get hold of a *pua kumbu* that you did not weave?"

Still, no reply was given.

Kumang stared at Sibat straight in the eye. "You said you want to get well again. I can see that you do not mean what you said. Enjoy the rest of your life." She let her eyes travelled over his face. "A few days more, I reckon."

"No!" Ramih exclaimed.

Kumang ignored her. She turned to Lulong and Rikok. "We are leaving now. We have wasted enough time for them."

THE GRAVE OFFENSE

"No, please, don't go!" Ramih begged Kumang, who had stood up. "Sibat! Tell them what they want to know! Let them help you get well!" She shook her grandson's arm.

Kumang had turned her body towards the *bilik*'s door when Sibat finally owned it, "All right! I bought it. There! Are you happy now?"

Rikok stood tall in front of him. "From whom?"

"Some man I know." Sibat diverted his eyes from Rikok.

"A man can't weave a *pua*. Don't lie to us! Give us a straight answer!" Kumang took a step towards Sibat.

Nara laughed softly. "Who says a man can't weave a *pua*." She looked up to the three standing guests. "After all, it is just a matter of learning and practicing."

"Are you telling me that men weave *pua kumbu* these days?" Kumang did not believe what she had heard.

"They sure do, too few of them, much to my regret. But yeah, they do. I have taught one or two men to weave. They are really good." Nara smiled weakly to see her flabbergasted expression.

"You? Teach men how to weave? You, who have never been visited by a Spiritual Guide, could teach anyone to weave? Who gave you the authority?" Kumang was appalled.

"Authority? Who holds the authority over teaching the art of weaving? Oh, I see. You are saying that because I never dream of a pattern, and therefore, I have no right to teach anyone. You are one of those people from the old school. Well, what you believe is completely irrelevant in today's world. The fact of the matter is I know how to weave despite never having dreamed of a pattern. I have been weaving for years, successfully I might add. You can ask

86

anyone who knows my work. Why can't I teach others to weave? I want to teach. Somebody wants to learn. That settles it," Nara answered back.

Kumang stared at Nara in disbelief for her bold answer. When she finally directed her eyes to Ramih, the old woman only dared to stare at the floor underneath her and whispered, "We are sorry. We are truly sorry. Please forgive us."

Rikok touched her hand. "Mao, we must focus on the curse," she reminded her softly. She asked Sibat, "Who is this man? Where can we find him?"

Kumang wondered why Sibat was so reluctant to reveal the man's identity.

"Answer the question, Sibat!" Ramih hissed.

"He's from Batu Terkura longhouse," Sibat mumbled.

"*What?*" Nara turned sharply to Sibat. "You never told me this."

"You never asked!" Sibat snapped.

"You told me the weaver is dead. You told me it is perfectly safe to claim it as my work. You convinced me that nobody can ever trace the *pua* back to her."

"And nobody can. Duat was a petty thief, and so were his mother and his sister. They all were. They took people's things and sold them to get some extra money. Everybody knows about it. He would never admit what they had done. That's the same as admitting their crime. He would not want them to go to prison. And now he's dead, and so are his mother and sister. Everyone in their *bilik* died. Nobody can say anything about where the *pua* came from."

"Do you believe me now?" Ramih pleaded to Kumang. "The *pua* is cursed! People who have seen it died. You must help us."

Before Kumang could respond, Nara asked Sibat urgently, "What about the weaver? Is she dead?" She shook his arm.

"She is as good as dead! Has been for years," Sibat said curtly.

Nara's eyes grew big. "It's hers, isn't it?" Her voice rose. "You have the heart to pass *her* work to me? You know what she said about me, what all of them said about me. They smeared my name all over Skrang and beyond. How could you do this to me? Do you have any idea how insulting this is?"

"You can't produce new patterns! The only thing you can do is to redo what your family has done. And you have done them all. Daniel kept asking for something new! His buyers want something new. You need help! I have to do something."

"And you went to *her* for help? You know I'd rather die!" Nara wailed.

"I don't want you to die! I want you to produce new patterns for Daniel's buyers."

"My family has enough patterns to produce and sell. Their patterns have fed us and this whole longhouse well over the years! Have you forgotten how many pieces of *pua kumbu* this longhouse has produced? They were sold out worldwide to the highest bidders the moment we finished weaving them! All of them are my family's patterns! So don't you dare look down on them!" Nara shouted out her anger.

"I do not forget nor do I look down on your family. But people are bored with the same patterns over and over again. They don't sell as well as before. There are too many of them in the market because we produce them non-stop. The money is no longer good. We need new exclusive patterns to make sure that the money keeps on coming."

"I never care about the money. I just want to weave. I am good at it. People recognize what I am good at. That is more than enough for me," Nara said tearfully.

"But it is not enough for me!" Sibat responded heatedly. "Do you think you can look like the way you look," he sighed at the sight of hers. "The way you looked before we had this illness, whatever it is, came from having money – lots of them. And I like the way I used to look too. And I need money to maintain that look! Do you think this longhouse can be built like this for everyone in it to enjoy if we have no money? Do you think we don't need money to maintain it? Be realistic! We need money!"

"I understand that we need money. But I can't accept that for the want of money, you crawled back to her!" Nara burst into tears.

"I did not crawl back to her! I did not even contact her. I bought the *pua* from Duat. He needed some cash and he offered it to me. He said it belonged to his family. I saw the pattern and knew it was different from anything you have produced, so I bought it. I thought you could study it and reproduce it. It is exactly what you need." Sibat softened his voice to see his wife sob harder. "I never think of her. Not even in a minute. I have erased her from my memory. Nara, dear, believe me ..." he reached out to her.

Nara pushed his hand away. "His family is her! Everybody in that longhouse is related to her one way or another. Why do you pretend that you don't know! You must know it is her work! Yet you still took it and gave it to me. You... you... how could you ..." She stood up abruptly and ran inside crying.

"Nara ..." Sibat followed her as fast as his frail body could cope.

Kumang witnessed what transpired in front of her in silence. She was too dumbfounded to react. When she finally could refocus, she asked the trembling Ramih, "Is everything they said true?" She was not quite sure what she had heard. However, she understood enough to be aghast.

Ramih nodded meekly.

"This longhouse has been reproducing the sacred patterns that the Spiritual Guides gave to their apprentices for the want of ..." Kumang turned to Rikok for clarification.

"... money as an exchange of valuables," Rikok explained somberly. "Money makes them wealthy. Wealth increases their social status."

"... exchanging the sacred patterns for your own personal glory without any regards as to why the Spiritual Guides gave you those patterns, without acknowledging and honoring those who inspired you to be well-known." Kumang could feel her own anger building inside her. "Did you ask for permission to pursue wealth this way?" she had to ask even though she knew the answer to that.

"Permission? From whom?" Ramih stumbled to catch up. "Oh, you mean from the Spiritual Guides." She folded her body smaller. "The girl does not have a Spiritual Guide.

"If she doesn't have a Spiritual Guide, she couldn't have reproduced the sacred pattern," Lulong interrupted.

Ramih looked nervous. "She only wove …"

"She couldn't have! It is impossible!" Lulong insisted. "She has not been given the authority to create the sacred patterns. The designs would fail to emerge."

"She modified the designs." Ramih's voice trembled.

"What?" Kumang frowned.

"She modified …"

"What does that mean?"

"She changed the original patterns, turned it into something else she could weave," Rikok helped to clarify.

"She changed the sacred patterns?" Kumang closed her eyes to calm herself. "She changed the sacred patterns without asking for permission."

Ramih gulped. "She has no one to ask for permission from the spiritual world. Not only that, she is not a believer"

"That means she does not perform a *ngar* ceremony every time a sacred pattern is about to be woven?" Kumang's voice was dangerously low.

She was referring to a sacred ceremony which encompassed all acts by which the loose cotton threads were prepared for weaving.

Ramih gulped. "Not always."

"Not always? Without performing *ngar*, the rest of the weaving procedure would not bear the intended results. How can anyone start weaving *pua kumbu* without performing *ngar*?" Kumang demanded.

"She knows another technique to treat the threads so that they can absorb dyes without performing *ngar*," Ramih answered.

Kumang turned to Rikok. "Can *mensia* do that now?"

Rikok nodded promptly. "Yeah, they have found a new way to bypass *ngar*, but the results are of less quality," she explained. "With the new technique the threads cannot absorb the dyes fully and the colors faded quicker. *Ngar* is still the best technique to prepare the natural ingredients needed to be applied to the threads so that they will fully absorb the dyes."

Lulong asked something that grabbed her attention. "You said 'not always'. Does that mean sometimes she performs *ngar*?"

Ramih nodded vigorously.

"What for? You said she has had a new technique that can bypass *ngar*?" Lulong continued her line of questioning.

"Sometimes tourists come here, and they want to see how the traditional weaving is done. That's why the longhouse women perform *ngar* as a show for them to record in a film so they can bring it back home for others to watch."

"I don't know what she is talking about," Kumang said to Rikok.

"Tourists are people from faraway places who come for a visit. They do not know our traditions, but they are eager to learn, so they want to see how we practice them. These tourists bring good money."

Kumang still had more questions about how these faraway people could bring the ceremony back home for others to watch. Unfortunately, she did not know how to ask. She could not restate Ramih's words to Rikok.

Therefore, she asked more questions about what she knew, "What you are saying is that many people from faraway places want to see her performing our rituals. This is my question: she does not have a Spiritual Guide. She has no right to perform *ngar* in the first place. How does she know how to perform it if no spirit guides her?"

"She comes from a long line of Master Weavers. She grew up watching her mother and her grandmother performed it. She knew all the steps by heart," Ramih said with shaking voice.

"I still don't understand. According to you, she is not a believer. So when she performs *ngar*... -- I expect she also performs *miring*? The offerings for the spirits are a must in a *ngar* ceremony," Kumang asked Ramih, who nodded meekly.

"Which spirits does she give the offerings to if she is not a believer?" Kumang finished her question.

Ramih bit her lip. "No one."

"In other words, she just chants empty words to the open space?" Kumang was shocked.

"She doesn't know any of our chants." Ramih fixed her eyes to the floor.

"You mean she simply places the offerings in various places without saying anything?" Kumang could not believe the silliness of it.

Ramih's eyes went left and right in panic state. "She says something. She is expected to say something. It is the procedure, so she says all the appropriate things to say. She usually asks for a blessing for the work she is about to do, wishing it to be a success, or something similar to that."

"Asking for a blessing? A blessing from whom? She is not a believer! What is the point of doing it?" Kumang raised her voice.

"It is only for a show. It is all for a show," Ramih's voice was hardly heard. "She says nice things. They don't necessarily mean anything. The tourists don't understand what she is saying anyway. They only want to see exotic rituals. She gives them what they want."

Kumang stopped asking questions for fearing that she would burst into rage if she heard any more of the atrocities these *mensia* had committed.

"Are you aware of what this longhouse has done to offend the spiritual beings of our world?" Lulong appeared to have more patience than Kumang.

Ramih did not dare to say a word. Even her nod was hardly noticeable.

"And nobody in this longhouse can advise them accordingly?" Lulong was blaming Ramih.

Ramih knew. She trembled from head to toe. "I tried. I have tried so many times. She doesn't listen to me. Neither does my grandson. They call me superstitious. They said I am uneducated, that's why I cling to old customs that are no longer relevant in the modern world." She crouched on the floor upon seeing Kumang's face. Her head was on her knees. "Please forgive me for not trying harder to make them see the truth. Don't let it stop you from helping us."

"I don't think there is anything I can do to help your longhouse. It is doomed." Kumang looked down at the back of Ramih's head with disgust.

"Noooooo, please! Please. Please reconsider." Ramih crept forward to touch Kumang's feet. "Have mercy on us."

Kumang moved her feet out of Ramih's reach. "You brought this calamity on to yourself. Live with it." She turned to go, but Rikok held her arm to stop her.

"Who was the 'her' they were talking about? The woman from Batu Terkura longhouse?" Rikok asked Ramih.

Ramih appeared sad. "She is my grandson's first wife. He left her to marry Nara. It made her very bitter. She created a lot of nasty rumors about Nara, her longhouse residents helped her spread them."

"Is she a Master Weaver? With a Spiritual Guide?"

Ramih nodded. "She is the best weaver in the area. She took Nara to be her apprentice despite the knowledge that she never received a dream from a Spiritual Guide. That's how Sibat met Nara. He should have never left his first wife for her. I had warned him more than once. Sadly, the pull of youth was too difficult for him to resist."

"What's the other woman's name?" Lulong asked.

Ramih's answer came at the same time Rikok whispered the name:

"Tenang anak Tinggi."

93

A NEW EXCUSE

"What are we going to do now?" Rikok questioned Kumang as soon as they had reached the forest border. She reached out to grab Kumang's arm. "Mao, can we stop for a while to discuss what to do next?"

Kumang stopped moving, and because she did, Lulong and Rikok did too.

"What is there to do? There is nothing to do," Kumang said flatly. "They deserve what has befallen on them." She frowned at Rikok. "Are you suggesting that they did not do anything wrong? They broke all the laws that govern our world regarding weaving. Or have you forgotten about them?"

"I haven't," Rikok replied quickly. "Don't look at me as if I am trying to offer excuses for their wrongdoings. I am well aware that they are wrong."

"And therefore, they deserve to be punished," Kumang stated firmly. "I am not going to do anything to lift the curse. It's good enough that I do not give them extra punishments of my own."

"All right, point taken."

"Then, what do you want from me? Why do I get the feeling that you are blaming me for something?"

"We shouldn't have left so abruptly like that," Rikok said mournfully.

"I couldn't bear to stay in that longhouse any longer after I found out what they did." Kumang could feel her anger brewing inside.

"At least we should stay long enough to ask more questions about where the *pua* is now."

"Why do we need to know about it?"

"We need to know if it is indeed cursed."

"Does it matter now?"

"If it is, whoever sees it will get the curse."

"Let it happen the way the curse is intended to."

"I can't believe you are so heartless, Mao," Rikok chided her. "Don't sacrifice innocent lives."

"Whose innocent lives are you referring to? They're all guilty. The whole longhouse is guilty."

"Nara of Lubok Sawo admitted that the *pua kumbu* is not with her anymore. I am willing to bet that it is now with Daniel somewhere in the city. He's getting it ready for the exhibition. That is where the innocent lives come in."

Kumang frowned. "I don't know what you're talking about."

"What is …err... exhibition?" Lulong asked. "Why is it a danger to innocent lives?"

"An exhibition is an event whereby someone shows a collection of beautiful and valuable things to anyone who is interested in viewing them." Rikok let her explanation sink in. "You see? If Daniel really puts the cursed *pua kumbu* in this event, everybody who comes to the event to see it, or to see something else, but he accidentally sees the *pua* on display will get the curse." She stared hard at Kumang. "That is not right, Mao. Those people have never done anything to offend the weaver's Spiritual Guide."

"They will if they purchase the sacred *pua kumbu* so that Sibat and Nara can accumulate personal wealth!" Kumang argued.

"The art collectors who enrich Sibat and Nara don't usually come to an exhibition, Mao. They purchase these beauties for personal viewing. The ones that come to the exhibitions are the ones who cannot afford to buy. They can only see and enjoy the art works during the exhibitions. They are very respectful of our culture. They wish to learn and understand our customs. They don't deserve to get the curse. If we don't try to stop it from being displayed in this exhibition, many innocent people will die." Rikok shook Kumang's arm. "Think about it."

Kumang eyed her sister-in-law. She had no idea what an exhibition was like. She did not know if Rikok was telling the truth or not. She asked Lulong, "What do you think?"

"It's up to you, Mao. I'll go with you to look for this *pua kumbu*. I'll go home with you if that is what you wish," Lulong replied.

The thought of going home made Kumang cringe. "Let's say we'll try to stop this cursed *pua* from being displayed, where do we even start?" she asked Rikok.

"Let me think." Rikok leaned on a tree trunk. "It should be in the city. I am certain of it. An exhibition must be held in a city – nowhere else. But first we need to find out which city," she mused aloud.

"Siti? Are you talking about the woman that Ramih told me about? The one who owns a lot of cats?" Kumang did not know why this Siti woman was suddenly the topic of their conversation.

"Huh?" Rikok stared at her as if she had been slapped. "Of course!" She lifted her back from the tree trunk. "A woman called Siti who has a lot of cats. Didn't you tell me that?"

"That's what I said." Kumang wondered what the sudden excitement was about.

"The exhibition is in Kuching City!" Rikok clapped her hands. "Yes! That helps a lot."

"I don't see how. We still don't know who this Siti is."

"Not Siti, but 'city' as in Kuching City. You know – 'Cat City'. That's what the world 'Kuching' refers to – 'Cat'. Why didn't I think of that?" Rikok patted her forehead.

"I still don't get it."

"A city is a word to describe a large area of *mensia*'s settlement."

"Like a longhouse?"

"Not like a longhouse." Rikok inhaled deep. She stared at Kumang in silence for a while. "All right, let's make it simple. A city is an area that covers a group of longhouses."

"Does that make it a combination of territories – all merged into one? Under the rule of one Chief?" Kumang could not grasp how it was possible.

"Something like that, but..." Rikok was lost for words. "… never mind that. We know that it is in Kuching. That is what matters."

"Do you know where it is?"

"I know where Kuching is. I can find out where the exhibition will be held. An event like this must be announced to the public long before it will be held. It won't be difficult."

"Good! After you find out, we will go there and get hold of it before it is being displayed. Ah, even before that, we also can lend you a hand to find the place," Kumang offered generously.

Rikok was speechless again.

"Yes, Endu? Is there a problem?" Kumang tried her best to maintain her civility. What was supposed to be the problem with her suggestion?

Rikok grimaced. "Err… I don't think the two of you should venture into the city."

"And why not?" Kumang's jaw tightened.

"It will be too much for you to cope."

Kumang raised her eyebrows. "I'm sure I can handle it."

"I beg to differ. I saw how you reacted in Lubok Sawo just now. That was only because you heard what they said about how they live their lives. I helped Gerinching find a longhouse to live on the land because she is ostracized, remember? And she could not stand it. I found her a considerably traditional longhouse, mind you, deep inside the forest. That's why I don't think you should go to the city. I don't want you to see for yourself what they have done to their lives and to the land."

"What could possibly happen if I see it?" Kumang challenged her.

"I am afraid you'd die of a broken heart."

Kumang had to laugh despite her annoyance. "I never knew you are such a drama queen, Endu."

Even Rikok smiled. "All right, maybe I exaggerate a bit. But I still don't think you should enter the city. Your heart will break, even if you won't die because of it. On top of that you will feel powerless."

"How so?"

"Our power as shape-shifters comes from the pure energy of the forest. The city doesn't host a forest. *Mensia* cut down a large area of the forest to build a settlement for them to live. Only small and young trees live there. They are hardly enough to feed us power."

"Have you been there?"

Rikok nodded.

"And you could not use your power there?"

"I did not try to use my power. Whatever for? To scare *mensia* out of their wits? But I have never felt that weak in my entire life, I can tell you that."

"That bad?"

"You can't possibly imagine how bad," Rikok said firmly. "Were you not in agony to hear what they have turned the practice of weaving *pua kumbu* into?"

Kumang winced. "How can you stand living on the land with them?"

"I don't live in the city. I avoid visiting it as much as I can. I choose to live in the forest, whatever is still left of it. Even that is getting harder and harder. The changes happening in the city seep through the defense of the dense forest. The fact that the forest is disappearing fast doesn't help one bit. It can't be helped," Rikok said gloomily. "I'm sure you've noticed that we have less and less forest on the land."

Kumang sighed sadly. Yes, she had noticed.

"Surely there is something we can do to help you." Lulong tried to change the gloomy mood.

"Actually, I'm thinking of visiting Tenang anak Tinggi. The two of you can go with me," Rikok offered.

"Why?" Kumang was fast to catch up. "Ah, you want to ask her about her Spiritual Guide."

"Yeah, that is another angle we can try. If we know who the Spiritual Guide is, you can go and see her. Try to persuade her to lift the curse. At the same time, I'll see what I can do to get hold of the *pua*," Rikok explained her idea.

"Is Tenang's longhouse far from here?" Lulong asked Rikok.

"Batu Terkura? It's not too far. With our speed of travelling, we can be there in no time."

"Why don't we visit her in her dream?" Kumang offered a more obvious solution. Once again, she was surprised Rikok did not think of it.

Rikok hesitated. "It is past midnight," she admitted. "It might be too late to visit them physically. It's not proper according to *mensia*'s norms."

"Then, we'd better visit her dream now." Kumang stood up.

Rikok stood with her. "Wait. We are on the land, remember? We take physical forms. If we want to visit Tenang in her dream ..."

"We have to leave our physical forms behind." Kumang heaved. She could see what the problem was.

"One of us needs to stay and guard our *mensia* bodies. We don't want some wild animals disturbing them when our souls are not here."

"Why don't you stay on?" Kumang asked Rikok.

"Me? Why me?" Rikok did not look pleased.

"This is something that Lulong and I can do. You said we can't help you with your search of the *pua kumbu*. Let us do what we can. You can take care of Siti and everything related to her." Besides, this was her mission, not Rikok's.

Rikok gave her a long penetrating look before agreeing. "You're right. I suppose it is fair enough."

"Excellent! That's what we'll do." Kumang smiled with satisfaction.

"Do you know how to find Tenang in Batu Terkura?" Rikok asked.

"We can randomly visit someone's – anyone's – dream and ask which *bilik* Tenang lives in. There can't be two Master Weaver called Tenang anak Tinggi in Batu Terkura," Lulong suggested.

"Good idea, Lu," Kumang said happily. She asked Rikok, "Will you be all right staying here by yourself, guarding our bodies?"

"Sure thing. Don't worry about me," Rikok assured her. "You go and find Tenang. I can take care of myself and your *mensia* bodies."

Kumang nodded her agreement. She still did not fully understand the importance of saving these *mensia*. However, any excuse she could use to stay longer on the land was more than acceptable.

THE NEED OF AN ADDITIONAL ALLY

Skrang forest, the Land

The dark forest was perfectly still after Kumang had finished retelling her encounter with Tenang's soul.

"Inik Bikhu Bunsu Petara?" Rikok whispered the name as if she was scared to let the words out of her lips.

Kumang nodded grimly.

"How in the world did Tenang get to have a Spiritual Guide that powerful?" Rikok closed her eyes. "Inik Bunsu is the supreme Goddess of Creativity. She doesn't trouble herself by taking a human apprentice. I can't believe it."

"Tenang has to be one extremely talented weaver," Lulong commented.

"Do you think she is suffering from a curse?" Rikok asked Kumang.

"I can't tell. But I could hardly see her soul. It was so faint. It's almost gone." Kumang shook her head as she recollected her meeting with Tenang's soul.

Rikok knitted her eyebrows. "You mean she is dying?"

"She said she is. She moaned a lot about so many things that went wrong in her life. It's difficult to tell which ones are true, which ones are her own imaginations. She strikes me as someone who likes to play the victim. Everything that goes wrong in her life is someone else's fault, not hers. She enjoys harvesting pity for herself. But I have to agree with her on this. I don't think she will last very long."

"What did she say about the *pua* she wove? Did she know that it is the last battle at the end of the world? Or if it is really the battle?" Rikok asked.

"It is the battle at the end of the world. She boasts that she knows who the boy is." Kumang bit her lip and paused. "If you believe what she said, that is," she quickly filled in the silence she created.

"Really? Who is he?" Rikok asked. "Don't tell me he's a shape-shifter."

Kumang shrugged her shoulders. "She doesn't know, I tell you! She just likes to

100

feel important and said that she knows. I doubt Inik Bunsu can tell who the boy is, so how can anyone?"

Rikok threw her eyes to Lulong, asking the same question in silent. However, Lulong chose to fix her eyes on the canopies above their heads rather than answering her curiosity. Therefore, she redirected her eyes back to Kumang. "What now?"

"I thought we have agreed that you will go and find the *pua kumbu* from this Siti while Lulong and I will try to break the curse. Why do you ask again?" Kumang answered.

"Yeah, but that's before we know we are dealing with Inik Bunsu." Rikok frowned. "Surely you're not thinking of confronting her? You know what she's like." She shook Lulong's arm to get her attention. "Can't you talk some sense to your sister?"

Lulong made a face. "She is right, Mao."

"Lu!" Kumang protested.

"I'm sorry, Mao. I don't think we should interfere with Inik Bunsu's wish. We have heard stories about what happened to those who upset her." Lulong shuddered.

"They're just stories. They may not be true. You know how stories tend to be exaggerated and blown out of proportion. She may not be as bad as they describe."

Rikok rolled her eyes. "My concern is not how bad she is. I am worried about her mood swings. She could be so nice and generous in one blink of an eye and turned nasty and cruel in the next blink – without a reason. I don't think we should risk being in her presence when the latter happens."

"Well, you are the one who insists that we protect *mensia* from the cursed *pua kumbu*. Now you don't want to do it. You'd better make up your mind. Do you want to save *mensia* or not? If we don't ask Inik Bunsu to lift the curse, how do you propose we help them?" Kumang challenged her.

"We can still get the *pua kumbu* from *mensia*'s hand, but we don't need to ask Inik Bunsu to lift the curse," Lulong tried to find an alternative.

"What do we do with it, then?" Kumang asked. "We can't destroy it. It will only make the matter worse. Inik Bunsu will definitely take it personally on us."

"I know!" Rikok patted her thighs. "We'll hide it."

"Hide it?" Kumang frowned upon the idea.

"We'll find a place where no man can find it and put it there. As long as nobody sees it, the curse is useless, isn't it?" Rikok looked at Kumang, then Lulong. "In fact, you can keep it in the sky."

"I don't think we should bring the curse back home," Lulong objected right away. "Especially a curse from Inik Bunsu. I doubt that the shape-shifters are spared from it."

"I didn't mean bring it home to Panggau Libau or Gelong longhouse," Rikok clarified. "You can bury it somewhere in the sky. No human beings will find it there. That's what I meant. There must be plenty of places in the vast sky where you can keep it away from eyesight."

"Never mind. We can think about what to do with it. But first, we need to find it," Kumang decided.

"So you agree with me that we leave Inik Bunsu out of this?" Rikok wanted a confirmation.

"Yes, we leave her out of this," Kumang agreed. "Do you know how to find the *pua*, though?"

Rikok was confident. "I will ask a friend to help me find it."

"A friend?" Kumang raised one eyebrow. "A *mensia* friend?"

"Yes, of course, he is a *mensia*. How else can I get help in the city if it is not from a *mensia*," Rikok answered sharply.

Kumang received the message that she did not want to talk about her *mensia* friend, so she kept quiet.

Lulong's curiosity, on the other hand, proved to be too much that she had to ask, "Is he the boy who was prophesized to open all the realm doors?"

"Where did you get the idea?" Rikok asked with irritation. "Ah, from you, I guess." She eyed Kumang. "And you must have heard it from Watt."

"If the *pua* really tells the story about the boy who will destroy the world, it means the boy exists somewhere in this world. If the boy who will destroy the world exists, it means the boy who can open all the realm doors also exists. The two of them come in a package. That's what the prophecies foretell." Lulong explained her reasoning. "Come now, you have to admit that I am right."

"All right, you may be right. Both boys could exist somewhere in this world. But it doesn't mean the boy who can open all the realm doors is Adam. Millions of boys live in this world. It doesn't have to be him. Where did your suspicion come from?"

"Watt said…" Kumang started.

"Oh, we're discussing Watt now, are we?" Rikok cut her off.

Kumang shut her mouth. No, she did not want to talk about Keling. "How long do you think it will take you to get hold of the *pua*?" She changed the topic of their conversation.

"I don't know. It depends on a lot of things. Why? Oh, you want to know how long you must wait for me. You can go back to the sky first. I'll let you know as soon as I have it with me," Rikok answered.

Kumang had no interest in going back home. "You can go back home first, if you'd like," she told Lulong.

"I don't want to leave you alone on the land," Lulong expressed her reluctance.

"It won't be long. I am afraid that your Indai is worried about you staying on the land too long. It can't be difficult to know where the *pua* is, can it?" Kumang asked Rikok.

"I don't see why it would be a problem," Rikok replied.

"Did you hear that? You can come down to the land again when we have received the news about the *pua*'s whereabouts," Kumang persuaded Lulong to accept her idea.

"What are you going to do on the land by yourself?" Lulong was still unsure.

"I'll find something to do." Kumang smiled at Lulong. "When will you start your search for the *pua*?" she asked Rikok.

"Let me see … what is the day today?" Rikok squinted.

"What do you mean?" Kumang did not know what Rikok wanted to know.

Rikok waived her hand in the air as she dismissed her question. "Ah, it's Tuesday … he is working. He won't come to see Apak in the longhouse. He only comes on weekends, which is still 4 days away. No, that's too long. Still, I can see him before that if I…" her eyes stopped at the giant tree trunk in front of her.

"…visit him in the city?" Kumang finished her statement.

Rikok blinked. "Huh? Oh, yeah sure, that's how I'll contact him." She avoided Kumang's eyes. "All right, give me at least 7 days to find the news. Where can I find you?"

"Here is as good as any." Kumang spread her arms around.

"Why don't we meet at Jang's den?"

"What's wrong with this place?"

"Nothing. But I want to see how he's doing. If I need to come here and see him, I'll need two different excuses to tell my adopted parents. I'd rather give them only one excuse. It makes things easier for me. Why do we have to meet here? What is the significance of this place?"

Kumang shook her head. She really did not have a reason to choose that place.

"So, I'll see you at Jang's den. Wish me luck. If all goes well, I might be able to get hold of the *pua* by then." Rikok stood up to bid goodbye to Lulong. "Goodbye for now, Lulong. Have a safe trip home. See you in seven days."

"Bye, Endu. Take care," Kumang bid her goodbye.

"I always do." Rikok waved her goodbye and disappeared from sight.

MEETING A MILLIONAIRE FRIEND

"Why can't we meet him somewhere else?" Rikok eyed her surroundings warily. The place was filled with *mensia* who were sitting down next to separate round tables that scattered all around the room. The big space was crowded with furniture rather than *mensia*. She was grateful for the absence of walls all around the structure. At least she could still inhale the faint smell of the forest.

Adam lifted his shoulders. "He specifically asked for this place. I don't know why, but since we need his help, I thought we'd better comply." He whispered, "Are you all right? Can you handle this place?"

Rikok was a little taken aback. "Why yes, I certainly ..." she lowered her voice down. "Ah, you are referring to my shape-shifter power."

Adam looked concerned. "This is a *mensia*'s place. I'm sorry I had to drag you all the way to Kuching, out of the deep forest. You told me once how all these concrete buildings affect you."

"They still have the same effect." Rikok scanned the room, trying to feel more comfortable in her own skin. "This is a very nice place, considering that it is a *mensia*'s place. It is very open to the outdoors. Does he own this place?"

Adam shook his head. "His family owns a lot of properties around Borneo island, but this one is not one of them. I am wondering the same thing you are. Why did he choose this place of all places to meet? This is a restaurant outside the Semenggoh Nature Reserve, an orangutan sanctuary. This place is surrounded by a forest – not the same type of forest located around your longhouse, of course, but it is still a forest."

"He likes the forest, does he not? This millionaire friend of yours?"

"He used to work with me and Apak at Lanjak Entimau Sanctuary. I would say he is passionate about the wildlife, especially the endemic birds of Borneo."

"Did you tell him why we want to talk to him?"

Adam grimaced. "I didn't think it was something I could tell him over the phone. He is not ... how to say ... a traditional man."

"But he is Iban, didn't you say?"

"He is a full-blooded Iban man. By that I mean both his father and mother are Ibans."

"But he doesn't believe in the Iban traditions?"

"Not in the slightest. That's not how he was brought up. His family is extremely rich. They lead a different life than the rest of us, mortals. I was actually quite surprised that he still responded to my phone call."

"Why? You know each other from work!"

"Yeah, that's the reason I know his personal number." Adam picked up his cup of coffee from the table. "But it's not like we were the best of friends. And ever since he took over his father's empire, we never met or contacted each other. You could say that we went our separate ways. I was just trying my luck when I called him up. I didn't expect him to agree to this meeting and I certainly did not expect him to be able to spare some free time so soon. It was only 4 days ago when your ..." he paused because he was suddenly conscious of something. He lowered his voice down, "... soul met mine." He hurriedly put the cup down. "Ah, there he is." He stood up.

Rikok followed him to stand up. She saw a young man, more or less Adam's age, walking swiftly towards them.

"Adam!" The young man extended his hand to Adam, who grasped it and shook it politely. "How have you been? It's been a while since we last met."

"It certainly has, Ezra. If my memory serves me correctly, the last time I saw you was when you were packing your things at the parking lot of the office. It was your last day of work."

"Ah, yes ... the office, how I miss that place." Ezra smiled dreamily. "I've taken several jobs afterwards, but I would say that my favorite workplace is still the Park."

Rikok had the chance to observe Ezra since he was busy talking to Adam about 'the good old days'. She did not venture into the towns or cities on the island often, so she was not well versed with how city men should look like. Nevertheless, judging from the neatly combed hair on top of his head to his shinny polished shoes, he was definitely much better groomed than Adam.

Ezra might have felt Rikok's eyes on him. He shifted his eyes to find her standing a step behind Adam. His smile froze. He seemed to have been struck by something.

Adam turned to where Ezra's gaze went. "Oh dear, I am very sorry. Let me introduce you to my friend. This is Imah. She is Apak's daughter. Do you still remember Apak from the office?"

Ezra dragged his eyes from Rikok to Adam. "Apak?" He blinked several times before his eyes went back slowly to Rikok. "You are Saing's daughter?"

"Yes, I am," Rikok, whose *mensia*'s name was Imah, replied politely. "It's nice to have finally met you. I heard a lot about you from Apak." She extended her hand.

Ezra looked at it warily before he accepted the handshake. "Did you?" His laugh was a bit awkward. "I'm scared to ask what he said about me."

Adam joined Ezra's laugh. "Your father has a very high standard when it comes to evaluating new rangers at the office," he told Rikok. "I'm sure he doesn't have anything nice to say about any of us." He grinned at Ezra.

"Why made you say that? He has the highest regards towards all the young men he works with," Rikok defended her adopted father. She pulled her hand away from Ezra's grip.

Ezra readjusted his manners and brought his smile back. "Come, come, come, sit down. Have you ordered anything? Those? Only drinks? That won't do, Adam. Order some food. I haven't had lunch today. I'm famished. Now, don't be so heartless to let me eat alone." He took a seat and looked around. He waved at the waiter who readily came to him and handed them the menus. "Order anything you want. Meals are on me today…no, no! No argument. I chose this place. I'll pay. You can buy me lunch some other day at a place of your own choosing." As he opened the menu and his eyes scanned the list of food, he asked Adam in somewhat absent-minded manner, "How's everyone at the Park?"

"Everyone is fine, I guess. We're losing more and more park rangers, including your friend, Lucky. What happened to him? Why did he suddenly disappear?"

Ezra glanced from behind the menu in his hands. "I have no idea."

"I reckon since you were the one who recommended him to us, you would know his whereabouts. I heard …"

Ezra lowered the menu down to stare at Adam. "What did you hear?"

"People said you settled him at Hilton Resort Hotel."

"I did."

"So where is he now?"

Ezra shrugged. "One day he just left everything behind." The smile he directed towards Adam was a little too stiff. "We don't live in each other's pocket, you know. He can do whatever he wants with his life. Why? Did he commit an offense at the Park? Did he steal something? Did he do something he should not have?"

"No, no, nothing like that. I'm just curious, that's all."

"Then, I am not under any obligation to know his whereabouts."

An awkward silence ensued following Ezra curt remark about Lucky.

Adam cleared his throat, grappling to start a new conversation. "Other than that, it's the same routine, day in day out."

Ezra lowered the menu down once more. "Really? I don't think so. Now it's my turn to tell you what I heard. I heard you guys managed to bring down the network of illegal hunting – or something to that extent. That's a big feat, man! Congratulations to all of you at the Park! How did you do it? Did the cameras I donate to the Park help in any way?" he asked seriously.

"Yes, of course, they do," Adam replied quickly.

"Tell me how it went down." Ezra put the menu on the table.

"Eh, I thought you've heard? Besides, the story was all over the newspapers a while ago." Adam looked embarrassed to receive the praise.

"The newspapers do not always tell the whole truth. There are stories that were not covered by the news, am I right?" He nodded with satisfaction when Adam did not reply. "I heard about the unexplained dead monkeys, for instance."

"Who told you about it?" Adam frowned. "Lucky? Oh, yeah, he was the one the people who found them. What did he say?"

"Not much. He said he could not tell me why they died. He also said Apak would ask Adriel to arrange a postmortem on the remains. He disappeared before he could tell me anything about the findings. So? What was the cause of death? Were they poisoned? Like the pigmy elephants in Sabah? Tsk! That was gruesome business! Lucky told me he did not see any sign of the monkeys being slaughtered, nor did he hear or see any trace of gun shots. That means we can't blame the poachers for this tragedy. Now, you work there. What was the verdict on their death?" He added hurriedly when Adam hesitated, "Come on, I don't gossip. This is something that I care about. I want to know." Suddenly, he remembered something. "Wait! First, let's order some food. After that, you can tell me all about it while we eat." He picked up the menu and this time he gave full attention to it.

THE UNFORTUNATE TRUTH

Semenggoh Nature Reserve, Kuching, the Land

"Dessert, anyone?" Ezra asked both Adam and Rikok. "No? How about another round of drink, Adam?"

"No, thank you. Really, I don't think my stomach can accommodate another drop." Adam rubbed his flat belly in contentment.

"But we are still going to be here for a while. We haven't even started to talk about why you called me. You said it is very important." Ezra waived his hand to the waiter. He ordered another drink for himself. He looked at Rikok briefly, who shook her head, and then at Adam, who told the waiter, "None for me, thank you."

As soon as the waiter left them, Ezra asked again, "So? What do you want to talk to me about?"

"Oh, that." Adam was suddenly tense.

Ezra leaned back on his chair. He folded his arms in front of his chest.

"Well…" Adam gulped.

"Yes?"

"The reason I … we …" Adam waved his hand to indicate himself and Rikok, "… we want to talk to you is that …we want to ask you for a favor." He became more and more careful as each word left his lips.

Ezra did not make any response – verbally or physically.

"You see …," Adam fidgeted uncomfortably on his chair. His laugh sounded forced. "This is rather difficult … I don't know how to put it…"

Ezra stretched out his arms and clasped his hands behind his head. "Let me help you then … you want to ask me to give a job for your girlfriend here." His eyes went straight to Rikok. "Am I right?"

Rikok smiled, "I am sorry, but you are mistaken."

Ezra seemed slightly relieved. He leaned forward and propped his head on hand. "Oh? Am I? Wrong about what? The job?"

"No, no, we are not here to ask for a job." Adam waved his hands frantically in front of his chest.

Ezra raised one of his eyebrows.

Adam cleared his throat. He sat forward to put his elbows on the table. "I ... we want to talk to you about ... the Pua Kumbu Exhibition in Kuching."

"Eh?" Ezra looked completely perplexed. He put his hand down.

"I understand that the organizer, Daniel, is your relative?" Adam probed.

"Yeah ..." Ezra replied slowly. "He is family, so to speak. He is married to my cousin. What about it?"

"We are wondering if you could talk him into letting us borrow the master piece?"

"Borrow?" Ezra's eyes grew big. "What does that mean? Borrow? The master piece? Are you talking about the *pua kumbu*? What do you want to do with a few thousand dollar fabric?"

"We want to ..." Adam heaved, "cleanse it."

"Cleanse it? Like ... cleaning it? You don't think Daniel, or the owner of the *pua kumbu*, knows how to take care of it? What makes you think they need your help?"

"No, that's not what I mean," Adam corrected him right away.

"Then, what do you mean?"

"I ... you see ... we ..." Adam bit his lip.

Rikok touched Adam's arm. "Let me try."

Adam was worried. "I don't think ..."

"No, Adam, let her try. You obviously cannot explain yourself well," Ezra interrupted. He gave his full attention to Rikok for the first time ever since they had met.

"The *pua kumbu* is cursed." Rikok went straight to the core of the issue.

111

"I beg your pardon?" Ezra frowned. He would have said more if the waiter did not come by to the table.

"I told you not to tell him *that* version," Adam whispered to Rikok while the waiter placed the newly ordered drink on the table.

Ezra asked as soon as the waiter walked away, "Ah, so there are many versions of the story? Which version are you planning to tell me, Imah?"

"The truth. Adam doesn't think you can handle it," Rikok explained.

"Hmmm…" Ezra stared at Adam, who looked abashed. Then, he said to Rikok, "and you think I can."

"Not only that you can, but you also deserve to know the truth." Rikok was very composed.

Ezra threw his hands in the air. "All right. Try me."

"You see…" Adam started.

Ezra held his hand up. "I want *her* to tell me her version of the truth." He picked up the glass and cradled it in his hands. "Go on, the *pua kumbu* is cursed … and?"

"And anyone who sees it will get the curse," Rikok continued. "That's why we want to ask your help. We are hoping that you would persuade your family to surrender it to us."

"Borrow, you mean? Let me guess. You want to try lifting the curse, that's what he meant by cleansing it just now." He made a hand gesture towards Adam. "Yes? Afterwards, after it is cleansed, you will give it back to Daniel. Correct?"

Rikok shook her head.

"No?" Ezra knitted his eyebrows. "Don't tell me you mean to keep it for yourself?"

"We cannot lift the curse."

"Your …err… *manang* cannot do it?"

"You have heard of our *manang*?" Rikok was surprised.

Ezra scowled. "For a very long time, my father had a *manang* in his life. His spiritual advisor – that's what he said the man was for. That part of his life is over now, thank God." He let his eyes run up and down Rikok's stature as if he tried to place her in a particular category. "You haven't answered my question. Can't your *manang* help?"

"Sadly, no. We are dealing with a power beyond the power of our *manang*."

To Rikok's surprise, Ezra's face changed. It turned into a blank mask. Rikok could not guess what he was thinking about as he turned away to stare at the forest outside.

"Please." She reached out to touch his hand on the table. He was startled when he felt her hand on his. "People who had seen this *pua kumbu* died. We want to prevent more innocent people from dying."

"Died, you said? How did they die?" Ezra lifted his eyes to meet Rikok's.

She let go of his hand. "They had nightmares that frightened their souls until the souls couldn't stand it anymore. They had to leave their physical bodies. You know what happens when a man's soul leaves its physical body, don't you?"

Ezra leaned back to his chair. "He goes into a coma like my father."

"You are right." Rikok nodded. "That's why we need your help to prevent more people from being exposed to this curse. The spiritual beings can be quite heartless when it comes to delivering punishments."

"Can they?" Ezra's eyes lost their warmth.

"Unfortunately, yes. Will you help us?" Rikok asked even if she could guess what his answer would be judging from his looks.

Ezra's face hardened. "Why should I? My father has been on a vegetative state for years. What help has he ever got from you lot? What did he do wrong until he has to be punished like that?" he glared at her.

Adam intervened. "Err ... Ezra, your father was involved in a boating accident, there's nothing anybody could do for him. It was an accident. Besides, *manang* cannot help much with physical injuries as severe as that of your fa ...," he faltered as Ezra's fierce gaze was aimed at him. "I mean ... that's what I read in the newspapers..." he added in a much softer voice, "I could be wrong."

"What happened to your father?" Rikok inquired gently.

Ezra did not answer her question for a long while. When he finally did, he sighed. "He was involved in a boating accident," he mumbled.

113

"The doctors cannot help?"

Ezra shook his head slowly. "It's been years since he lies on the bed – unconscious. There's nothing they can do to wake him. They said he is brain-dead. The only thing that keeps him alive is his strong heart."

"You mentioned that your father had a *manang* friend. What did he say about your father's condition?" Rikok probed further.

Ezra laughed helplessly. "The man disappeared after the accident. We can't find him anywhere. Believe me, I've tried. I wish that's because he himself is already dead. All those years my father showered him with money, how did he repay him? He abandoned my father in the hour when he needed him the most." He stared hard at Rikok. "Don't call him my father's friend. He is none of that."

"You hate him," Rikok stated her observation out loud. "And everything he believes in."

"Can you blame me?" Ezra challenged her.

"No," Rikok answered softly. "I am sorry that you and your family have to experience such grievance, but what happened to your father …"

"My father spends his whole life entertaining the idea that the spiritual world exists. More than that, he lets it rule his life. And it …," Ezra swallowed hard. "…and it destroyed his life."

"Are you saying that you do not want to help us?" Rikok looked at Ezra straight in the eye.

"I …" Ezra's eyes were locked with Rikok's. "You believe in the existence of the spiritual world, don't you? Just like my father."

"Yes," Rikok replied with conviction. She was a spiritual creature after all.

"Have you encountered any of these spiritual creatures?"

"I have, if you must know." She had lived surrounded by spiritual creatures. She read his troubled eyes. "I dare say that anyone who has spent a considerable time living in the forest would have seen a spiritual creature or two. Haven't you?" She wanted to test her suspicion.

Ezra's pupils dilated. "Sometimes I thought I imagine things," he murmured almost to himself. "But her face haunts my dreams. I can't …" He blinked and the lock was broken. He shifted his eyes to Adam. "What about you?"

"Me?" Adam pointed at his own face.

"You're a city boy, aren't you? I mean, you grew up in the nation's capital city. Not in a longhouse inside the deep jungle like she." Ezra pointed at Rikok.

"True."

"I expect you were brought up with values that come with living in a metropolitan city."

"I guess."

"And you still can say you've encountered a spiritual creature or two in your daily wandering in the Park?"

Adam took his time answering. "I have." He chose his words carefully. "Not in the Park, I haven't. But I have."

"Which means, just like my father and she, you also believe that the spiritual world exists?"

"After everything I've seen …" he smiled ruefully at Ezra. "You don't want to know what I've seen in my life. There was a time I thought I was cursed because of this … this … some people call it 'gift'. Let just say that right from the start, I was never given the choice not to believe."

Ezra let his eyes linger at Adam's slumped body before he pulled the chair forward and shifted the glass on the table to his right. "All right, this is what I am going to do. For the sake of my father and everything he believes in, I am offering you a deal, Adam." His voice was suddenly business-like. "You bring my father's soul back to his body, and I will give you the master piece you want."

"Huh?" Adam's mouth gaped opened. "How can I do that?"

"You're the expert in this spiritual thingy. You tell me. I'll prepare everything you need for the ceremony, or whatever it is you call it. Just let me know what you want. Expenses are not an issue, do you understand? I want my father to wake up."

"But …"

"It is not negotiable, Adam. If you want the master piece that bad, give me what I want. Take this deal or leave it."

"If we …" Rikok stopped talking when Ezra's body emitted a loud buzz followed by a popular song that she often heard on the radio.

Ezra rolled his eyes. He took out a mobile phone from his pocket. He waived his hand to Rikok. "Sorry, I must get this. It's my mother. Give me a second."

He swiped his finger through the surface of the phone and put it next to his hear. "Mom? Can I call you back in a few minutes? I'm in a middle of …. Huh? Mom?"

Even from across the table, Rikok could hear the hysterical voice of a woman.

"Mom, calm down. I don't understand what you are saying. What happened?" Ezra closed his other ear with his finger. "What? I can't hear you." He stood abruptly. "Excuse me," he muttered as he hurriedly went outside the building.

Adam leaned over to Rikok. "Can you wake his father up from a comma?"

She looked at him. "You know I'm not a *manang*."

"Do you think Apak can? He is a very powerful *manang*. He brought back the soul of a logger who was taken by *antu gerasi* once. Can he do the same for Ezra's father?"

"I doubt his father's soul was taken by *antu gerasi*. Besides, I don't think we should involve Apak."

"Why not? He is a *manang*. You and I are not. We can't heal wounded souls. Let Apak try."

"And how will you explain to him about our deal with Ezra without mentioning the cursed *pua kumbu*?"

"Oh … I see your point. You don't want him to know about the background story of the cursed *pua kumbu* and the involvement of your … spiritual creature family."

"You got that right. He doesn't even know that I am a spiritual creature. As far as he is concerned, he found a human child in the forest. He thought my parents abandoned me, so he took me in and raised me as his own child. He has no idea that I am a shape-shifter. And I'd like to keep it that way."

Adam scratched his head. "If that is the case, what can we do?"

"I can find another *manang* who might be able to help."

"We still have to explain to this other *manang* about the *pua kumbu* and your family …" he stopped to see her face. "Ah, you are talking about finding a

116

celestial *manang* – not a human *manang*."

Rikok nodded. "But we must know what happened to his father."

"I suppose I can find the news about the accident. It's been a few years back, but with the news goes digital nowadays, it will not be a problem to trace it back."

"What people wrote in newspapers might not be what actually happened," Rikok cautioned him.

"Ah, Ezra admitted as much," Adam agreed.

"I personally believe it has something to do with spiritual creatures. Did you see how he reacted when he asked me about the existence of the spiritual world?"

"Yeah, that was eerie. Do you suspect that he saw a spiritual being or two that day? He was with his father when it happened. I've heard different rumors about the incident, but he is in it in each of them. He was also wounded because of it although his injury was not as bad as his father."

"He must tell us what happened. We can't ..." Rikok stopped talking upon seeing Ezra walking quickly towards them.

"I am very sorry, but I must leave now." Ezra did not bother to sit down.

"Is everything all right?" Adam stood up.

Ezra grimaced. "I can't say until I see my mother. That's why I must rush now. Bye, Adam." He offered his hand to Adam, who promptly shook it. He then offered his hand to Rikok. "Nice meeting you, Imah."

Rikok stood up to hold his hand with both of hers. "We take the deal."

Ezra nodded. "Great." He pulled his hand away.

Rikok refused to let it go. "But you must tell us the truth about what happened to your father."

Ezra froze.

"Otherwise, no deal," Rikok said firmly.

Ezra nodded again, more firmly this time. "I'll be in touch. Now, I really must go." His eyes went to his hand, clasped inside Rikok's hands.

Rikok let go of him and took a step back. "Goodbye. I hope everything is all right with your family."

Ezra managed a faint smile. "Thank you. I also hope for the same thing."

He went half-running out of the building into the parking lot.

AN OLD ENEMY

Kayan River, Mentarang Terrain, the Land

Kumang gathered her silky long hair to the right and gently squeezed water out of the thick strand. She just finished her bath by the Kayan River. She looked up to the sky for a home she could not see. Panggau Libau longhouse was situated on the first layer of the sky, just above where she was at right now. She could not explain why of all the places on the land she chose that spot to wait for news from Rikok. She did not want to accept that it was because she missed home, or – heaven forbid – her husband. She cast her eyes around the mountainous scenery. The land was still the best place to be, she realized with a feeling of fondness. She might not love the land as much as Rikok did, but at that very moment she felt like she could almost understand why her sister-in-law chose to sever ties with her family just to be on the land. Their home in the sky was only a mirage of the land. Naturally, the original was always the best.

The forests in Mentarang terrain were more than a hundred years old. She eyed the hovering clouds that framed the upper waves of misty mountains around her. She was grateful that the steep slopes of sandstones valleys protected the ancient forests like a fortress that *mensia* found too troublesome to penetrate. She felt at peace here, alone with the forests that fuelled her shape-shifter's power to the maximum.

Her dreamy look disappeared abruptly as soon as she detected the presence of a *petara* not far behind her. She closed her eyes in desperation. Why couldn't he get the message that she wanted to be left alone? Didn't he know how difficult it was for her to keep pushing him away? Why did he love to torture her so? This had to stop! She had to stop him! Her desperation turned into anger. She got on her feet so fast that the drops of water from her hair had not reached the ground when she stood in front of the man she detected as a *petara*.

"I've told you ....," she halted. Whatever she planned to say to her husband did not materialize.

She could not pinpoint what it was to be exact, but something was off. The man was definitely a *petara*. There was no mistake in that. His handsome face might as well be Keling's. Only he knew what kind of appearance he was assuming right now. But that smile was not Keling's. Keling never smiled at her like that –

119

like he thought he was far superior to her. She inhaled to get a calmer composure. She imagined things – over a smile! Who else could the man be if he was not Keling? This world did not have many *petara* walking about. And for him to think that he was better than her …

She was about to restart what she wanted to say to him with a renewed fire when she caught a glimpse of a female not far behind him. As her eyes zoomed in on the female, she shook her head in disbelief. "You!" What was the female doing with her husband? No, her real concern was what was he doing with her?

"Hello, Kumang. Long time no see. How have you been?" The female stepped forward to stand next to the *petara*. She made a face. "Aw, don't look at me like that. I'm not trying to steal your husband away from you, unlike a certain female, so you don't need to get so workup, dear." She smirked. "This is not your husband," she touched the arm of the male affectionately.

Kumang's jaw tightened. "You've got the nerve to show your face in front of me, Cherurai."

"Why should I be afraid of you?" The female she called Cherurai offered her an indulging smile.

"I am expecting you to feel ashamed of yourself for what you've done to us. We took you in, protected your life from your own brothers. And how did you repay us? We still suffer from the consequences of your actions until this very day. Yet, you don't seem to feel a slight of remorse," Kumang said coldly to the female. "A normal creature wouldn't even dare to show her face, out of guilt. Not you, it seems. Never you." She shifted her eyes to the male. "Oh, I see. You dare because you have a *petara* by your side. I am Kumang of Panggau Libau," she addressed the male. "And you are?"

Kumang had the impression that the male was surprised she needed to ask. "My name is Lium," he answered curtly.

Once again, Kumang received the unspoken message that he expected her to know him. And she admitted that he had the right to feel that way. She should have known him. The male was a *petara,* for heaven's sake! How many *petara* was there in their world? Why did she not know him?

"Nice to meet you, Lium of …?" She decided to find out by asking which longhouse Lium was from. Every shape-shifter came from a longhouse. The real question was which of the existing seven shape-shifter longhouses did Lium come from? Because she had never heard of him, her best guest was that he came from either Bukit Bangkai or Lubok Naga longhouse.

120

For centuries, the shape-shifters had endured long and bloody wars against each other. The winners of the wars took in their surviving enemies as their slaves in their respective longhouses – mostly the children, and the females who surrendered for the sake of protecting their children. By the time peace was successfully brought upon them, only five longhouses survived: Panggau Libau, Gelong, Batang Rajang, Nanga Langit, and Ulu Tinting. The peace also brought freedom for the slaves. They were given two choices, either to be adopted by the family who used to be their masters or to go freely. It was not surprising that the majority of the slaves opted to break free. They got together to form Bukit Bangkai longhouse. The first Chief of Bukit Bangkai set a nonnegotiable rule that no resident of his longhouse was allowed to form any acquaintance with the other five longhouses. Anyone who was found violating the rule was dealt with utmost ruthless punishments. That was the reason why, apart from the Chief himself, the other five longhouses' residents did not really know who was who in Bukit Bangkai longhouse. Another thing that came out of this strict rule was a group of residents broke away from Bukit Bangkai to form a new longhouse: Lubok Naga. Lubok Naga longhouse's Chief welcomed any shape-shifters who ran away from their original longhouses for all sorts of reasons. These runaways usually arrived at Lubok Naga with a new identity which the Chief never bothered to investigate. Lubok Naga longhouse prided itself to be the place where its residents could build a brand-new life that they had always wanted to have. As a longhouse that host former slaves and runaways, naturally the residents avoided any dealings with the longhouses filled with their former masters and their past. Thus, the other longhouses hardly knew the identities of Lubok Naga residents.

Upon his silence, she clarified her question, "Which shape-shifter longhouse are you from?"

"I am not a shape-shifter," Lium said rather vindictively.

"Oh?"

"I'm a *bunsu baya*," Lium stated.

Kumang did not catch any pride resonating in his words. "A *bunsu baya*?" One of her eyebrows rose. He was not a spiritual creature from the crocodile kingdom! She could detect his shape-shifter's presence through and through as she was certain he could fully detect hers. So why did he admit that he was a creature he knew that she knew he was not? Was he a recluse that even Lubok Naga longhouse rejected? His crime had to be unforgivable!

As if he could read her mind, he said, "Families are not always formed based on bloodlines. My own bloodline disowned me. The *bunsu baya* took me in. I am one of them now. Does that answer your curiosity?"

One more time, he gave her the vibes that she should have been able to guess who he was by giving out that piece of information. She wanted to hit her head for not knowing the answer.

"Apparently not," Cherurai commented dryly to Lium. "She is not as bright as she wishes people to think she is. Not as pretty as she thinks she is either. Otherwise, that pathetic husband of hers would not have looked at another female, would he not?"

Kumang gritted her teeth. "You still can't stop yourself from spreading lies, can you, Che? It's true what they say, old habits die hard."

"Lies? Every resident of the water kingdoms knows about your husband and that female water spirit!"

"But you are not a resident of the water kingdoms! You are an *antu raya*. You do not live under the water. You live in the sky …ops, I forgot. Your family cast you out. Even your own brothers cannot stand your lies!"

"I don't live under the water. You are right. But he does." She touched Lium's arm. "He told me what happened that day with him and the water spirit. Unless you want to accuse him of lying, you'd better stop the denial. Your husband has another female on the side, or maybe more. Who knows? You'll never know with a male like that."

Something Cherurai had said caught Kumang's attention. "You were there?" She stared at Lium with sudden comprehension. "You were the other *petara!* You fought Keling in Batang Kapuas."

Lium nodded. "And wounded him so badly that he almost went to Sebayan."

The smile that made Kumang uncomfortable just now came back to his face. She could see it for what it was now. It was pride, bordering on arrogance. "Why did you fight him? What offense has he ever done to you?"

Lium scowled. "What has he done? He shouldn't have …"

Che cut him off, "Why do you always point finger at someone else? Has it ever occurred to you that it was your husband's fault? He challenged the King of Baya for a life and death duel. He asked for it. He got what he asked for." Che clasped her hands into fists. "Almost," she hissed. "It was close – so close. I was so close to see him die. For a moment I thought he did. Until that wretched female came and rescued him!"

"So you were really there when it happened." Kumang caught Cherurai's lie.

"Do you think I wanted to miss the opportunity to see him go to Sebayan with my own two eyes? I would have gladly sent him there myself had I had the power. Unfortunately, I had no choice but to wait for other creatures to finish him off!" Che snapped.

Kumang raised her eyebrows at her. "Be careful, Che, you are showing your true color." She addressed Lium, "I wonder if you really know the company you are keeping. This female *antu raya* …"

"Ah, he knows all about me," Cherurai dismissed her warning.

"Do you?" Kumang continued talking to Lium. "And you can cope with all the lies, the cheats, the schemes, the …"

"Stop painting me as a villain, Kumang. I am the victim here. Your heartless husband killed my twin sister, don't you forget it."

"That's because your sister threatened to kill me! Oh, I know now. Is this why you are here with your *petara* friend? You want to avenge your sister's death?"

Cherurai snorted. "We are not here to kill you. Get real! You are not that important!"

"You tried it before. Don't deny it. You also used the *gerasi* to try killing Sampurai so that Keling would feel the pain of losing a sibling the way you lost your sister." She said to Lium, "And now she wants to use you to get her revenge by hurting me. I hope you know what you're getting yourself into. Haven't you heard what happened to the *gerasi* she used to hurt one of us?"

Lium's eyes narrowed upon hearing her warning.

"Resorting to threats now, are we?" Cherurai purred. "Are you scared you'll lose your life today, Kumang?"

"Threats? I merely stated a fact. You failed the last time you tried to kill me. Your sister paid for your folly with her life. The *gerasi* failed the last time they tried to kill Sampurai. Again, they paid for your folly with their lives." She let out a pretend sigh. "Still, I have to give you credit for your amazing skill of finding creatures who are willing to be used for your own personal gain. Unfortunately, you will fail again today."

"Don't be so sure of that, Kumang." Che smiled smugly. "You don't have your

123

good for nothing husband with you now to save you."

"You did not think he was 'good for nothing' when you wanted to use him to kill your brothers, did you? Or when you persuaded him to rule over *mensia* to fulfil your crazy ambition of saving the world, did you? He only became 'good for nothing' in your eyes after he refused to help you get what you wanted," Kumang said sharply.

"Why did you say the idea of saving the world 'crazy'?" Lium asked out of the blue.

"I'm sorry?" Kumang was distracted by his question.

"Lium agrees with me that this world needs saving." Che's smile was serene.

"No!" Kumang could not believe it. This mentally unstable female *raya* finally found a powerful ally who believed in her delusional idea to rule the world. "Not you! The *gerasi*, I can understand. They are simple creatures. She could've easily manipulated them. Not you …" a shape-shifter should have known better. But a memory of a young shifter of Gelong longhouse who became a victim of Cherurai's scheme flashed back. Still …"You look like a sensible male, how can you support her idea to rule over *mensia* in the pretext of saving the world?"

Lium looked at her as if she just insulted him. "I am not interested in ruling over the insipid *mensia*. They are not a danger to our world. It's so easy to wipe them out of the face of the land if I want to."

"What do you want to save the world from?"

"The boy."

"From a boy? A *mensia* boy? I thought you said *mensia* are insipid."

"Not a *mensia* boy. The boy who will destroy the world." Lium nodded calmly to reaffirm his intention. "I am hunting him down," he admitted. It looked like he meant every word he said.

Kumang was speechless for a while. "Are you telling me that you know who the boy is?"

"Ah, that is why we are here."

"I don't understand."

"I want you to tell me."

"Me? I don't know who he is. What gives you the idea that I know?"

"You have spoken to Tenang anak Tinggi about the *pua kumbu* she wove – about the last battle at the end of the world, haven't you? She described to you the story that she wove on the *pua*." He smiled to see her face. "The forest has many ears. You should've been more careful about what you said while you are in it. Pretty much every living thing in the forest is aware of the *pua*'s existence by now. The news has spread. Everyone is worried about the apocalypse." He waited for her to say anything. When she did not, he repeated his command, "Tell me about the boy."

"I don't know who he is! She didn't tell me his name! That's because she doesn't know his name!"

"I'm not asking for his name. I want to know what the *pua* shows."

Kumang shook her head. "Go and find her yourself. Visit her dream. You're a shape-shifter." She raised her voice when he started shaking his head. "You *are* a shape-shifter. You know how to do it. Ask her!"

"I can't. I tried. I couldn't find her. Her soul is already in Sebayan. Now, before you suggest I visit the others who have seen it, as if I do not have the capability of thinking for myself, let me tell you that I did. Unfortunately, they do not know what the image is about, including the old woman who could recognize it as a battle. She didn't weave the *pua*, so she did not create those symbols. She doesn't know what they mean. They're just lowlife thieves. They know nothing of the sacred meaning in a precious *pua kumbu*. They are totally useless. It's a good thing they won't linger in this world for much longer. Our precious air is totally wasted on them." He paused to let the information sink in. "So, you see. You and your sister are the only ones who know about it now. Tell me!"

"I can't!"

"Why not? Surely you do not wish to protect this boy who is about to destroy all of us? What's the matter, Kumang? Do you find that he is too close to home?"

Kumang was worried to see his knowing smile. "What?"

Even Cherurai got the implied message. "What are you saying, Lium? You mean the boy comes from her home? But who could it be? I know all of them. I've lived with them once. Who could ..." she asked him with wonder. "Oh! I know! I know!" She clasped her hands in delight. "I bet the boy is that ghastly half-breed brother-in-law of hers. Oh, yeah! I can see that it's him! He and that

125

awful temper of his. You're right, Lium. It's him. It's definitely him. There can be no one else. Mark my words. We don't need her help after all. You'd better prepare yourself to hunt him down. He is on the land right now, you know, serving his punishment. It will be very easy to find him and send him to Sebayan."

"Leave Sampurai out of this! You are just saying that because he is hunting for your head," Kumang said angrily to Cherurai. Then, she turned to Lium. "Don't let her use you to get rid of her enemy! She doesn't know that it is him! Nobody knows who the boy is. You can't kill him for something he hasn't done. You can't go after his life based on wild speculation. It is not right! That is a crime in itself!"

To her surprise, his face changed abruptly. The trace of arrogance was gone. "Such action is indeed a crime," he agreed. Kumang wondered why he looked so sad. The next time he spoke, his voice was almost gentle, "Don't worry. I will not do that to him."

Cherurai screamed. "Lium! Don't listen to her. You don't know what he is like. I do. And I'm telling you …"

"Silence! You don't know what you are talking about. I do!" he barked at her. His high and mighty attitude came back in a flash. "Be quiet from now on. I want to talk to her. Go somewhere you can't be seen and heard!"

Kumang watched in amusement how Cherurai squirmed before she made herself scarce. It was too bad that she was not given ample time to enjoy the scene. She was instantly alarmed when he took a few steps towards her.

"That is why I want … I am asking you to tell me what Tenang said about the boy. Please, I implore you. I want to minimize the chance of hunting the wrong boy. As you correctly said, it is not right. I am asking you to help me do it right," Lium said urgently.

"It would be wrong of me to tell you about the boy. Look, hear me out, all right? Tenang had a dream about the day of the apocalypse. She interpreted that dream into an image on a *pua kumbu*. That in itself is already a distortion of the truth because personal interpretation is very subjective."

"Come now, Kumang. I am a shape-shifter, as you'd like to remind me. I know how a piece of *pua kumbu* is made. I've seen my mother wove them. The weaver may have her own interpretation of the dream she had, but her spiritual guide is always by her side to make sure the image does represent the dream. No distortion of the truth happened here."

126

"You are right. The image on the *pua kumbu* is not distorted from the message in the dream because the spiritual guide will make sure that it is not. But how a weaver describes the image to someone else about it might. Words have multiple meanings. We only hear what we want to hear. And that someone who listens to the explanation of the image will interpret it to her own understanding and form a somewhat distorted idea about the image."

Lium sighed. "Why do you females like to complicate things? Just tell me what she told you. In her own words, in your own words, it doesn't matter. Let me be the judge of what is the truth, what is not."

"How can you tell which information is the truth, and which one is not?"

"Do not underestimate me. Hasn't it ever occurred to you that I'm asking all these questions because I know something you don't?"

Kumang blinked fast. "Such as?"

He smirked. "If I tell you, I will have to kill you." His face turned serious. "That was the promise I made when the information was passed on to me. I always keep my word."

"I seriously doubt that you can kill me," Kumang commented lightly.

"You're not asking me to put the idea into a test, are you?" Lium squinted. "Let me remind you that I almost sent your husband to Sebayan."

"I am not my husband."

"Hmmm … so you are determined not to tell me what you know?"

"I have made up my mind. I appreciate what you are trying to do, Lium. But this is not the way to do it."

"You're forcing me to find another way. It's a pity. I believe this is the easiest and also the safest way."

"There has to be a better way."

"Naturally there is always another way, but I doubt you would call it better."

"What way is that?"

"I can find your sister instead. I'll persuade her to tell me what I want to know."

"What? My sister is not on the land! Go to the sky to find her if you dare!" She was more than sure he would not dare. She was so grateful Lulong was at home

127

right now, fully protected by both Gelong and Panggau Libau warriors. She had to warn them about this.

"She's not? All right, I will have to find another alternative to make you agree with me, won't I? Something like …hmmm… I give you no choice but to tell me?"

"I don't know what you're talking about."

"How about this? Say, you tell me what you know in exchange for your sister-in-law's life? She's the one on the land, isn't she?" Lium nodded with satisfaction to see a glimpse of panic in her face. "Yes, she will do just nice. I'll see you soon, Kumang." He turned away. "Let's go, Che!" he flicked his head to Cherurai, who waited for him upstream.

"No! Hey, wait up!" Kumang called out.

He stopped to face her. "Yes, Kumang? Have you changed your mind?"

"No! I won't have a hand in you killing an innocent male."

"I do not want to kill an innocent male! That is why I ask you tell me what you know. By not telling me, you are forcing me to guess and I might make the very mistake you do not want me to make. For the last time, I am begging you. Tell me what you know!"

"I can't!"

"Tsk! The stubbornness of a female is beyond my comprehension." He shrugged and walked away.

"Leave my family alone!" Kumang shouted at his back.

"It's your choice, Kumang. Don't go around later saying it's my fault when something you do not like happen to your family. I have given you enough chance to avoid it." He did not stop walking away as he spoke.

Kumang moved so fast she blocked him from walking further.

"Leave my family alone! I'm warning you," she said sternly.

He was not impressed by her threat. "Or what? You'll kill me? I can assure you that you cannot. Now let me go through. I have things to do somewhere else." He took a few steps to his right to walk past her.

Kumang moved to stand in front of him one more time. "Give me your word that you will leave my family alone."

"Move aside! Or I will move you by force!" He gave her an ultimatum.

"Not before you give me your word!"

He straightened his posture. "Very well! Since you insist."

He stomped his right foot to the ground and the earth beneath his feet bounced up and down to form a wave that travelled fast towards Kumang.

THE ARGUMENTS BY THE RIVER

Kumang did not move away from where she was standing. She imitated what Lium did, stomping her right foot to the ground, and the wave subsided. The ground was flat once more. "Give me your word that you won't disturb my family," she told Lium. "That is all I ask."

"Then, tell me what Tenang told you." Lium was not less stern than she. The moment he lifted his arms dried leaves and tree branches were lifted from the ground. When he pointed his arms to Kumang, the leaves and branches gathered to form a gigantic spear that flew straight to her.

"I've told you I won't help you kill an innocent male!" Kumang swiped her arms in the air and the gigantic spear was dispersed into its original forms – countless leaves and branches, which flew back to Lium with lightning speed.

Lium scooped the air around him to form a whirl wind that protected him from the coming debris. The wall of wind deflected the debris to all possible directions and hit the nearest things that stood in the way – the plants of the forest.

"If that is your decision, let me go. Let me do what I want to do. I don't stop you from doing what you want to do," he shouted from behind the whirlwind.

Kumang could hear the distressed moans of the plants around them. She understood that the animals nearby had run for their lives at the first sign of trouble, but the plants were rooted to the ground. They could not get away from the newly formed battlefield. All they could do was to scream their protests without much hope of getting their wish heard. She pitied them. She had to take the battle away from the forest. She unbuckled her metal belt.

"I don't intend to interfere with what you want to do. Just promise me you will leave my family out of it," she repeated her request.

"I can't make that promise. I'll do anything to stop the boy. I won't even spare my own family members, let alone yours. Look, we don't need to fight today. If I don't need to disturb your family, I won't do it. I'm not unreasonable." The whirlwind thinned so that Kumang could see Lium's figure behind it.

"Do you expect me to wait until you hurt one of them?" Kumang asked incredulously.

"In other words, you'd prefer we settle this today, once and for all?"

"You can't threaten a life and get away with it! Which world system do you follow? Is that how you've lived your life?"

Kumang did not expect him to roar in anger as a response.

"Why do you need to ask how I've lived my life? Do not pretend you do not know what all of you have done to me!" The ground trembled violently. Everything around them that was not rooted to the ground was lifted and spinning wildly in the air.

Kumang quickly manipulated the earth beneath her feet to root herself to the ground before the strong wind lifted her up like the rest of the forest debris. She was anchored safely to the ground. However, she had to protect herself from the onslaught of the moving debris that did not seem to notice she was standing there. She whipped her metal belt around to fend off the debris from hitting her body from all directions. Soon she realized that she had a problem. She did not have eyes at the back of her head to know which debris could give her a fatal wound, or when it would strike her from behind. That her feet were planted to the ground made it more difficult to get a good angle to see what was going on behind her back.

She screamed when a thick dead trunk hit her right arm in its way to make a complete turn in the air. It caused her to drop her belt to the ground, leaving her defenseless. She knew if she wanted her belt back, she had to bear more hits from the debris. Before she could make up her mind, she heard a male voice said to her, "Pick your weapon from the ground. I'll cover you!"

She did not know why she obeyed the instruction given by an unknown male, but she did as she had been told. A battle never gave anyone the time to think and reflect what course of action was the best under the circumstance. Every decision was made on instinctive mode, especially when one was under intense attack the way she was at the moment.

As soon as she straightened her back with her belt in her hand, she saw an orangutan near her swinging from one piece of flying debris to another while at the same time kicking and pushing the bigger debris away to make room for the two of them. The orangutan caught her eyes and smiled at her.

"Look out!" Kumang shouted at him when the same tree trunk that hit her

131

swirling back behind him. She wrapped the end of her belt around the trunk and sent it flying outside the whirlwind that surrounded them. She bit her lip. This madness had to stop.

"Cover me one more time, will you?" she asked the orangutan. She did not wait for an answer. She left the debris to the orangutan to handle while she focused her eyes to find Lium. Ah, she could see him standing to her left. She calculated the movements of the debris in the air, waiting for a window of opportunity to deliver her attack. As soon as she saw a clear passage, she threw the end of her belt towards Lium. With her power over metal, the belt was extended in length as it travelled with high speed.

A moment before the belt reached his chest, he caught it deftly in his hand. What he did not calculate was that the top of the belt changed form into a sharp blade that cut the flesh of his hand mercilessly. As soon as he let it go in reflex, it continued its travel to plant itself on his upper arm.

And just like that, all the debris dropped to the ground. As soon as the air was clear, Kumang released her feet from the stronghold of the ground.

Before she could pull her belt out of his arm, he did it for her. In a blink of an eye, he transformed his human body so that his wound stopped bleeding.

Kumang pulled the loose belt back to her. She could feel the presence of the orangutan by her side. She did not see him for she could not afford to take her eyes off Lium.

"I will make you pay for what you just did." Lium gritted his teeth. His hand involuntarily went to touch his free-from-wound forearm.

"I expect nothing less from you." Kumang tightened her hold on her belt.

"I don't think it is right for a male to fight a female," the orangutan commented.

Lium glared at him. "And who asked for your opinion? I do not need to hear a speech about what is right or wrong from a useless creature like you! If you know what's good for you, be gone!"

The orangutan shifted his eyes to the ground. He muttered, "I'm just saying that it is not right for you to …"

Lium snapped his fingers in the air and a huge rock rose from the ground. It took a swing on the orangutan and sent it flying towards the river.

"What are you doing?" Kumang shouted as her eyes followed where the orangutan's body went. She predicted that it would land in the middle of the deep river.

Orangutans had high body density, so they could not help but sinking in the water. Apart from that, they were known to be such lousy swimmers that there were a lot of stories of them drowning. She could not risk it happening to this orangutan that had helped her fend Lium's attack. She ran at full speed to the riverside. As soon as she got there, she used her power over water to make it rise from the river. It formed a hand that would have caught the orangutan if it had not suddenly turned into an iceberg that was shattered to pieces in an instant.

"Noooooo!!!" She screamed in dismay to see the orangutan fall straight to the river. She knew it was Lium who had stopped her from saving the animal.

Just when the orangutan was about to plunge inside the river, an explosion was heard from underneath the river. A net made of water emerged. The orangutan bounced back in the air and fell hard on her. She was pushed to the ground due to the unexpected weight of the animal on her lap.

She did not comprehend what had just happened. She pulled the unconscious orangutan closer to her as she looked up to Lium, "What do you want to do to him?"

He stared down at her haughtily. "I did not mean to send him to the water to die. He annoyed me, but that is not a reason to kill him. It was my fault that he faced a mortal danger, so it was my responsibility to save his life, not yours."

Kumang shook her head in confusion. "You ..."

"What is going on around here?" A voice emerged from the water, followed by the shape of a man.

Kumang instantly recognized him as Ribai.

And he recognized her in return. "Oh, it's you." He frowned at the unconscious orangutan on her lap. "Fighting again? Now, who do you accuse of casting a curse this time?" He turned his head around. "Lium? Why did you pick up a fight with them? What will the creatures of the land say about us? Don't give the water kingdoms a bad name because you bully defenseless female species."

Kumang was intrigued to see how Lium dropped his arrogant manner in front of Ribai. However, she soon remembered that he identified himself as a *bunsu baya*. Of course he had to respect his King.

133

Lium bowed slightly to Ribai. "I do not wish to fight this female shifter, my King. She forced me to fight with her. I wanted to leave. She forbade me. I was merely defending myself. And she is most definitely not defenseless."

Ribai raised an eyebrow at Kumang. "This particular female is certainly not defenseless. In any case, don't fight with a female! What are you doing here anyway? You are a long way from Batang Lupar. Have you done what I asked you to do there?"

Lium looked nervous. "No, my King, I haven't." He continued as soon as he saw Ribai knit his eyebrows, "I was about to, but she would not let me go!"

"Ignore her! Go now! And Lium," Ribai added as Lium started to retreat. "Try your best not to create suspicion there. If Simalungun is really preparing to do what I heard he is trying to do, he won't welcome your presence, to say the least. However, you have a good ally." Ribai directed his eyes upstream. "Use her skills wisely to your advantage. I trust you know what to do."

Lium smiled proudly. "Thank you for your confidence in me, my King. I will not disappoint you."

"Don't do anything rash there. Report to me what you've found out. We'll decide what to do afterwards."

"You can count on me, my King." Lium bowed one more time at Ribai before he hurriedly walked away.

"You can't go without giving me your word!" Kumang suddenly remembered. She would have gotten up to catch up with Lium if the weight of the orangutan on her lap did not obstruct her.

"Let him go!" Ribai pushed her shoulder down. "You can't possibly think he casts curses here and there. He doesn't have any curse to give away. If you know what's good for you, don't look for trouble with him. He is a dangerous creature."

"He can't hurt me! And I am not defenseless. He may be a *petara*, but so am I!" Kumang hissed.

Ribai gave her a mocking smile. "Dear me, why are you so touchy? I was not talking about you when I mentioned defenseless female. Anyway, I'm not referring to your shape-shifter power or his. I am talking about his state of mind." He pointed at his forehead. His smile disappeared. "He's not quite right in here. Plus the company he keeps. That female he is with is also a dangerous creature. No, she doesn't cast curses here and there either. But then, you know that already. My point is the two of them combined is bad news. Stay away from them! That's the best advice I can give you when it comes to them."

"Why are you harboring dangerous creatures in your kingdom?" Kumang half-scolded him.

Ribai shrugged. "I promised my Apai I would take him in if he wished to stay with us. If it were up to me … hmmm! Still, a promise is a promise. Besides, he has skills that I can use. As for the other one, I let her stay because …"

"You can't resist her charm?"

Ribai looked genuinely offended. "Oh please, what do you take me for? Give me some credit, will you?"

"She does have a charm that most males can't resist. And she knows how to use it to her advantage."

Ribai's eyes widened. "Don't tell me she and your husband …?"

"They did not! But not because lack of trying on her part!"

"Ah!" That was all his said, but it spoke volumes to Kumang.

"I am not saying this because I am jealous. She *is* that kind of female," she said sharply.

"I am aware of that. That is why I said she is dangerous." Ribai shook his head. "Are you always this defensive?" He walked closer to look down on the creature on Kumang's lap. "How is she?"

"It's a he," Kumang corrected him.

"A he?" Ribai squatted in front of Kumang. "Oh, I see, an unflanged male orangutan, huh? No wonder his fighting skill is not impressive."

Kumang quickly put her hands on the orangutan's ears while she shushed Ribai. "Don't say such a thing. You'll hurt his feelings."

"Hurt his feelings? He is unflanged! He doesn't have puffy cheeks. That is a fact! That's why he looks like a female orangutan."

"Give him time. He'll conquer a territory one day and his puffy cheeks will grow within a few cycles of moon."

"He doesn't have a chance if you keep babying him like that. Spare his feelings!

135

Hah! He needs to toughen up if he wants to be a real male! How can he beat all the other contenders and rule over a territory if he only nurtures his feelings! No females would want him. She wants a male who is strong enough to fend her and her children. We live in a real jungle here. This is not *mensia*'s amusement park."

"Really? You reckon you know what it is that we, females, want, don't you?" Kumang gave him acidic remarks.

"It is public knowledge."

"Has it ever occurred to you that all we want is a peaceful life with our significant others, a peaceful world where we can raise our children..." she choked on her own words when the words 'children' went out of her mouth.

Luckily Ribai did not notice it. "And how do you think you can get that peace?" he asked forcefully. "By being considerate towards other creatures? Don't be so naïve. Tell me, why did you marry your husband? I bet it is because he is a *petara*, not because of his sensitive soul. Whatever peace you have in your life is because the others fear his power, not because they appreciate his gentle heart."

Kumang smiled faintly. "Actually, I married him because our parents arranged it."

Ribai was taken aback. "Oh yeah, the shape-shifters do arrange their marriages. I forgot about that."

Kumang was curious. "How can you forget? You used to be one of us."

"Ah, it was eon ago. I hardly remember what it was like to be a shape-shifter." He smiled ruefully. "Now that you mentioned it, though, I do remember something. My Apai actually wanted to arrange our marriage, yes – you and I – that's why your face is familiar to me -- but your parents preferred your husband. My Apai never really gets over it, you know. That's why I remember this particular bit. He is very bitter about it. He can't accept that your parents think your husband's family is better than his."

"I'm sorry if my parents' decision offended your Apai and his family. It was not their intention. And it's not about which family was better. My mother and my mother-in-law had dreams that Keling and I should marry. That's the reason my parents chose his family over yours. We take our dreams very seriously. They are the message from the universe about how we should conduct our lives."

"I know about the importance of dreams. Apai still holds on to that value until now," Ribai said seriously.

Kumang noted how he spoke of his father as if he was still up and about. "How is your Apai?" she asked gently.

"He is unconscious, but he is stabilized," he replied. His aggressive voice was gone. "Luckily I knew he had a dragon's pearl in his possession. I managed to make him swallow it before he slipped to Sebayan. It keeps his condition as it is. I don't know how to improve it, unfortunately."

"What are you planning to do?"

"Find a way to wake him. I don't know how to do it today. It doesn't mean I won't know tomorrow. One day I will find a way to wake him. It is not what I want, but I can live with it for now." He stared at her. "Thank you for asking about his condition, despite everything."

Kumang understood what he meant. "Your Apai is my husband's uncle after all, that makes him family. Families fight. It's normal."

He grimaced. "I don't think it's normal that brothers kill each other."

"That is unfortunate," Kumang agreed. "I wish it could have been avoided. I wished they could have come up with a peaceful solution."

"We can't turn back time, can we?" Ribai asked a question that needed no answer.

"Do you know why?" Kumang asked after a short pause.

"Why? You mean why my Apai and Apai Sabit killed Apai Laja and Apai Keling?"

"Yes. We in Panggau Libau don't know what happened that day. We never understand how it had to come to that end. Has your Apai ever told you about it?"

"My late sister cornered him about this issue once because Laja of Panggau Libau accused Apai as a cold-blooded male who killed his own brother."

"Did your Apai explain to her?"

"He did. And my foolish sister told the story to Laja. Didn't he tell the rest of you about it?"

"He didn't say anything about it." At least not to her knowledge. A story like this would have been the talk of the *ruai* in Panggau Libau and Gelong longhouses had Laja told anyone about it.

137

"Really? I wonder why. Don't you?"

Kumang did not know how to wonder about something that she was not aware of existing. "Can you tell me what your Apai said?"

"He said Apai Keling knew who the boy is, you know who I'm talking about, don't you? – the boy who will destroy the world. Apai asked him to give the boy up for the sake of all the residents of Panggau Libau. Apai Keling refused. Apai Sabit took Apai's side. Apai Laja took Apai Keling's side. They fought life and death duels. Apai won. Apai Sabit won. It was that simple. Yeah, I know. Something that simple had horrific results."

By now Kumang's interest was on what was implied. "Was your Apai suggesting that the boy who will destroy the world is from Panggau Libau?" she asked in disbelief.

Ribai did not respond well to her tone of voice. "Why not? Why is it impossible?"

"Because he is not!"

"My Apai would not have made a serious accusation like that if he had not been absolutely sure. He would not have sacrificed the life of his own brother for a mere speculation!" Ribai raised his voice.

"I am sure he really believed he was doing the right thing. But it doesn't mean that he is right. Obviously he is wrong."

"The boy is not your husband. He is not your brother either. So why are you so adamant in defending this male who will destroy our world?"

"I am not defending the boy who will destroy the world! I am saying that you won't find him among us in Panggau Libau."

"In other words, just like Laja of Panggau Libau, you are accusing my Apai of committing a cold-blooded murder." Ribai clearly took offense.

"Don't put words in my mouth. I am merely rejecting the idea that Panggau Libau hosts the boy who will destroy the world." She was sure that was exactly what the late Apai Keling and Apai Laja had done.

Ribai stood up abruptly. "You know why your life is full of never ending fights, Mao? You don't want to face the truth even if it stares at you in the face." He pointed at the river. "That female water spirit who tried to steal your husband did not cast a curse on *mensia*. Still you insist that she did." He shifted his finger at the orangutan on her lap. "That male is unflanged because he has lousy

138

fighting skills. He will remain unflanged for the rest of his life because you keep on fighting battles on his behalf." He pointed to the sky. "And the boy who will destroy the world *is* from Panggau Libau. Yet you are determined to shield him. If you don't want to accept those facts, even the best of luck this world can offer cannot give you the peaceful life you want!" He stormed to the river and his body was dissolved in water within an intake of breath, giving Kumang no chance to reply.

She caressed the head of the orangutan while she set her eyes to the surface of the water that had swallowed Ribai. "He is wrong about you and he is wrong about the boy, just like his father was wrong. And one day we will make him admit that he is wrong, won't we?"

THE SPREAD OF THE CURSE

The chatter in the *ruai* stopped immediately as soon as someone noticed a figure standing under the door frame of the entrance door on the right. That person quickly notified the others, and the news spread throughout the corridor in a matter of seconds. The reason why the residents of the longhouse aimed their eyes in wonder towards the young man was because he was not one of them. Not only that, they had never seen him before. From his appearance, he was definitely a man from the city. Their longhouse was not accustomed to have uninvited visitors from the city.

The young man greeted the nearest crowd, "Good day, I am looking for Imah daughter of Saing. Does she happen to be at home?"

Because of that greeting, all eyes went to Imah, who was sitting in front of her family's *bilik* further inside the long corridor of the longhouse.

One old man stood up to answer the young man, "Yes, she is. Please come in. Welcome to our longhouse." He extended his hand to offer a handshake.

"Thank you." The young man stepped in and accepted the handshake with a slight bow. He shook hands with every resident he passed by with a polite smile and a slight bow until he reached the person he was looking for.

He shook hand with Imah, who instantly turned to her mother who was standing next to her. "Mak, this is Ezra. He used to work in the Park with Apak and Adam." She looked back to Ezra, "This is my mother."

Ezra extended his hand to Imah's mother, who accepted his offer of handshake with a bright smile, "Are you looking for Apak? He is at work in the Park." Lenya's husband was the oldest staff in Lanjak Entimau Wildlife Sanctuary. All his colleagues, especially the young ones like Ezra, called him Apak – a word that meant 'father' in the local language.

"I would imagine that he is at this time of day." Ezra smiled back at Lenya. "I came here to talk to Imah."

"Oh, I see. Please come inside our *bilik*. You can talk more comfortably there."

Lenya had started heading to her own family apartment when Ezra hesitantly said, "Err…actually, I would rather that we go somewhere else to talk," he said to Imah. He quickly addressed Lenya, who stopped walking. "If that is all right with you, Aunty."

Lenya did not say anything but looking at her daughter who also did not say anything but looking at Ezra.

"And you too," Ezra added solemnly to Imah.

Imah smiled at him before she turned to her mother. "Can I go, Mak?"

"I don't see why not," Lenya answered although Imah could see uncertainty on her face.

"We won't be long," she said to her mother. "Will we?" she asked Ezra.

"No, no, no, it won't be long. I will bring her back within a couple of hours, long before the sun sets," Ezra assured Lenya.

"All right. You may go." Lenya shook hands with her daughter and Ezra as a gesture of goodbye.

And Ezra had to repeat his shake-hands with the same group of people all over again to get out of the longhouse.

"They will be busy speculating why you came," Imah said to him as she walked down the ladder of the longhouse to reach the ground.

"I imagine they would," Ezra did not turn back to talk to her. He was concentrating on getting to the ground safely since the ladder was carved of a fat tree trunk. It did not have any handrails on either side. He really had to watch his balance. "I have lived in a longhouse before, you know. I know how it is with the longhouse folks." He sighed with relief as soon as he reached a solid ground. Then, he turned back to wait for Imah to reach him.

"Where are we going?" Imah behaved as if the journey down was so easy she could do it safely in her sleep.

"Anywhere you feel comfortable going with me." Ezra spread his arm to his left, showing his flashing red car. "I have transport. We could drive around and talk in my car …" he paused. "Or anywhere else you prefer. I just want to talk to you without anyone listening. What I want to talk to you about is… private matter."

"Is this about our deal? Shouldn't we wait for Adam?"

"It is about our deal and something else …" Ezra paused. "I don't mind if Adam hears what I have to say, but he is working right now. I don't want to go to the Park. Too many people know me there. I want to keep this as quietly as possible and I don't want to wait until he has the time to come here. I need something done fast. Besides, between the two of you, I gather you are the expert when it comes to this. Well? Shall we go?" He stepped aside to give Imah a pathway to get to his car.

She hesitated.

"You'd rather go to the quiet and dark jungle with a man you hardly know?" Ezra was surprised.

"I am more comfortable in the forest than being in a car with a man I hardly know," Imah answered truthfully. However, Kumang had warned her in her dream the other night that the forest was not a safe place for her to be at the moment.

Ezra stared at her for a quite a while before he smiled faintly. "I see. The forest it is." He nodded. "After you." He extended his arm to signal Imah to lead the way.

"No, we can drive around in your car." Imah made up her mind as she walked past him toward his car. Although she was not particularly worried about this Lium, who was after her to make Kumang do what he wanted, she did not like the idea that she could be used as his leverage. As much as she resented the idea of obeying Kumang, she admitted that she had better spent less time in the forest for the time being. "It is the best option." She smiled at him.

"If you say so," he muttered behind her. He walked faster to open the left front door for her. After closing the door with care, he walked over to the right side and slid smoothly inside the car.

They did not speak during the drive out of her longhouse's compound.

Imah cast her eyes to the moving forest outside the window. She turned to Ezra. "I think we are far enough from my longhouse now. What do you want to talk to me about?"

Ezra fixed his eyes to the road ahead. "The *pua kumbu* that you said is cursed," he started.

Imah waited for he paused as if he was unsure of what to say next.

"What did you say happen to those who have seen them?" he finally asked the question.

"They get recurring nightmares."

"What kind of nightmare?"

"They don't seem to be able to say what it is about. They only know it scares them to bits." She scrutinized the side of Ezra's face. "Who is having recurring nightmares? Daniel?"

Ezra shook his head weakly. "My mother and my sister," he muttered.

Imah's eyes widened. "Have they seen the *pua*?"

"When I asked my mother, she said she had. Daniel showed it to her, to all of them. He arranged for a private preview of the exhibition for his family and close friends, which included my mother and my sister."

"You are worried that they get the curse."

Ezra hit the steering wheel with his right hand. "I don't know. I just don't know. My mother … she … ever since my father had the accident, she's changed. She becomes highly paranoid, especially over our safety… my sister and me, I mean. She calls me at odd hours, asking where I am, what I am doing, if I'm okay. If I don't reply immediately, she can have a panic attack. I had to take her to see a doctor more than a few times because of it." He tightened his grips on the wheel. "I don't know if these dreams she is having is just an extension of her nerves or it is something else. But my sister should not have them too if this is another case of my mother's panic attack." He gave Rikok a quick side glance. "Adam said you know how to lift the curse."

"Eh? Oh, no, I don't …"

"He said you know how to cleanse it. That's why he wanted to 'borrow' the *pua*," Ezra insisted.

"You misunderstood him, I don't …"

"I can give you the *pua*, you don't need to give it back. Take it. It's yours. Just stop my mother's and sister's nightmares."

"But I really …"

"I have lost my father! I can't lose my mother and my sister, too!" Ezra raised his voice in desperation.

"You haven't lost your father," Imah tried to pacify him.

"I might as well have with the state he is in now!" His grip on the wheel tightened as he fought to get a calm composure. "And we have a deal. I give you the *pua*, you'll wake him up."

"Then you'd better tell me what happened to him," Imah asked for what he had promised her.

He nodded. "I will tell you everything that happened that day." His right hand reached into his shirt pocket and took out a pack of cigarettes. "Do you mind?" he asked Imah, who immediately shook her head. He swerved the car to the left side of the road and stopped it.

He scrolled the windows down and switched off the engine. Instantly, they were bombarded by the chirping sounds of birds and insects from the nearby forest. He lit his cigarette before he started speaking. "We were on a boat, travelling downstream on Kapuas River. The weather was good." He inhaled the cigarette. "The sky was perfectly blue without a spec of dark cloud around. The river was very calm. Upon my father's constant pestering, the man who owned the boat told us that he was confident we could reach Putussibau in no time, and then we could start our journey on land from then on. My father does not like travelling on the river, you see. Being surrounded by water makes him nervous. Then …" he extended his right hand out of the window as he rested his head on the car seat. "Then, the river burst out of the blue as if there was a bomb exploded inside it. The boat was thrown to the air and so did we. I fell down and hit the water. My father fell down and his head hit the boat that reached the water first. That's what I found out later. He lost consciousness and never regains it until today."

"The owner of the boat?"

"He had similar experience with my father. His body hit the boat. He died on the spot."

"I don't know what you expect from me. When it comes to physical injuries, the doctors in the hospitals have far superior skills than the longhouse people. If the doctors can't do much to help him …"

"But you people have your own specialties, don't you? Skills that doctors don't have? Don't deny it. I know what I'm talking about."

"I dare say that we specialize in illnesses caused by spiritual creatures, such as the cursed *pua kumbu*. I don't see how we can help when there's no spiritual creatures involved in the injuries."

144

"Oh, there was … there were spiritual creatures involved in this," Ezra said with conviction. "A calm river did not burst out without a reason. And the reason was not an explosive the local fishermen used to catch fish. I fell inside the river. I saw what happened. They were all inside, attacking us!"

"Who are you talking about?"

"The King of Baya and his troops!"

"You saw the King of Baya?"

"Yes! Don't tell me you've never heard of him!"

"I have. He is part of our belief system. I know of his existence. I am just surprised that you have. I thought … Adam said you don't believe in the traditional Iban belief."

"I didn't. Until that day!"

"How did you know he was the King of Baya? Did he introduce himself to you?"

"He wore that crocodile suite … just like what my father described. I knew instantly it had to be him!"

"Your father could describe the King to you? How come?"

Ezra heaved. "I told you before that my father had a *manang* as an advisor. Well, it turned out that's not what the man was for. My father kept a secret from us – all of us, including my mother – that he needed the *manang* to protect him from the King of Baya. He told me that very morning when I refused to followed him home."

"Why did your father need protection from the King of Baya?"

"The King claimed that my father owed him, for feeding his family and the rest of his longhouse residents with fresh food from the river throughout the drought years– food from his river, he said. My father was just a poor longhouse boy back then. So, yeah, he met the King of Baya in his dream. The King asked for payment of some sort, a regular offering that the *manang* continuously performed. That's how my father knew how the King looks like."

"If you said the *manang* never fails to perform the offerings, there should not be a problem. Why would the King want to attack your boat?" Imah still did not see how Ezra's father injury had anything to do with spiritual creatures.

"The King was after me, that's what my father said. My father's company won the contract to build dams in Sarawak. To build the dams, he had to relocate some group of indigenous people. They lost their homes, their ancestor's land. They were very angry with him. It turned out that the King hated the dams as much as these people. They told the King it was my father who was responsible for building the dams."

"It doesn't mean ..."

"My father told me that the King came to him in his dream, specifically mentioning my name, threatening him with my life. What do you think the King meant by that?"

"All right, so the King was after your life. Then, why are you alive and your father is the one lying unconscious in the hospital? Why didn't the King take your life when you were inside the river?"

"The only reason I am still alive today is because Lucky protected me."

"Who?" Imah's mind went blank for a while before it started working again. "Lucky? You mean Lucky from the Park? Who worked with Apak? Did you know him before the day of the accident?" What kind of *mensia* was powerful enough to stand between the King of Baya and his intended victim?

Ezra grimaced. "I first met him on that unfortunate day inside the river. I don't know his real name. We did not meet in a circumstance that allowed us to exchange names and contact numbers. You see, after the ordeal inside the river was all over, I woke up on the riverside. I saw my father and Lucky unconscious somewhere nearby. I went to find help. Long story short, I got them to a hospital in Kuching. Lucky went into a coma for a long time, just like my father. But one day he woke up. Doctors can't explain why he did and my father did not. He suffered bad head injuries when he woke up. He couldn't remember anything, not even his name. We couldn't get any information out of him about his past. It was my sister who called him Lucky."

"Adam told me you got him a job at the Park."

"That's the least I could do for him. He needed help to get back on his own two feet."

"And you still don't know anything about him? Where he came from? Who he is?" Imah still could not believe Lucky was a *mensia*. No amount of luck could protect a *mensia* from the wrath of the King of Baya.

"He never regained his memory until the last time I saw him."

146

"Eh, this Lucky... wasn't he ... yeah, he was the one Apak found in the forest with the dead monkeys."

"Now wait a minute!" He threw the cigarette bud recklessly outside the window. "I know what you're thinking. But you're wrong. He did not do it. How could he? He was half crippled. If you want to accuse someone, accuse the other guy! He is a more likely suspect. Apak suspected him, too. Lucky told me." He took out a new cigarette and lit it.

"Which other guy?"

"There was another guy there with him. What's his name again ...tsk! ...It's an old Iban name ...oh! Ponggo?"

"Ponggo? Are you sure?" It was not an Iban name. Imah searched for the nearest possible name. "Don't you mean Pungga?

"Ah, yes! Pungga."

The bits and pieces of new information were a little bit too much for Imah to digest. Her brain was working overtime to place them into the frame that she already had.

Upon Imah's silence, Ezra grew impatience. "So? Can you wake my father?"

"Oh! That!" She bit her lip. "All right, let's discuss his situation. Your father is still alive, but he is unconscious. In our belief it means his soul has left his body. He is not dead yet because his physical body system is still working. The question is what happens to his soul? Where is it? If it is in Sebayan, he is already dead. If it is not in the land of the dead, where is it?"

"The King of Baya took it!" Ezra offered the answer he believed.

"The King is dead, Ezra."

"What?" The cigarette almost fell from his lips. Luckily he caught it in time. He scowled when he held the burning end. "Does that mean there's no King of Baya now?" He threw the new cigarette out of the window and lit a new one.

Imah frowned. "You're throwing rubbish to the road outside," she pointed it out to Ezra.

"So?" He did not seem to understand her concern. He blinked slowly to see her face. "Oh God, you're one of those environmentalists, huh?" He groaned. "I'll pick them up later. All right? Now, don't change the topic of our discussion. The King of Baya – is there not a king now?"

147

"His son succeeded him, naturally. But the King of Baya who dealt with your father is dead."

Ezra nodded firmly. "Then, ask the son to return my father's soul!"

"I doubt the son knows anything about it."

"Go and ask him if you're not sure!"

"I can't just go and ask the new King of Baya about the location of a certain *mensia* soul."

"Why can't you? Isn't that what you do? Contact the spiritual beings and make arrangements of this and that? Sort things out between our world and theirs?"

"It is not that simple."

"Simplify it, Imah! Do you want the *pua kumbu* or not?"

She did. "I'll see what I can do. When can you give me the *pua*?"

"It's at the back seat." He pointed his thumb over his shoulder.

Imah could not conceal her surprise. She looked back and saw a thin rectangle box. She turned to Ezra. "You managed to persuade Daniel to give it up? How?"

"You don't need to know how I got it! What matters is it's yours as of now if you promise you'll wake my father and stop my mother and sister from having nightmares."

"I can't wake your father and lift the curse today. These things take time."

"I know. I am willing to give you advance payment. I hope you and Adam will keep your promise."

"Thank you for your trust in us."

"Imah," Ezra called her to make sure that she looked at him when he said, "Don't make the mistake of taking me for a fool. I am willing to give you time to repay me, but I won't wait forever. I will demand my share of the bargain."

"I understand."

"Right." Ezra reached out to the back seat and snatched the thin rectangle box. He placed it on Imah's lap. "Your *pua kumbu*."

Imah was almost scared to touch it. Her fingers hovered around the shape of the box.

"Aren't you going to open it?"

"Eh?"

"Don't you want to see if I gave you the correct *pua kumbu*?"

"You want me to expose myself to the curse?" She lifted her eyes to Ezra. "Did you see what is inside this box?" she asked anxiously.

He shook his head. "I don't know if that is the *pua kumbu* you want, cursed or not. Thea said … she's Daniel's wife, …she said that's the master piece. I took her word for it."

"Has she seen it?"

"How could she tell that's the one if she has not? Before you ask, yes, she also has nightmare now, and that includes Daniel's family members – his parents, his siblings, their spouses, their children, everyone who's seen it. That's why it was easy for me to ask her to give it up." He pointed at the box. "I won't force you to curse yourself. I just want to be fair. I'm giving you a chance to verify that I have done my part of the bargain. If you want to accept it without checking it first, that's fine with me. But I want you to know that once you accept it, it means I have the right to demand that you will give me what I want in return."

Imah stared hard at the box on her lap. She bit her lip. "It is only fair that I have a look if it is the correct *pua*," she said softly.

"Your call." Ezra threw another cigarette bud out of his window. For some reasons, he did not reach out to take a new cigarette stick. He focused his eyes on the box on Imah's lap.

Imah inhaled a big bulk of air and slowly lifted the lid of the box to see what was inside.

A heavy thud on the roof of the car stopped her from opening the box. The car shook violently as a series of thuds landed on the roof. Before Imah could figure out what was going on, loud screeching of monkeys hit her ear drums, and multiple tiny claws reached out to her from the opened window.

THE AFTERMATH OF THE MONKEYS ATTACK

Batang Ai, the Land

In reflex, Imah dropped the box's lid to cover her face. The claws scratched her hands and arms instead. She knew she had to start defending herself from her assailants before they created too much damage to her human body. The main problem she had was the confined space of the car. It did not give her enough room to fight back. She had to get out. She took the risk of lowering down her hand to grab the door handle. The vicious tiny claws immediately scratched her face. She gritted her teeth to bear the pain while her fingers grappled to open the door. Fortunately, the door was not lock. She jumped out while she took out the wooden bangles she wore on her wrists to transform them into weapons. The monkeys continued their latch on her body. With an elastic whip on her right hand and a wooden spear on her left, she hit each and every monkey she could while she fled to the nearest forest.

Imah, or Rikok of Panggau Libau, was a fifth grade *bunsu kayu*. She might not be a Panggau warrior, but the monkeys had no chance of winning when the fight occurred inside a forest where the source of wood was limitless. It was not long before the last monkey that attacked her disappeared without a trace behind the thick rows of trees.

She did not inspect her flesh wounds because she remembered that she had left Ezra inside the car, under the attack of the monkeys. Using *mensia*'s speed, she ran as fast as she could to the car.

She did not see any monkeys there. She rushed to get inside the car through the opened door. She reached out to Ezra, who cowered to his side of the door with his arms covering his head.

"Ezra," she touched his shoulder gently.

He screamed in response.

"It's all right. It's me, Imah. The monkeys have gone."

In response, he pushed the door opened and jumped out.

Imah followed him to get out of the car from the passenger seat's side. "Ezra?" She began to walk around the front of the car to get to him. "Don't worry. You're safe now."

He moved back to put some distance between them. "Don't come any closer!"

Imah stopped.

Ezra pointed at her. "You're not human!" he almost shouted his accusation.

Imah's heart beat a little faster. "Ezra, come now. Get a grip of yourself."

"No! You're not human! I saw what you did!"

Imah inhaled deep to maintain her calmness. "What exactly did you see? You were under attacked. We both were."

"I know what I saw!" he insisted although he did not look too sure of himself. "You jumped out of the car…"

"So did you."

"You …" unexpectedly, he ran inside his car, locked the door, ignited the engine, and drove off.

Imah watched his car disappear on top of the slope. Oh dear, she hoped beyond hope that he would not stop by her longhouse and started telling her parents about his accusation. Not that anyone would believe him, she was sure of that. Still, it would be better if he did not say anything at all.

Alone by the roadside with nothing to do, she examined her wounds. None of them was fatal, but she needed to get them cleanse to avoid infections. Some of them bled out. She scanned the forest in front of her. There had to be something there she could use to stop the bleeding.

She went straight inside the forest and asked the first animal she met where she could find a soursop tree. A friendly bird on a tree gave her direction to the nearest tree it knew. It was quite a distance from where she was at. Nevertheless, it was not an issue for a shape-shifter with her power level who could travel as fast as the wind. She had no problem getting there and with the soursop tree's permission, took a few of its leaves so that she could attend to her wounds. Then, she went to find the nearest spring water to wash herself.

As a shape-shifter, she could make the minor cuts disappear with her power of transformation, but physical wounds were still wounds that had to be healed. Covering the outer looks with a new appearance did not heal the real wound underneath it. She had to think of the best explanation to give to her *mensia* parents why she came home alone with cuts all over her limbs.

She decided that the best thing to do was to go back home using the main road. It would take longer time which gave her more time to think of a better excuse. She went out of the forest to find the nearest road. When she had found it, she looked left and right, trying to identify where she was. She was not too far from her longhouse. A quick check on the sun's location told her that she could walk back with *mensia*'s speed and reached home before the sun set. She inspected her wounds one more time. She believed she did not look too alarming for her parents to see.

She walked absentmindedly along the roadside, trying to understand why the monkeys attacked Ezra's car. Monkeys did not have the habit of attacking unmoving car. She wondered what brought the aggression on. Suddenly she heard a car screeching behind her. She looked back in surprise. Surely she was not in the car's way. Her surprise escalated to see that it was Ezra's car.

The man came out fast from the car. "Ah, there you are! I've been driving up and down the road looking for you," he said anxiously.

"Why?"

He approached her with caution. He halted when he saw Imah's face. "I am terribly sorry for my behavior just now. You were right. We were attacked. I was in shock. I was wrong. I did not know what I saw, nor did I know what I was talking about. I really shouldn't have just left you behind, alone next to the jungle, in the middle of nowhere on a deserted road. Forgive me. It's just that … all the things that happened to me lately, I am afraid I have become as paranoid as my mother has. It's a lame excuse, I know. But that's the only one I can offer." He paused. "Please allow me to drive you home. I promised your mother I would bring you back home safely to her before sunset."

Imah did not make a move to get to his car. "Are you sure you feel safe with me inside the car?"

Ezra winced. "I should be the one asking you that question. I am sorry you were attacked while you were in my car." He took a few steps nearer. "I went back to the place I left you, but you weren't there. I panicked. I thought something terrible happened to you. Where did you go?"

"I went inside the forest to get something to stop the bleeding." Imah showed him her arm.

He went to her instantly. "How are you? Ouch, that looks like a nasty wound. Have you got more of that?" His eyes scrolled up and down her limbs. "Tsk! And on your face, too," he commented with upmost concern.

She pulled her face away from the reach of his hand.

He pulled his hand back. "Oh, sorry, I did not mean to … Do they hurt? Why do I bother asking? Of course, they hurt."

"I feel much better now. They don't sting as much. What about you? Did they hurt you, too?" she asked him.

He showed her his limbs. "Not too bad, actually. Just minor cuts. I plan to see a doctor anyway." He shook his head. "I don't understand why they attacked us without a provocation like that. Do you know why?"

Imah also shook her head. "I've never experienced monkeys attack in all my life going in and out of the forest."

"Never mind that. Let's talk inside my car. I'll drive you to the nearest clinic before I take you home."

"I'm fine. Just take me home."

"No. You need to see a doctor as soon as possible. Those wounds … did any of the monkeys bite you?"

"I don't think so."

"But you can't tell for sure. We'd better go to see a doctor. Don't take those wounds lightly. You know how it is with monkeys. Their saliva is full of bacteria. One bite is all it takes to give you rabies."

"I don't think any of those monkeys has a disease."

"Even a bite from a healthy monkey poses a health risk. We'd better get ourselves vaccinated, just to be on the safe side." He looked at her one more time. "How am I going to explain to your parents about your wounds? I hope they won't think that it was I who attacked you."

Imah laughed softly. "I'm sure they can differentiate between monkeys attack and human attack. Besides, if we go to a clinic, the doctor can vouch for you."

"We are going to see a doctor," he said firmly. He did not make another attempt to touch her.

Imah walked swiftly to his car. She glided gracefully on the passenger's seat. "Let's go!" she called out to Ezra, who just stood rooted to the ground.

Her call woke him up from his state of daze. He came half-running to his car. He started the engine with ease and his car purred to the main road. "What are we going to tell your parents and the rest of the longhouse residents?"

"The truth is always the best," Imah replied.

Ezra cast a glance at her. "The whole truth? Are you sure?"

"Why not? I'm sure they will believe our story about the monkeys attack. All right, that was not the usual behavior of monkeys, but," she eyed her limbs. "These wounds were caused by animals, not by humans."

"Not by me, you mean." Ezra smiled weakly. "No, I was referring to our deal. I don't like the idea that the whole longhouse knows about my family's problems. I'd prefer that you do not tell anyone from your longhouse about it." He paused. "That includes Apak … if it is possible." He threw a glance at her again.

"Oh, yeah. That." She remembered something. "The cursed *pua*? I'd better not get it out of my sight, just in case anyone from my longhouse finds it by accident." She turned around to the back seat. It was empty! "Where is it?" she asked anxiously.

"I gave it to you!" Ezra was almost defensive in his reply.

"I know you did." She tried to look down under the front seat. She could not see the box.

"You had it with you on your lap before the monkeys came to attack us."

"I remember. But then, I jumped out of the car when the monkeys attacked me…" she paused. "Ezra, stop the car!"

"What? Why? We need to get to the clinic as soon as possible."

"We need to find the *pua*! I can't search this car properly when it is moving."

Ezra stopped his car by the roadside.

Imah quickly got out. "Can you see it underneath your seat?" She bent down to see the base of the car. Her hand went groping inside the dark compartment underneath. "Anything?" she asked Ezra who more or less did the same thing.

"No, it's not here."

"It's gone!" Rikok whispered in fear. "The cursed *pua* is gone!"

THE UNEXPECTED TURN OF EVENT

Ulu Katibas, the Land

"What do you mean the *pua* is gone?" Sampurai commented on Rikok's last meeting with Ezra. "It doesn't have legs. It can't run away from the monkeys by itself!"

"I never said it ran away," Rikok corrected him. "I couldn't find it inside the car. That's what I meant."

"You don't suppose that it fell outside when you jumped out?" Pungga gave a suggestion.

"It crossed my mind," Rikok admitted. "That's why we went straight back to the place where it happened. We searched the ground. It's not there."

"Oh, dear ..." Gerinching closed her mouth. "You don't think ..."

"What? What do you think happened?" Sampurai asked her.

"You see, Ezra went away with his means of transport and Endu Rikok went inside the forest. If the *pua* had fallen down to the ground, it would have been left there unattended. Is it possible that someone picked it up?" Gerinching expressed her suspicion.

"Why would the monkeys want it?" Sampurai asked again.

"Monkeys are well-known collectors of things they find. They might not know what it is, but it never stops them from taking what they find. And no, I did not mean the monkeys when I said 'someone'," Gerinching explained.

"Are you talking about *mensia*?" Kumang guessed.

"Precisely!" Gerinching nodded vigorously. "It is possible, isn't it?" she asked Rikok.

Rikok groaned. "It is very much possible. I am afraid that was exactly what

156

happened." She hid her face behind the palms of her hand.

A short silence filled the air until Sampurai broke it. "So? Now what?"

"Mao and I don't know. That's why we are here. We are hoping that you can help us figure it out. How can we find the *pua* now? Any ideas?"

Gerinching, Sampurai, and Pungga looked at each other in silence.

"We can't track down *mensia*, especially when we don't know his identity," Pungga said slowly.

"Hah! Even if we know his identity, it is still very difficult to find a *mensia*. Believe me, Igat and I did that. It was a painful effort. Count me out of this." Sampurai lifted his hands in the air.

"If we don't try to find him, what are we to do?" Kumang asked.

"Forget about the whole thing and go home," Sampurai answered without hesitation.

Kumang widened her eyes.

"You said it yourself that they deserve what's coming to them, did you not?" Sampurai continued.

"Yeah, but that was before Endu Rikok said the *pua* would put a lot of innocent lives at risk." Kumang fought for a reason to stay on the land.

"It is missing now. It is not going to be in a … a…" Sampurai failed to say the word, "it will not be seen by many people now, will it?" he asked Rikok, who promptly nodded. "There! End of story. Let whoever has it now gets what he deserves, for taking something that is not his." He nodded firmly to stress his point. "I am right. You know I am. There is nothing else for you to do here but to go home! Go back to Panggau Libau!"

"I still want to stay on the land." Kumang was defiant.

"To do what?" Sampurai pressured her to admit that she had no reason to stay on the land.

"Well, for one, I am concerned about this Lium."

"He is hunting the boy who will destroy the world. Let him be. What has it got to do with you?" Sampurai continued his pressure.

"He threatened that he'd find Endu Rikok to force me into telling him who the boy is." Kumang found a sound reason.

"Do you really know who the boy is?" Gerinching asked carefully.

"Not you, too," Kumang complained. "Of course not! I've told you what I told him. I don't know."

"I know, I know," Gerinching replied quickly. "But don't you have a guess?"

"No!" Kumang said curtly.

Sampurai leaned over to Gerinching. "Yes, she has her suspicion. She just doesn't want to say it." He stared at Kumang boldly. "Why didn't you tell him that the boy is me?"

Kumang was shocked. "Because it is *not* you!"

Gerinching was aghast. "Sampurai! I hope you're not suggesting that …"

Sampurai frowned at Gerinching. "Of course I am not the boy. Why would I want to destroy this world?"

"That's why I couldn't say it's you. It's not right! If I had said that, he would have come after you," Kumang warned him.

"It is better that he comes after me than he comes after Endu. He wants a boy from Panggau Libau. Give him what he wants. You shouldn't have allowed him to get the idea that he should go after Endu," Sampurai criticized her.

"I was thinking that he is a *petara* and you are only a fifth grader," Kumang explained to him. "I know you are a great warrior, Jang, but I don't think you can survive a *petara*. I should not put your life in danger."

"I spent my whole life facing fingers pointed at me, accusing me for being the boy. I survived that. I will survive him." Sampurai belittled her concern.

"You don't know that for sure!" Kumang insisted that her worry was justified.

"You don't know if I might not survive either." Sampurai glared at her for doubting his fighting skills.

Rikok coughed softly. "You don't know if I might not survive him either, Jang. I am also a fifth grader like you."

"*What?*" Sampurai shifted his attention to his sister. "You might be another fifth grader like me, *Endu*," he stressed the word 'Endu' which generally used to address a young female, "but you don't fight like I do." He continued quickly as soon as he saw her open her mouth to protest. "No, you don't! All of you females do not fight the way we, males, do."

"And what way is that?" Rikok challenged him.

"When we fight, we aim to kill. This is not a question of power level, all right? You may have the same power level as I do, but how many times have you taken a life? No, no, no, the fish, the chicken, and the boars, that you eat, they don't count. You kill them for food consumption. That's different. I am talking about taking a life purely for the sake of taking a life. Do you think it is easy to take a life? You don't wake up one morning and suddenly feel that you want to kill someone. Do you think it is easy to live with the knowledge that you have taken a life? Eh? You don't have it in you, Endu! Most females don't have it in them. Let me give you a clear example. She has *petara* power." He pointed his thumb at Kumang. "And yet we all know that she can't kill him."

"Excuse me?" Kumang was offended.

"You can't, can you? You didn't fight him to kill him. What were you doing aiming your weapon at his arm? You gave him a minor wound. It did not even cripple him. What could you have accomplished from that? Do you think if the role had been reversed, he would have aimed for your arm? In your dreams! He would have aimed straight to your heart! And that would be the end of the battle right there and then, with you dead!"

"All right, point taken, I will remember it next the time I fight him," Kumang admitted grudgingly.

"You don't have a second chance in a battle," Sampurai said fiercely. "Either you kill your opponent or he kills you. If you don't have it in your heart to end a life, don't start a battle. You will only lose your life."

"Some males don't have it in them either, Jang." Rikok was adamant to prove him wrong. "And I do believe that some females have it in them."

"They sure do," Kumang agreed wholeheartedly. "Cherurai would have taken so many lives, if she had had the power in her hands to do it. Fortunately for all of us in this world, she doesn't have any."

"And I am glad that you don't have it in you," Sampurai said to Kumang. "Look, it's not a bad thing. It's not like it's a flaw or something. You should not be ashamed of not having it. You don't need to prove otherwise to anyone."

"Lium may be one of those males who don't have it in him," Rikok picked up the topic they had left behind.

"How can you tell?" Sampurai asked with irritation.

"He saved Sugie, didn't he?" Rikok pointed at the orangutan at Kumang's feet. "He did not need to. Doesn't that show that he is not ruthless?"

Sampurai frowned at Sugie. He opened his mouth as if he wanted to say something to the ape, but he ended up snorting and directed his question at Rikok, "What is your point?"

"There is still a chance that I could win if I fight Lium."

"*What?*" Sampurai exclaimed.

"That's what you said …," Rikok argued.

Pungga cut her off unexpectedly. "You are wrong, Endu. He has it in him. He has taken many lives without qualms."

"How do you know? You've never met him." Rikok pouted.

"I have met him. I've seen with my own eyes how he ruthlessly ended the lives of those macaques in the forest just because they refused to tell him where the *remaung* was."

"Come again?" Kumang did not see it coming. "The *remaung*? Are you talking about the *remaung* whose *gerasi* followers gave Jang his present wound?"

"The one and the same. Lium hunted the *remaung* down because he thought the *remaung* might be the boy who will destroy the world."

"The *remaung*? The boy who will destroy the world?" Gerinching wondered. "He can't be," she quickly corrected herself.

"Why not?" Sampurai asked. "He was a spiritual creature. Does it make him less likely to be the boy because he took the form of a clouded leopard on the land? We know his father was a demonic *antu gerasi*. We also know he had been born without a conscience. He could very well be the boy!"

"If he had been the boy, Lium would have stopped hunting the boy now, wouldn't he? The *remaung* is dead," Gerinching clarified her stand.

"He doesn't know who the boy is. He was only guessing with the *remaung* boy," Pungga elaborated. "That's his way of eliminating possibilities."

"What you are trying to say is that Lium knew that the *remaung* might not be the boy, but he still killed him?" Gerinching summarized Pungga's explanation.

"He didn't kill the *remaung*. Pungga did," Sampurai corrected her.

"Oh, yeah. That's right." Gerinching nodded to acknowledge him. She turned to Pungga again. "So, Lium knew that the *remaung* might not be the boy, but he hunted him down anyway?"

Pungga nodded.

"That's the same as killing an innocent life!" Gerinching exclaimed.

"Precisely. So you can imagine how ruthless he is." Pungga's face was grim. He addressed Rikok, "Therefore, Endu, don't fight him. You have no chance of winning."

Rikok was displeased. "I still think ...wait a minute, wait ... the killing of the macaques in the forest, you said? You mean the forest where my *mensia* father works? You were there? Oh, that's right, Ezra said there was a man called Pungga there. So that Pungga was really you? And you are saying that Lium was with you at the time?"

Pungga nodded multiple times to answer a series of her questions.

"I thought it was Lucky who was with you." Rikok widened her eyes. "No way! Lium is Lucky?"

161

"Yes," Pungga confirmed.

Rikok held her cheeks in the cradle of her hands in shock.

"Who? I'm sorry I don't follow," Gerinching asked Rikok. "Can you explain?"

Rikok lifted her hand in the air. "Give me a minute a sort all the information we have." She closed her eyes. When she opened them, she said very slowly. "This is what we know about this character Lium from all the stories we've heard.

It started with Watt and the late Chunggat going to the land to avenge the late Apai's murderer – that's Apai Ribai. Watt found Apai Ribai in Kapuas River, but he ended up fighting with another *petara* who was with Apai Ribai at the time, and that *petara* was Lium." She looked at Kumang, who nodded.

"He said the *bunsu baya* adopted him as one of them. And he admitted the other *petara* in the battle who wounded Watt was him," Kumang confirmed.

Rikok continued, "During their battle, a boat that carried Ezra and his father passed by. It got caught in the middle of the battle. The boat was hit by, what I could only guess, a *petara*'s power – we don't know whose power, whether it was Watt's or Lium's. The boat broke into pieces and the passengers fell inside the river. Ezra said Lium saved his life under the water, that's why he survived. In the meantime, because of the battle, we lost Chunggat to Sebayan. Apai Ribai would have gone there too if Ribai had not given him the dragon's pearl. Watt and Lium were severely wounded. Watt's body was washed away to a lake, then found by a fisherman …" Rikok cast a glance at Kumang, who instantly look uncomfortable. "Lium and Ezra's father were found by the riverside by Ezra, who then, took them to a hospital in Kuching. The three of them – Watt, Lium, and Ezra's father were unconscious for a long time until one day Watt and Lium woke up while Ezra's father did not. Unfortunately, both Watt and Lium lost their memories. They did not even remember who they were. Even the doctors could not explain why Lium could wake up considering his injury. Because of that, Ezra's sister called him 'Lucky'. Ezra helped Lium get a job at the Park where Pungga met him as Lucky. And according to you, he was the one who killed those macaques because they refused to tell him where the *remaung* was?"

"Yes, that is correct." Pungga confirmed. "He worked at the Park because he wanted to find the *remaung* boy."

"Wow!" Rikok was speechless.

"Does that mean Ezra knows that Lucky or Lium is a shape-shifter?" Gerinching asked.

Rikok appeared to consider the idea. "I don't know about that. He never mentions anything like that. If he does, I don't think he wants to admit it. He encountered a spiritual creature or two during the accident. I am sure of it. I don't know if it means he knows that Lium is a spiritual creature."

"Do you think Lium asked Ezra to get him a job at the Park?" Pungga asked more questions. "Does Ezra know about Lium's real intention in the park?"

"How could Lium not remember his own identity, but he wanted to find the boy who will destroy the world? Are you sure he really lost his memory? Or was he just fooling this *mensia* boy who owed him his life?" Sampurai added more questions.

"I don't know the answers to any of your questions, Jang. I did not ask Ezra about Lium. I didn't connect him with Lucky at the time." Rikok frowned.

"All right, now that we've established that Lium is Lucky. Where does it leave us?" Sampurai asked impatiently.

"What do you mean, Jang?" Rikok asked.

"I mean, how does it help in you making a decision about what to do next?"

"I really don't know. What do you think?"

"Do you really believe that Lium would go after Endu?" Sampurai asked Kumang.

"I do."

"Then, we'll find him first. We'll tell him I'm the boy." Sampurai made an instant decision.

"We can't do that," Kumang disagreed.

"Why not? He's a *petara*. It's easy to locate a *petara*. You go home to Panggau Libau and ask Inik Anong to locate him. We'll find him, and we'll tell him I'm the boy."

163

"But you're *not* the boy!" Kumang protested.

"It doesn't matter. We can't just wait until he actually comes after Endu, or your sister!" Sampurai swept his eyes around. "Where is your sister anyway? I thought she was supposed to come here with you."

"She's in Gelong."

"Good. Tell her to stay put."

"I did."

Sampurai looked sideways to Rikok. "You should go home to Panggau Libau until we sort this thing out with Lium."

Rikok was flabbergasted. "Never!"

"Endu, it's been a few hundred years. Why can't you let bygones be bygones? Whatever happened between you and Indai was water under the bridge – as they said. Get over it. Go home! Dom! Tell her," Sampurai urged Pungga.

Rikok beat Pungga in giving a reply, "No! Indai told me that she would never welcome me home if I chose to marry Rengga. I did choose him over her. I'm not the one who refuses to go home. She is the one who doesn't want me home. I am not going home until she asks me to!" Her eyes were suddenly glassy.

Sampurai winced to see the sign of tears. "Can't you talk to Indai about her request?" he asked Kumang.

"Why me?" Kumang did not want to get involved in this delicate matter. The conflict between Indai Keling and Rikok had been going on for centuries ever since Indai Keling objected Rikok's wish to marry a *mensia* called Rengga.

Sampurai knitted his eyebrows. "I can't go home even if I want to! I'm ostracized on the land. Besides, we've agreed that you should go back to Panggau Libau to ask Inik Anong to locate Lium."

"We haven't agreed to that," Kumang rejected the one-sided decision. "Ask Pungga to go home to talk to Indai Keling about inviting Endu Rikok home! He's good at persuasion. And while he is there, he can talk to Inik Anong."

"Whoa, I'd rather not," Pungga turned down the idea.

"See? Even Dom knows that there's no way Indai would want me home again!" Rikok's voice trembled.

"That's not what I meant, Endu." Pungga was not comfortable that the burden of building a new bridge between Indai Keling and Rikok was pushed to him.

"Tsk! Fine! I'll look for Lium myself! Without Inik Anong's help." Sampurai shook his head in annoyance.

"You are barely healed!" Gerinching was not happy.

"I can move about to find another shape-shifter, especially a *petara*. It should not be difficult." He was not about to be deterred.

"You are not fit enough to fight!"

"I am fit enough to handle an *antu raya*."

"Oh!" Gerinching forgot about the significance of the female *antu raya*.

"If I can find Lium, that means I can find Cherurai. She is with him, isn't she?" Sampurai asked Kumang.

Upon Kumang's nod, he continued, "That means I can give Indai Perunu her wish: Cherurai's head. That means I get to go home to Panggau Libau!" He shouted the next few words, "I want to go home!"

Gerinching gulped and she was suddenly lost for words.

"Wait! What about the cursed *pua*? What are we going to do about it?" Rikok reminded them.

"Nothing! It's gone. Let it be gone! Forget it. There are more important things to do, like finding Lium and Cherurai." Sampurai turned to Kumang. "Where did you say you met him? Kayan River? That's Panggau Libau's territory at the moment. Yup, I know the area quite well."

"He might not be there anymore. He's a *petara*, remember? He can move faster than the wind," Rikok cautioned him.

"With a powerless *antu raya* in tow? No way. They will still be around

165

somewhere near the area." Sampurai jumped up. "I'd better get going now."

"No!" Gerinching found her voice again.

Sampurai aimed his eyes at her. "Oh! You can't go with me. Ah," he turned to Kumang. "Can I ask you a favor? Can you stay here with her until I get back?"

"No!' Gerinching was the one who answered him.

"You can't come with me. Things will get ugly when I meet them. You don't need to see any of it."

"No!" was the only word that Gerinching could utter.

"Well, Mao? Can I count on you? I won't be long. She can go with Endu, I suppose, but she doesn't like living in her father's longhouse. She likes the forest. Endu can't stay here too long, her *mensia* parents will notice her missing," Sampurai argued his case.

"What about Pungga?" Kumang asked.

"Dom will go with me! Why do you need to ask? Right, Dom? What?" Sampurai rolled his eyes to see Pungga's facial expression. "You'd rather stay put with them?"

"I'll go with you, Jang." Pungga smiled to see his face.

Sampurai frowned at Kumang. "If you don't want to help …"

"I'll keep her company until you come back. Don't worry," Kumang gave him her word.

"Great." Sampurai nodded with satisfaction. He walked closer to Gerinching, who still could not find any other words to say. "I'll get us home. I promise you." He waved to Rikok. "I'll see you soon, Endu." He turned around and walked away. "Let's go, Dom!" he shouted.

Pungga stood up. First, he went to Gerinching, "Don't worry, he'll be fine."

Gerinching looked sad. "I don't suppose there's anything I could have said to stop him."

Pungga shook his head slowly. "There's nothing anyone could have said to stop him." He reached out to her. "Hey, he has gone to a battle with much worse condition than this, and survived. There's no reason why it should be any different now."

"DOM!!!" a loud shout from deep inside the forest make Pungga let go of Gerinching's hand.

He nodded his goodbyes to the three female shifters who were now standing in front of him. "Goodbye, then." He turned around to follow Sampurai. He instantly found Sugie was on his way. He stopped to address the male orangutan. "You're the male in charge now, Sugie." He roamed his eyes to the canopies above his head. "You and Mayas are, to be exact. I'm counting on the two of you to keep these females out of mischief." He nodded his goodbye to the orangutan and disappeared from sight in a blink of an eye.

BEING HOMELESS

"What are you thinking of?" Kumang sat herself down next to Gerinching, whose eyes were glued to the canopies above their heads. She knew Gerinching was not admiring the lush green roof over their heads. Since Rikok had gone back to her longhouse, it was only the two of them left there, if she did not count Mayas and Sugie, who were nowhere to be seen at the moment.

Gerinching lifted her back to leave the solid support of the tree trunk.

Kumang watched in amazement how the soft branches of the tree cradled Gerinching's back gently until she had sat upright independently.

Gerinching directed her eyes at Kumang. "I'm sorry?"

Kumang smiled and repeated her question.

Gerinching seemed to have a problem finding words to say.

"Are you worried about Jang? Don't worry, he'll be fine. He'll find Cherurai. The two of you can end your punishment on the land and go home," Kumang offered her reassurance.

Looking at Gerinching's face, Kumang realized that she gave the wrong reassurance.

"No? You don't think he can find her? Dom will help him. I'm sure …" She suddenly got it. "Oh! You are worried that they *will* find her."

Gerinching swept her bang aside to tuck it neatly behind her ear. She looked away quickly.

"You are worried about going home." It was more of a statement than a question.

Gerinching swallowed hard. "I …"

"Why don't you want to go home?"

"It's a long story," Gerinching said sadly.

"You have days to tell me about it before Dom and Jang come back," Kumang encouraged her. "Unless you don't feel comfortable talking about it."

Gerinching's smile was as sad as her eyes. "I'm sure you already know about the pathetic story of my life. I believe every shape-shifter in the whole dome of the sky has heard about the pathetic story of my life," she sounded tired.

Kumang had heard, of course. "You are talking about your engagement with Chief Tait's son?"

"Failed engagement," Gerinching corrected her. "He is married to someone else now."

"He was the one who broke the promise, not you. He was the one who should be ashamed of himself, not you," Kumang said passionately.

"Dom, I mean, my brother, Dom Jilan, said it was my fault."

Kumang nodded her resentment. "They always put the blame on us when something like this happens. It is always the female's fault. Even when it is obvious that it is the males who cannot control their wandering eyes, it is still the female's fault." She thought of Keling, and she could feel her heart contracted painfully.

"He said Ajie chose to marry his wife because she is a better cook and a better weaver than I. It is my fault that I never spent enough time in the kitchen to cook or in the *ruai* to weave."

"Those are just lame excuses the males like to use to justify their wrongdoings." Kumang was upset. She could cook well and weave extremely well. Her husband still found another female.

"I know that's not the reason Ajie married someone else."

"Did he tell you why he did what he did?" Kumang was curious.

Gerinching shook her head. "He never came to see me to explain why. He was already married by then, he couldn't come and see another female to have a

169

private conversation. It is inappropriate. You know our norms do not allow it."

"Why do you think he did it?" It had better not be another 'it just happened' excuse.

"I suppose it was because for once he wanted to have a life of his own choice."

"Do you not resent his choice?"

"I was hurt. But my pride aside, I can understand. I know him well. We grew up together. His parents' *bilik* is just next to my parents' in Nanga Langit longhouse. I know how much he did not want to leave Nanga Langit to live with his real parents in Batang Rajang longhouse." Gerinching paused. "You know the story about his parentage, don't you?"

"Yeah, I've heard. He is actually Chief Tait of Batang Rajang longhouse's son."

"Youngest son, to be precise."

"They lost him one day, and he was found by a Nanga Langit resident who then adopted him."

"Nobody can love him more than Apai and Indai Ajie in Nanga Langit." Gerinching smiled. "His real mother would disagree with me."

"She demanded to have her son return to her, didn't she?"

Gerinching nodded. "As soon as she found out that Ajie was actually her son."

"And Indai Ajie refused to give him up."

"Any mother would!"

"That's when your parents had the idea to arrange for the two of you to be married."

"Both mothers would not stop fighting over their son. Every new meeting held to solve this issue ended up worse than the last. It had turned so bad that my Apai was worried Nanga Langit would end up fighting a new war with Batang Rajang because of these two mothers. It was my Indai's idea that they should arrange for Ajie to marry me when the right time came. In the meantime, Ajie would live in Batang Rajang with his real family. They meant to arrange that he would end up living in Nanga Langit after the wedding took place. He would have inherited Apai Ajie's *bilik*. That way, Indai Ajie could have her son back."

"And both mothers agreed to this."

"It took a while for them to agree, but they eventually agreed it was the best compromise under the circumstances. Unfortunately, they forgot to ask how their child felt about the whole arrangement."

"Ajie didn't like the idea?"

"He hated it. He was very young when Apai Ajie found him. He had no memories of his real family. They're practically strangers to him. Nanga Langit was the only home he knew, the only life he had. And just like that, everything and everybody he loved was taken from him."

"He was still allowed to visit Nanga Langit, wasn't he? To visit his adopted parents?"

"That was the original agreement, but his mother resented the idea, so visitation never happened. She was jealous of Indai Ajie, I suppose. She knew how much Ajie adored his Indai in Nanga Langit while he saw her as nothing but a stranger. I can't really blame her for harboring such feeling. Anyway, it was a long time before he was old enough to travel on his own that he could come more often to Nanga Langit. After all, he had the perfect excuse."

"You."

Gerinching barked out a short laugh. "He had a fiancé in Nanga Langit, who just happened to be me. He came to see me for *ngayap* as often as he could. The truth is he just wanted to go home to Nanga Langit. He couldn't stand Batang Rajang. I didn't know it then. I thought he came because he was so eager to see me."

"If he wanted to go home so much, he should have married you and settled down in Nanga Langit. He shouldn't have married another female from a different longhouse. His wife is from a different longhouse, isn't she?"

Gerinching nodded. "She is from Lubok Naga longhouse."

Kumang closed her eyes. Ajie had chosen a former slave as his wife. It was a

171

great insult to Gerinching, whether or not he meant it. "I can't believe his parents allowed him to break his engagement to marry someone else," she muttered. It was a grave offense in their norms to break a promise as important as an arranged marriage.

"He went *bejalai,* and he came home bringing a wife. She was already with child. His parents had to agree. They had no choice. We would never allow a child to be illegitimate. You know that."

Kumang's hand went voluntarily to hold Gerinching's. She could imagine how humiliating it was for Gerinching that her fiancé chose to marry someone else, and that someone used to be their slave was pouring salt over the open wound. Nevertheless, the ultimate blow came from the news that the other female gave him a child, while she did not. Kumang's heart ached at the thought. She knew exactly how it felt.

"I still think he should have come to apologize to you personally for everything he put you through. I don't care if our norms do not allow it to take place, he should have come and begged for your forgiveness, in public if necessary!" she said fiercely.

"His parents from Batang Rajang came to see my parents and me. They apologized through and through until my Apai felt uncomfortable about it." Gerinching smiled weakly. "Apai and Indai Ajie came and apologized, too, for failing to raise a better son until I was completely uncomfortable about it. I believe Indai Ajie was more broken-hearted about the whole thing than I."

"It should've been him who apologized. It was his fault – not his parents! Why didn't he come? If he did not like you from the start, he should have said 'no' to the whole arrangement when it was first proposed, not to bail out halfway like that."

"Saying 'no' to the arrangement? And let a new war rage between Nanga Langit and Batang Rajang? It was too big of a burden for a young shifter to carry. Besides, I'm sure he liked me. His marriage to his wife was not about him disliking me. He didn't do it to spite me. That's the reason I can't bring myself to hate him even after what he has put me through. He just didn't want a life dictated to him by others. He is tired of living a life thrust upon him. He wanted to have a say in how his life should be like."

172

Kumang did not know what to comment. Was that how Keling saw their life together? As a life dictated upon him by others? Their marriage was arranged by their parents, not by his choice. He would have probably married that female water spirit had he been given a free choice. Was he tired of living a life that was thrust upon him? Was that the real reason he agreed to marry another woman on the land? Oh sure, he claimed that he lost his memory at that time, but who knew, maybe somewhere deep in his subconscious mind, that was his way of rebelling to the circumstances of life that he did not want.

"Can you really accept what he did? He hurt you when you did nothing wrong," Kumang asked Gerinching what troubled her.

Gerinching held her folded legs closed to her heart. "It hurt very much to be humiliated like that. I cried a lot. My tears could have form a river bigger than Batang Rajang. But I can accept what he did."

"Really?" because Kumang could not accept what Keling had done.

"Yes. I can confidently say that I have forgiven him completely now."

Kumang could only stare at Gerinching. Why could she not forgive Keling when Gerinching could forgive Ajie? Did she not have a big enough heart to forgive? She bent her head to hide her sorrow.

Gerinching misunderstood her gesture. "Hey, it's all right. Whatever happened, I'm sure it is the best for the both of us."

"Is it?"

Gerinching smiled nervously. "I have to believe that it is. How can I move on with a new life if I don't?"

Kumang quickly picked up the missing pieces of the story. "But Ajie is now living in Batang Rajang longhouse with his wife, is he not?"

"Naturally, he gave up his chance to come back to Nanga Langit."

"Then, what stops you from going home to Nanga Langit?"

Gerinching's face turned grim again. "Dom Jilan said I made too many offenses that humiliated my family. He said it is best that I do not go back home."

173

"We have established that your failed arranged marriage is not your fault!"

"According to him, it was. And it is not just that. After Ajie's marriage became known to the world, it was the talk of our *ruai*."

Kumang rolled her eyes. "Did he say it was your fault that the longhouse residents gossiped about it? You had no control over what they wanted to talk about in the *ruai*. How could he not know that?"

"He said I had full control about how I reacted to it. You see, I decided to run away from home because I couldn't stand the way they talked about Ajie and me."

"Oh, was that when you met Jang?"

"Yeah, I met Sampurai on the land during that time. He …" she laughed softly, "… he would tell you that he saved me from a demonic pig. I was not in any danger, by the way, but that's how he likes to remember it."

"He thought you were a male shifter."

"I was assuming the form of a man at the time," Gerinching confirmed the story.

"And that's how the two of you got entangled in the *gerasi* war."

"It was precisely at that moment that a group of *gerasi* came and captured us. They actually only wanted him, but since I was there, they brought me along."

"You met that female *antu raya*, Cherurai, in the *gerasi* camp."

"Yes."

"What do you think of her?" Kumang remembered Ribai's comments about Cherurai.

"She scared me. She was so bitter about losing her twin sister. Keling killed her, she said. So she wanted to make sure that Keling understood how it felt to lose a sibling who meant so much to him the way her twin sister meant to her. That's why she wanted Sampurai dead. I have never met a creature who was so full of hatred."

"I bet she was the one who gave the order to the *gerasi* to find Jang and kill him. I don't believe the *gerasi* – what's his name again?"

"Guroh."

"I don't think Guroh could come up with such an ambitious plan to unite all the *gerasi* clans under his rule. And look at how they planned to kill Jang. The *gerasi* could never think of something like that. They were simple creatures. If they had wanted him dead, they would have killed him in a battle, then and there. End of story."

"Guroh almost did just that. But for Cherurai, killing Sampurai was not enough. Before that, she wanted to ensure that his name was smeared among the shape-shifter communities. That's why she arranged for him to kill another shape-shifter."

"And Si Ganti of Bukit Bangkai lost his life because of it." Kumang shook her head.

"Yes, poor him. He was at the wrong place at the wrong time. Sampurai tried his best not to kill him, but sometimes …"

"Yeah, I know. Sometimes, bad things just can't be avoided," Kumang said mournfully. "And how was that your fault, according to your brother? You did not kill anyone that dreadful night."

"No, because Sampurai did it for me. It should've been me who killed Si Ganti. He was fighting me at the time. Sampurai interfered in time to end it."

"But the fact of the matter is it was not you. They decided during the hearing among the Longhouses' Chiefs that you did not commit any murder."

"Si Ganti's family still holds me accountable for it. Therefore, both Sampurai and I are now ostracized on the land."

"I still don't see what your offense is."

"The thing is, because I am ostracized on the land, the first thing my Apai did was to ask Keling to help me settle down here. Therefore, Keling asked Endu Rikok to find me a longhouse to live."

"Yeah? So?"

"One day the longhouse was swept away by a big flood. I lost the longhouse I lived in."

"Was the flood your fault?"

"No, a big dam broke and it caused a flash flood. That's not my offense. According to Jilan, my mistake was I chose to live in the forest with Sampurai afterwards."

"How did Jang come to the picture out of the blue?"

Gerinching laughed again. "He would tell you that he saved me from the flash flood."

"Did he not?"

"I was swept away under the water, along with my longhouse's debris. He tried to drag me out of the raging flood. But it was Laja who got both of us safely to the dry land."

"All right, fine, so you decided to stay in the forest with Jang. Why was that an offense?"

"Dom Jilan said it was not proper."

"Hmmm…if he put it that way …" Kumang said grudgingly.

"He is right. It was not proper. I made a bad choice, that's what he said."

"But…hold on. You lost your longhouse. What did he expect you to do?"

"Found a new longhouse to live."

"Could you? I mean, can anyone just turn up in a longhouse and live there? Is that how *mensia* live their lives nowadays?" When Kumang had lived on the land among the *mensia* centuries ago, they were on constant wars with each other. A stranger who suddenly turned up in a territory would most probably end up dead. It was better-safe-than-sorry attitude that they adopted.

"I could. It would be tricky, but it could be done, Endu Rikok said so. I did not want to. It was my choice not to stay with *mensia*. I don't like living with them. I can't cope with their new lifestyles."

"Your brother would rather see you suffer living with *mensia* than see you happy living in the forest with Jang like a couple of nomads? All right, I understand that Jang might not be the best choice of a companion for you, but considering your special circumstances, wouldn't it better for you to have him around rather than you living alone in the forest? Didn't your family worry about your safety?" Kumang actually did not understand how Gerinching could be happier living in the forest like a nomad than a proper home such as a longhouse. The wild forest was not a permanent house for the shape-shifters. But hey, if she could not stand *mensia* and their lifestyle – she shuddered when she remembered her own experience in Lubok Sawo longhouse – why couldn't her family allow a little diversion from their usual norms?

"He said it looked like as if my family did not care enough for me until I have to ask protection from a ... a non-family member. He said our *ruai* was once again buzzing with chatter, about me, and Sampurai, about how I made my family look bad."

"Tsk! Your family was in the sky, what could they do for you on the land? Say, why didn't your brother come down to the land to be with you since he did not want a non-family member to be with you?"

"It is my punishment, not his. Anyway, I suppose things became unbearable for them in Nanga Langit, so Indai sent Indai Tuai – she's my Apai's older sister - to be with me to replace Sampurai. She was hoping that Nanga Langit residents would stop talking about him and me afterwards."

"That was the end of it, then. It was not a big offense."

"Unfortunately, that's not it. Indai Tuai got an accident not long after that. A hunter shot her on the neck."

"Oh yeah, I remember! That's when Jang broke the terms and conditions of your punishment."

"Yes, he went back to the sky, which he was not allowed to. But how else could we have saved Indai Tuai? She needed a shape-shifter *manang* to heal her wound."

"How could your brother blame you for this? The hunter shot your Indai Tuai. Jang broke the agreed punishment. Which one of them was your fault?"

"Indai Tuai shouldn't have been on the land in the first place."

"Your Indai sent her down to be with you! You did not ask for her to come!"

"That's how Dom Jilan sees it. He told me I keep on making bad choices in life and my family has to pay for the consequences of my actions. He said enough is enough. He doesn't want to take any responsibility for my actions anymore."

Kumang's eyes widened. "What does that mean?"

"He said he doesn't welcome me home anymore."

"What?"

"He said when the time comes for him to inherit Apai's *bilik*, he will not welcome me to live there with him and his future family. He will not endanger their lives with the bad choices I keep making."

"He can't do that!"

"Yes, he can. My family's *bilik* will be his one day. I was supposed to marry Ajie and live next door with Ajie and his parents, remember? It has always been arranged like that. Jilan will inherit Apai's *bilik* and I will have Apai Ajie's *bilik* through my marriage with Ajie. The problem now is the marriage did not happen. I can't move next door. I can't go back to my parent's *bilik*. Now you see why I am not excited about the thought of going home. I don't have a home to go to. Where will I go?"

"The *bilik* still belongs to your parents!"

"For now. What will happen when Jilan inherits it?"

"You have plenty of time to find a new home until then."

"What new home? Oh, you mean *if* I get married?"

"*When* you get married!"

"Who would want to marry me now after everything that has happened?"

"Don't say that! I'm sure there's a male shifter ..."

"Who wants to take me in knowing that I will bring 'danger' to his family with all the bad choices I continue to make."

"That's what Jilan thinks. It doesn't mean everyone thinks like him."

"Do you think there is a soul in the sky up there who has not heard about what happened between Ajie and me? About me running away from home? How I pretended to be a man? How I almost killed Si Ganti of Bukit Bangkai in a battle field? How I am now ostracized on the land for my offense? Who has not heard of these stories?"

Kumang could not think of one. The offense that Sampurai committed by killing Si Ganti of Bukit Bangkai broke the peace agreement among the seven shape-shifter longhouses in the sky. Gerinching might not commit the offense, however, she was considered to be an accomplished in the whole incident. To determine their guilt and punishment, all the Chiefs of the seven longhouses and their entourages held a meeting in Ulu Tinting longhouse. Everyone who attended the meeting had heard the full story of what happened. And Kumang believed beyond the shadow of doubt that they went home to their respective longhouse and recounted the whole story. Knowing the shape-shifter communities well, Kumang was certain that they did not stop only at the facts presented at the meeting. Their personal views on the matter would be included to create additional colors to the story that could only shine strikingly brighter from one storyteller to the next.

"Now you see that there isn't a single family in the whole dome of the sky who would risk taking me in." Gerinching repeated her statement, "I don't have a home to go to."

FORGIVE BUT NOT FORGET

Kumang was concerned. "Did you tell Jang about this?"

Gerinching looked perplexed. "Tell Sampurai about what?"

"That you are worried you have no home to go to. Does he know that you dread going home?" Something distracted her chain of thought. "And why do you keep calling him Sampurai?"

"I'm sorry?"

"Why don't you call him Jang? All of us call him Jang."

"He never asks me to."

Kumang had to smile. "Do you need him to give you permission first before you can call him Jang?"

"I don't think I should unless he says so."

"Why not? You can meet him for the first time in your life and call him Jang. It is perfectly proper." Jang was a common nickname to call a boy – any boy for that matter. There was nothing improper to call a male - any male - 'Jang'.

"It's not about propriety. It's … He doesn't want to call me Endu. That's how my family calls me. I asked him to call me Endu. He refused."

"Oh? Why?" Endu was a common nickname to call a girl – any girl.

"I have no idea. He flat out refused, down right adamant about it. He … I … I don't understand him sometimes."

"You're not the only one, dear." Kumang patted Gerinching's hand lightly.

"He is … I feel like he holds a different set of norms than ours."

"That is a very nice way of putting it. I cannot describe him better than that."

"I don't know what this nickname thing means to him. To me – to us, it is a simple meaningless thing, but he seems to feel strongly about it. I don't want to offend him by calling him Jang unless he tells me it is all right. I don't think I should cross a line that should not be crossed."

"Have you?"

"Have I what?"

"Crossed a line that should not be crossed?"

Gerinching wrinkled her nose. "He was so offended that he ignored me for days."

"Which particular line did you cross?"

"I'm not sure. It's not like he wanted to talk about it. He hates talking about our rules and regulations. He avoids them as much as he can."

"How do you know you've crossed a line you should not cross if he doesn't want to talk about it?"

Gerinching raised her shoulders and lifted her arms in the air.

Kumang sympathized with Gerinching. "He must be difficult to live with." And this female shifter was stuck with Sampurai for as long as they were ostracized on the land. No wonder Rikok had asked Sampurai to give Gerinching a break for once.

Gerinching shook her head. "Not really. He's quite all right."

"Do you think so?" Now Kumang was surprised.

"Uh-uh. I get use to all his quirks and antics after a while. Other than that, he is a decent male."

That was the best complement Kumang had ever heard a female said about Sampurai. It made her wonder if one day this female would really end up marrying him instead of Lulong. Rikok obviously thought it was a possibility. Not only that, she fully supported the idea that Gerinching would become their

181

family member. Kumang, of course, would prefer Lulong than any other female. She could not tell how she would feel if Rikok turned out to be right.

"Why do you look so surprised? You live with him, don't you?"

The question cut Kumang's chain of thought. "He lives in the same *bilik* with the rest of us. The *bilik* is my mother-in-law's at the moment. All her children lived there until they moved out when they got married. Let's see, Endu Rikok left to marry *mensia* on the land, and Wai Mayang went to Gelong longhouse when she married the late Chunggat. Only Watt Keling stayed put when he married me. Sampurai is not married yet, so he is still a resident of the *bilik*. Why do you ask?"

"Because you look so surprised when I said he is a decent male. Do you not agree with me?"

"I do. He truly is a decent male, that is if one is willing to spend time and efforts to get to know the real him underneath all the rough exteriors he displays to the world."

"You mean his explosive temper, his bluntness, his bigger-than-a-mountain ego."

Kumang eyed Gerinching with interest. "I suppose you have spent enough time with him to know them by now. Anyway, back to my original question, does Jang know about your situation? How you feel about going home?"

"No."

"Why don't you tell him?"

"What can he do?"

"He is trying his best to find a way to go home. I bet he thinks he is doing it with the thought that the both of you can go home to the sky, that you want to go home as much as he does."

"I know. There's nothing he wants more right now than going home to Panggau Libau." Gerinching smiled wistfully at Kumang. "He must love his family so much."

Kumang raised her eyebrows. "Don't you?"

182

"I do, but apparently they don't think that I do. Dom Jilan said everything I had done showed that I didn't care enough for them. That's why I kept embarrassing them with my actions. I never meant to make them lose face. I was just being me. Jilan thinks it is selfish of me to do only what I want. What about what they want? What about what they expect of me? Sadly, I can't be what they want me to be. Apai understands me to a certain extent. At least I would like to think that he does. He tolerates me as much as he can. Indai…ah! To her I am a major disappointment. I am definitely not the daughter they wish to have, a daughter they could be proud of."

"Did your parents actually say that you are a disappointment to them?"

"They did not need to. I know!" Gerinching tightened her hold around her legs. She buried her face in between her knees.

Kumang moved closer and put her arm around her. "I am so sorry. I am sure it is just a big misunderstanding. That is why you need to go home to Nanga Langit and talk to them about it. They may not think what you think they do."

Gerinching lifted a teary face. "Sampurai doesn't have any problem being accepted by his family for being … for …"

"…holding a different set of norms than the rest of us?" Kumang helped her finish what she wanted to say.

"Yeah."

Kumang pondered at the question. "No, I don't think he does. The longhouse residents are a different story, mind you, but the residents of his *bilik*, they all root for him through and through."

"That's what I thought. He clearly worships his late Apai. It shows every time he talks of him. He is fond of his Indai. He adores all his siblings, Keling especially."

"You got that one right."

"And I could see how much his Indai loves him from the way she defended him during the Meeting of the Chiefs. That included his brother and sister, too. They all tried their best to get him out of every single punishment."

"That is true." Kumang could not argue with that.

"Oh, and he likes you, too."

Kumang laughed softly. "You don't need to add that in to make me feel better."

"No, it's true. He does. That's why he is desperate to end his punishment on the land. He has a loving family to go home to."

"He does," Kumang agreed.

Gerinching wiped her nose with her hand. "So why don't you want to go home to Panggau Libau?"

Kumang let go of her.

"They are nice family. You are part of the family. Aren't they nice to you, too?"

Kumang turned away. "They are."

Gerinching let silence fill the air before she said, "Sampurai said …" She stopped abruptly the moment Kumang turned to her.

"The two of you followed Keling around at that time, did you not? When he lost his memory after his battle with Apai Ribai?" Kumang's voice was sharp.

Gerinching blinked slowly. "We did not know if he was Keling back then. There were two *petara*, remember? We did not know which one was Keling. Pungga followed one of the *petara*, whom we know now as Lium, and yes, Sampurai and I followed the other *petara*, whom we know now as Keling."

"They said the two of you stayed underneath the longhouse he lived in at the time."

"We shadowed him around to protect him from the attack of the *remaung*, yes."

"Did you know that he had a wife in that longhouse?"

Gerinching's face displayed guilt.

Kumang did not need to hear an answer. "Did you know that she was expecting a baby? His baby?"

Gerinching gulped.

Kumang covered her face with her hands.

She could hear Gerinching's frantic explanation, nonetheless. "I did not know for sure, though. From under the longhouse, we could not see what was happening inside the longhouse. We could hear things, bits and pieces of conversations, their movements, this and that, and ... I only ... guessed ... I did not know for sure that he was Keling ... and ..."

Kumang put her hands down. "And the two of you had a good time having lengthy discussions to fill your days, talking about the possibilities ..."

"We did *not* discuss the things we heard from the longhouse above." Gerinching shook her head firmly. "Sampurai would've cut his tongue out so that he was incapable of having this conversation with me even if I had dared to start it."

"Then what did he say to you?"

"Pardon me?"

"You were saying something when I cut you off just now. I am sorry I did that. So, what did Jang say to you?"

Gerinching blinked several times to recollect her thoughts. "Oh ... he said you always run away from home every time you are upset with Keling about something. And he has to chase after you all over the land to bring you home."

Kumang raised her eyebrows high.

"Is that why you don't want to go home now? You are angry with him? Because he had a wife on the land?"

"And you think I should not feel hurt that he married someone else because you can accept and even forgive Ajie for marrying another female." Kumang's defensive mode was up again.

"Oh! It took a long time before it stopped hurting! It took longer to accept it, and it took so much longer to forgive him."

Kumang stared at Gerinching. "So you're not blaming me." Unlike the others.

Gerinching waved her hands in front of her chest. "Not at all. Hey, I also ran away from home right after it happened, didn't I?"

Kumang smiled faintly. "Will it stop hurting someday?" she finally asked.

"Yes." Gerinching nodded firmly. "It is true that time heals all wounds, no matter how cliché it sounds. One day, you can think of it without feeling the pain. It will never be a happy thought, but you won't feel the tinge of pain anymore."

Kumang directed her eyes to the ground. "I don't know if I can ever forgive him for giving another female a child while he never gives me one. I doubt that pain will ever go away every time I think of it."

It was Gerinching's turn to extend her hand to hold Kumang's.

Kumang patted the hand placed on top of hers. "I think it is time we do something less depressing. Let's prepare something nice to eat!" She laughed to see Gerinching's face. "Ah, I forgot, you don't like cooking, do you?"

Gerinching pouted. "It's a public secret, isn't it?"

"Don't worry. I can do all the cooking. You can sit down, relax, and talk all you want," Kumang assured her.

"Talk?"

"They said you liked talking."

"By 'they' you mean Sampurai?" Gerinching pursed her lips. "Anyway, I can't let you do all the cooking. It is not proper."

"We are not in a longhouse, Endu. We can ignore propriety for once. This dinner is on me." Kumang got up and turned around. She lifted her foot a little bit higher to avoid tripping over the net of buttress roots. She almost kicked an orangutan which happened to sit behind her. "Sugie! I didn't know you were there. I'm so sorry."

Sugie gave her the saddest face she had ever seen from an orangutan.

"Oh, dear, did I kick you?" Kumang caressed the top of his head. She was pretty sure she had not, but what else would make Sugie look so miserable?

The orangutan went closer to hug her legs.

"Sugie, what happened? Did Mayas bully you?" Gerinching came to squat next to Sugie. She looked up to the canopy above. "Mayas! What have you done?" she shouted to the nowhere-to-be-seen ape.

Sugie let go of Kumang to plead to Gerinching, "No, no, he didn't do anything. Please, don't scold him because of me," he sounded frightened.

Gerinching did not seem to believe Sugie. "Why are you scared of him? Did he threaten you in any way? Does he refuse to share this territory with you?" She added sternly, "I'll have a word with him if he had."

Sugie took her hands in his. "He did not do anything. He really did not. Please, I do not want to cause any trouble."

Kumang joined Gerinching to squat in front of Sugie. "You will not cause a problem, Sugie. Why don't you come with me? Help me prepare dinner. What say you?"

Sugie let go of Gerinching's hands and went closer to Kumang.

"Come, then. Let's go." Kumang got up and extended her hand to Sugie, who took it at once. "We go first, Endu."

"Are you sure you don't want me to help?" Gerinching also stood. She looked guilty.

"It's all right. Sugie and I will be back soon with all the cooking ingredients. You and I can have a chat while I am cooking." Kumang smiled to Gerinching. "Don't worry, Endu. We are going to enjoy our time on the land."

FINDING CHERURAI

Lupar River, the Land

"Do you think this is the place?" Sampurai scanned the broad lining of Lupar River.

Pungga looked around. "I suppose so."

"I don't detect a *petara* around. Do you think he is long gone by now? Mao met him days ago, and we wasted time going to Mentarang terrain before we decided to come here," Sampurai grumbled.

Pungga did not want to point out to him that had he been more patient and discussed where they should have gone first, they would not have wasted a couple of days in Mentarang terrain. Instead, he smiled and answered, "I doubt it."

"Why do you say that?"

"From Mao's story, I gather that the task Ribai gave him is complicated. I don't know what it is, but if it involves Simalungun …," Pungga shook his head. "I don't believe Lium could accomplish the task within a few days. He should be here somewhere. Batang Lupar is big. He could be at the other end of the river."

"Should we travel down the river?"

"That's one way to do it."

"In it or by it?"

Pungga chuckled. "This is Batang Lupar, Jang. It is vested with vicious crocodiles. I am certain they will not welcome a couple of shape-shifters in their territory."

"Why are we afraid of Simalungun? He is only a *mensia* who committed unjust murder, and therefore, he is cursed to be a crocodile. So what if he grows so big

188

and now has an army of crocodiles behind him? He still does not have our shape-shifter powers and neither does his crocodile army."

"We need to conserve our energy to face Lium and Che. We spare the crocodiles for today. We'd better travel along the river bank."

Sampurai scowled.

"Don't look so discouraged. I'm sure we'll have our share of fight when we meet Lium and Che." Pungga knew better than to remind Sampurai that he was not in his best condition for any kind of battle.

Sampurai snorted, however, he did not argue further.

"Try to avoid fighting Lium. It's Cherurai we are after. There's no need for unnecessary battle." Although Pungga realized that his advice would fall on deaf ears, he felt he was obliged to say it.

As expected, he did not get a reply for his reminder.

"Do we go down or up the stream?" Sampurai looked left and right, considering their options.

Pungga squinted at the wide river of Lupar. "We'll try our luck downstream first. What do you think?"

Sampurai shrugged. "Whichever side is fine with me as long as we can get moving right away."

"All right. Let's get moving!" Pungga turned to his left and started walking.

They travelled slower than what their fifth grade shifter power allowed them. Pungga convinced Sampurai that they needed to move in a slower speed to ensure they did not overlook anything. Lium's *petara* power could be detected easily from afar, but they might miss spotting Cherurai. As shape-shifters, they could not detect an *antu raya*.

They did not chat much. It was more because of Sampurai's brooding mood. Pungga had no idea what brought it on. He thought Sampurai was more than eager to go home to the sky. He expected to see a more enthusiastic manner that was now lacking from his cousin. If anything, Pungga was the one who was reluctant to go home to face his sister-in-law and her accusation that he wanted to reclaim their family *bilik* from his brother.

189

Pungga was about to ask him about it as they walked around a big bend. He did not get the chance. Sampurai stretched his left arm to block him from walking forward.

"Look!" Sampurai whispered and his nudged his head towards their right. "Is that her?"

Pungga's eyes went to the river bank. "That's a female, all right. She could be a *mensia*," he whispered back to him.

"She's not *mensia*." Sampurai was confident.

"You don't know that."

"I do. I can smell a *mensia*'s soul. If I can't smell hers, that means she is not *mensia*. Come!" Sampurai moved in haste.

But Pungga stopped him. "You can smell *mensia* soul?" He thought he heard it wrong.

"I can smell souls in general, *mensia* especially." Sampurai added when he saw Pungga's surprised reaction, "You know, I am half-shape-shifter-half- ..."

"*Gerasi*," Pungga muttered in awe. Of course, the *gerasi* could smell *mensia* soul since it was their food intake. That much he knew. It never occurred to him that the *gerasi* could smell other creature's souls. Thus, Sampurai who had *gerasi* bloodline also inherited this ability. All the time they grew up together, had adventures and shared bloody battles, he had never heard a whisper of this. He found the reasoning for it almost instantly. He should have known. Sampurai's adopted family never wanted to discuss his *gerasi* bloodline. They chose to overlook the fact as if it was not a part of him at all. Talking about his *gerasi* bloodline and anything related to it was considered as a taboo for them. Thus, Sampurai never talked about it either. What Pungga could not figure out was how come Sampurai now talked about it? What brought this change?

Sampurai hissed impatiently. "Are you coming with me to check her out or not?" He made a move towards the female without waiting for Pungga to answer.

Pungga followed Sampurai in haste. His cousin was not known for possessing tact. He was worried about how Sampurai would approach the female, especially if she turned out to be someone else other than Cherurai.

He heard Sampurai call out to the female even when he was still a few stone throws away from her.

"Hey, Che!"

The female turned around. It took her a few intakes of breath to identify the caller. When she finally did, she screamed in fright.

Pungga had never met Cherurai before, so he did not know what she looked like. Nevertheless, the terror he saw in her face and the way her body trembled until she dropped to the ground gave him the confirmation he needed.

"Hello, Che!" Sampurai greeted her rather happily. "Long time no see. Glad to have finally found you. It is time you bring me home."

Cherurai began sobbing although no tears came out of her eyes. She moved frantically on her four towards the river.

Sampurai sighed at her feeble attempt to get away from him. "Oh, don't make this more difficult than it is necessary." His long strides to grab her arm were stopped by a swift movement from the river. A crocodile went up to the land and positioned itself in between Sampurai and Cherurai.

Sampurai pointed to the river. "Go back to where you belong. This is none of your business."

Cherurai crawled to the crocodile. "No, no. Don't let him take me away. He wants to kill me," she begged.

The crocodile asked Sampurai, "Is that true? Do you want to kill her? Why?"

Sampurai gritted his teeth. "Don't interfere with something that does not concern you. Go away!"

"Does not concern me?" The crocodile made a noise that sounded like a cough. "If you were a man, I could understand. They are like that – *mensia*. Their principles are totally off. They don't know how to live together with the rest of the creatures of this world. But you're not a man since you can talk to me. You must be a creature of the forest. Then, you should know better. What kind of male are you, wanting to kill a powerless female?"

Sampurai's face turned darker than the murky water of Lupar River. "I want to go home! I can't go home without her head!" he shouted his frustration out in

191

the air. He unbuckled the handle of his *parang* from his belt and expanded its blade fully. "Go away! Or I will go home with your head too!"

He took a few steps back when a couple of crocodiles climbed up to the dry land to join the crocodile in front of him.

The first crocodile laughed. "Not so brave now, are you? You need to call a friend to back you up." He referred to Pungga, who now also had his *parang* ready to face the crocodiles.

"Hah! I don't need a back up to fight you lot! Dom! Stay out of this fight. I can take them on myself!" Sampurai shouted to Pungga while he took a fighting stand.

"Jang, you need to focus! We are here to find Che, not to fight with Batang Lupar residents," Pungga cautioned him. He pointed to Cherurai. "Look! She is getting away!"

Sampurai let out an expletive to see Cherurai head fast towards the river. "Oh no, don't you dare! DOM! STOP HER!"

Pungga raised his eyebrows. "Who? Me?"

"I've got these crocodiles to handle ... why ... NO! ..." he shouted in frustration to see Cherurai dive into the water.

"You!" Sampurai pointed at the crocodiles with his *parang*. "This is your fault!" he shouted angrily. "The whole residents of Batang Lupar will pay for hiding her. I will find her in there. And any creature who dares to stand in my way will pay with his life!" He waved his *parang* wildly in the air. "I will start with the three of you if you don't get out of my way!"

"I don't think so." A male voice from behind them caused Pungga and Sampurai to turn back.

Pungga recognized Lium in an instant. However, that was not why he gasped. It was the female he had in his clutch: Lulong of Gelong.

"Let her go!" Sampurai's aggressive strides stopped the moment Lium put his hand on Lulong's throat.

"No, no, no. Stay where you are. Let's settle this amicably, shall we?" Lium was perfectly calm in responding to Sampurai's demand.

"Amicably? You are chocking her and you call that amicable?" Sampurai pointed his *parang* at Lium. "Get your hands off her!"

"You are the one holding a *parang*, not me. As you can see, I am unarmed. Now, why don't you put down your *parang* and leave? When I cannot detect you anymore, I will let her go. Don't bother coming back to look for Che afterwards. She won't be in Batang Lupar anymore by then. Leave the residents of the river alone."

Sampurai put his *parang* down. He eyed Lium with distrust.

Pungga went to Sampurai's side. "How do I know you will keep your word – that you will let go of her unharmed after we're gone?" he asked Lium.

Lium frowned. "What do I have to gain by hurting her? I have no use of her anymore. She has given me what I want."

"What is that supposed to mean? What did you do to her?" Sampurai's *parang* went up in the air again.

"I did not do anything to her. Tsk!" Lium sighed. "Why don't you tell them?" he urged Lulong. "They don't seem to believe a word I said."

"He is telling the truth. He will let me go." With Lium's hand on her throat, Lulong's voice was hoarse.

"She doesn't look all right to me! Answer my question! What have you done to her?" Sampurai shouted.

"That was not my doing! You can't hold me responsible for her condition. Now, why don't you just go away. And no harm will be done here. All is good between us." Lium shook her head in dismay when Sampurai did not stop glaring at him. "Why are all the shape-shifters so stubborn and won't listen to reason?" he said to Lulong as he tightened his hold around her neck. She squeaked as he pushed the air out of her throat.

"We'd better go, Jang!" Pungga urged Sampurai.

Lium smiled brightly at Pungga. "Thank you, Pungga. That would be the wisest thing to do. Off you go now! The faster you are out of my detection, the faster she gets her freedom."

Pungga grabbed Sampurai's arm and said to Lulong, "Find Endu G, we'll be there waiting for you." Then, he dragged Sampurai away before he had a chance to challenge Lium for a duel.

THE CURSE OF THE WEAVER GODDESS

Ulu Katibas, the Land

"Sugie, what's wrong?" Kumang asked when the orangutan jumped up from the forest ground. She did not need an answer because she could detect three fifth graders travelling fast towards them.

"Who are coming, I wonder?" Gerinching, who also detected them, asked.

"My best guess would be Dom and Jang," Kumang replied. She got to her feet.

"They're back so soon? And who's the third shifter?" Gerinching followed her to stand up.

"Igat, perhaps?"

"How did Laja get involved in this all of a sudden?"

"We can ask them when they got here. Let's meet them half-way." Kumang took Gerinching's hand in hers. "Are you ready for this?"

"Eh?"

"They're back. It could mean you're going home soon."

Gerinching bit her lip.

Kumang squeezed her hand. "Don't worry too much. We'll figure it out together."

Gerinching nodded with lack of enthusiasm.

Kumang pulled her to greet the coming shape-shifters. She let go of Gerinching's hand as soon as the shape-shifters came to sight. "Lu! What are you doing on the land?" She rushed to her sister. "How come she is with the two of you?" she asked Pungga. She did a quick scan on him and Sampurai. They did not find Cherurai. She shifted her eyes from Lulong, to Pungga, and then to Sampurai when none of them answered her questions.

Gerinching went to Sampurai. "What happened?" she asked timidly. She, too, had to feel the dark mood they brought in with them.

195

He did not answer her question. He spoke to Lulong instead, "You shouldn't have come down to the land, just like your sister asked you to. That's the problem with you females nowadays. You don't do as you're told!"

"Jang!" Pungga chided him. "It's no use talking about what should've been done. That's not what matters now."

"What is going on?" Kumang asked one more time. "Lu, what are they talking about?" She came closer to her sister. "What is that you have with you?"

Lulong stepped back as soon as Kumang was within reach. "Don't!" she said shakily.

"Lu? What's wrong? Will someone tell me what is going on?" Kumang's anxiety escalated. "Dom! What happened?"

Pungga pointed his right thumb to the box in Lulong's arms. "That's your cursed *pua kumbu*."

"It is?" Kumang was surprised. "Where did you get it from?" she asked Lulong.

"Lium," Lulong answered. Her voice was still shaky.

"Lium? How did he get hold of it?" Kumang was astonished. "How did you get it from him?"

"Mao, we'd better go in first. I think Lulong needs to lie down," Pungga reminded her. He turned to Gerinching, "Endu G, would you be so kind to prepare …"

"Yes, yes, of course, of course." Gerinching ran inside the den before Pungga finished his request.

"I don't need …" Lulong said weakly at the same time Kumang asked Pungga, "Why does she need to lie down?"

"Let's talk inside, shall we?" Pungga extended his arm towards the entrance. "Mao, you might want to help Lulong get inside."

"Why? Lu, are you not well?" Kumang now noticed that Lulong looked a bit pale. "Did you fight Lium to get the *pua*?" She did a quick scan on Lulong's body, from the top of her head to the *spata* on her feet. She did not see any wound. Still, if Lulong had fought Lium, she could not have won.

Lulong shook her head. "I'm all right."

"No, you are not! You are far from all right!" Sampurai said sternly.

196

Pungga frowned at him. "Jang! Let's go inside first. We'll talk about it later."

"But …" Kumang could not wait to hear an explanation.

Pungga cut her off gently. "Mao, please. It will only take a while for us to go inside. Our priority now is to get Lulong comfortable."

"All right, all right, come, Lu, let's get you inside first."

Kumang ushered Lulong inside, although she did not know why Lulong needed her help to walk.

Gerinching was ready to receive them the moment they passed the curtain of creepers. "Over here, come, you can lie down here." She waved her hand to Lulong. She indicated something that looked like a woven rattan mat big enough to sleep on in between the tall buttressed tree roots of the giant tree.

"I don't need to lie down, thank you." Lulong offered her a smile. "I am sorry. You shouldn't have taken the trouble."

"What trouble?" Sampurai dismissed her concern. "She loves doing these things. You can't stop her even if you try. And if you really appreciate what she has done, you'd better use it to lie down."

"I really don't feel like …"

"At least take a seat, Lu. You may not feel it now, but you need it," Pungga assured her.

Lulong relented and took a seat.

Kumang noticed how Lulong clung to the cursed *pua* as if her life depending on it. The others chose their own choice of seats from the various flat surfaces of the roots. Kumang sat herself next to Lulong.

"Now, tell me what happened," Kumang said to Lulong. "How did the three of you meet?"

Lulong threw her eyes to Pungga, and then Sampurai.

"We are sitting down now. It is time to tell me … and Gerinching, what is going on," Kumang began to lose her patience. "Jang! How did the three of you meet?" Out of the three of them, Sampurai was the only one who could not lie. She could always rely on him to tell the truth no matter how bad it was.

"I was about to fight the crocodiles by Lupar river that protected Cherurai …" Sampurai started.

"You found her?" Gerinching, who was sitting next to him, placed a hand on his arm.

"We did," Sampurai nodded grimly.

Gerinching looked around in alarm as if she expected to see Cherurai's head.

He must have noticed her concern because he added hastily, "She escaped to the river because the crocodiles were in my way. So, I told them that I'd get rid of them first, and then I'd go into Batang Lupar to find her. That's when they showed up."

"They? More crocodiles?" Gerinching asked for clarification.

"Lium and Lulong." Sampurai frowned at her mistake. "He threatened us with her life if we didn't leave immediately. So we did what he asked."

"What were you doing with Lium?" Kumang asked Lulong.

Lulong closed her eyes briefly. "I reached the land through the portal in Katibas."

"How do you know there is one there?" Kumang did not know about the portal.

"Igat told me he used the portal once to get to the land to find Jang," Lulong explained. "It's nearer than where the *pintu langit* is, so I went there."

"Igat? Igat Laja?" Kumang clarified.

Lulong nodded.

"What made you come down to the land? I thought we have agreed that you stayed in Gelong."

"I was worried about you. Lium is obviously a dangerous creature. I could not stay at home while you risk your life ..."

"You should have stayed in Gelong!" Sampurai snapped. "What can you do that we cannot? You think ... ouch!" he glared at Gerinching.

Gerinching gritted her teeth and shook her head at him.

"*What?* Why did you pinch me?" He clearly did not get what she was trying to tell him.

She put a finger on top of her lips.

"I …" he moved to the next flat surface on his left to avoid her outstretched hand.

Pungga filled the gap in the conversation. "Lium found her in Katibas."

"How did he know you'd be there? Don't tell me he has the gift of visions like Igat?" Kumang did not like the idea that Lium was so powerful.

"No, he doesn't. He … apparently he has spies all over the forest. He told me this. He is very proud of it," Lulong clarified.

Kumang frowned. "What do you mean by 'spies'?"

"He has animals that report to him about what is going on in the forest, the movements of *mensia*, animals in and out of the forest, that sort of thing. So, that day, when I reached the land, I was spotted by his spies, which then reported to him of my presence on the land. That's how he found me."

"I bet he got the idea from the *remaung* boy," Pungga commented.

"Do you mean that Lium took over the *remaung* poaching network after his death? Is he their leader now?" Kumang's frowned deeper. Lium identified himself to her as a *bunsu baya*. Why did he rally the animals on the land?

"No, he does not support the hunting of animals for trade. He believes what the *remaung* boy did is wrong," Pungga contradicted her guess. "I think he formed his own followers, those who believe in what he believes. Then, he imitated how the *remaung* network worked."

"What does he believe? Oh! He wants to save the world from the boy who will destroy it." Kumang nodded as the memory struck. "Is he really working on finding the boy or was it just crazy talk? I mean, how in the world can he find the boy?"

"Lium is dead set in finding the boy," Pungga confirmed.

Kumang turned to Lulong. "So he wants you to tell him about the design of the *pua*, because Tenang told us about the *pua* design." Her eyes fell on the box in Lulong's arms. "But he had the *pua* with him, didn't you say?"

Lulong nodded. "He told me his followers took it from Endu Rikok."

"That's before or after he found you on the land?"

"Before."

Kumang did not understand Lium's way of thinking. "Why can't he see it for himself if he had got the *pua* before he found you?"

Sampurai snorted. "He doesn't want to get himself curse, does he? A coward that he is!"

Kumang suddenly felt the canopies of the forest were closing down on her. She found it hard to breath.

"Did you see it? Did you see the cursed *pua*?" She dreaded to hear Lulong's answer.

Lulong gave a single nod.

Kumang closed her eyes in despair. "He made you see it so that you could tell him about the boy. That wretched male-shifter!"

"He asked me to do it. I agreed," Lulong said.

"Why? I mean, if he doesn't want to get cursed, he can always ask one of his followers to see it."

"He said they're all innocent. He couldn't do that to them."

"You are also innocent. Why did he choose you?"

"I am your sister."

Kumang's eyes widened. "Because I wounded him, he targeted my sister?" She groaned. "He told me I would pay for that. As he said, he always keeps his word."

"He said if I refused, he would kill me and then, he'd go after the rest of your family members one by one and repeat the same thing until one of them is willing to see the cursed *pua* and tell him the story on it. I could see that he meant what he said. I decided that it had to stop with me. I saw the *pua* and then I told him what I saw."

"Lu …," Kumang did not know what to say. "I'm so sorry. I should have just told him what I know. It's just that, I really believe it is wrong of me to say anything about the design."

"No, you are right. You shouldn't have. You never see the *pua*. You only heard Tenang talk about it. I told him the exact same thing," Lulong said firmly. "He agreed with me. That's why he asked me to see the real *pua*."

"But now you suffer because of my decision!" Kumang covered her face with her hands.

"I am in this condition because of Lium's decision and mine, not yours," Lulong disagreed with her. She caressed Kumang's shoulder. "Mao, it's all right. It's over now. He's got what he wants. He won't come after any of us anymore."

"How could you say it is all right now? You've got the curse of Inik Bunsu Petara! How are we going to lift it?" Kumang shook her head. "I doubt that Sindun can help with this although she is one of the most powerful celestial *manang* we have in our world."

"The only creature that can lift the curse is the one who cast it, isn't it?" Gerinching asked quietly.

Sampurai hit his knees. "We'll ask Inik Bunsu Petara to lift the curse! That will settle it!"

Pungga smiled ruefully. "It is not that simple, Jang."

"What is not that simple? Inik gave the curse because *mensia* defiled our sacred traditions. She wants to punish them. It has nothing to do what-so-ever with her." Sampurai pointed his thumb to Lulong. "Her situation is completely different. Inik can lift the curse just for her. It is that simple."

Pungga shook his head. "We are talking about Inik Bunsu Petara, Jang. Nothing is ever simple with her, even if it is really a simple straight forward issue."

"You've met her before, haven't you?" Kumang asked Pungga. "I mean, when you lived in Tansang Kenyalang Longhouse with your wife, you've met Inik Bunsu?"

Pungga nodded. "We've met a couple of times. That's how I know that she is difficult to reason with. She makes decisions based on her mood, not reasoning."

"Can you talk her into lifting the curse?"

Pungga's face was not encouraging at all.

"Just for her." Sampurai pointed at Lulong with his thumb. "If Inik is angry with *mensia*, let her be. It's none of our business. We do not want to interfere with what she is doing to them. She can continue unleashing her wrath at them. We don't care. We just want her to spare her. Just her!"

"I suppose ..." Pungga was still not sure.

"Can you, Dom? Please?" Kumang pleaded.

201

"I can't promise, Mao." His eyes found Lulong's. "Please don't think that I refuse to help. I do want to help. But Inik Bunsu Petara…" He threw his arms up in the air.

"I understand," Lulong smiled faintly. "We have heard of what she is like."

"At the very least we should try. We must try. We won't blame you if it turns out that you can't persuade her," Kumang promised Pungga.

Pungga heaved. "All right, I'll take you to see her." In an instant he remembered something. "Are you going to be all right, here?" he aimed his eyes at Gerinching, and then Sampurai.

"Why won't I be all right?" Sampurai was already on his feet. "I've told you, my wounds have healed."

Pungga looked up to his tall stature. "You can't go with us. You need to stay here with Endu G. That's why I ask if it is all right that I leave the two of you on your own."

"Why can't I go with you?" Sampurai put his hands on his hips.

"We are ostracized on the land," Gerinching reminded Sampurai.

"Inik Bunsu Petara lives in the second layer of the sky," Kumang said almost at the same time Gerinching did. "You are forbidden to go there."

Sampurai's face turned sour. He dropped to the ground and crossed his legs. "Fine! I'll stay here and be useless," he grumbled. "Why can't I go to the second layer of the sky? I am banned from the first layer of the sky. That's the agreement. Nobody said anything about the second layer."

"You'd better not risk it," Gerinching warned him. "You could end up getting more punishments."

"We don't even know if the terms of our punishment cover the second layer of the sky. That is my point!" Sampurai argued. "Why can't we go and ask someone …"

"You know what you should do, Jang?" Pungga stopped the potentially never ending debate.

"Don't tell me to stay here and do nothing. I won't accept it!" Sampurai punched the tree root with his fist. It shuddered violently due to the brute force he used.

"Don't do that to the tree!" Gerinching got hold of his fist as if she expected him to continue hitting the tree.

He might have done it if Pungga had not said, "Inik Bunsu has a dwelling on the land. She could be there right now instead of in her dwelling in the sky. Why don't you go and check it out?"

Sampurai beamed. "You're right! We can go there!" He was already on his feet.

"You know where she lives, don't you?" Pungga asked. "You know how to get there?"

"Everybody knows where she lives!" Sampurai waved his hand in the air. "It's just that I've never been there before. I had no need to look for her. But I know where the place is. I can find it."

"After you've met her, let Endu Jie do all the talking," Kumang suggested.

Sampurai's eyes grew big. "Why? You don't think I can talk?"

Kumang secretly sighed. "That's not what I meant, Jang." She just wanted to increase the chance of Inik Bunsu agreeing to help Lulong.

Gerinching touched her arm gently. "Don't worry. We'll do our best to persuade her to lift the curse for Lulong. How do plan to go to her place in the sky?"

"The nearest portal to get to our own realm in the first layer of the sky is in Katibas. We should go there. From there, we'll have to find the *pintu langit* to cross over to the world in the second layer of the sky," Pungga turned to Kumang. "What do you think, Mao?"

"Why bother going through all the trouble looking for a portal or a sky door? You're wasting time," Sampurai grumbled. "Mao can create a shortcut to go to our realm. Watt always does it."

"What kind of shortcut?" Kumang was intrigued.

"The shortest cut would be using his realm rock. You'll reach Inik Bunsu's dwelling at once. Ask him for it." Sampurai squinted when she hesitated. "Your sister's life is at stake and you still don't want to talk to your husband, even if it means it could save her a lot faster?"

"Watt lost all his belongings when he got injured. He told me that. I don't think he has the realm rock," Kumang defended her decision not to talk to Keling.

"You don't think he has it? Or do you know it for sure?" Sampurai pushed for his idea. "Find him and ask him!"

Pungga interfered. "He lost it, Jang. He told me the same thing. He lost all his possessions. The only thing he had on was the clothes he was wearing at the time. At least that's what the people who saved him told him."

"Does that mean *mensia* has the realm rock now?" Gerinching guessed.

"Maybe, or a resident of the water kingdom has it," Pungga answered. "It doesn't matter now."

"We'd better focus on getting Lulu to see Inik Bunsu Petara as soon as possible." Kumang patted Sampurai's knee to get his attention. "Jang, what kind of shortcut do you have in mind? How do we get to our realm as soon as possible?"

Sampurai was ready with his answer. "Watt likes to create rainfall from the sky. All of you can use the rain drops to walk up to the sky. No need to waste time travelling to Katibas to find the portal. You can go from here."

"That's an idea that might work," Pungga told Kumang.

Sampurai frowned. "It does work. It always works with Watt, why can't it work with you? You are also a *petara*. You know how to create rain. Or don't you?" he asked Kumang.

"I do know how to make rain fall, Jang," Kumang said with amusement. "But I'm not going to wet your home. I'll do it right outside." She smiled at Gerinching.

"Get on with it, then. What are you waiting for?" Sampurai drummed on his knees. "Go now, go! All of you! Go!" He waived to Sugie, who was sitting behind Kumang. "You, too, go with them. Go!"

"Sampurai," Gerinching caught one of his hands that were swinging wildly in the air. She said to Sugie, "Don't mind him, Sugie. You can stay here until they come back. He's just upset that he can't go with them."

"He wants to go with them! See?" Sampurai stretched his arm to show how Sugie hurriedly stood up with Pungga, Kumang and Lulong.

"An orangutan is a physical being on the land. He can't go to the sky and leave his physical body behind. He is not like us," Gerinching hissed as she pulled Sampurai up to send their guests off.

"He can if he has the realm rock!" Sampurai widened his eyes at Gerinching.

"But he doesn't have it, does he?" Gerinching sighed. "We have established that Keling lost it, and now *mensia* has it." She directed her eyes to Lulong, who suddenly looked worried. "What is the matter?"

"You remind me of something." Lulong bent her head to the box she clutched in her arms. "I can't bring this *pua kumbu* to the sky. It is a physical object." She hesitated. "I wonder if you don't mind taking care of it while I am away." She added quickly, "You don't need to worry. As long as you don't open the box, you won't get the curse. I don't mean to trouble you, but I really don't feel I should leave it on the land unattended."

"It's all right. You can leave it with us." Gerinching offered her hand to Lulong.

Sampurai snatched the box from Lulong's outstretched arm before Gerinching could reach it. "You should get going now. You need to travel further than us," he said to Pungga.

"You are right," Pungga stood up. "It is best that we go as soon as possible. Are you ready to go Mao? Lu?"

"Sure." Kumang helped Lulong get up. "Jang, contact us as soon as you have any news about Inik Bunsu being on the land."

"No problem!" Sampurai nodded. "Bye! Take care!" He waved his hand to them.

They said their goodbyes and left Sampurai and Gerinching behind.

As soon as they were out of sight, Sampurai turned to face Gerinching. "We also had better get going. We might not have to travel further like them, but we will have to travel slower. Time is of the essence here."

"Because I am only a third grader? Therefore, I can't travel as fast as you?" Gerinching's sweet smile was purely artificial. "If you are in such a hurry to save her life, I don't need to go with you."

"You know I can't leave you behind!"

"Oh, I'll be fine here. If you think saving her life is so important ..."

"Naturally saving a life is important. What is your point?"

"My point is I can't travel at your speed. If you want to find Inik Bunsu as soon as possible, it is best that you go alone."

"You are coming with me. There is no other option!"

"There is."

"No, there isn't! I promised your Apai that no harm will come to you while we are ostracized on the land."

"I know, I know! Apai will send Nanga warriors to go after your head if anything happens to me on the land. You've told me about it so many times." Gerinching sounded bored.

"If you know, why are we still having this conversation? You're coming with me and that is it!"

"I will only slow you down."

"That is why we have to start moving now! And you want to waste time arguing!" He looked up to the canopies above their head. "Yas! We are going to Inik Bunsu's house." He shouted to Mayas. Then, he looked down at Sugie. "Are you going with us? No? Good, you keep an eye of this box." He threw the box recklessly to the ground in front of Sugie. "We're going now!" he said to Gerinching. He started moving without waiting for her reply.

Gerinching would have followed him if it was not because she saw Sugie standing alone, looking forlorn. She went to him. "Don't be so sad, Sugie, Kumang will be back soon with good news."

Sugie stared at her with sadness in his eyes. "I wish I could go with her. She needs help. I wish I could help her. But I'm just a useless creature. How I wish …"

"You wish you have the realm rock with you so that you can go with her to the sky, huh?" Gerinching caressed Sugie's shoulder.

"Let's go! Let's go!" Sampurai's voice boomed in the forest.

Sugie smiled sadly at her. "You'd better go with him. I'll be fine here."

"Bye, Sugie. Take care of yourself, all right? Don't think too much of the realm rock. Nobody knows where it is. There's no point spending time wondering who has it now." She ran to the forest where Sampurai had disappeared into.

206

THE REALM ROCK

Lupar River, the Land

Cherurai sat alone on the damp ground of a dark cave. It was a cave underneath the riverside. She had to dive in and swim through a long and winding tunnel to get there. Devoid of light, the cave was chilling. However, that was not the reason she shivered. She could not shake off the dreadful feeling she had when she saw Sampurai a while ago. She closed her eyes in despair. He was still looking for her. He would never stop looking for her until he had her head as a trophy to bring back home.

She opened the palm of her hand to stare at a small green rock that glowed in the dark. The shape-shifters called it the realm rock. They said it had the power to take the bearer to any place they wanted to go — any place in their world: under, above, and beyond. What she needed was the presence of the five elements of nature: water, earth, air, wood, and metal to make it work. At least, that was what she heard. She had never tried to use it. For the thousandth time ever since she got hold of it, she thought of using it. She had never been able to summon enough courage to try. She had never seen anyone use it. What if something went wrong? What if she ended up somewhere she should not have? What if she ended up neither here nor there? Who would come to her rescue? Nevertheless, what had happened just now really shook her to the core. Maybe this rock was exactly what she needed to run away from Sampurai.

She was always a firm believer of the notion that everything happened for a reason. And the realm rock in her hand only solidified her belief. She had been inside Kapuas River to witness the King of Baya and Lium fought Keling of Panggau Libau and Chunggat of Gelong. She had waited for that moment for a long time. To see Keling go to Sebayan where he had sent her twin sister was a long-awaited dream. She had to see it with her own eyes. Therefore, despite Lium's warning for her to stay clear of the battlefield, she lurked in the dark water to see her dream turn into reality. She shed tears of joy as Keling's unconscious body sank slowly towards the bottom of the riverbed. She was waiting to receive him with open arms when the female water spirit snatched him away half-way through and took him away with her. In the end, only a tiny pouch landed gently in one of her palms. She was so disappointed that she ignored the pouch for weeks. When she finally inspected its content, she realized with a surge of hope that everything did happen for a reason. She recognized the small green rock almost immediately. At first, she had thought of using it to go to Sebayan so that she could visit her sister. She missed her terribly. Who knew, maybe – just maybe – if what they said about the realm rock was true, she could go to Sebayan and took her sister back with her to the land of the living. The thought gave her excitement as much as anxiety. It was an extremely ambitious quest.

She bit the tip of her little finger. Perhaps, she could try to use it first to go to another place on the land. That would be useful to avoid Sampurai. Yes? It should be safe enough to try the rock within the same realm. She inhaled deep. She needed to … she heard footsteps coming towards her. She quickly slipped the rock inside the pouch hanging on her belt.

"Ah, here you are. I've been looking for you." In the dark cave, a male voice came within hearing distance.

She recognized who he was. She got on her feet to approach him. "Has he gone? Have they all gone?" she asked anxiously.

"They have gone." Lium's figure came so close she could almost see him.

She smiled with relief. "Thank you for saving my life, Lium. I don't know how to repay your kindness, but one day I will. I promise you."

"You can do it today by leaving Batang Lupar as soon as possible."

Cherurai blinked rapidly to hear his expressionless voice. She could never tell his mood when he was like this. She had to be extra careful. Lium was unpredictable. "Where are we going? I thought the King of Baya gives you an assignment to do? Oh, I don't suppose that is important anymore. You've got what you need to look for the boy, haven't you? If that's the case, we need to …"

"You are leaving Batang Lupar. I am staying here. As you said, I have an assignment to complete."

"But … I don't understand. If you're staying…"

"You can't stay here. The shape-shifters may come back to look for you here, and they will create chaos in Batang Lupar in order to find you. I can't have that at the moment. You must leave!"

"But Lium, where can I go? You know he is looking for me. You heard him. He is after my life!"

208

"I know. That's why I suggest you leave now. Go as far away as you can before he comes back for you."

"Why can't I stay here? He can't fight all the crocodiles in Batang Lupar."

"Batang Lupar is not my territory. It is Simalungun's. I can't risk his residents to shelter you. It won't do me any good to antagonize him. The King gives me a task to do here."

"A task from the King? Your task is to save the world from the boy who will destroy it! Listen to you! I can't believe you are willing to be a servant boy to the King of Baya!"

"I am a *bunsu baya*. It is an honor to do bidding for my King." His voice sounded harsh.

"What about the safety of the world? Have you forsaken it to gain favor from your King?"

"I have not forsaken the world. I will never forsake it. That is precisely why I must complete this task in Batang Lupar without flaws."

"I don't understand."

"You don't need to. Saving this world is a fate given to me, not to you."

"I can help you save the world. Let me stay."

"If you want to help me, leave now. Don't create a problem for me by staying here."

She reached out to hold his hand. "You know I don't have any power to defend myself from him. Why are you doing this to me? After everything I've done for you!"

He moved away to put a distance between them. "What have you done for me?"

She could not believe he could be so ungrateful. "I nursed you to health after the shape-shifter killed your Indai Tuai."

"I just saved your life in return, didn't I?" His voice was emotionless again.

She realized she had lost her bargaining power. She could only plead for his compassion. "Lium, please! Don't make me leave! You are all I have in this world. I don't have anybody in this world. You know what it's like when your family, the creatures who are supposed to protect you turn their backs on you.

209

You are also like me. You understand …"

"Look, you can stay here if you want. But if the shape-shifters come looking for you, don't expect me to protect you. If I can save a life of a Batang Lupar resident by handing you over to him, I will." Lium walked closer to hold her shoulders. "Don't cry. I don't want to do that. We are friends, are we not? Yes?" He gave her a gentle shake. "Now, I suggest that you leave while you still have the chance. Go to the deepest part of the forest. Find a place where no creature has ever dwelled in. As a shape-shifter, he can't detect you. I know that for a fact! Chances are he will never find you. You are a smart female. I know you are. You will find your way in this world."

"Lium!" She caught the hand on her shoulder to put it on her wet cheek in her last attempt to seek for his pity.

He wrenched his hand from hers. "Goodbye, Che! I wish you the best of luck!" He walked away without missing a step, leaving her sobbing on the wet damp floor.

What was she to do? Where would she go? How could he be so heartless towards her? What had she done to deserve this? Why was this world so merciless to her? Everyone was against her. Everyone who was nice to her was taken away from her. She swallowed hard. All her life, there was only one creature who was sincerely kind to her – her twin sister, Cherembang.

She took out the realm rock from the pouch. She stared at it hard. This was not the time to think too much. This was the time to act. She clasped it in the palm of her hand with determination. She would use the realm rock to go to Sebayan and bring Cherembang' soul back with her to the land of the living!

THE VALLEY OF THE DEAD

Kumang stopped because Pungga, who was travelling at the very front, halted abruptly.

"What is the matter, Dom?" She peered to the narrow path in front of them. She did not see anything alarming, nor did she sense any danger approaching.

"This place is not right," Pungga sounded unsure. He squatted to place his hands on the ground.

"What do you mean? This is just another forest on a hill that *mensia* called Bombalai," Lulong, who was standing right behind him, arched her neck to see as far ahead as she could.

"That is the strange thing I'm talking about. This soil can't possibly grow those trees" Still squatting, Pungga pointed at the trees around them. He looked up to Lulong, who was a *bunsu kayu*. "Do you think these are the types of trees that should grow at this height?"

Lulong scrutinized the forest more closely. "Now that you mention it, why didn't I notice it before?"

Pungga stood up and closed his eyes. When he opened them, he turned to Kumang and Lulong. "What do you hear?"

Kumang shrugged. "Some birds are chirping. That's normal to hear in the forest."

"You don't think the voices are too faint? The forest is here, right next to us." Pungga spread his arms around. "Why do the voices sound like they come from afar?"

"I can hear a clear sound of knocking on wood." Lulong tilted her head to one side. Then, she frowned. "I don't think that is a woodpecker."

"No." Pungga shook his head. "That's definitely not a woodpecker. That's the sound of someone working on wood."

Kumang walked forward to stand next to Lulong. "Do you think we are near Inik Bunsu's dwelling?" As the knocking of wood became louder and faster, she wondered where the sound came from.

"I don't …" Pungga could not finish what he wanted to say because a deafening creaking sound broke the fast rhythm of the wood knocking. Something huge was falling down to the ground. "Watch out!" he shouted.

Without knowing what was falling, Kumang grabbed Lulong's arm and dragged her to a direction she predicted to be safe. Unfortunately, her prediction was wrong. She took Lulong right underneath the falling object. She used the only fraction of time she had to make up her mind whether she should use her hands to manipulate the air above their heads to brace the falling object or to drag Lulong to the opposite direction.

The falling object would have crushed their heads had it not because of a strong gush of wind that passed through the narrow distance between their heads and the object, giving her time to execute her decision to take Lulong away.

They reached Pungga's side at the same time the object landed heavily on the ground, shattering the earth and lifted dust in the air.

Kumang's first thought went to the gush of wind that saved their lives. She could have sworn that it was not a natural phenomenon. It had to be sent by another creature. Who was it? Keling? She quickly detected her surroundings. She did not find a *petara* around. She swallowed. Of course Keling was not around. He was not there to keep her safe. Silly her! How could she think that he would trouble himself to watch over her after everything she had said to him?

She forced herself to stop thinking about Keling. She shifted her attention to the fallen object on the ground. Before she could figure out what it was, a movement from up the hill caught her eyes. A male with a ponytail, holding a big wooden hammer, was running down the path towards them.

"Are you all right, ladies?" He was out of breath when he reached them. He directed his question to Kumang and Lulong although he fixed his eyes at Kumang.

"Yes, we are fine," Lulong's answer was polite.

The male with a ponytail shifted his eyes to Lulong as if he just noticed her presence. "Oh, good! I did not know you were on the other side of the fence."

"Fence? Was it a fence what fell down?" Lulong pointed to the ground.

212

"Yours?"

The male with a ponytail made a face. "Err ... you could say that. I mean ..."

Kumang scanned the new scenery after the fence had fallen. She saw a barren pyroclastic path. She was instantly reminded that the hill was actually a sleeping volcano. The thought roused her curiosity.

"Why did you put a fence up here? What was it for?" Kumang walked closer to the fallen fence.

"To keep intruders like you from finding us obviously." A female's voice sounded acidic to the ears.

Kumang looked right to find the owner of the voice. She was startled to see the female who was coming towards them. From far, she looked like she had uneven skin tone, which made her appearance look odd. However, as soon as she stood next to the male with a ponytail, Kumang could see that it was paint splattered randomly all over her body, also on top of her clothes, that created the uneven skin color illusion. She hooked her arms around the male with a ponytail's right arm.

"Us? The two of you live somewhere near?" Pungga asked the male with a ponytail.

"Oh, we ..." the male with a ponytail pulled his arm out of the female's grip. He took a step aside to distance himself from her.

The female pouted. "Whatever gives you the idea that our house is nearby?"

Pungga pointed his thumb at the male with a ponytail. "He said that's his fence. Therefore, I assume he lives nearby. And since you are with him, I take it that both of you live together."

"That was her fence, not mine," the male with a ponytail's denial came too quickly.

"So why did you fell a fence that was not yours?" Kumang asked. The situation was getting more and more confusing.

"She asked me to. She's not happy with her paintings." The male was mournful.

"Paintings?" Lulong turned to the forest. "You mean ..." She left the narrow path to approach the forest border. She extended her hand carefully. "Oh dear me!" she exclaimed as she touched the flat surface of wood instead of three-dimensional tree. "These are all paintings? Mao, come here and have a look.

213

These are amazing! Did you paint all these?" She turned around to the female with a painted face.

The female only offered her a smug smile.

"See? I told you there is nothing wrong with your paintings. There was no need to fell the fence," the male with a ponytail grumbled.

"Do I give you advice about how to do your carpentry? I do not, do I? Don't start giving me advice about how to paint!" The female with a painted face glared at the male with a ponytail.

The male frowned. "I would not have said anything if you had not involved me in building the fence. I spent weeks building a frame for you to paint. It was solid woodwork. Why did I have to destroy it? Why can't you paint on top of the painting you're not happy with?"

"Paint on top of the old paintings?" The female almost spat at the male in her rage.

Kumang caught Pungga's worried look directed at her when the female continued her rant on the male, who in return shouted back at her. She did not know what to do. It would not be wise to get involved in a quarrel between these two creatures who seemed to be a couple.

The verbal argument soon escalated into a physical fight. The moment the male with a ponytail shoved the female with a painted face a little too hard, Pungga did not wait for a cue from Kumang about what he should do. He filled in the empty space that the male created from pushing the female away. "Hey, hey, hey! Calm down, Jang."

The male swung his hammer at him as a reply.

Pungga caught the male's wrist with ease. The hammer changed hand with a mere twist of arm. The male was clearly not a brawler. Nevertheless, Pungga had another problem coming. The female screamed and jumped on his back.

Wrapping her arm around Pungga's neck, she screamed, "Give him back his hammer!"

Kumang felt that she had to interfere. She swiftly went to the female, disentangled her from Pungga's back, and dragged her away.

The female screamed even louder, "Intruders! Intruders! We have intruders!"

In a blink of an eye, four more creatures appeared within sight.

Kumang let go of the female, who instantly ran to join the new arrivals. The male also did the same, but not before he snatched his hammer from Pungga's hand.

Kumang went to stand next to Lulong, while Pungga positioned himself a step in front of them.

The unnatural sounds of the forest disappeared along with the appearance of the new arrivals, creating a dead silence all around. Because the six creatures in front of them were not shape-shifters, Kumang could not detect their power levels. The only thing she could do was to scrutinize their appearances to gauge the level of danger each of them could pose.

She did not know what to make of the row of creatures in front of her. The creature on the far left was a lanky male whose face showed great misery. He wore black clothing from the top of his head which was covered with a strip of black cloth to the bottom of his wrapped-in-leather-straps feet. Everything about him shouted out misery, except for the weapon he was holding in his left hand. The sword had an extremely long blade full of colorful decorations. Kumang had never seen a sword with so many ornaments as the one he was holding. The shape-shifters' *parang nyabor*, although were also crafted to the last detail, was designed in such a way that each curve was aimed to create the most effective and efficient weapon to kill an opponent. She could not imagine how the male could fight effectively with a sword which carried too many embellishers.

The next creature was a plump female holding a giant wooden spoon in her right hand. Her appearance was also odd. Her body seemed to be made of round objects. Her radiant face was the exact opposite of the grim face of the first male. The way she put her hair up in a tight bun on top of her hand accentuated the roundness of her face, which reminded Kumang of the moon. She even had the dark bluish shade on the right side of the face, the same exact shade found on the moon when it was seen from the land.

Next to her was a sturdy male with a big head. His body sported wide shoulders that took a sharp turn inward towards his waist, and from that point downward, it took a triangle shape to the bottom of his large feet. He reminded Kumang of the drum he was cradling in his right arm.

Next to him was the female with a painted face, who called herself a painter. And then, the male with a ponytail, whom the female called a carpenter.

After the carpenter was a female covered in ornaments. She was not as tall as

215

the male on the far left, but her appearance gave the impression of extra length. Her black hair, mixed with strikes of silver, was let loose down to the back of her knees. Kumang was not sure it was the length of her hair or the thick silver rings she piled up on her neck, or the heavy metal earrings that pulled her earlobes down to her shoulders which created the impression of an abnormal length. Her clothes were of many shades of green and brown, the main colors of the forest. Her body was covered in painted beaded necklaces of various lengths. Kumang wondered how this female could move around at ease with such heavy jewelry weighing down her whole body.

Kumang heard Pungga conduct the introduction on their behalf. "Good day. I am Pungga of Panggau Libau. I am here with Kumang of Panggau Libau," he pointed his thumb to his left to indicate Kumang, and moved it to the right, "and Lulong of Gelong."

The creatures in front of them exchanged curious glances among each other. It had to be the names 'Panggau Libau' and 'Gelong' that they recognized.

"We are not here to cause any trouble for you. We are looking for Inik Bhiku Bunsu Petara," Pungga continued.

"Mistress? What do three shape-shifters want from our Mistress?" The bubbly round female asked with excitement.

"We need her help." Pungga took a step forward. "May I enquire if she is at home at the moment?"

Most of them shook their heads.

"Do you happen to know when she will be back?"

The male who looked like a drum snorted. "She is our Mistress. She doesn't report to us about her movements."

"But this is where she lives, is it not?"

"When she is around," the drum-like male gave a non-committal answer.

"Do you mind if we stay at her place while we're waiting for her?"

They erupted into chatter all at once.

"Whoa! Whoa! Whoa! That is not going to happen! Just go away!" The painter waived her hands in the air as if by doing that she could erase their presence from the scene.

"Oh! It would be nice to have visitors for once." The bubbly female clapped her hands in delight.

"She hates uninvited visitors! I don't think it is a good idea," said the long female to the bubbly female.

"We can't host them for indefinite time!" The carpenter shook his head vigorously.

"They can stay as long as they don't disturb me making my music." The drum-like male nodded his head in a steady beat.

"They can't stay! What will we say to Mistress if she comes back and finds them at home?" The long female made a loud clunking sound by waving her hands in the air.

"They want Mistress's help. I want to see what she is going to do to them when she meets them." The grim male turned around to walk away without waiting for response.

The other five was stumped to hear his statement. Their eyes followed him leaving for a while.

Then, the bubbly female broke into a giggle. "That is really something I'd love to see." She moved quickly to approach Pungga. "Come, come! Let's wait inside the house until she comes back." She hooked her arm around his while she smiled to Kumang and Lulong. "Follow us, you two. You are here in time. I just finished creating new recipes. I need someone to try them."

"I am sure they are delicious." Pungga smiled politely to her.

As she walked behind Pungga and the cook, Kumang caught the sight of the long female shook her head as a warning signal. She was not sure if they were doing the right thing by going to a house full of peculiar creatures. However, what better option did they have to meet Inik Bunsu?

"You can't possibly consider letting them stay in our house? After what they've done to me!" The painter wailed.

"What did they do to you?" The long female's voice was almost buried under the noisy clunk of her jewelries as she started moving along with the cook.

"She attacked me!" The painter pointed accusingly to Kumang .

"I am very sorry. I only wanted to stop you from chocking Pungga because he was trying to stop you from getting hurt." Kumang did not stop walking as she

217

explained herself to the painter, who was walking next to the long woman.

"Me? Getting hurt? Who was about to hurt me?" The painter frowned. "Ah! You mean him?" She pointed at the carpenter, who walked in front of Pungga and the cook. "Pah! He would never hurt me! He cannot hurt me even if he wants to. I don't believe you. I still think you attacked us on purpose just now. And I must say that I am disappointed that my housemates invite hostile guests to a house where I live."

"Stop being overly dramatic!" The long female's body clunked in the same beat of her movements. "The two of you fight every day. Even we, who live in the same house with you, don't know if your fights are genuine or not. Don't blame these strangers for thinking the worst of you."

"Why you ..." the painter pointed her brush at the long female.

Kumang stopped listening to her grumble because she caught the sight of the grim male up front pushing a tree. A door frame appeared from the forest and the male went inside. Was the whole forest made of paintings? Or were they going to another realm from that door? Should they be worried about where they were about to go?

She glanced at Lulong and caught her doing the same thing to her. She got hold of her sister's hand and squeezed it as they went nearer to the door.

Pungga and the cook reached it first.

The cook held the door opened and said cheerfully, "Welcome to *Lebak Pemati*!" She bowed slightly and stepped aside to let Pungga go through.

Still holding Lulong's hand, Kumang followed Pungga to step inside the door frame. The first thing that hit her senses was the strong smell of sulfur. That was not the reason she gasped. It was the realization that they were standing on the edge of a crater.

Lebak Pemati, or the Valley of the Dead, was a vast barren grey crater with no living plants or animals inside its huge round bowl. Apart from a tiny house in the middle of the crater, there was nothing but ashes around them.

"See you down there!" The plump female jumped down and disappeared from sight. All they could hear was her cry of delight.

"I think we need a much safer way to go down." Pungga grinned at Kumang and Lulong. He stomped his right food to the ground and a staircase unfolded from underneath the surface along the steep wall of the crater. Pungga stared down to assess the situation. "We still need to be careful. The blow of wind is too strong here. Who wants to go down first?" He turned back to the female shifters.

Kumang shook her head. "Just help Lulu, please, Dom. Thank you. I think I can manage."

Pungga offered his hand to Lulong, who took it without hesitation. They began walking down the stairs, with strong wind pushing them from behind.

Kumang waited to make sure that they were travelling steadily down before she followed them. She grabbed the nearest air around her. With her *petara* power, she transformed it to a steady hand so that she could brace herself from being dragged down too fast to the bottom of the valley.

Even the cool air that caressed her cheeks gently could not erase the dreadful feeling she had that they were walking towards their doom.

THE DREADFUL WAIT

Lebak Pemati, the Sky

"How much longer do we need to wait here?" Kumang whispered to Pungga. "We've stayed in Lebak Pemati for more than two weeks, there's no sign of Inik Bunsu is coming home soon."

"You need to be patient, Mao. Where else should we wait but here?" Pungga whispered back to her.

Kumang threw her eyes to the nearest *bilik* door where she knew Lulong was resting inside. "I don't know how much longer she could take it. Her nightmares are getting worse with each passing night."

"I know." Pungga also fixed his eyes on the same *bilik* door.

"Gerinching visited my dream last night. She and Jang met Inik Bunsu on the land a few days ago. She said she had asked Inik Bunsu for help and Inik said she could only decide after she met Lulong. Do you think we should go down to the land? The two of them could meet sooner."

"The problem is she might not be on the land anymore now. Where should we look for her?" Pungga gave her a patronizing look that she hated. "Look, I know it has not been easy for you to wait here."

"You're absolutely right when you said it's not easy! I mean, what kind of place is this to begin with?" Kumang spread her arms around to indicate the *ruai* of the longhouse.

Pungga's eyes roamed the *ruai*. "It is a longhouse, Mao. It is a short longhouse, with only eight *bilik* under its roof, but it is still a longhouse."

"That is the only thing that qualifies it as a longhouse. Everything else about this place does not feel like a longhouse. They practically abandon us here all by ourselves. Nobody stays inside to entertain us. They go in and out of this house without acknowledging us. We would never do this to our guests." Kumang

220

stared at the empty *ruai*. "And the noises they made, it gets on my nerves!"

It was actually the absence of the natural forest sound that gave her the uncomfortable feeling. Without them, the air sounded empty. It was unsettling to feel that they existed in a hollow place. That the drummer male continuously produced unnatural forest sounds with his musical instruments only made the whole thing worse. No matter how much they matched the original sounds to perfect pitch, the knowledge that they were artificial was enough to cause discomfort.

"You are worried about your sister. It is the most natural thing in the world. I don't think even Panggau Libau can be a comfortable place for you to wait. Now, why don't we focus on the good things we have here, so we can make this waiting time more bearable. Look! At least the cook never fails to feed us." Pungga opened his palm at the wooden floor in front of them.

Kumang narrowed her eyes. "All the food she cooks tastes funny. What does she cook anyway? We are in the middle of a vast barren land. There isn't a living thing around us. No river or lake to fish. No forest to hunt. No plant to harvest. What are these things?" She pointed at the multiple plates of dishes with her hands. "I have come to the conclusion that she ..." she paused to see Pungga shake his head vaguely. "What?"

"Good morning, Sunshine!" The plump female dropped down to sit next to Kumang. Her eyes went straight to the untouched plates on the floor. "Hello!!! You haven't touched any of the food. What's wrong? Are they not good enough to eat?" The twinkle in her eyes faded and her dimmed eyes were framed by a deep frown.

"It's not your food, Wai," Pungga's answer came quickly. "We're waiting for all of you to join us for breakfast. It feels wrong to finish all the food for ourselves, and we do not leave any behind for our hosts." He changed the topic of the conversation smoothly. "Where are the others, by the way? Are they not having breakfast with us?" He swept his hand to the plates of food on the floor.

The cook kept her frown. "They practically don't live here. They only come back to sleep, that is not even every night. The blacksmith and the jeweler always leave before the crack of dawn to the hot springs to work."

"The nearest hot spring is quite a distant." Pungga nodded his agreement. "Why do they need to work there?"

"They need the hot spring to wield metal and rocks, of course." The cook's eyebrows lifted and her frown disappeared.

"Of course they do. I'm sorry for my ignorant question." Pungga smiled.

"And the rest?" Kumang was intrigued now.

"Ah, the carpenter is always outside, working overtime to help the painter with her fence. If you ask me, that's only their excuses. I mean, how many times do you need to get your paintings right? The musician, err..., as you can hear for yourself, is practically living outside, trying to reproduce the forest sounds."

"What he is doing is amazing." Pungga kept the smile on his face.

"Oh, be real! Any creature can tell they're artificial. You are so easily pleased." The cook stared at him fondly.

"I know we can still tell the difference between the real sounds and the ones he produces. However, considering the types of musical instruments available, it is amazing he can produce those sounds." Pungga defended his opinion.

"He makes a lot of adjustments to the original instruments we usually have, adding this and that." The cook wrinkled her nose. "He is making great progress, now that you mention it. You were not here when his experiment started, though. It was quite a torture to the ears."

"And you? How do you spend your days outside? How do you find ingredients for your cooking? Don't you need to go somewhere to get them considering there's no forest, no river, or lake nearby?" Kumang wanted to put her worries to rest.

"Err... Sometimes I do, but it's too troublesome. I don't like the idea of travelling far. I'd rather adjust my ingredients." The cook grinned sheepishly. She shifted her eyes from Pungga to Kumang, and lastly to the food served on the floor. "Is that the real reason you haven't touched the food? You are suspicious of what I cooked for you?" She peered at them like a clouded leopard eyeing its potential preys.

Pungga waved both hands in front of his chest to calm her. "Oh, no, Wai. It is not what you think. I am very sorry. I know you have spent so much time preparing this lavish food for us. It may look like we do not appreciate your efforts, but we do. We truly do. It's just that, we have no appetite to eat."

"No appetite? How come?" The cook's eyes grew bigger. She threw her eyes at Kumang. "Oh! It's your sister, isn't it? She's the reason you are here to see Mistress."

"What makes you think she is the one in trouble?" Kumang asked sarcastically. After weeks of being ignored, somebody suddenly took an interest!

"Haish! All of us can hear her screams of fright night after night. Our wooden walls are thin. What is wrong with her? Is she ill or something?" The cook nudged Kumang's arm. "Why are you looking for Mistress? You came to the wrong place, dear. Mistress is not a healer. You should go and see her sister, you know, the one who lives in Tansang Kenyalang longhouse. She is the *real* Mistress of Healer."

Kumang inhaled deep. "We came to the right place." She lowered her voice. "My sister was exposed to Inik Bunsu's curse. We are here to ask her to lift it."

The cook's eyes could not be rounder. "Mistress's curse? Ay, ay, ay! What did your sister do?" She grimaced. "Mistress is usually very kind. She easily feels sorry for a creature, but if your sister has upset her in any way." She shook her head firmly. "Don't ask for her compassion. You're wasting your time."

"She didn't do anything to offend Inik Bunsu!" Kumang was quick to defend Lulong. "Inik cursed a *pua kumbu* her *mensia* disciple wove, so anyone who has seen the pattern woven on it gets the curse. My sister was unfortunate that she was exposed to the pattern. I really don't think she deserves to die because of it."

The cook's mouth formed a round shape. "Are you talking about the *mensia* Master Weaver?"

Kumang nodded. "Tenang anak Tinggi."

"Ouh, I don't know her name. But I have heard Mistress talking about her. The *mensia* has great talent, but her family's situation did not support her to develop it to the fullest. Mistress felt she needed to interfere so that the *mensia*'s in-born talent would not go to waste."

"She wasted it anyhow," Kumang muttered grudgingly.

The cook was flabbergasted. "Who? Mistress? You think Mistress wasted her time teaching the *mensia* how to weave exquisite designs?"

223

"No, the *mensia* wasted the talent she had. She turned into a drunkard. She could not work on weaving a *pua*."

"Did you say 'the talent she had'?"

"The *mensia* died because of the curse."

The cook hissed. "That's Mistress. I won't deny that she is capable of such thing because she is. After all the time she had spent to train the *mensia* to prove that Mother Nature is wrong, the *mensia* chose to ignore her own talent. Mother Nature must have laughed at her. Mistress must be livid with fury."

"What has Inik Bunsu got against Mother Nature?" Pungga was curious. He had never heard of a story about it during his days in Tansang Kenyalang longhouse.

The cook smirked. "Ah, both of them are getting along just fine, generally speaking. It's just that Mistress doesn't like the idea that we all must succumb to what Mother Nature has in store for us. Mistress is a strong believer that each of us is responsible for our own destiny in life. That translates to the idea that each of us can do something to change our course of life, even if it means we must defy Mother Nature's wishes."

"Do you think she will lift the curse for my sister?" Kumang suddenly saw a ray of hope.

The cook blinked fast. "Err... I never said that..." Her face showed her worries.

"You know her well. Can't you predict what she would do? What are my sister's chances?" Kumang refused to let go of her hope.

"I don't know..." The cook wiped her wide forehead with her hand. "Let's see. One thing for sure, if Mistress likes your sister, she will move the sky and the land to help her."

"Will Inik like my sister? You've met her. Do you think she is the type Inik would like?"

"Err..." The cook blinked slowly.

"What type of creatures does Inik Bunsu usually like?" Pungga helped the cook find an answer.

The cook seemed confused. "Ah!" Suddenly she beamed. "Mistress likes those who have talents. Does your sister have a talent?" she asked Kumang.

"Of course she has a talent. She has many talents." Kumang was a little bit offended.

"Like what?" The cook absentmindedly picked a piece of food from one of the plates.

"Let's see. She can weave. She can cook. As a *bunsu kayu* she has extensive knowledge of plants ..." Kumang could not concentrate on listing Lulong's talents since half of her attention was focused on the cook. She wanted to know how the cook would react after she swallowed the questionable looking food.

The cook's hand that was holding the food changed direction, from going to her mouth to wave wildly in the air. "No, no, no, no, those are regular talents. Mistress is not interested in the regulars. She is into special talents. Is there something your sister can do that others can't?"

"Such as?" Kumang had no idea what the cook was looking for.

"How should I know? That's why I ask you." The cook tilted her head to the right and shrugged her shoulders. "Well, I can't help you, if you don't know." She took a bite of the food in her hand and started chewing.

Kumang did not realize that she held her breath in suspense waiting for what would happen next. She exhaled in relief that she did not taste any of the food served for them when the cook's eyes bulged in horror, and she almost spat the food out of her gaping mouth.

Within the next intake of breath, Kumang realized that it was not the food quality that chocked the cook because she scrambled to stand with wobbly legs to rush to one of the front doors of the longhouse.

Kumang turned around, curious to see what prompted such a frantic reaction. From the shady *ruai* she was in, her eyes caught the sight of a figure that filled the door frame. The sun that shone too brightly outside made it difficult for her to identify the creature that sent the cook into a panic state. However, as soon as the figure stepped inside the *ruai*, her detailed appearance came to light. Her jet black hair was arranged in a neat bun which hosted the base of the *sugu tinggi* – a silver headgear for females. The multiple silver strands of the *sugu tinggi* were spread in a full arch form just like the tail of a great *argus* bird. Her limbs were equally heavy with chains of thick silver. Even her exquisite woven cloth was fully adorned with arrays of silver chains. She exhibited the presence of elegance and grace.

Kumang bit her lower lip as soon as she figured out who the creature was. Her heart contracted instantly. She did not know if it was due to excitement or worries. The time had come to face Lulong's fate.

Inik Bhiku Bunsu Petara had come home!

INIK BHIKU BUNSU PETARA

Lebak Pemati, the Sky

"Mistress ..." The cook's voice shook a little. "I didn't know you'd come home today. I didn't prepare..." she stopped talking the moment she noticed that Inik Bunsu's head were shifted to her left to stare at Kumang. "Mistress, it was not my idea that they are here." She almost touched Inik Bunsu's arm, but her hand stopped midway and hung in the air. "I've tried my best to ..."

One frozen look from Inik Bunsu was enough to clamp the cook's mouth. Bowing slightly, she took a step back. The next raise of eyebrow from Inik Bunsu sent her running outside the longhouse.

The sudden departure of the cook left only three creatures in the spacious *ruai*.

Inik Bunsu walked further inside the *ruai* with such stealth that Kumang had to suppress the urge to take a fighting stand. That was what they always did when suspicious visitors came to their longhouse.

Luckily, she remembered in time that she and Pungga were the visitors in Inik Bunsu's house. Their standing positions were exactly the opposite what it should have been. As the guests of Inik Bunsu, Kumang and Pungga should have stood facing the inner of the *ruai*, introducing their arrival while Inik Bunsu, as the owner of the house, should have stood facing the opened front door, welcoming them.

Pungga was quicker than she. He moved forward to start the introduction. "Good morning, Inik. I am Pungga of ..."

Inik Bunsu did not even look at him while she walked slowly towards Kumang. "I know who you are. You are a male shifter who stole my niece's heart, gave her a child, and then abandoned them in the pretext of protecting Panggau Libau. And you must be ..."

"You're wrong!" Pungga protested. "How could you say such things?"

Inik Bunsu frowned when she finally directed her eyes on him, most probably because she resented that he cut her off. "Which part of what I said is not right?

227

Are you accusing my niece of not loving you?"

Pungga shook his head. "I know she loves me."

"So? Are you denying that the child is yours?"

"Of course he is my son!"

"Oh, so you're saying that you did not leave them behind in Tansang Kenyalang so that you could go down to protect Panggau Libau longhouse?"

Pungga swallowed. "Yes, I did." His eyes avoided Kumang.

"Then, what was wrong with everything I said?" Inik glared at him. "And you can't protect it from what is about to happen. You know you can't. No creature can. It makes one wonders about the real reason you left your family behind."

Pungga clearly did not want to pursue the subject. He shook his head firmly. "I disagree with the way you say it. You made me sound so …"

"Selfish?" Inik Bunsu finished his statement when he struggled to find the right word. "Well, that's exactly what you are as far as I am concerned." She waved her hand to dismiss him. She returned her attention to Kumang. "And you are Kumang of Panggau Libau. You ran away from home, to avoid a husband that you have wronged."

"*I* have wronged him?" Kumang's eyes grew big. "After what he has done to me, how come it is my fault now?"

"What he has done? What he has done is the result of what you have done to him!"

"What have I done to him until he had to repay me like that?" Kumang's voice rose unintentionally.

"You defied Mother Nature." Inik Bunsu stood a step away from Kumang so that she could see directly into her troubled eyes. She stared at them hard as if she wanted to find something there. "Did you not defy Her? Because you wished to keep him with you? You pulled him out of limbo to the realm of the living before his time came."

"I …" Kumang suddenly understood what Inik Bunsu was talking about. She wanted to explain herself, but she was aware that Pungga was listening to every word.

"Do you think She would not find out? Do you foolishly believe She would let you get away with it?" Inik Bunsu reached out to touch Kumang's cheek. "You poor thing, I admire you for your courage to defy Her. But what you did afterwards is cowardice! You must face the consequences of your action."

"I am. I am paying the price now, aren't I?" Kumang pulled her face away from Inik Bunsu's hand. She fought hard to regulate her breathing. She would not cry in front of Inik Bunsu!

"Are you? The way I see it, you are avoiding payment. You left him, didn't you? You let him suffer by himself – a suffering he has to endure because of what you have done to offend Mother Nature. You let him pay for your mistake!"

Kumang forgot about Pungga. "I do not let him suffer! It was not my decision to punish him. Mother Nature should have punished me! She shouldn't have punished him! She is not playing fair!"

Inik Bunsu laughed. "And who are you to tell Mother Nature what She should or should not have done? You are not in a position to decide which punishment is fair and which one is not. You decided to play a game when you do not know what the rules are and now after the top has been spun, you throw tantrums because you don't like the results. Oh child, you are so silly that it is almost cute."

Kumang clenched her hands so tight she could feel her nails dig into the palm of her hands. She wanted to scream her protest, but she could not find her voice. She felt like a gigantic rock was pressing down on her chest.

"Now, where is your sister? In one of the *bilik* there?" She pointed at the rows of *bilik* doors behind Kumang.

Kumang was glad that the conversation took a different turn. She inhaled a big bulk of air. "Yes, she's in there." She pointed at the door right behind her. "Do you know about my sister's condition?"

"Ah, I met a female shifter in my longhouse on the land. I'm sure you know I'm talking about the peculiar female shifter who talks to the trees. She told me about your sister and my curse." Inik Bunsu's face broke into an amused grin. "Now she is an interesting creature. I offered her my home should she feel she needs a roof over her head since her own longhouse has disowned her." Her sigh was also filled with amusement. "But the male she was with," she threw a quick glance at Kumang and clicked her tongue, "your brother-in-law if I'm not mistaken – he insisted that she left with him, using the most pathetic excuse about his promise to her father or something to that effect. Did he think that any creature, let alone *me*, could believe that was the real reason? I extended my offer to him too. He was, after all, a special creature – one of a kind." She nodded dreamily. "I would love to personally mentor him on how to navigate through all the sneaky traps Mother Nature has in store for him along his path. But alas, he refused adamantly, saying something about he's had a home. I guess he meant Panggau Libau." She laughed softly. "Isn't it funny? You wish to help some creatures by giving them the very thing they need, and they refuse your kindness, in such a rude manner in this particular case, simply because they think they have something that they don't actually have. What do they know about what they have and not have? It is so difficult not to frown on them when you know better than the rest of them, but they behave as if they know better than you."

Kumang found it difficult to keep up with Inik Bunsu's chain of thoughts. "I am afraid I do not understand what you are saying, Inik."

Inik Bunsu gave her a condescending look. "You are not supposed to. Anyway, the next time you meet him, tell him that my offer still stands. He, and the female, too, if he insists that she must go where ever he goes. Tsk! Tell him to use a better excuse next time. It insults my intelligence to hear such an insipid reason. But I don't' suppose he meant to lie to me. He is just slow to catch up in this particular area. He'd better be hurry. This is a matter of extreme importance. Time will not wait for any creature. He needs to make the right move. And he needs to make it fast. He must start collecting all the allies he can possibly have if he intends to mess with Mother Nature's plan."

Kumang still could not follow what Inik Bunsu was talking about. She seemed to jump from one topic to another without using proper transition. Whatever message she was trying to convey, it sounded like she offered Sampurai help. "Thank you for your offer, Inik. I will tell him." She nodded her thanks.

"You make sure of that!" Inik Bunsu told her firmly.

"That is very generous of you, Inik," Pungga commented.

Inik Bunsu smirked at him as if he just caught her in an act of wrong doing. "It is not about generosity. Any creature who tries to defy Mother Nature always gets my support. It is not easy to get away from Her wrath when She finds out you refuse to walk the path She has laid neatly for you. To be fair to Her, it is really not easy to create a path for every single one of the creatures in our worlds and make sure that a creature's path crosses another in a particular time frame so that each of them can fulfill his destiny. Uh-uh, I don't envy Her. I can understand if She goes berserk every time a creature thinks he knows better and wants to create his own path in life. Because once you change a path, the others' paths will be affected, too. She can be unforgiving at times. Ask her!" She eyed Kumang with amusement.

"I'm sorry I have to say that I don't feel your support for me in this matter, Inik," Kumang replied dryly.

"Ah, what I do not support is how you deal with it." Inik Bunsu touched the tip of Kumang's nose lightly.

Kumang gritted her teeth. "How do you suppose I should deal with it?" She could not resist the sarcastic question.

"You should stand by him through thick and thin. Both of you should go through this together. What? Is it too painful for you? Of course it is painful. It is going to be painful for a very long time. Do you think you can offend Mother Nature and feel no pain? Seriously? Wake up, Kumang. What realm are you living in right now? She is laughing at you as it is - laughing at your misery, laughing at his misery. You get exactly the opposite of what you wanted when you defied Her, don't you? Show Her that She is wrong. Show Her that there is nothing – *nothing* – in this world that you would not do to be with him. Is it too much to ask? Don't you want to be with him? Come on, Wai. You defied Mother Nature to be with him. Don't you want it anymore?" Her eyes narrowed at Kumang

Kumang gulped. "I wanted to be with him. I tried to make it work after what happened. I really did. I did my best. I can't. It's too painful."

"You will not succeed at the first try. And I am not asking you for a successful result. You can't control the results." She put up her hands as if she wanted to strangle her. "Why can't you and the rest of you understand? This is the root of all your problems, I'm telling you. You don't want to accept that you have no say in the results, none at all. You are responsible for trying your best. That's it! You leave the rest to those who know what is best for you! You will get what you are working for when the time is right, not sooner, and not later. No, you don't get clever and decide when the result should come. There's nothing you can do to speed it up. Just keep doing what you are supposed to be doing faithfully and consistently. Results will come at the perfect time." She let a pause linger before she continued, "You are aware that the female water spirit is doing exactly that? She is showing Mother Nature that there is nothing in this world that she will not do to be with Keling. Oh, he is not in her path. Not the present path anyway. But she believes that one day their paths will cross, and she can keep him for good. She is working on creating that intersection faithfully, waiting patiently for time to give her the result she wants. She might get exactly what she wants one day if she keeps it up and you keep on doing what you are doing now."

The mere mention of Ennie gave Kumang a sudden pounding headache. "She can have him if she wants," she hissed.

Inik Bunsu clasped her hands loudly. "Then what do you seek my support for? When you do not even want to fight for him? When you give up?" She praised Kumang with her eyes. "After all the stories I've heard about you, Kumang of Panggau Libau, I expect you to have more grit than this." She moved swiftly towards the *bilik* door. As she passed her by, Kumang could hear her mutter under her breath, "I hope this one has a much better fighting spirit to brighten my mood!"

The wish for Inik Bunsu to lift the curse was the only reason Kumang kept her mouth shut. She walked behind Inik Bunsu in silence.

However, Inik Bunsu stopped at the opened door only to tell her, "You stay outside. I must talk to her in private."

Then, she slammed the door at Kumang's face.

A CURSED LIFE

Kumang closed her eyes in agony. Without thinking, she turned around. The moment she opened her eyes, she found Pungga staring at her.

"Don't look at me like that, Dom. Not you, too." She suddenly felt tired.

"I'm sorry. I don't know what you're accusing me of." Pungga did not move from where he was standing, which was quite far from the *bilik* door.

"Just like Inik Bunsu, you blame me for leaving Watt."

"Come now, 'blame' is a strong word. I might not agree with your decision …"

Kumang looked at him warily. "Isn't that the same thing?"

"Aren't you the one who blames him for what he did on the land when he lost his memory?"

Kumang's jaw tightened. She did not say a word.

"Is it true what Inik Bunsu said? That you pulled Watt out of limbo when he was badly wounded after his battle with Apai Ribai on the land? How did you do it?"

Kumang shrugged. "What does it matter now?" She sighed to see his determined face. "All right, if you must know, I went to see Sindun. She said she saw two *petara*'s souls in limbo - that's where Chief Saga said he saw him, remember?"

Pungga nodded. "And you asked her to pull Watt out of limbo. I did not know Sindun can do that. How could she know which soul was Watt's and which soul was … Lium's? The other *petara*'s soul had to be Lium's."

"Yeah, at that time I didn't know whose soul was the second one. I didn't know of a *petara* named Lium then. Anyway, Sindun couldn't tell which one of the two souls was Watt's, so she brought both of them back to the realm of the living. Oh, she has the ability to do that, so she can, but she is not supposed to, that means she can't. It is not up to her who stays in limbo and who gets out."

233

"She did it anyway."

"I begged her to do it. She did it for me."

"Didn't she warn you about the repercussion of it?"

"Of course she did. She was not irresponsible."

"Let's just say that if my sister asks me to pull a soul out of limbo, I will talk her out of it. It's a bad idea. Sindun is a celestial *manang*, she should have advised you better."

Kumang had to smile. "She is not you, Dom. She couldn't talk me out of it."

"Why didn't you wait for Watt's soul to come back naturally to the realm of the living? It's just a matter of time until his body healed."

Kumang frowned. "I didn't have your confidence that his soul would've ended up in the realm of the living. What if it had ended up in Sebayan instead?"

"In other words, Inik Bunsu was right when she said you defied Mother Nature to keep him with you."

"Are you going to blame me because I fought for his life?"

"Not at all. I just want to understand why you left him after all the efforts you put in to pull him out of limbo."

"You know why I left him!"

"Because after his soul came back to his body on the land, he lost his memory of his past life? Because he didn't remember who he was, didn't remember his family, didn't remember that he had a wife? Because he married a *mensia*'s daughter who had saved his life and nurtured him back to health when he was totally defenseless? Because she bore him a child – a child who was stillborn because he left them to save his brother's life, that's why he couldn't be there for them when they needed him the most? You think he did you wrong based on those things?"

Kumang smiled sadly. "Now you sound like Inik Bunsu." Her voice rose unconsciously. "Yes, it's my fault! All right? Everything is my fault!"

"I am not trying to put the blame on anyone, Mao."

"Then what are you trying to do by having this conversation?"

"I am trying to understand why you left him. It is not his fault he lost his memory. Come on, you know it is not! He didn't do anything to deserve it. Therefore, everything else that happened as the result of it is also not his fault. No, don't get me wrong. I'm not saying that it is your fault. You couldn't have known it would happen." Pungga paused because she winced. "Wait ... you knew? You knew he would have lost his memory?"

"Sindun warned me that a lot of things could go wrong because what she was about to do was not the natural process for a soul to come back to its body."

"And you still insisted on it?"

"I didn't think he would lose his memory! I surely didn't think he would marry a *mensia* so soon, before any of us could find him on the land and bring him back to Panggau Libau safe and sound. I never thought ..." She bent her head in defeat.

"It never occurred to you that she would give him a child," Pungga muttered.

Kumang could hear him sigh.

"Why can't you forgive him? It is not his fault. He didn't mean to hurt you, oh yes, I know, I know, it doesn't hurt less because he didn't mean it. Still, I have to agree with Inik Bunsu. What's done is done, Mao. It can't be undone. You have a chance to start a new life with him now that he has lost his wife and child, wasn't that what you wanted when you pulled him out of limbo? Don't you want it anymore? Don't you care about him anymore?"

Kumang grimaced. "I do."

"Why did you leave him? Why did you say things like 'she can have him if she wants'? Don't say such things. A force in this world might be listening and think that you wish it. It may come true."

"If that is what is best for him, let be it!"

"Mao, you can't mean that!"

"I do."

"You pulled him out of limbo, knowing that Mother Nature would be angry with you. How could you give him up to some other female so easily?"

"I pulled him out of limbo so that he could live! Above all, so that he could live a happy life. I just assumed it would be a life with me."

"I don't see why the two of you can't have a happy life now."

"I am cursed, Dom! Don't tell me you haven't figured it out by now."

She saw panic in Pungga's face. "Cursed? What do you mean? Do you get the same curse as your sister? How? Because you know about the pattern woven in the cursed *pua*? If that is the case, you should …"

"I never see the *pua*. I don't get *that* curse."

"What other curse are you talking about? I'm not aware there's another curse going around."

"I defied Mother Nature. She is punishing me for it. It is the same thing as a curse. I won't die because of it, but she will make sure I will suffer for the rest of my life."

"I don't see what it has got to do with you leaving Watt. Are you worried that because Mother Nature is angry with you, he will leave you? He won't! He'll stand by you to face it all. She's not going to scare him off."

"I know he will stand by me. That's why I am the one who has to be strong and leave him."

"I still don't get it."

"She is punishing me, Dom. She is punishing me through him. Look at how his *mensia* wife and child died. It crushed him. He is suffering so much because of me, because I offended Her. I can't live with the knowledge that I give him so much pain. He is better off without me. Mother Nature will not target him anymore if he is not with me."

Pungga did not answer her this time although his face still showed that he was troubled.

"I am right, Dom. You know I am. This is how it is supposed to be. I have to let him go. I do love him, and therefore, I have to let him go. It's his only chance to live a happy life."

236

Pungga frowned. "It doesn't feel right," he finally said something.

"It does to me. If you love someone, you'll sacrifice your life to protect him from harm. That's how it should be."

He shook his head slowly. "What are you going to do next? Disown your family? Abandon your aging mother? Your sister? Leave Panggau Libau? Leave Gelong? Leave everyone you love in this world for the sake of shielding them from Mother Nature's wrath?"

"If that's what it takes to keep them safe. I can't bring Mother's Nature's wrath to Panggau Libau, or Gelong with me so that the innocent residents pay for my decision. It is wrong. You know it is. Now I will sort out this curse on Lulong. After that I will be gone from her life, from everyone's lives."

"Mao! You can't …"

"I can. I have made the decision and there is nothing you can do to change my mind."

"You don't know what you're getting yourself into, Mao. It might seem like a good idea to you right now, but you'll soon find out that …"

"This is how it will be done, Dom. I will live my life alone for the rest of my life. Don't you worry, I can be content with it. There shouldn't be a reason why I can't be, especially when I know that everyone I hold dear in my heart …" She chocked and without warning tears came streaming down her cheeks. She tried to stop. She had to be strong. She was not as weak as Inik Bunsu had accused her of. Sadly, her tears could not be contained when she thought she would never see any of her family again. She covered her face with her hands and sobbed hard.

She did not hear Pungga call her name, nor did she realize that he had come to hold her in his embrace while her sadness burst out of control.

It was the chilling voice of Inik Bunsu that finally penetrated her deep sorrow. "My, my, my, don't tell me this is the real reason you left my niece behind in Tansang Kenyalang, Pungga of Panggau Libau."

Kumang took a few steps back to distance herself from Pungga. She turned around to see Inik Bunsu standing at the door frame, frowning at her and Pungga. Her hands frantically wiped her wet face and nose while her eyes looked for Lulong. Was she all right now? Had Inik Bunsu lifted the curse for her?

"You know very well why I left Tansang Kenyalang, Inik." Pungga's voice was steady, free from any trace of guilt. "Do not be mischievous to suggest something that only exists on your wish list."

"Hmmm…" was the only answer Inik Bunsu gave him.

"Lu?" Kumang strained her neck to look for Lulong.

"Ah!" Inik Bunsu rolled her eyes and stepped outside the *bilik*. By moving forward, she exposed Lulong to Kumang and Pungga.

"Lu!" Kumang rushed to her. "Are you all right?"

"Yes." Lulong smiled as she squeezed Kumang's hand.

"Are you … still cursed?" Kumang looked at Inik Bunsu from the corners of her eyes.

"I'm afraid I am." Lulong nodded slowly.

"Then why did you say that you are all right? Inik, please, why can't you …" Kumang turned to Inik Bunsu.

Inik Bunsu lifted a hand. "Say no more. I have said everything that I have to say to her. She can repeat it to whomever she wants. Now, be gone, all three of you. I have pressing matters to attend to." She flicked her hand to them as if she shooed chicken out of her house.

"Oh but …" Kumang wrinkled her nose. What pressing matter was there for Inik Bunsu to do? There was nobody else in the house but the four of them.

"It's all right, Mao." Lulong patted her hand. "She has told me everything I need to know. We can go now." She nodded with respect to Inik Bunsu. "Thank you for your advice, Inik. Goodbye."

"Hmmm…" Inik Bunsu folded her arms in front of her chest. "Don't forget what I said. Your survival depends on how much you remember everything single detail I told you."

Kumang did not find it comforting. She stared at Lulong. "Is there anything …"

"No, there's nothing you can do here." Inik Bunsu's voice was dismissive.

"You'd better get going now. No need to thank me. We don't know if she can survive or not."

"What does that mean?" Kumang asked Lulong.

"It means the longer you linger here, her chance of survival is getting lesser," Inik Bunsu answered.

"If that is the case, we'd better go now, Inik." Pungga nodded his goodbye.

"I've told you more than once that you'd better get going and here you are – still here!"

"Thank you for helping my sister, Inik. Goodbye." Kumang bowed slightly.

"Yeah, yeah, yeah…when are you really going? Go! Now! Go!"

Since there really was no reason to stay any longer, Kumang, Lulong, and Pungga left the longhouse.

INIK BUNSU'S ADVICE

"I feel so guilty because I've asked Dom to go away." Lulong focused her attention to screen both banks of Mahakam River.

"It was not a nice thing to say, but I don't think you had a better choice. Inik Bunsu specifically said you could only take one more creature with you to go to this secret forest," Kumang, who was using her power over water to navigate the longboat they were in through the rapid of Mahakam River, did not turn to speak to Lulong. The scattered big rocks located in the river forced her to concentrate on which direction the longboat should move forward. "I'm sure he understands that you did not mean to slight him in the least."

"Do you think he is right when he said we need to be extra cautious with Inik Bunsu's help?" Lulong's eyes went fleetingly to the back of Kumang's head.

"I don't see anything worthy to be cautious about with her advice. It's perfectly harmless," Kumang readjusted her sitting position so that she controlled the water with more ease. "Why? Do you think her advice could potentially hurt us in any way?"

"Not at all. She only gave me directions about where to go, which is a forest known as Mystical Forest, where a *manang* who is specialized in healing disturbed minds lives. To reach this forest, we need to travel through Mahakam river from its spring up in the Muller range, until we find the second pier by the river, which according to her is the where the entrance of the forest lies."

"Which part of her directions do you find suspicious?"

"I don't think any of them sounds suspicious. But I would say that Dom knows Inik Bunsu better than we do. If he feels that something is odd, shouldn't we heed his warning, or at the very least, consider his worries?"

"All right, to put our mind at ease, let's scrutinize her directions through and through from the very beginning. What is the first one?"

"We shouldn't take Dom in our journey."

"Did Inik Bunsu tell you why?"

240

"The bigger the crowd, the lesser chance I get to persuade the *manang* to help. Ah, here is the thing. The truth is she asked me to go alone. I bargained with her to take you with me."

"Good."

"I don't mind going alone, but I knew you would never let it happen, so Inik and I came to some kind of compromise that I bring you along with me. Regretfully, I couldn't bargain for Dom."

"That's all right. You win some, you lose some. That's what bargaining is. Besides, I'm sure the two of us can cope with this journey. What's next?"

"Like I said, she instructed me to travel along Mahakam River ..."

"Is there anything we should be worried about in this river?"

Lulong looked around. "I don't think so. The river might be a little bit wild, but what is rapid to us?"

"True. And then?"

"We should find the second pier along the river ..."

"We've passed the first pier. It must be the next pier we see after this."

"The pier will lead us to a village."

"Is this village a *mensia*'s settlement?"

"I believe so."

"We shouldn't be worry about *mensia*, should we? I mean, what kind of danger can they pose to us?"

"Nothing that I can think of."

"Splendid. What's next?"

"The village is the only entrance to Mystical Forest known to men."

"How come? Shouldn't we be able to enter a forest from any side of it?"

"I do not know why. The only thing she said was that not just any man can enter this forest. I made the assumption that the layout of the land forbids multiple entrances, you know, just like Nanga Langit longhouse territory up North. It only has one access."

"Nanga Langit only has one considerably easy access, not that it doesn't have multiple accesses. The shape of the terrain makes it almost impossible to be travelled through. Yeah, you're right. It could be the case with this forest. We are still up in the mountain, mind you. I don't think many men can handle this terrain, but we are not men, aren't we? We are shape-shifters. We might be able to enter the forest from different sides of it."

"Inik Bunsu said this village is the only entrance known to men."

"Maybe there are other creatures who know a different entrance to Mystical Forest."

"Maybe, but since the only clue we have is the second pier from the spring of Mahakam, we'd better find it. Or do you want to look for an alternative entrance?"

"We don't even know who to ask, how can we find them?"

"That's what I thought. So we proceed with the original plan, don't we?"

"Definitely. It is the fastest way to get there right now. And what is next?"

"After that, enter Mystical Forest, find this *manang*, and persuade her to heal me."

"Is this *manang* a *mensia*?"

"No, Inik Bunsu said she is an *antu raya*."

All right, this was where it did not feel right somehow. "How come we've never heard of her if she is a spiritual creature?"

"We're not *manang*. We don't know who is who in the *manang* circle. Sindun might know her, or at least hear her name. Do you want to ask Sindun if she knows anything about this *manang*?"

"It would be best, but looking for her and speaking to her would take time. I don't want us to waste time. Here's the thing, if she has a special skill the way Inik Bunsu describes, we must certainly have heard of her. But we have not.

242

Why is that? And why should we persuade her to heal you? She is a *manang*. It is a *manang*'s duty to heal whoever comes to see her." The more Kumang thought about this *manang*, the more she believed that the possible danger they could encounter would probably come from her.

"Inik Bunsu addressed her to me as Inik Tuai, so I automatically assumed that she is a lot older than us. As to why she might not want to help, Inik Bunsu told me it's because Inik Tuai doesn't want to use her power anymore. Rumor has it that she made a mistake with one of her patients that cost him his life. She felt guilty for what happened that she punished herself by living with hardship on the land and became a recluse. It must have happened long before our time, that's why we did not hear about it."

"Her choice of never use her power to heal anyone again would be a problem for us, no doubt. Still, I would not classify it as a danger. As an *antu raya* she should have the power to control lightning. It is a different power than ours. But based on our previous encounters with the *antu raya*, I am confident I can handle this *manang* and her *antu raya*'s power. We don't need Dom."

"It isn't because I think we need his help that I feel bad he is not coming with us. It's just ..."

"Sorry, Lu, but I can see a pier ahead. We must stop at the second pier, must we not?"

"That's what Inik Bunsu told me."

"Let's bring this longboat to the bank." Kumang looked up to the sky as soon as she felt drops of water fell on her head. "Oh, come on. This is really not the time. Can't you wait until we reach the bank?" she shouted at the sky.

Her plea was ignored. Rain began to pour heavily. And just like that, they lost the sight of the river bank.

"This is ridiculous," Kumang grumbled. Drenching wet, she turned around to Lulong. "Do you think somebody up there does not want us to find this Mystical Forest?"

Lulong shouted at her in the midst of the heavy downpour. "It doesn't matter, Mao. This longboat is filled with water very fast. We must reach the bank as soon as possible."

Or, she could stop the rain from falling, Kumang thought. She stood up and reached out to the sky. The rain stopped effective immediately. The sky cleared up, and she had clear enough vision to bring the longboat safely to the river bank.

Kumang jumped out of the boat as soon as its tip touched the pier. She looked around to assess the surrounding area.

Standing up inside the longboat, Lulong smiled at her. "Nicely done, Mao."

Kumang did not smile back as Lulong joined her on the pier. "I did not stop the rain."

Lulong stopped smiling. "Eh? But just now … the sky couldn't have cleared up by itself all of a sudden like that. And I saw you reach up to the sky."

"Someone else did it before I had the chance."

Lulong stood still next to Kumang. Involuntarily her eyes wandered around. "Do you think …?"

Kumang's jaw tightened. "No, it's not Watt. I can't sense his *petara* power anywhere. It can't be him."

Lulong leaned closer to whisper, "Who do you think did it? Who helped us? And why?"

Kumang shook her head faintly. She whispered back, "I don't know. But one thing for sure, we are not the only spiritual creatures in this forest. We don't know what kind of power they have and what their intentions are. We'd better be extra careful from now on. Come, let's find this village."

THE VILLAGE OF MENSIA

Mahakam Terrain, the Land

Holding Lulong's hand tightly in hers, Kumang observed the village in the shallow valley in front of them. "These *mensia* do not live in a longhouse."

"That is what Inik Bunsu told me."

"Did she say how we should approach them? Should we let them know of our arrival, and that we do not mean them any harm?" She threw her eyes fleetingly at Lulong. "Or should we just pass by without letting them know? We can find the entrance to the forest ourselves."

"No, she said, we should ask for directions from the Chief of the village. We must face these *mensia*. Only they know where the entrance to the forest is. Inik Bunsu also said that these *mensia* have some sort of map of the forest that can help us find where the *manang* lives."

"Why do we need a map?"

"She did not say. But if a map can help find this *manang* faster, why not?"

"All right if that is ... look! Some people we can ask for direction!" Kumang called out to a couple of boys she spotted coming out of a path on her right, "Hey!"

The boys, who appeared to be in their teens, froze on their track as soon as they saw Kumang and Lulong. They looked petrified.

"Hello there," Lulong used her gentlest voice. "Don't be scared. We are not here to hurt you, or cause you a problem."

The boys took a few steps back as Kumang and Lulong went to approach them. They tried to run to the direction where they came from, but Kumang was faster. She blocked their path.

Kumang exerted all the charms she possessed to smile at the boys. "Hi, my name is Kumang. And that is my sister, Lulong. We are looking for the Chief of the village down in the valley. Would you be so kind to show us where he lives? We would be very grateful."

245

Realizing that Kumang and Lulong blocked both their way outs, the taller boy inhaled deep, and then he hesitantly took a step forward to extend his hand to Kumang. "Hello, I am Jayan."

Kumang accepted Jayan's hand although her eyes went to the shorter boy because he muffled some sort of scream to see her action. "Hello. I am happy to meet you, Jayan." Her smile went back to Jayan.

Jayan did not smile back. He pulled his hand out of Kumang's grasp. He turned around to Lulong and extended his hand to Lulong, who took it without hesitation.

Again, Kumang heard a muffled scream from the shorter boy as Jayan's hand touched Lulong's.

Jayan quickly pulled out his hand out of Lulong's grasp. He inspected his hand, and then he smiled with relief to the shorter boy. "They're all right. See?" He showed his hand.

The shorter boy cowered behind Jayan as Kumang went near. "I am sorry. I do not understand. What did you expect to happen if you shake hands with us?" She tried not to sound offended.

"Ah, I am sorry, Miss. I did not mean to accuse you of anything, but I had to be sure. We never know these days. Once again, I apologize." Jayan became talkative all of a sudden.

"What did you want to make sure by shaking our hands?" Lulong also came nearer towards the boys.

The shorter boy clutched the back of Jayan's collar tighter. "That you are not the creatures from the forest."

Jayan squirmed under the tight clutch of the other boy. "Let go of me, Saban. They are not going to burn us. They are just human beings, like us." He turned to Kumang, "You are, are you not?"

Kumang would rather comment on his earlier statement than answer his question about their state of being. "Burn you? You think you will get burnt by shaking our hands? How is that possible?"

Jayan wrinkled his nose. "Now you think we are crazy for saying things like that." He dramatized an exhalation.

"I'm sure you have a good reason for it." Kumang kept her charming smile.

"A good reason? You mean you want proof?" Saban shouted from behind Jayan. "You can see the dead corpses for yourself if you want proof." He showed his head from behind Jayan's shoulder. "See if you still call us crazy." Then, his head disappeared again from sight.

"We never call you crazy, Jang." Kumang calmed him down. "We asked because we do not understand."

"Where are you from? You can't be from around here." Jayan scrutinized Kumang's appearance. "Come on, Saban, let go of me. You're going to kill me if you don't stop chocking me with my own shirt." He scolded the other boy.

"No, we're not from here. That's why we do not know what is going on." Lulong addressed Jayan, "Do you mind taking us to see the Chief of this village?"

"What do you want to go to my house for?" Saban, who was forced by Jayan to stand next to him, asked nervously.

"Your house?" Kumang shifted her attention to Saban.

Jayan touched Kumang's arm to get her attention back to him. "His grandfather is the Chief of the village."

"Ah, I see. So, can we …"

"No you can't," Saban cut Kumang off at the same time Jayan said, "Sure you can."

"It's my house! You don't decide who can go there and who can't." Saban glared at Jayan.

"The only reason why it is not my house anymore is because my father passed on before your father did. Otherwise, it would have been my house, not yours." Jayan turned to Kumang. "The Chief is also my grandfather. Saban is my cousin."

Kumang exchanged glances with Lulong. "Would you be so kind to show us the way to the house, Jayan?" Kumang smiled.

"Sure, that's not a problem. The village is not far from here. Follow me." Jayan walked past Lulong to show the way.

247

"Jayan!" Saban protested because he was left behind.

Jayan waved his arm. "Come along, Saban. The sun almost sets. We don't want to be found wandering around outside after dark, do we?"

Saban was half-running down the hill to catch up with Jayan. Kumang and Lulong walked closely behind the two boys.

"Are you not allowed to play outside after dark? How old are you?" Kumang could not help asking. She guessed that both boys were old enough to take care of themselves. Why, a male shifter their age would have done his *bejalai*, a young male's rite of passage in the form of taking a journey outside their longhouse to prove that he could live independently on his own.

"I'm sixteen." Jayan smiled at Kumang without stopping his quick strides. "Saban, here, is seventeen. No, Miss, it has nothing to do with age. Nobody goes out of the house after dark."

"Does it have anything to do with the creatures from the forest?" Lulong asked carefully.

Even from behind him, Kumang could see Saban shudder at the mere mention of the creatures.

"Who are the creatures from the forest? What kind of creatures are they? Have any of you seen them? What do they do to you?" Kumang wanted to know about these mysterious creatures. Were they the ones who stopped the rain just now?

Saban looked back at them and rolled his eyes. "We have never seen them, of course. That's the reason we are still talking to you."

"You are saying that these creatures from the forest kill everyone that sees them?" Kumang never heard of such creatures in their world.

"They don't want to leave any witness, do they?" Saban answered incredulously.

"If there is no witness, how do you know it is the work of the creatures from the forest?" Lulong asked. "Ah, all their bodies have burnt marks?"

"Their hands – up to here." Jayan circled his wrist with his fingers. "...turned as black as charcoal."

248

"What did they die of?" To Kumang's knowledge, *mensia* could survive a burn up to their hands. They would suffer a great deal, but it should not be the cause of death. *Mensia* died when their heart stopped beating.

"We told you they got burnt," Saban mumbled.

"At the hand? And as a result of it they died?"

"That's what we said!" Saban almost shouted at her.

Kumang exchanged more looks with Lulong.

"How long has this been going on?" Lulong asked.

"For as long as we can remember," Jayan answered.

"Why didn't you move out of here?" Lulong asked more question.

Now it was the boys' turn to exchange looks.

"This is our home! The land is our land, passed down to us from our ancestors. Nobody and nothing can chase us out of here!" Jayan was suddenly very excited. He waved his fist in the air.

Saban grabbed his hand and pulled it down. "Do not challenge them in the open like that!" he hissed. "You know what happened to those who dare to oppose them."

Jayan wrenched his fist from Saban's grip. "If it is my fate to die in their hands, I will give them a fight they will not forget." He kept his voice low.

Saban sighed. "You can't give them that. They have magical power that you don't have. Forget about fighting them. Concentrate on how to survive as long as we can, and do what we are supposed to do."

"We can't just wait until they take our lives one by one! We just buried Jemut yesterday, who is next tomorrow? If you don't mind waiting for them to take your life, it's up to you. But I do mind. And as for what we are supposed to do, I …" Jayan stopped talking because Saban nudged his ribs with his elbow and threw his eyes fleetingly to the back, where Kumang and Lulong were following them.

Kumang did not know if she should comment on what they were talking about since they talked softly between the two of them as if they did not want to be

249

heard.

"Ah, we have arrived. Let me present our village to you." Jayan turned around and spread his arm in a welcoming gesture.

Jayan and Saban parted to make way for Kumang and Lulong to pass through.

Upon close proximity, Kumang had a completely different impression of the village. Naturally, the twilight sky was not generous in giving out light. However, she had the sense that the gloomy sight in front of her was not caused by the lack of light. The village in front of them consisted of a collection of old wooden houses which were built a little too close to each other. The way the houses stood reminded Kumang of how the female shape-shifters took their stand to circle the children inside it when their enemies managed to enter their longhouse. The village was under siege. At least, that was it looked like to her. She wondered what kind of creatures lurked inside the forest. Her eyes scanned the surrounding forest. Which part of it was Mystical Forest? Was the village at the center of it?

"Excuse me, Miss! You said you want to see my grandfather." Saban's voice brought her back to the present.

"Yeah, we do," Kumang replied promptly.

"You shouldn't stand there daydreaming, should you? Let's get moving." Saban's eyes went to the horizon. "We only have very little time left before the sun sets."

THE CREATURES FROM THE FOREST

Mahakam Terrain, the Land

"Why do you want to go to Mystical Forest?" The Chief's frown was deep. The flashes of lightning from outside the house added extra light through the windows.

"We are looking for a healer who lives there," Lulong answered politely.

The instant murmur that broke in the crowded living room was muffled by the roaring thunder.

Kumang swept her eyes around the room. According to Saban, this wooden structure had sheltered his family for more than 5 generations. No wonder it looked so old and crooked. Although one would expect that the family should have replaced the old wood with the new one at least once in every generation. The room was dark, poorly lighted with small sticks of white tubular that emitted gentle fire on top of them. The heavy thunderstorm outside filled the room with the sound of thunder. When the thunderstorm took a breath from roaring, the room was filled with the sound of inharmonious drops of rain water that fell into metal buckets on the floor. Under the dim light Kumang still could identify the faces of residents in the house. Only old people and children were there. They did not have the presence of the second generation - the parents of the children. Where were there? Were they not worried to be outside after the dark?

"There is a healer who lives in Mystical Forest, isn't there?" Lulong directed her question to the Chief.

The Chief tapped his fingers to his knees. "Not to my knowledge."

"Are you sure? Because we heard …"

The Chief interrupted Lulong, "If there is, I certainly have never heard of her."

"How do you know the healer is a woman if you have never heard of her?" Kumang quickly pointed out his mistake.

The Chief blinked fast. "I don't know. A healer is usually a woman. Are you saying that this healer is a man?"

"Did she not heal your youngest brother once, Chief Jurong? When he was a child, he got very sick. Men could not find out what was wrong with him, let alone heal him. Did your late father not take him to Mystical Forest? And he was completely healthy after that," Lulong recited the information she heard from Inik Bunsu.

Chief Jurong went white. "How … how did you know about my brother's illness? Nobody outside this village knows about this. Who are you? Are you one of them?"

Kumang felt movements on the floor as the result of the residents distancing themselves from her and Lulong.

"What do you mean by 'them'? Who do you think we are?" Kumang asked the people around them.

"They are not creatures from the forest, Grandfather," Saban spoke from where he was sitting.

"And how do you know that?" One of the elderly men from the crowd asked him.

"Jayan touched their hands, and he is fine. Look! Look!" Saban held up Jayan's right hand. "No burnt marks."

"It doesn't mean anything. They could still be the creatures from the forest. You must remember how cunning they are. They have tried so many tricks on us. This could be their latest scheme. Haven't we learned enough lessons as it is?" An old woman spoke with a trembling voice.

"I can assure you that we are not the creatures from Mystical Forest. We do not have any intention to hurt any of you. We are looking for the Healer from Mystical Forest. My sister," Kumang placed a hand on Lulong's knee, "… has an illness that only she can cure. I am asking for your help to find her. After we have found her, and my sister is healed, we will leave you alone. We will not disturb any of you. I give you my word."

Kumang did not get any verbal response. The residents only looked at each other, shook their heads, and whispered among themselves.

"Please," Kumang implored them, "all I ask is for you to tell me where the entrance of Mystical Forest is. And we won't bother you anymore. Why can't you do that?"

The Chief lifted his chin in pride. "We don't betray those who have saved our lives, the lives of our children, and grandchildren. We don't turn our backs on those who have protected us from one generation to another in this god-forsaking land. We might be insipid villagers in your eyes, but we have our dignity. We know what is right and what is wrong. Giving you the very means to find her is the same thing as giving you the opportunity to kill her. It is wrong. There is no justification for it. You can kill all of us if you wish. We know you could, with your power and all. But you will never get to know the entry to Mystical Forest from us. Never! She preserves our lives so that we can live longer than we should have. If we lose our lives because of her today, it is only fair."

Kumang swept her eyes around and found faces that had the same expression with the Chief: defiant. "Kill her? We don't want to kill the Healer. Look here," she pointed to Lulong. "My sister is dying. I am only interested in getting her cured."

"That is what you said," the Chief dismissed her. "For all I know …"

A young girl came forward. "Grandfather, allow me to confirm what she said about her sister."

Jurong shook his head decidedly. "No, child, I don't think it is a good idea that you …"

"Grandfather, we can never resolve this with 'they said' and 'we said'. We must know if they are telling the truth or not." Although the girl was young, she was obviously strong-minded.

When Jurong finally nodded, the young girl went to Lulong. "Do you mind if I examine your health?"

Lulong's eyes went to Kumang's for approval. As soon as Kumang nodded, she answered the girl, "Sure, how do you want to do it?"

"Just sit still, please." The young girl reached out to place her hand on Lulong's forehead. She closed her eyes.

Kumang had never seen any of their *manang* did what the girl was doing to check someone's health. What could this young girl find out by placing her hand on Lulong's forehead?

The young girl gasped out loud and pulled her hand abruptly from Lulong. She was panting heavily. Her body was shaking.

Jurong rushed to her side. "Ipah, are you all right? What happened? Bring her a blanket! Quick!" he shouted to the crowd.

Another young girl dashed out of the living room. She came back running with a square piece of cloth. Jurong snatched it from her hand and quickly wrapped it around the young girl who was shivering on the floor.

When the young girl finally opened her eyes, she looked for Lulong's face. "You are going to die because of that memory, are you not?" she asked in a shaking voice.

"Did you see it?" Lulong was concerned. "Oh no, you really shouldn't have."

"Why? What's wrong?" Jurong was anxiously. "Ipah, what is she talking about?"

"That memory is a curse. I want to ask the Healer from Mystical Forest to erase it from my memory so that I can live." Lulong placed her hand on the girl's shoulder. "I'm sorry you saw it. I didn't know you were about to read my mind. I would've stopped you otherwise."

"What do you mean?" Jurong's voice rose. "Have you just transferred the curse to my granddaughter?"

"I don't know. I don't know how it works. I don't know what just happened. Did you actually *see* my memory?" Lulong stared helplessly at Ipah. "I'm very sorry."

"What good comes out of you saying sorry?" Jurong shouted. "Oh, I see, you did it on purpose. You're pressuring us to tell you where the Healer lives by giving my granddaughter a curse."

"Jurong! Jurong! Calm down!" An old woman gripped Jurong's arm.

"Excuse me, did we ask your granddaughter to see my sister's memory? We did not, did we?" Kumang swept her eyes around the crowd. "She volunteered to do that. We did not know that what she was about to do. She did not ask my sister's permission first, did she? As far as we know, human beings are not supposed to have this kind of power. Are you human beings?"

The silence that followed Kumang's accusation was filled by the roaring thunder.

"I take it as a 'no'," Kumang concluded calmly. "So what kind of spiritual creatures from the forest are you?"

"We are human beings!" Jurong hissed. "Of course we are human beings. What else would we be if we are not human beings?" He sounded anxious though.

Kumang could see that she had the upper hand now. "Let me repeat my statement one more time. Human beings do not have the ability to …"

"Some humans can! Just because we have extra abilities that most humans don't have, it does not make us less humans!" The old woman next to Jurong exclaimed.

"Are you telling me that *all* of you have the ability to read people's mind?" Lulong was astonished.

After an awkward pause, Jayan finally replied, "No, not exactly that ability, and not really all of us."

"What do you call what she just did if it was not reading my mind?" Lulong pointed at Ipah.

"Oh, *she* can. Not all of us can do what she does. I can't." Jayan smirked.

"Do you mean to say that the others have different abilities?" Kumang probed.

"More or less."

"What kind of abilities?" Lulong pressed on. "Can you … let's say … manipulate water? I mean, you can freeze the water inside a bucket there, for example?" she pointed at a bucket at the corner of the room.

The residents made indescribable noise.

"Eeeeewww! We're not freaks!" Saban rolled his eyes. "Who does that anyway?"

"If that is the case, what kind of abilities do you have?" Lulong repeated her question.

Saban pouted. "Jayan can feel someone's intention."

"Eh? You said you can't read mind." Kumang turned to Jayan.

255

"I can't. I don't know what you're thinking about when I shook your hand. But I can sense that you are not a threat." Jayan wrinkled his nose. "Do you really think I would have led you to my family had I not been sure that you mean us no harm?"

"I see. That is the real reason you wanted to shake our hands."

"Pama, a girl from a house at the end of the road, can see someone's aura," Saban continued.

"Aura?" Kumang asked for clarification

"She can tell if you're going to die or not, or something like that. Pity she's not here right now. She would be able to tell if you are telling the truth about your sister's condition. Then, Ipah did not need to see inside your head and get a curse."

"Does that mean you made up the story about the creatures from the forest that burn people's hands?" Lulong asked Saban.

Kumang could hear a loud inhale of air in the room when the creatures from the forest were mentioned.

"That story is true, unfortunately." Jurong's face was grim.

"They're killing the villagers? For what?" Kumang asked.

"They want to know how to find the Healer," Jurong answered.

"Why can't they find the Healer if they live in the same forest?" Lulong asked.

"They do not live in Mystical Forest – that's the forest where the Healer lives." Jurong paused. "Why do you think the forest was called Mystical Forest?"

Kumang shrugged. "I assume that's because it is beautiful? No?"

"It is beautiful – no doubt about it. That is not the reason it is called mystical." Jurong explained further when Kumang raised her eyebrows, "It is full of magic – good magic, all right? For protection purposes only. That is all."

"Protection from … ah, I see, the creatures from the forest. Am I right?" Kumang guessed.

"Yes, they've been trying to find the Healer for as long as we can remember."

"And you know how to find the Healer in Mystical Forest. That's why the creatures are after you."

"We can go inside Mystical Forest and come out unharmed. That is true. But that's just the outer layer of the forest. The Healer lives deep inside the forest. She usually finds us, not the other way around."

"Do you know why these creatures want to find the Healer?"

"We don't know. They are ancient creatures, both the Healer and the other ones. What happened between them occurred long before we existed on this land. But they mean her harm. That much we know." The old woman caressed the gray hair on top of her head.

"Why don't you move out? Wouldn't that be safer for your people? Why do you stand in between these creatures that fight each other?" Lulong asked Jurong.

"Where can we go? Live among other human beings? Do you know what they did to our ancestors when they found out about their extra abilities – the abilities that were passed on to us?"

"But you are hunted down here!"

"I don't suppose you understand if you have never gone through this life the way we do." The old woman looked sad. "Of course it is not safe here, but so is anywhere else in this land for us who are different from the rest of them. At least when the worst happens, we can take comfort - if you can call it comfort - in thinking that it is those foul creatures that do it. It is more bearable because they are not one of us. You have no idea how it feels when your own people have it in their heart to exterminate you."

"Your own people? You mean humans? What wrongdoings do they accuse you of until you need to be exterminated?"

"As you said it yourself we have abilities that most humans don't have."

"So what? All right, you are a little bit different from the rest of them. Why is that a crime? Every creature of the forest, be it the physical and spiritual, has different abilities. We can live together, accept our differences, and share this world." Kumang frowned. *Mensia* used to live with the shape-shifters on the land. They had seen abilities that they did not have more than often enough.

"Listen to you, talking about physical and spiritual creatures of the forest. What

257

century are you from?" Saban rolled his eyes.

"Excuse me?"

"How come you don't know how it works with the people out there? Where have you been?"

Once again Kumang exchanged looks with Lulong. "We … we have lived far away from people, to tell you the truth."

"I can tell from all the comments you made. Why did you live far away from people?"

"Well, we …" Lulong hesitated.

"Let's just say that we also have extra abilities that most people don't have," Kumang finished what Lulong started.

"Abilities like ours?" Jurong tilted his head to the right.

"No, nothing like yours, but …"

"You can manipulate water. Wasn't that what you asked us just now? You want to know if we can freeze water, just like you can." Jayan was fast to catch up.

"Something like that," Kumang said slowly.

The residents murmured among themselves to hear her answer.

Saban ran to get a bucket of rain water. "Freeze it!" He pushed the bucket to Lulong.

"We want proof that you are who you said you are," Saban stated when Lulong hesitated.

Kumang made an instant decision. She dipped her hand inside the bucket. Then, she pushed the bucket to Saban.

"Ooooohh!" Saban's face was full of wonder. He passed the bucket to Jurong.

"When did your people separate yourselves from the rest of them?" Jurong enquired as he stared at the frozen water inside the bucket. He passed the bucket to the old woman next to him.

"I can't tell exactly, but it was centuries ago." Kumang's eyes followed the bucket that was passed on from one hand to another. Simultaneous exclamations were heard as the bucket changed hands.

"Was it before or after the arrival of the White Rajahs?"

Kumang's eyes went back to Jurong's face. "Who?"

"The white people who came from a distance shore. They came here and declare themselves Kings of the land. Ah, if you have never heard of them, it had to be before they came. Whoa, that was really a long time ago. You had to have found yourselves a very remote area such that they never found your settlement."

"Many settlements are still not found until today, Jurong. This island has places that most modern men never step foot on," the old woman reminded Jurong. She turned to Lulong, smiling. "I suppose yours is one of them."

"I dare to say that it is," Lulong returned his smile.

"Do you still practice the old way of life? Ah, why do I ask? You still believe in the spiritual beings of the forest. Of course, you do. Am I right?" The old woman winked.

"You are absolutely right." Kumang beamed.

"It is a blessing for your community that you stay hidden. I hope those who call themselves modern humans will never find your home, dear," the old woman said wistfully.

"I doubt that they will ever find it." Kumang was confident.

"Good! Well now, since you have been away for so long, allow me to keep you updated with the latest development. This is the 21st century, ladies. People don't believe in the spiritual creatures of the forest anymore," Jayan said.

"But you just told us about these creatures from the forest and the Healer from Mystical Forest. Why do you talk about not believing the existence of the spiritual creatures?"

"Oh, we believe in their existence all right. That is why we are hunted down."

"I don't understand."

"The people out there found new profound beliefs they call religion and science. Spiritual creatures of the forest do not fit into these new belief systems. Everything that cannot be explained from these new systems is called evil. That's what they call our extra abilities – the work of demons. They hunted our ancestors down because according to them our ancestors practiced dark magic." An old woman shook her head to express her hopelessness.

"I don't know what to say." Kumang was disturbed to hear the news.

"It's awful, I know. What can we do? They are the majority. They have the power to force their will on us, to make us believe what they want us to believe. That is why we prefer to live here, away from them, where we can practice whatever belief we want. We are free to live our lives the way we were born to be."

When Kumang and Lulong could not find a word to say, Jurong filled the silence "Ah, but you are here not to discuss how unfair life is to all of us, are you?" He flicked his chin to Lulong. "You are here to find the Healer so your sister can go on living."

"Yes, will you help us?" Kumang was hopeful.

"As I said just now, we are only familiar with the outer layer of Mystical Forest while the Healer lives deep inside the forest. The best we can do is to let you know what we know."

"You are willing to lend us your map?" Lulong asked.

"A map? No, we don't have a map. We remember it by heart. A map can easily be stolen by the creatures from the forest."

"Then, what can you give us?"

"You will spend time here to learn what we know. I will tell you and you must memorize them."

"But time is what we don't have."

"I can start telling you about it tonight. How fast you can memorize everything is up to you."

"Thank you. I really appreciate it. When can we start?"

"Right after dinner." Jurong laughed to see Kumang's face. "I don't know if your extra abilities diminish your need to eat, but I must eat. That is not negotiable. My memory doesn't work well without the boost from proper meals." He patted his round belly with affection.

The roar of thunder was matched with a roar of laughter inside the house.

MYSTICAL FOREST

"We should turn left." Lulong pointed her thumb to the intersection.

Kumang squinted at the foggy path. She shook her head. "No, we should go straight."

"No, this is where we should turn left."

"Jurong taught us about the paths repeatedly last night! You know we have not reached the junction yet." Kumang was agitated.

"Yes, we have! This is the junction!"

"How could you not remember what he said? This is not the junction."

"You were the one who insisted that we leave Jurong's house even when we were not ready."

"I was only concerned about your health. We need to find the Healer as soon as possible." Kumang stared at Lulong. "And you agreed with me on this. I asked for your opinion. You agreed with me. You said so."

"I did."

"Then, why are we arguing now?"

"Because you said we should go straight when we should turn left! I memorized every detail Jurong said. And I remember vividly that according to him we should take the left path. I do understand how you could jumble up all the information he gave us. They are extremely lengthy."

Kumang frowned. "I remember them just right. We should go straight at this point. We should go to the left only after the next junction!"

"He said turn left after the fifth junction. This is the fifth junction."

"No, this is only the fourth junction. The next one is the fifth."

"I can count until five, Mao."

"What are you saying? That I can't?"

"I'm saying that maybe the fog and the rain cloud your vision, and therefore, you missed the junction behind us."

"Excuse me, I am not wrong and I did not miss a junction. This particular forest curiously has clear paths, unlike the usual forest. Look at that!" Kumang pointed at the path in front of them. "Not a single branch of tree protruding towards our walk way, the ground is perfectly flat. The people from the village must have worked very hard to maintain these neat paths. We can find our way very easily here. A thin fog and a little rain do not make it harder to see where we are going. I'm telling you, this is the fourth junction. We must go straight. Trust me. I am right."

"And because I disagree with you, it automatically makes me wrong?"

"Look here, Lu …"

"No, *you* look here, Mao. This is my life at stake, not yours. Stop the patronizing attitude for once and let me decide where we should go."

"Patronizing? *Me?*" Kumang eyes widened.

"Oh, don't look so surprised as if you do not know that is how you always behave towards others. Just because you are a *petara*, you think you have power above us, but you don't know *everything*. You can't even stop this stupid rain from falling and drenching us wet!"

"Forgive me for trying to save your life! Next time …"

"Oh please, do not use me as an excuse for refusing to go home! You are here on the land simply because you can't find it in your heart to forgive your husband for the wrongdoings you think he has committed. Because you always think that you are never wrong, you can't tolerate it when someone makes a mistake."

Kumang's jaw tightened. "Do not give me advice on things you do not know about," she hissed.

263

"Just listen to you! Did you hear yourself? You are always like that. You place yourself above others. You, who know it all. To you the others are blind simpletons."

Kumang was aghast. "I will not stand here and listen to all your insults!"

"And where will you go if you are not here? Home? I don't think you dare to face your husband and his family."

"I can go somewhere where I can be by myself."

"You can, but I bet you won't."

"And why not?"

"If nobody else is with you, who will you look down upon? You can't feel you are superior when there is nobody else whom you can treat as lesser than you. That is why you are still here, stuck with me."

If Lulong really wanted to know why she stayed put, she might as well tell her. "I am still here because you can't make up your mind. You need me to make the choice for you."

"I don't have problems making up my mind." Lulong's hand went to pluck a thin tree branch from her right.

Kumang thought she saw the air pop as the thin tree branch was taken from the main tree trunk. She would have said something about it if Lulong had not thrown the thin stick towards her direction.

"That junction is the correct junction!"

Kumang moved to her left to avoid the stick. "Hey, watch it!" She glared at Lulong. Her temper flared. "You do not know how to make up your mind. You never do. If you knew, you would make a choice between Igat and Jang long ago. Yet you let the issue hanging. It's the same thing with these junctions. You don't know which one to take."

"Do not twist the situation. I don't have a choice to make for that particular issue. None of them is interested in me! What choice is there for me to make? There are choices here in this forest. And I know which one to choose." Lulong's hand plucked another branch, and she threw it to the junction. "It's

264

that one!"

"It's *not* that junction. And it is not because none of them is interested in you! They both are. It is you who don't know how to choose. One would think that the choice is obvious. But not you, you don't know how to choose. You never do. That's why I have to be here and make it for you."

Lulong narrowed her eyes. "Are we talking about the junction? Or are we talking about Igat and Jang? Yeah, you are still talking about the two of them. And when you said 'one' you mean 'you'? It is obvious to *you* which one of them you would choose? Ah, yes, of course, why do I need to ask? I know without a shadow of doubt who you would choose. Heck, the whole Panggau Libau and Gelong longhouses know exactly who you would choose. And you use that as a point of reference that you have the ability to make a better choice than I?" She walked a couple of steps forwards. She plucked another tree branch to throw. "I choose that junction! My ability to choose is better than yours."

"What is that supposed to mean?" Kumang stood her ground.

"Oh, now you – the one who knows it all – suddenly do not have a clue of what I am talking about."

"Are you referring to the rumors about Igat and me?"

"Naturally, I am. Nobody talks about you and Jang!"

Something Lulong said distracted Kumang. "Why do you keep calling him Jang?"

Lulong was startled. "What do you mean? It is his name."

"It is not. His name is Sampurai."

"I mean, that's how everyone calls him."

"Not everyone, no."

Lulong knitted her eyebrows. "What is your point?"

"Does he allow you to call him Jang?"

265

Now Lulong's eyebrows rose. "Huh? Allow me? I don't need his permission to call him Jang. Anyone can call him Jang. All right, if you must know, he asked me to call him Jang."

"Why?"

Lulong said the words one by one, "Because. Everybody. Calls. Him. Jang."

"Did he say that to you? Did he actually say *that*?"

Lulong rolled her eyes. "What is the purpose of these pointless questions? Are you trying to change the subject? You are worried that I can prove to you that I am right and you are wrong. That is the correct junction." She threw another branch to the junction as she walked forward.

"I can prove to you that you are wrong. Jang is interested in you. I just gave you the proof. Because Gerinching said…" Kumang stopped to see Lulong's face. "What is the matter?"

Lulong did not answer. She walked past her, heading towards the left junction.

"Lu, that is *not* the correct junction!" Kumang followed her in haste.

However, Lulong did not go to the left junction. She stopped at the intersection.

"Are you looking for something?" Kumang asked her because Lulong was preoccupied with scanning the ground.

"Where are the sticks I threw to the junction?"

"You mean the sticks you threw at me?"

Lulong gave her a slight glance. "I threw them at the correct junction." She pointed at the ground. "Where are they?" She walked to enter the left path. "They should be here. Where did they land on? Don't tell me they sink underground." She halted abruptly to stare at the ground.

Kumang stood right behind her. She peeped from behind Lulong's shoulder. "Do you think that is quick sand?"

"There's only one way to find out." Lulong's right hand plucked the nearest tree branch.

Kumang shook Lulong's arm. "See? See? Did you see that?" She pointed at the tree.

"See what?" Lulong stared at her.

"The air popped when you pulled a branch off the tree."

"What do you mean the air popped? Air doesn't pop!"

"But this one does. Take another tree branch to see that I'm right."

"Wait, first things first." Lulong held out her hand. "I want to see if that is quick sand." She dropped the branch to the ground. "No, it is not. It stays solid on the ground, which means ....Whoa! Whoa! Whoa!" She stepped back, dragging Kumang with her, when the stick disappeared out of sight. She whispered to Kumang, "Mao, what just happened there?"

Kumang did not let go of Lulong's arm. "Look! Look at what I am doing!" She pulled a branch off a tree. "See? Did you see that? The air popped!"

Lulong looked at her wide-eyed. "What does that mean?"

"We are in Mystical Forest, Lu. This forest is full of magic. That's what the *mensia* from the village told us. Remember?"

"I still don't know what that means." Lulong widened her eyes. "Give me the stick!" She grabbed it from Kumang's hand to inspect it. "It might not be a real tree branch." She walked over to the nearest tree to place her hand on the tree trunk. She caressed it gently. "I don't …" She looked up to observe the tall tree. "This is a living tree, all right. It's not a painting like the forest we saw near Inik Bunsu's house. But I don't know… I don't feel the usual pulse of life a tree usually emits. Something is not right with it. Come here and feel it, Mao. You also have power over wood."

Kumang came closer to the tree. She touched it the way Lulong did. "You're right. It doesn't feel quite right." She arched her neck to address the tree, "Is everything all right with you?" She grimaced. "I wish I could converse with the trees like Gerinching."

Lulong took a step back to have a better view of the tree. "Do you think this tree is not really a tree?"

Kumang looked around her. "Does that mean the forest here is also not a real forest?"

"You said it yourself, forest ground is not supposed to be perfectly flat like this."

Kumang eyed the ground. "You are completely right."

"You have power over the earth, Mao. Try to do something with it. See what happens," Lulong suggested.

Kumang bit her lip. "I suppose I could try." She gave the ground a calculated look before she stomped her right foot.

The solid ground formed a gentle wave before it returned to its flat form.

"That looks all right," Lulong commented.

"No, that's not what I wanted the ground to do." Kumang squatted. She pressed her right palm to the ground, channeling her power over the earth to it.

A narrow wall rose from the ground, but just like the wave, it went down to form a flat ground once more.

Kumang stood up. There was an unknown power being used in the forest that prevented her from using her power to manipulate the earth. That suggested the presence of another spiritual being in the forest that was blocking her shape-shifter's power. What kind of creature had the power over the earth strong enough to stop her from manipulating it?

"Mao?"

Kumang was too preoccupied to hear anything. As Lulong had said, she was a *petara*. Only a handful of creatures in this world, above, beyond, and under had power that matched hers. Thus, the opportunity to use her power to the fullest was very scarce. That she was a female and fighting battles was not part of her life made the opportunity so limited. Had she ever wondered how powerful she was to be exact? Her fingers twitched. Had she ever had the curiosity to find out just what exactly she could do with the power she had in her hands? The muscles in her hands flexed.

268

She dropped to the ground and slammed her hands on the flat ground. The earth trembled and cracked open to let a pole emerged slowly. Just like the wall, it halted midway and started to sink to the ground as if there was an opposite power pulling it from the inside.

"Oh no, you won't this time," Kumang muttered under her breath. She kept one hand on the ground while the other hand went up. She flicked her wrist in the air, which twisted and formed the shape of a hand. The hand managed to grip the top part of the pole before it was fully buried under the ground. She controlled the force of air to fight the pulling force that came from within the earth. She smiled with satisfaction as the pole was slowly but surely lifted upward once again.

Her smile did not linger. The hand she formed out of air dispersed fast. As it faded away, the pole sank back slowly to the ground. She was dumbfounded to see what was happening. Did this other creature have power over air as well? She let go of her hand from the ground so that she could stretch out both her arms to the sky to gather the drops of air that relentlessly fell from the sky. With her hand movements, she wove the water flow to form a thick rope that wrapped itself tightly at the top of the pole and started pulling it upward. She stood up as soon as she felt an opposite force from underneath the earth. Whoever this creature was, she was determined to draw him out of his hiding place to face her!

The tug of war continued until Kumang stopped it with a scream as she used all the power she had to make the rope of water pulled the pole out of the ground. It went flying out of control because the rope of water dispersed itself to merge with the rest of the rain drops.

Kumang staggered backward. Luckily Lulong was behind her to catch her from falling hard to the ground.

As soon as she had her balance back, Kumang noticed a figure standing behind the thin fog. As she always did with an unknown opponent, she tried to detect the power of the other creature right away. She found out immediately that he was not a shape-shifter.

She straightened her posture and got herself ready for the next stage of fight. However, Lulong grabbed both her arms and pulled her backwards. She realized in a blink of an eye later that the pole she pulled out of the ground had come down. It dropped horizontally on the ground, covering half of the hole. The earth shook and dust went up to mingle with the water in the air, creating a black flog which hid the sight of the figure on the other side of the pole.

Kumang pulled Lulong behind her. She was fully ready to continue the fight with this unknown assailant. Even with a massive pole separating them, she would not take any chances against an opponent who apparently had similar powers to her own.

INIK TUAI

As soon as the dust settled back to the ground, Kumang had a clearer view of who was standing on the other side of the pole. The assailant was not at all as she had expected. She was a tiny female with jet black hair that was tied into a neat bun at the back of her head.

"You have got my attention now. What do you want from me?" The female's voice was very gentle, far from aggressive.

"I'm sorry? What makes you think we want something from you?" Kumang asked with caution.

"Why did you enter Mystical Forest if you are not looking for me?"

Kumang blinked fast. Was this female Inik Tuai? She looked too young to be someone's grandmother. "I am Kumang of Panggau Libau and this is my sister, Lulong of Gelong." She indicated Lulong, who had stepped forward to stand next to her. "We are looking for the Healer from Mystical Forest, known as Inik Tuai."

"Then, you had better answer my question: what do you want?"

"Are you Inik Tuai?" Lulong asked. "I am sorry, I do not expect you to look …" she was lost for words.

"What do you expect I look like?" The female sounded and looked amused.

"Inik Bhiku Bunsu Petara said that …"

The female's face lost all trace of amusement. "Bhiku Bunsu Petara? She sent you here?" Now she was all serious. "It has to be a matter of extreme importance. Or …" She eyed Kumang and Lulong with speculation. "… the two of you must be creatures of extreme importance."

Kumang and Lulong exchanged glances before Kumang answered, "My sister was exposed to the curse of Inik Bunsu. She told us to look for you. She said you are the only creature in our world that has the ability to heal her."

"What? First, she cursed you. And then, she sent you somewhere else to get healed? Why didn't she just lift the curse if she wants to spare your life? That's the easiest way to heal you," the female said to Lulong.

"It's more complicated than that, Inik." Lulong hesitated. "Is it all right if I call you Inik?"

"Why?" the female chuckled. "You don't think I am old enough to be your grandmother? Don't get too fixated with appearance, dear. The packaging rarely represents the content inside. Anyway, you can call me Inik if you wish." She smiled. "Now, what is this complicated thing that Bhiku Bunsu Petara has created?"

"It is a long story." Kumang expected that Inik Tuai would invite them to her dwelling. Instead, the female walked over to the pole on the ground and sat herself comfortably on it.

"I am all ears." She folded her hands neatly on her lap and sent them an encouraging smile. She patted the pole as an indication for Kumang and Lulong to sit next to her.

Inik Tuai stared at Lulong after Kumang had finished telling the story. "Let me restate your intention of coming here. You want to erase the cursed memory from your mind."

Lulong nodded. "Inik Bunsu said you are the only creature in our world that has the ability to do that," she stated, half-asking for a confirmation.

Inik Tuai did not say a word, but saying, "Hmmm." She kept her eyes fixed on Lulong.

"Can you, Inik?" Kumang wanted to hear the confirmation right away.

Inik Tuai inhaled. "It is not a question of 'can'."

Kumang was prepared to hear this. She nodded. "What do you need us do for you?"

Inik Tuai did not answer her question. "And both of you are ... shape-shifters, did you say?"

"Yes. I am from Panggau Libau and my sister is from Gelong. I don't know if you have heard of our longhouses ..."

"As a matter of fact, I have. If I'm not mistaken, the Head of Panggau Libau longhouse is Si Gundi."

"Si Gundi is my late father-in-law. His son, Keling, is now the Head of the longhouse," Kumang corrected her.

Inik Tuai genuinely looked surprised. "Si Gundi has passed on to Sebayan? When?"

"It happened a long time ago, Inik."

"Not a natural death, I presume? Ah, yes. You, shape-shifters, practically do not die unless someone decapitates your head, do you? That means he died in a battlefield."

"He did." Kumang nodded solemnly.

Inik Tuai looked troubled. "I am so sorry, I didn't know. It's one of the drawbacks of living a secluded life. I don't get to hear news from the outside world. Your late father-in-law was a decent male." She touched Kumang's hand briefly.

"Have you met him, Inik?" Kumang was curious.

"I've met him and his brother-in-law. Now, what is his name...?" Inik Tuai's smile was bright. "I don't know how I could forget it. He was one charming young male. How is he doing?" She stopped smiling to see Kumang's face. "Not him, too!"

"I'm afraid so." Kumang could not decide if this conversation would benefit them or not because Inik Tuai seemed so disturbed by the news.

Inik Tuai suddenly grabbed her hand. "And Nuing? How is he? He turned out

273

all right, did he not?" she asked anxiously.

With Kumang's silence, Lulong asked, "Who is Nuing?"

Inik Tuai raised her eyebrows. "Who is Nuing? What do you mean? I thought … Si Gundi said …eh! Did he not say …" Inik Tuai covered her mouth with her hand. "Oh no! He didn't make it, did he?" She shook her head in dismay. "I can't believe that after all the efforts we put in, we still lost him."

Kumang turned her head to Lulong, who returned her clueless gaze with equally incomprehensive stare. She was digging her memory trying to find neutral comforting words that could be applied to all depressing scenarios when Inik Tuai suddenly snapped out of her misery.

"And you still come here to ask for my help. Are you sure you want my help? Are you not worried she will end up like Nuing? Or maybe like …" She made a face that showed displeasure. "The other one?"

Kumang had no idea what had happened to the two creatures Inik Tuai mentioned. "Inik Bunsu recommended you. She said you are the best there is."

"What you are asking is not without risk. Are you aware that there are other ways to lose that cursed memory? You can find the Queen of Water Spirits. She has charms that can take your memory away."

Kumang inhaled deep. "We are well aware of that charm. But my sister rejects using it."

Inik Tuai leaned forward to Lulong. "Oh? Why? That way is a lot safer."

"It will wipe up my entire memory! I won't be able to remember anything and anyone. It will erase my entire life," Lulong argued. "I don't want to lose my life!"

"You will have a new life, make new memories. What you ask of me can also end up with you losing your life."

"You mean she could die?" Kumang was worried now.

"It's possible."

"How come?"

"Look here, you ask me to extract a particular story from your memory clumps. Do you know the implication that comes with it? Your memories – past and present – are entangled with each other. That is how they manage to exist. Why do you think you remember some things, but you don't remember other things? Memories that cannot connect themselves to another existing memory will perish like morning dew – vanish without a trace. If I extract a story from the whole clumps, it means I take away a single clump. I will have to disconnect it from the other existing memories associated with it. Do you understand what I am trying to tell you?"

Lulong frowned. "You are saying that if you take out the cursed memory, chances are I will lose some other memories that have a connection with it?"

"First of all, you must understand that you are a living being, and your memory clumps are also alive, that is why they keep changing forms as new memories come in and reshape them. I can't predict how important this particular clump is to the rest of the clumps. That being the case, it is impossible to say for certain how the whole clumps will react to the sudden loss of a clump. Yes, you will lose some memories. Which ones? I don't know. How much? That remains to be seen. Still, that is the least of your worries."

"What should I worry the most?"

"I think it is best if I just show you." Inik Tuai stood up. She stood and walked to the edge of the hole. "Tell me what you see." She pointed to the ground.

Standing next to her, Lulong stated the obvious, "It's a hole."

Inik Tuai pointed to Kumang. "She took the earth out of its compact condition and created a hole there. Look at it now, is it an empty hole?" She asked Lulong.

Lulong shook her head. "It's filled with water."

"Precisely! Because it is raining now, the rain drops and fills the hole, so do dust, dead leaves, and everything else that happens to drop in. It will not stay empty. Will this ground be exactly as it was before? Not a chance."

"All right," Lulong said slowly. "As I understand it, you are saying that my memories will change?"

"You can't have a permanent hole in the clumps of your memories. That's not how it works. The clumps will refill the empty space of the removed clump. That's the only way the whole construction of clumps survives. What will they use to fill it? That is the problem."

"I don't understand. Surely, she will have new memories that will soon fill the empty space. Where is the danger in that?" Kumang asked.

"If you are so lucky, your new memories will fit perfectly into that particular space. You won't have a problem. You can continue your life as it is. We are not discussing success here although it is a possibility. We are exploring the possible damages you might suffer. Now, what if the new memories do not fit?"

"What is your worst scenario, Inik?" Kumang did not want to play the guessing game.

"My worst worry is that your memory clumps will fill in the empty space by readjusting the old memories you've had, forcing connections that are not meant to connect. Do you understand what I am trying to tell you? If that happens, you will have memories of things that never happened. But you'll believe them wholeheartedly because they have become your memory clumps."

"I don't really understand what you are telling me."

"For example, you may end up hating your sister for something she never did to you, because you remember she has wronged you for some reasons."

Lulong bit her lip as she fixed her eyes at Kumang. "But … that is not the definite result of it, is it not? This is only a possibility. It may not happen to me the way you predict it."

"That is not my prediction for you, dear. That is only a possible scenario. I can give you millions of possible scenarios. None of them is my prediction of the outcome. I don't know what you have in your memory clumps. I can't predict what memories they could invent." Inik Tuai eyed Lulong seriously. "You come to me believing that I am the best creature to help you with your problem. And this is the advice I can give you for your problem: the memory charm belonging to the Queen of Water Spirit is the best option to take if you want to erase this cursed memory."

"Are you saying that you don't want to help her?" Kumang asked.

"I did not say I don't want to help. I said what you ask me to do is not the best option for your sister."

Kumang turned to Lulong. "Lu?"

Lulong shook her head. "The memory charm will definitely erase my whole memory. There is no other possibility. This way ..." She stared at Inik Tuai. " ... there is still a chance that I will be all right, isn't there? I mean you will only take one particular memory. I still can keep the rest. I still can have my life. I still can be me. Yes, all right, I understand, I will lose some memories. But I get to keep the big bulk of them."

"Lu ..."

"If I completely lose my memory, I will have to restart my life. I won't be able to remember my father. He's gone from our lives. I can't restart getting to know him. And to continue my life without memories of what he has done for me, without being able to think of him and feel the gratitude of his love for me. No, I can't do that to him. I won't do that to him, to my mother, to my brother. No, I won't!"

Kumang patted Lulong's hand. "All right, all right! Calm down. We won't use the memory charm." She turned her face to Inik Tuai. "Inik, if you really don't mind helping, please. Unless you have another concern in mind?"

"Mind? It is not my memories that are going to be messed up. It is not my life that is going to change. No, I don't mind." Inik Tuai sighed. "I just don't want you to blame me later if the result is not how you picture it to be right now."

"I understand, Inik. Don't worry, no matter what, I will not blame you," Lulong assured her.

Inik Tuai was far from convinced. "That's what they always said before the treatment began. When they didn't get what they wanted afterwards, they turned nasty towards us."

"Us?" Kumang was confused. Did some other creatures live with Inik Tuai in Mystical Forest? Perhaps the creatures that were involved in the tug of war with her just now?

"To me and the forest, of course. Do you have any idea what they have done to this forest that has faithfully protected me over the past centuries?"

Kumang recalled Jurong's story about the creatures from the forest and Inik Tuai. Their animosity could stem from a treatment gone wrong. She reached out to hold Inik Tuai's hand. "We won't be like them, Inik. I give you my word."

Inik Tuai clicked her tongue. "All right, since you insist. Let's do this. Sit down there." She pointed to the horizontal pole next to the hole.

"You're going to heal her here?" Kumang was not comfortable with the idea.

"Where else should we do this?" Inik Tuai tilted her head to the right.

"I thought maybe we would go to your house or something …"

"This forest is my house." Inik Tuai raised one eyebrow. "Do you really come here to get her healed or do you come here to see my house?"

"I come here to be healed, Inik," Lulong answered hastily.

"Let's get to it." Inik Tuai spread her right arm, swinging it to the pole. "Take a seat."

THE COMPLICATIONS

Mystical Forest, the Land

"How is she?" Inik Tuai whispered.

Kumang turned her head back to the thick curtain of gigantic palm leaves. "She is still sleeping over there. I don't want to wake her. Last night was nightmare free. She hasn't had a good sleep for quite a while. That is a good sign, isn't it?" She also kept her voice low.

"It is a good sign. What about the rest of yesterday? Anything happened that caused you to be concerned?"

"You mean after you left us alone here?"

"I have done what you asked me to do. What do you want me to hang around for? You should've left right away. I don't know what you wish to accomplish by staying here."

"I think we'd better stick around until we know that she is really all right. You are the one who said that there might be complications. Isn't it easier for you to address them while we are still here?"

"Please don't tell me you will stay here for years to come, waiting for possible complications that may never occur! There's nothing else I can do for her. I've done my best."

"Well, we are not leaving until I know for sure she is all right."

"That's why I asked. Was she not all right after I left yesterday?"

Kumang bit her lip. "She remembered me, her family, her home, her childhood."

"In other words, no harm done. And you said she has lost her nightmare. That means everything is all right. What is your concern?"

279

"It's just … there were times when she went blank, you know what I mean? She looked like she was disconnected from where she was and went into the void."

"How long did it last?"

"Not long, I could get her attention back by asking her questions about her life. She gave me all the correct answers."

"What are you saying? She doesn't remember the latest memories?"

"She remembers what happened yesterday."

"What *is* your concern, then? Look, she lost a memory clump. There's a hole in her life that she cannot explain. I would say that it is normal that she behaved that way."

"Do you think so?"

Inik Tuai moaned. "I've told you she is fine and you don't believe me. Why do you waste my time by asking the same question again and again? If you are determined to live here in this forest, suit yourself. Remember that I don't invite you to come here. Don't expect me to play the role of welcoming hostess." She turned around abruptly without waiting for an answer.

Kumang knew better than to stop her from going away. She scanned the surrounding forest with troubled mind. She could not explain in words why she was uneasy with Lulong's condition. She just had this uncomfortable feeling that Lulong was not all right just yet. The feeling would not go away even when all the signs indicated that she was fine. She inhaled and let out a big bulk of air from her *mensia* lungs as if by letting go the air from the lungs, her worries would go along with it.

She parted the curtain of leaves to check on Lulong.

"Ah, you've woken up!" she said cheerfully when her eyes met Lulong's. "How are you feeling today?"

Lulong got up from the comfortable cuddle of the tree roots. She massaged the back of her head. "I feel refreshed." She smiled at Kumang.

"Did you have a good sleep last night?"

"The best in weeks." Lulong beamed. She stretched her arms up and yawned. She bent her head down and began rotating it to the back. She stopped as she looked up to the top of the tree poles. "What is that sound?" She pulled her head back to stare at Kumang in confusion.

"Eh?" The warning bells inside Kumang's head made noise. She intensified her hearing sensor. She did not hear anything extraordinary. They were inside a forest. Naturally, the forest residents made noises. The forest was never absent from sound. It was normal, so normal that they never paid attention to it. "I only hear the sound of the forest. What do you hear?"

Lulong's face lit up. "Ah, yes, of course. I can recognize the sound of the leaves rippling against each other. It always gives me comfort. Then, there are the animals, let's see, that's ......"

Kumang went back to the state of relaxation. Inik Tuai was right. She was worried for nothing. Lulong was fine. She just needed time to rearrange her memories and placed everything to its rightful place. Maybe it was time to leave Mystical Forest. She should send Lulong home. And then … She felt a pang of anguish for she knew what was waiting for her. She had made a decision to leave her life behind after Lulong was healed. Maybe that was the root of her rotten feeling. She did not want to start a new life without everyone she loved. That was the truth. It had nothing to do with Lulong's health.

"Mao?" Lulong touched her hand. "Are you all right?"

Kumang tried to show the brightest smile she could possibly muster. "I'm fine. I'm better than fine." She was not. She was far from fine. She was dying inside. "I'm so glad you're all right." She squished Lulong's hands. That was the truth, so it lifted her spirit a little bit. She was doing this for them. She would leave them so that they could have a happy life. She nodded firmly. Yes, she could be content with that. "Let's get you home." Then, her heart sank deeper.

"Do you still remember how to get out of here?" Lulong smiled sheepishly.

"We didn't wander around too far from where we were when we met Inik Tuai, we should be able to remember our way back."

Lulong's face changed. "Mao," she touched Kumang's arm gently. "About what I said … you know … when we disagreed about which junction to take … I …"

"It's okay. Don't worry about it," Kumang waved her hand to dismiss her concern. She only had little time left to spend with Lulong. She cringed at the thought. She did not want to fill it with petty arguments.

Lulong was agitated. "No, you have to let me apologize for what I said. I don't know what came over me until I said those things to you. They are not true."

Kumang smiled faintly. "Are they not?"

"Of course not! That's not how I think of you, not really! I mean …"

"Forget it. It's all right."

"It's not all right. You are obviously upset!"

Kumang was not upset. She was devastated. But it was not because what Lulong had said to her. It was because of the thought that she would never see her again. How could she make her understand without telling her what she was about to do?

"Lu, don't make something out of nothing. I am not upset because of what you said."

"Are you saying that I imagine things? That I don't have the right mind? That I can't think for myself?"

Kumang was worried about how their conversation turned fast into an argument. "I didn't say that. You know I didn't say that. You worry about nothing. Look, let's just get out of here. I'll send you home. And then …" she chocked on her own words.

Lulong responded by screaming. She bent down and picked up a long tree branch from the ground. Without missing a beat, she swung it hard to a squirrel that jumped down from a nearby tree and landed next to Kumang's leg.

"Lu!' Kumang shouted as the squirrel flew up to the canopy of the forest, screeching in pain. "What have you done?"

Lulong grabbed Kumang's hand. "Don't worry. I will protect you. Let's go out of this forest. We must find somewhere safe." She started dragging Kumang with her.

"Lu!" Kumang pulled her hand back, trying to slow her down.

Apparently it was not necessary because Lulong halted instantly.

"Lu!"

"Shush!" She put her finger on her lips. "Listen! Did you hear that?" she whispered. Her head went around to scan the forest's canopy.

"What am I supposed to hear? Lu! What is going on?"

Lulong held both Kumang's hands in hers. "He is coming for you."

"Who? The squirrel?"

"Don't be silly. What does a squirrel want from you?" Lulong squished Kumang's hands firmly. "We won't let him get what he wants, will we? We will outsmart him." She restarted her walk, still dragging Kumang with her. "I know he is very smart, but we can be smarter than he."

"Who are we talking about? Lu! Can you stop for a while and talk to me?"

"I will tell you when we have reached a safe place. We have to get out of here as soon as possible. This place is bad news."

"What place? This Mystical Forest?" Kumang pulled her hand out of Lulong's grasp. "Lu! I'm not going anywhere until you explain to me what happens."

Lulong gave her an exasperated look. "This place is not real, Mao. Surely, you've figured it out by now. Look at the path." She pointed to the ground. "A real forest cannot possibly have such neat path. Didn't you say that you saw the air pop when I pulled a branch off a tree? That's because they are not real trees. This is a trap!"

"All right. Who wants to trap us?"

"What do you mean who? You know who…" Lulong looked up with alarm as the sound of thunder was heard behind the thick layers of canopies. She shook her head. "We don't have time to talk. They're coming for you." She got hold of Kumang's hand.

"They? Is it a he or they? Who is coming for me?" Kumang rushed to follow

Lulong's hasty footsteps.

Lulong answered her with a scream. "No! No! Get away from her!" She waved her hands wildly above Kumang's head.

"Lu! They're just raindrops. They're harmless. Water can't hurt me!"

"We must get out of this forest. Come!" Lulong ran along the path, taking Kumang with her.

Unfortunately, the sky was faster. It poured massive amount of water over the canopies such that even their thick layers were powerless to prevent the water from pouring in to the ground.

"No! No! Leave her alone!" Lulong pushed Kumang to the ground and use her body to shelter her. "You can't touch her. I won't let you hurt her."

Kumang was never worried about her sister more than now. "Lu!" She broke free from Lulong's clutch. It was not a problem because Lulong could not overpower her.

Lulong screamed louder to see how water drenched Kumang wet. "No! What are you doing? That's exactly what they want you to do! Get back down here! Take cover!" She pulled Kumang to her with no avail.

"Lu, listen to me. It's only water. See?" Kumang opened up the palm of her hand to let water fill it. She brought her hand to Lulong. "Water can't hurt us both. Calm down."

Far from calming down, Lulong's anxiety escalated. Realizing that she could not pull Kumang down to take cover, she picked a giant palm leave from the ground. She waved them above Kumang's head. "They're too many. I can't stop them all. I need help."

"Lu! Please, stop. Please, listen to me." Kumang managed to get hold of Lulong's hand. "We'll go back and find Inik Tuai once again. All right? She will fix whatever it is that went wrong." It was her turn to drag Lulong along with her.

"Why are we going back inside the forest?" Lulong cried in distress. "No, Mao! No! Don't go there! Please, believe me." She struggled to pull Kumang to the

284

opposite direction without success. "I'm on your side, Mao! I will always be on your side. I will never do anything to hurt you, not for anyone. Not even for him! Never! I swear! So, please, we have to get out of here! We can't go inside! Mao! Stop! Oh heavens, I need help to get her out of here."

Kumang hardened her heart to ignore Lulong's heartbreaking plea. "It's all right, Lu. You hang in there for a little bit longer. I'll get help. Everything is going to be all right soon." She kept dragging her struggling sister to find Inik Tuai.

She did not go far. Out of the blue, her body collided with another body. Her mind did not have time to register the impossibility of what happened. It automatically treated the other body as an assailant. She pushed Lulong back at the same time she took a few steps back. She waved her hand in the wet air to transform the raindrops into iced needles that she sent flying to the assailant.

To her surprise, the iced needles stopped in the air, certainly against her command. The moment they dropped to the ground as raindrops she recognized who had thawed them. It was Laja of Panggau Libau.

"Igat!" Kumang was beyond surprised. "What...? How ...? When ...?"

Lulong knocked her from behind in rushing to get to Laja. She clutched his arm. "Thank heavens you came. We must get her out of here. It's too dangerous here."

Laja threw Kumang a baffled look.

Kumang cut in before he had time to open his mouth. "No! We must go further inside the forest to get help!"

"No! Don't listen to her. She doesn't know what I know. We can't let her get inside the forest. Help me get her out." Lulong shook Laja's arm.

"She is not well, Gat," Kumang warned Laja. "We need to get her to a *manang*. She is inside this forest."

"No, we must get out of here!" Lulong pleaded to Laja, who looked worried to see her crying face.

"Lu!" Kumang came to approach Lulong. She addressed her with a gentle voice.

"Listen to me. Please, just talk to me for a while. Look at me."

"I've told you this is not the time for talking. They are coming for you!" She pointed to the sky. "Why can't you see what is in front of you?"

Laja looked up to see what Lulong was pointing at. And Kumang used that opportunity to strike Lulong unconscious.

"Mao!" Laja deftly caught Lulong's body from falling down to the ground. "What is wrong with you?" He was horrified.

Kumang pulled back her outstretched arms when Laja shifted Lulong away from her reach. "Gat, she is not well. She needs help."

"According to her, you are the one who needs help."

"She is not in the right frame of mind." She shook her head to see his distrust. "Oh come on! You know me. Why would I want to hurt my own sister?"

"I just saw you strike her unconscious without a reason!"

"We must get her help as soon as possible. She is resisting help. I don't know why."

"Why does she need help? Why did you say she is not in her right mind? What is going on here?" Laja wanted an explanation.

His questions reminded Kumang. "What are *you* doing here? I mean, how come you are here?"

"She asked me to come." His eyes went to the unconscious Lulong in his arms.

"She did? When? Oh, did she visit your dream last night and ask you to come?" Kumang wondered why.

Laja shook his head. "She called me using *batu besapak* a while ago. I answered her call. That's how I could get to where she was in an instant."

"You used a charmed rock called the internal twins?" It started to make sense a little bit.

"A pair of charmed rock to be precise. I got them from Umei." Laja's face twitched when he mentioned the name.

286

"The late daughter of the King of Baya?" Kumang stopped that line of questioning because Laja's face turned grim. She remembered that he had accidentally killed the female. She quickly changed the subject. "How did Lulu get to call you using them?" She wanted to know how the charmed rocks worked.

"She holds a piece. I have the other piece. We can call each other when one of us is in need by using the piece that we have." Laja lifted Lulong's body into the cradle of his arms. He stared at her face with concern. "What is wrong with her?"

"It's a long story. Come, follow me. I'll tell you what happened while we are looking for Inik Tuai."

"Inik Tuai?" Laja shifted his eyes to Kumang.

"The *manang* who can help her. She lives inside this forest. Make sure you follow me closely, okay? This forest is full of magic."

Laja chuckled. "Did I hear you said 'magic'?"

"Gat, please, I promise I'll explain everything. But right now we need to get moving. She is getting worse with each passing moment." Kumang fixed her eyes at Lulong.

"All right, all right. Lead the way. We'll follow you."

THE HEALER OF MYSTICAL FOREST

"A curse? She's got a curse? From Inik Bunsu Bhiku Petara?" Laja was flabbergasted. "Why wasn't I told about this?" he demanded.

Kumang looked back at him without stopping her walk.

He stammered upon receiving her look. "I mean … I met her brother in Gelong the other day, he didn't say anything to me about his sister getting a curse."

"Did you ask him about his sister?"

"Well… no. Still … if something like a curse befell on her …, was it not worth mentioning? It's Inik Bunsu Bhiku Petara we are talking about."

"Did you know that she's on the land?"

"He told me. But he only said she wants to keep you company while you are trying to help *mensia* with some weaving problems. It sounded harmless."

"Really? If you had heard that she was on the land to do something that had the potential to harm her, what would you have done?"

Laja had to have received Kumang's bemused look because his face's fair complexion turned into a reddish shade. Fortunately he was spared from giving an answer since they had arrived at the spot where Inik Tuai healed Lulong.

"Why are we stopping?" Laja asked Kumang.

"This is where we met her."

"She is not here."

"I can see that."

"Don't you know where she lives?"

"She lives inside this forest."

"Yes, but where specifically? She must have a house, or something that gives her shelter against this pouring rain, among other things." Laja gazed up to the sky, welcoming the rain to fall on his face. He was a *bunsu ai*, being soaked through and through by water only served to make him more powerful.

"I don't ..." Kumang inhaled in frustration. "Inik Tuai! Where are you!" she called out as loudly as possible. "My sister is in trouble! Please help her!"

She did not receive an answer. She turned sideways to Laja. "There is only one thing to do. We don't have much time to find her."

He shrugged. "Whatever you think is best, Mao."

Kumang looked around her to address the trees of the forest. "I don't know what you are. I don't know whether you are real trees or not. If you are, I apologize for what I am about to do to you. It is not my intention to hurt any of you. I will not do this unless it is absolutely necessary. My sister 's life is at stake, so I must get her to Inik Tuai as soon as possible." She said to Laja, "You look for her at your right side. I'll do the left side. Ready?"

"What do I look for?"

"Anything you can see – a house, maybe? A woman? Anything other than the trees. All right?"

Upon Laja's nod, she spread both her arms to the left and right while she screamed, "Inik Tuai!" The trees on the right side of the path were bent down to the right and the trees on the left side of the path were bent down to the left.

It happened only for a blink of an eye. Then, all the trees went back to their original positions – reaching towards the sky.

"Did you see anything?" Kumang asked Laja.

"I didn't see anyone. It was too fast. The rain and the fog did not help give clear vision. The lightning strikes served more of blinds than source of light. Can you keep the trees down longer to give me time to scan wider area?" Laja suggested.

"I will try my best. Just so you know, I didn't command the tree to stand up when they did."

"The trees resisted you?" Laja was surprised.

"Inik Tuai has the power to resist my shape-shifter's power."

"Really? What kind of creature is she?"

"She is an *antu raya*, if I'm not mistaken."

"The *antu raya* do not have the power to resist our powers!"

"You are right. It could be this weird forest. Hmmmm…it doesn't matter whose power it is. Let's try again. I'll keep the trees down as long as I can." Kumang inhaled deep. "One more time?" she asked Laja.

"Yup."

She managed to keep the trees down longer this time.

"See anything?"

Laja frowned. "I thought I saw a shack somewhere upstream." He pointed south. "I'm not sure. You?"

Kumang grimaced. "I didn't see a thing."

"As I said I'm not sure what I saw. Can you do it one more time? I know where to look now. I should be able to focus on that direction."

"Upstream? There?" Kumang pointed south.

"Yes." Laja turned around to find the best position to have a look. "I'm ready when you are."

Kumang stretched her arms to get ready. "Okay, here we go."

"That is enough!" A stern voice was heard from inside the forest.

Kumang and Laja turned to the direction where the voice came from.

An old female came out from behind the fog that veiled the poles of trees. "I have come to answer your call. What do you want from me?"

Kumang quickly scrutinized the old woman. She carried a haughty appearance although Kumang would not describe it as hostile. "I do not want anything

290

from you." She chose her words carefully.

The old woman raised her eyebrows. "The whole forest and its residents could hear you calling me. You bent the poor innocent trees to see where I was. And you told me you want nothing from me?"

"We are looking for the Healer of Mystical Forest," Kumang corrected her.

"I am she." The old woman was very poised when she made the admission. The booming thunder sounded as if it wanted to confirm her statement.

"You are not Inik Tuai. I met her yesterday and this morning. And you are not she! Wait, can you change form? Are you a shape-shifter, too? You can't be. I can't detect your presence. You can't ..." Kumang halted the moment she saw Inik Tuai coming out from behind the forest trees. "Ah, there you are, Inik Tuai, I'm looking for you. Look there." She pointed at Lulong in Laja's arms. "Her mind got meddled. She keeps saying that some creatures are after me. I can't convince her otherwise. Can't you do something about it?"

Inik Tuai fidgeted under the closed scrutiny of the old woman standing next to her.

"What did you do to her, Bata?" the old woman asked sternly.

Inik Tuai hunched forward. "I suppressed her cursed memory, Mistress."

Kumang was aghast. "Hang on! You are *not* the Healer of Mystical Forest?"

Bata was downright defensive. "I never admitted that I am. You made your own assumption."

"You let us believe that you are! How dare you play around with my sister's life?" Kumang's voice rose instantly.

"How dare you come here asking for an exchange of life!" Bata shouted back at Kumang. "What makes you think your sister's life is more valuable than my Mistress's?"

"I did not ask ..." Kumang halted as the realization sank in. "Are you saying that if you ..." she shook her head and closed her eyes to adjust her thinking. "If Inik Tuai ..." she opened her eyes to stare at the old woman, who acknowledged it with a nod, "If you save my sister's life, you will die?"

"Don't pretend that you don't know! Isn't it the very reason Bhiku Bunsu Petara sent you here?" Bata glared angrily at Kumang.

"Bhiku Bunsu Petara sent you here?" The real Inik Tuai asked. She did not sound surprised though.

"That's her curse, Mistress!" Bata pointed at Lulong. "She sent you her very own curse!"

Inik Tuai was more interested in something else. "A curse from Bhiku Bunsu Petara? Bata, you should've known better! I'm not saying this to belittle your skills, but get real! You know you can't suppress her curse. Nobody can. Why did you do it still?"

"I can't take the memory out, Mistress. I haven't mastered the skill yet. And I can't let them find you! That's exactly what she wants."

Inik Tuai smiled. "I have been waiting for something like this for centuries. I wonder why it took her so long."

Kumang did not know how to plead for her sister's life without feeling guilty. "Inik, we did not come here to hurt you. I swear we did not know anything about your problem with Inik Bunsu. I just want to save my sister's life. That is all."

"I told you to find the Queen of Water Spirit! She can obliterate her cursed memory with her charm. I told you!" Bata was shouting again. "But noooo! It has to be my Mistress who heals her. Why is that? You are after her life. That's why!"

"We are not! I am terribly sorry. I ..." She turned to Laja in dismay.

He did not look happy either. He stared at Lulong in his arms. "Do we still have time to find the Queen of Water Spirit?" he whispered to Kumang as she came nearer to him.

"I can't ask Inik Tuai to die so Lulu could live. Can you?" She whispered back to Laja. She bit her lip to stop herself from crying. Finding the Queen of Water Spirit would take time, not to mention that she did not know how to persuade her to help. It was universally known that the Queen was cruel beyond belief.

292

Laja's jaw tightened. "No, it is not right. No matter how much we wish it is not the case, the truth remains that it is not right. We can't ask Inik Tuai to sacrifice her life for Lulong." He swallowed hard at the mention of Lulong's name. "We must go now. Kapuas is not that far from here. With our speed we can be there in no time. We can do this. Yes, we still have time." He sounded more like he wanted to convince himself than Kumang.

"Tsk! You are already here. Why do you need to go somewhere else to get healed?" Inik Tuai came forward to them. "Let me have a look at her, and then I'll see what I can do for her."

"Mistress! You can't!" Bata grabbed her arm to stop her.

Inik Tuai patted the hand on her arm. "I am a *manang*, Bata. It is my responsibility to heal." She smiled to the sky above and continued to address it, "I never turn away a creature that needs my help. Not even you can make me deny my true calling in life, Bhiku Bunsu Petara."

She came nearer to Laja since Bata let go of her to close her face in the palms of her hands. "We need to get her to my house. Do you think you can carry her all the way there? It is quite a distant."

Laja nodded without hesitation. "That won't be a problem, Inik."

"Good! While we are heading there, you can tell me all about the curse, how she got it, how long has she got it, how it has affected her life ..."

"I just got here, Inik. I don't know much about the curse," Laja informed Inik Tuai.

"Oh? Then, who can tell me about it? In order for me to know what course of action is the best for her, I must have all the information."

"I can tell you everything you need to know about the curse, Inik," Kumang chipped in.

"Excellent! Bata, after she has finished telling me what I need to know, you must tell me what you did to her, so I can repair the damage that you have caused."

"Yes, Mistress," Bata answered miserably.

Inik Tuai looked around. "Let's get moving." She snapped her fingers in the air. The pouring rain and the raging thunder stopped in an instant.

THE HEALER'S NEMESIS

Bata rushed to open the door of the house. She held the door open for Inik Tuai to come in.

"Welcome to our humble abode." Inik Tuai spread her arms to welcome her guests.

Kumang followed Laja to step inside the house. Because it was darker than the forest outside, her eyes needed time to adjust before she could see the interior. The house only had one spacious room. The floor on the left side of the room hosted a row of rattan mats. The back part of the house was supposed to be a kitchen, or a place where medicine was brewed. And the right side of the room was filled with racks full of jars. A ladder was placed behind the last rack. Kumang's eyes travelled up to find a loft. All the windows were situated so high on the walls such that they almost touched the ceiling. That was the reason why sunshine did not really reach the floor.

"You can place her down there." Inik Tuai pointed at the row of mats on the left side of the room.

"Which mat?" Laja asked.

"Any one will do," Inik Tuai answered curtly.

Laja followed her last instruction without uttering another word.

Kumang stood near the door without knowing what to do. "Do you have many patients, Inik?" she could not help asking.

Inik Tuai did not answer her. She went straight to kneel next to Lulong.

"Do you see many patients here?" Bata, who stayed by the door, asked Kumang acidly.

"I'm asking because I see a long row of mats there. I assume they were for

295

patients," Kumang defended her question.

Bata appeared sad. "There was a time when Mistress's healing skill was high in demand. All sort of creatures lined up here to be healed." Her face brightened a little as she recalled the memory.

"What happened?"

"What do you mean what happened?"

"Something must have changed that." Kumang spread her arm around the empty room.

Bata turned away in dismay.

"What about the *mensia* who live by the forest? They said they are protected by you, or is it by Inik Tuai?" Kumang remembered the village at the entrance of the forest.

Bata hissed. "Mistress does not need to lend a hand to deal with *mensia*'s health issues. I am also a *manang* although my healing skills are not as good as Mistress's. I am more than capable of taking care of them. It is my calling to heal the sick anyway. And they have proven themselves to be worthy of being saved. They are very loyal to us."

Kumang's attention was distracted by Inik Tuai, who spoke to Laja, "First, she needs to wake up. I can't do this treatment without her cooperation."

She left Bata to kneel next to Inik Tuai. "Is she going to be all right, Inik?"

Inik Tuai gave her a quick side glance. "That is entirely up to her. We shall see soon." She placed the palm of her hand on top of Lulong's head. She closed her eyes and her mouth moved to form a silent chant.

The moment she lifted her hand, Lulong's eyelids fluttered and her eyes slowly opened.

Kumang held her breath, fearing another episode of frantic screams. Thankfully, it did not happen.

Lulong lay still on the mat. Only her eyes roamed the room. The first creature she found was Laja, who was sitting cross-legged on the left of her mat. She smiled weakly at him. "You are here." She extended her hand to him.

He caught it and squeezed it gently. "Hey, you called, so I came. Didn't I tell you I would? Any time. Anywhere."

"Where am I?" Her eyes continued to scan the room. She found Kumang on the right of her mat.

"Hi, Lu." Kumang smiled at her. "We are at Inik Tuai's house."

"Inik Tuai?" Lulong's eyes went to the female sitting next to Kumang. She scrambled to get up.

"It's all right." Kumang reached out to her, but Lulong cowered back to Laja's side. "This is Inik Tuai, Lu. The *real* Inik Tuai."

Lulong's eyes moved to and fro from Kumang's face to Inik Tuai's. "Who was the female we met yesterday?" she asked in confusion.

"She is Inik Tuai's apprentice. There she is." Kumang pointed at Bata, who was still standing near the door.

Lulong arched her neck to find Bata. "Why did she deceive us?"

"There is something that Inik Bunsu did not tell us when she sent us to find Inik Tuai," Kumang broke the news to her.

"Oh?"

"Inik Tuai will lose her life if she heals you."

"*No!*" Lulong's eyes went to Inik Tuai. "Really?"

Inik Tuai smiled. "Not really."

"Not really?" Kumang touched Inik Tuai's arm. "Is there a way to avoid it?"

"I will not die because I extract a cursed memory from her."

"That is great news." Kumang clasped her hands in delight.

"But her life will be in mortal danger because of it," Bata argued from afar.

"I don't understand. How could it be?" Kumang turned her head around to

297

Bata.

"Inik, is there anything we can do to eliminate this danger?" Laja asked.

Inik Tuai smiled sadly. "I'm afraid the danger will only go away when I die."

"Yes, there is!" Bata came quickly to kneel next to Inik Tuai. "Are you also from Panggau Libau?" she asked Laja. She pointed at Kumang. "She said she is from Panggau Libau. Doesn't that make you a shape-shifter from Panggau Libau?"

"I am Laja of Panggau Libau," he acknowledged with humility.

"Are you a warrior?" Bata scrutinized his appearance. She did not seem to be impressed by what she saw.

"Bata …" Inik Tuai gave her a stern warning.

"I am a Panggau warrior," Laja admitted.

"The best that Panggau Libau has?" Bata continued her questions.

Laja's lips twitched. "The best that Panggau Libau has is not here at the moment." He threw his eyes to Kumang, who quickly looked away. "What do you need a warrior for?" he asked Bata.

"We don't need a warrior," Inik Tuai disagreed.

"Mistress! He can fight them off!" Bata cut in.

"Bata! You can't ask him to risk his life for me," Inik Tuai chided Bata.

"They ask you to risk your life! It is only fair that they do the same for us," Bata refused to let go of her idea.

"He is just one male. He can't fight all of them. It is impossible." Inik Tuai waved her hands.

"You're wrong. There are two of us to fight them. Would that be enough? How many enemies do you have?" Kumang asked.

"Two?" Bata repeated. "Do you have more warrior friends coming here?" she asked Laja.

"None of my fellow warriors is coming here as far as I know. I'm sorry," Laja added when he saw Bata's downcast face.

"Can you ask them to come? I mean, you arrived here out of the blue. Can't you do the same to call the others?" Bata did not give up easily.

Laja exchanged looks with Lulong. "No, the others can't come the way I did. Look, I can try to ask some of them to come, but the soonest they can come is … let's see, err …"

"Jang and Dom are in Pelagus." Lulong put her hand on Laja's knee. "How long do you think they can reach here?"

Laja shook his head vaguely. "Tomorrow morning maybe?" He looked at Inik Tuai for approval.

"We don't have until tomorrow," Inik Tuai said curtly.

"How about tonight? I'll get them here by tonight," Laja bargained.

Inik Tuai shook her head. "She can't wait until then. I managed to put her in a calm state of mind, but it won't last long. She must start her treatment right away while she still can get a grip of reality. I can't treat her when her mind starts to play tricks on her. She will resist me. No, you are all we've got young shifter."

"Not necessarily. As I said, there are two of us. By two I mean, there's him." Kumang pointed at Laja with her thumb. "And there's me."

"You?" Bata made a face. "Fight?"

"Yeah, I can fight." Kumang was offended to see Bata's reaction.

"She can fight, all right," Lulong said to Bata. "Don't underestimate her power."

"I have seen what she can do." Inik Tuai gave Kumang a calculative look. "She might be just what we need. You see, I don't want you to hurt them."

"Mistress! They are determined to kill you!" Bata protested.

"I know, Bata. It doesn't mean we have to treat them the same way they treat

299

us." She patted Kumang's lap gently. "No, I don't want you to harm any of them."

"Then, what do you want us do?" Laja asked.

"Prevent them from coming inside this house while I am treating her." Inik Tuai pointed at Lulong.

"Who are dealing with, Inik?" Laja asked more question.

Kumang suddenly remembered. "Oh! The people of the village talked about the creatures from the forest. Are they your enemies?"

"They have been trying to find use for centuries." Bata smirked. "The biggest problem they have is they cannot penetrate the forest stronghold."

"This Mystical Forest is not a real forest, is it, Inik?" Kumang expressed her speculation.

"No, Wai, there is no Mystical Forest. It only exists in your mind." Inik Tuai smiled.

"We imagine it? The whole forest?" Lulong asked in awe.

Bata chuckled. "My Mistress is the master of controlling minds, in case you haven't figured it out by now."

"That's the reason your house is difficult to find even though the paths are clear." Kumang understood now.

"That is also partly because what you see is only what your mind wants you to see, and everyone's mind is different." Bata's smile was smug.

When Kumang's eyes met Lulong's, she knew her sister was thinking of the same thing she was: their argument over which junction to take.

"The thunderstorms and the rain? Did we also imagine them?" Lulong asked.

Bata grinned. "We are *antu raya*. It is within our power to control them."

"If your enemies can't penetrate the forest stronghold, why do you need our help?" Kumang still did not see the cause of worry.

"The moment I start your sister's treatment, Mystical Forest will be gone. I need to concentrate fully on extracting the cursed memory. It's a very delicate procedure. Even Bata hasn't been able to master it after centuries of training. I can't spare any thoughts to maintain this fake forest. They will be able to see this house and find me. And they will come here as soon as the Mystical Forest disappears. I need you to keep them outside the house, for her sake. I don't think I need to explain to you what will happen to her if I get interrupted half-way."

Kumang nodded. "I understand, Inik."

"What kind of creatures are we dealing with?" Laja repeated his question.

"They are *antu raya*," Bata answered.

"Eh? Aren't you one?" Kumang asked Inik Tuai.

"I am. I know what you are saying. But in this case, it is precisely because I am one of them that they hate me more."

"Why?" Kumang blurted out the question. "I mean, if you don't mind telling us what happened."

Inik Tuai closed her eyes. "A long time ago, when I was a lot younger, I made a grave error of judgement. It cost them their daughter's life."

Bata instantly disagreed. "It's not your fault, Mistress! You did all you could for her. You are not the one who gets to decide who lives and who dies."

"But the child's parents cannot accept it," Lulong voiced out what was left unsaid.

Inik Tuai did not open her eyes. "The child's mother was completely heart broken. She lost the will to live."

Kumang put her hand on her mouth. "Oh dear, did she die in the end?"

Bata corrected her. "She died shortly after. Her husband vowed to avenge their deaths. Mistress's life for their lives. According to him, he is very generous. It is a life for two lives. His whole family supports his twisted mission. That's the problem with these creatures. They don't want to understand that we, healers, can't save all lives! We save some, we lose some. That's just the way it is. But

301

they don't want to know. They never want to know."

Inik Tuai opened her eyes to gaze at a glass window up in the ceiling. "I gave them hope, Bata. I shouldn't have done that in the first place. I promised to prolong the child's life."

"You gave them that. They kept the child alive with them for a few years because of you. She should've died on the day she was born, or soon after! You allowed them to have a few good years with that child. They should've got down on their knees to kiss your feet for all the good memories they get to keep! But some creatures just don't know how to be grateful," Bata grumbled.

"Those few good years only increased their pain in magnitude when they finally lost the child. I should've let her die when it was her time to die. I shouldn't have tried to defy Mother Nature. I knew I shouldn't have, but I still did it. I let my emotion got the better of me."

"What has the incident got to do with Inik Bunsu?" Lulong asked after a short pause.

"The mother of the child was Bhiku Bunsu Petara's apprentice," Bata explained. "Her favorite, they said. The most talented of them all, if you know what that means, because I don't."

Both Kumang and Lulong said, "Oh!" at the same time.

After a long silence, Inik Tuai clasped her hands. "Are you ready to start your treatment?" she asked Lulong.

"You'd better start as soon as possible, Lu," Kumang urged.

Lulong bit her lip. "All right." She turned to Laja.

He took her hand in his and gave it a squeeze. "I'll be right outside," he assured her. "If there's anything, anything at all, just calls me. I'll be here. You know what to do."

She smiled and nodded. "Be careful out there."

He grinned at her. "You know me. I am always careful."

Lulong turned to Kumang. "You, too, Mao. Be careful."

302

"I will. Now, you listen to everything Inik Tuai tells you to do, all right?" Kumang nodded her goodbye to Inik Tuai and Bata. "We go out first." She stood up. "Let's go, Gat. We need to figure out how we want to keep the *antu raya* at bay."

Laja also stood up. He bowed slightly to Inik Tuai and Bata before he followed Kumang to the door.

Kumang opened the door and took one last look at Lulong. She could see Inik Tuai ask Lulong to lie down again on the mat, and she heard her said, "Now, you will feel some discomfort when I enter your mind. Whatever you feel, do not - I repeat - do not try to resist."

"Yes, Inik," Lulong answered obediently.

"Bata," Inik Tuai called out to her apprentice, who ran to kneel behind her at once.

From the distance that separated them, Kumang could see that Inik Tuai closed her eyes, but she could not hear a word of what she was chanting as her body rocked slowly from side to side. She only knew that the rhythm of her chants got faster and faster, matched by the escalated swings of her body and head. The chants and the body rocks ended with a sharp intake of her breath, her head arched upward, and her body fell backwards towards Bata, who was ready to catch her in her lap. Although Kumang was not a *manang*, she understood that Inik Tuai had gone into trance, and that her soul had left her body to enter Lulong's mind.

Laja's hands on her arms startled her.

He pushed her gently outside. Then, he closed the door. "Come, Mao. It is up to us to protect them now."

She looked at his determined face and nodded. "Let's do this, Gat."

THE EXTRA HELPERS

"How do you propose we do this, Gat?" Kumang asked Laja.

"Since we are dealing with *antu raya*, we can expect that they will use lightning to fight us." Laja's eyes went up to look for the sky above. The thick layers of canopies perfectly covered it from his sight. "This forest is a disadvantage for them. But then again, this forest is not real, is it?"

"We've had experienced fighting battles with the *antu raya*. We know how to fight them." Kumang reminded him.

"Yeah, we should be able to …" He stopped talking because the vision of the forest shuddered.

Kumang scanned their surroundings. "The illusion begins to wean. That means we don't have much time until this house is exposed in the open and the *antu raya* can find it."

"I can't really say what we should do until I know the real landscape of our battlefield …" He stopped again because the trees around them disappeared. He turned his back on Kumang with his hand on the handle of his *parang nyabor*, expecting a group of *antu raya* to surround them. His body posture became more relax when he did not see any potential danger around.

"Are we in the real forest now?" Kumang wondered.

"I supposed so." Laja let go of the handle of his *parang*. "The forest now has the usual appearance we know, uneven grounds, cluttered tree branches." He gazed up to the sky. "We are more exposed now compared to the forest before this. I think …"

"Oi!" A loud voice from somewhere inside the forest overshadowed the other forest sounds. "Mao, is that you? Oi, Luloooooong!"

Laja widened his eyes to Kumang. "Did you hear that? Tell me I did not

304

imagine that voice. Let it not be another mind trick by Inik Tuai."

Kumang shared his excitement. "I heard him, too. I don't think it is our imagination."

Laja shouted back, "Oi! Jang! Over here! Come quick! We've got a battle to fight!"

Kumang laughed. "You can't make him come here faster than that. He'll be here as soon as he possibly can."

True to her prediction, Sampurai's voice was heard even when he was not within sight, "I'm coming! I'm coming! Wait for me! Don't start the battle without me."

As it turned out, it was Pungga who arrived first. "Are you all right, Mao? Where is Lulong? Hey, Gat, you're here!" he patted Laja's arm.

"Inik Tuai is treating her inside the house." Kumang pointed at the house with her thumb.

Pungga's attention was redirected towards Laja. "How come you are here, Gat?"

Laja did not answer his question. "And how come you are here? Don't tell me the Healer of Mystical Forest contacted you using her mind power?" He grinned. "How do you know that we need your help at this very moment?"

"We are here because I know they are here," Pungga pointed at Kumang. He smiled at her. "You don't think I would let you take the journey to Mystical Forest all by yourself, do you?"

"How do you find this Mystical Forest?" Kumang smiled back at Pungga. "Did the villagers tell you how to get here?"

"No, we travelled following Lulong's story, based on Inik Bunsu's directions. We looked for the second pier, the entrance to the village. We just reached the river bank when we saw the forest behind the village disappear. We could detect your whereabouts, of course. Your *petara* power level is easy to spot. We bypassed the village and the villagers and rushed to find you."

"How did you know we need you here?" Kumang repeated Laja's initial question.

"I dare say that I know Inik Bunsu better than you. Things are never straight forward with her. She would not offer help without getting something in return. So yeah, I thought you might need our help one way or another."

Sampurai finally arrived with Gerinching. He punched Laja's arm playfully without saying a word.

"Hi, Jang! How have you been?" Laja greeted him.

Sampurai did not bother to exchange empty pleasantry with Laja, so he did not answer the question. "Where are the enemies?" he asked the one question that was important to him.

"They are not here yet. But they can be here anytime," Laja gave him the answer he wanted to hear.

"I did not know for sure that you would face danger, mind you," Pungga continued his conversation with Kumang.

"So what made you come?" she asked him.

"After Lulong sent me away, I went to look for Jang and Endu G at our den in Pelagus. I was sure they were anxious to hear the latest news. I told them what happened in Inik Bunsu's longhouse," Pungga answered.

"I met Inik Bunsu. I don't trust her one bit." Sampurai nodded his head to stress his opinion.

"His instinct told him that," Gerinching added.

"I'm glad your instinct is right this time, Jang!" Kumang could not help grinning at him at the thought.

Sampurai frowned at her. "My instinct is never wrong! I told Dom that she is up to no good by sending the two of you to this Mythical Forest ..."

"Mystical Forest," Kumang corrected him.

"Huh? Whatever! I can't guess what her plan is, but it can't be good. So we decided to come here. And I was right, wasn't I? You do need our help." Sampurai looked around. "What kind of place is this? The forest can change form."

"We should've arrived sooner, but we had to travel at my third-grader speed. I'm very sorry," Gerinching apologized to Kumang.

"Don't be." Kumang touched her shoulder. "You arrived just in time."

"In time for what? What are we dealing with here?" Sampurai put his hands on his hips. "I don't see any enemy around!"

"All right, this is our situation," Laja took over. "Lulong is inside the house there." He pointed at the house behind him. "Inik Tuai and her disciple are treating her. She is in good hands for now. This is where we all come in. It will take a while for Inik Tuai to heal her, and in the meantime a family of *antu raya* ..."

"*Antu raya*? Oh, are we fighting them?" Sampurai rubbed his hands in excitement.

"Yes, Jang, we are going to face a family of *antu raya* who want to kill Inik Tuai. We can't let them disturb her while she is healing Lulong. Correction, we can't let them kill her even after she has healed Lulong. Therefore, it is our job to stop them from coming to the house," Laja gave explanation to all the newcomers.

"That won't be a problem. I've fought with them before. I know what to do," Sampurai said with confident.

"How many *antu raya* are we talking about here?" Pungga asked Laja.

"I do not know for sure," Laja told him. "Oh, one more thing, Inik Tuai does not want us to hurt any of them. Therefore, our task here is to chase them out of the forest without killing them."

"What? Why? That means they can come back some other time to finish the job. What happens when we're not here? We can't stay here to protect her forever! And what am I supposed to do to them if I can't even hurt them?" Sampurai was displeased.

"After she has finished healing Lulu, she can protect herself. She doesn't need us anymore. She has done it successfully for centuries. Therefore, our task is to protect her while she is using her energy to heal Lulong instead of protecting herself. As to why she wants to spare their lives, that is her choice, not ours. It is an old conflict. It has nothing to do with us. We shouldn't get involved. Our task is to make sure no life is lost from either side until Inik Tuai finishes healing Lulong, and she can defend herself again," Kumang clarified the task.

"Fine, I get it!" Sampurai snapped. "Chase them out of here! This battle is not fun at all," he grumbled.

"How many *pintu kayau* does this house have?" Pungga asked Laja. He was referring to the points of entry in the forest which led to the house. "Do we have enough warriors to guard each and every one of them?"

"Let's see. There's you, Jang, and me. Each of us can guard one *pintu kayau*. I just don't know if …"

"We've got Sugie and Mayas," Sampurai cut in.

Laja was baffled. "I remember Mayas of Nanga Langit. He is a first grade Nanga Langit warrior who assumes the form of an orangutan on the land, isn't he? But who is Sugie? Can each of them guard a *pintu kayau* by himself or will he need help from one of us?"

"Sugie can guard a *pintu kayau* by himself!" Sampurai was confident. "Oh, I don't think Mayas can be stationed at a *pintu kayau*. He would not want to leave her unprotected." He pointed at Gerinching.

"Sugie can't guard a *pintu kayau* by himself! But it's okay. I'll be there with him," Kumang offered an alternative.

"Sugie can guard a *pintu kayau* by himself. He doesn't need you to help him! Stop being overprotective towards him. Let him have his day in a battle. It would do him good. Besides, you shouldn't be at a *pintu kayau*," Sampurai rejected her idea.

Kumang's eyes widened. "Why not?"

"Isn't it obvious?"

"Because I'm a female?"

Pungga interrupted before a pointless argument started, "Because our main task is to protect the house, Mao. You are the most powerful among us all. You need to stay here to protect the house."

Laja supported Pungga. "He is right, Mao. Protecting the house is what really matters in this case. You are our last line of defense against the *antu raya* if all else fails."

Kumang relented. "Can the five of you handle all the *pintu kayau*?"

"Four," Sampurai corrected her. "Mayas won't be at a *pintu kayau*. He will be wherever she is, to protect her," Sampurai referred to Gerinching.

"And you accused me of being overprotective?" Kumang would have laughed at Sampurai if she had not been annoyed with him at the same time. "I'm sure Endu Jie can take care of herself. She doesn't need to be protected all the time."

Sampurai shrugged. "You talk to Mayas. Let us see if you can persuade him to leave her alone. Her father sent him to the land for one purpose and one purpose only: to protect her. I know better than to stop a warrior from doing a responsibility entrusted to him by his Chief."

"Mayas can guard a *pintu kayau*. I can be there with him," Gerinching imitated Kumang's suggestion.

"You will not go anywhere near a *pintu kayau*!" Sampurai frowned at her.

"You'd better stay here with Mao, Endu," Laja agreed with Sampurai.

"But I'm the least powerful among us. I shouldn't be guarding the house, should I? What kind of last line of defense can I offer should the *antu raya* reach here?" Gerinching used Pungga's previous argument to disagree.

Kumang smiled with glee at Pungga. She began to feel that she could like this Nanga Langit female as a sister-in-law if one day she ever ended up marrying Sampurai. She would be a good ally.

Pungga smiled back at her with confidence before he talked gently to Gerinching, "Actually, I am thinking of asking you to do something, Endu G. And for that, you need to stay here. I am sorry, I am afraid you are the only one

I can entrust with this particular task."

"Oh?" Gerinching was intrigued.

"Do you see that house?" Pungga pointed at the wooden structure behind them. "It sticks out like a sore thumb inside this forest."

Gerinching's eyes followed his pointing thumb. "Naturally. It is the only thing that is not organically growing in the forest."

"Do you think you can do something to hide it from plain sight? It will make it harder for the *antu raya* to find it," Pungga probed.

"What do you have in mind, Dom?" Laja clearly did not understand where Pungga was going with his idea.

"Ah, you want her to ask the forest to cover it." Sampurai was the first one to understand Pungga's suggestion.

Laja took a good look at the house and the forest around it. "But the house is not covered by the forest. How can the forest hide it from plain sight? Do you want her to move the house because it is made of wood? I don't think it is a good idea to move the house when Inik Tuai is treating Lulong."

"No, no, no, I believe he wants her to ask the trees to move to cover the house," Kumang explained because now she also understood what Pungga was asking Gerinching.

Laja was taken aback. "Move the trees? All those trees over there? How?" He swept his eyes around the forest near the house.

Kumang smiled at him. "You should have seen what she did to the forest in Pelagus, Gat!" Kumang turned to Gerinching. "I think it is an excellent idea. It is worth trying."

Gerinching stared at the house and the forest around it. "I don't know. I mean ... this is the first time I came here. I don't know the trees around here. I suppose I can try. Let me see ..." She bit her lip. "How much time do we have?" she asked Laja.

Laja shook his head. "I'm not sure. They can be here at any time now for all I know."

"Then, you'd better start talking to them now!" Sampurai urged Gerinching. "No need to concern yourself with the *pintu kayau*. Leave them to us. If you need help to get it done faster, Mao can help."

"Is there anything I can do?" Kumang asked Gerinching.

"You have power over wood, don't you? So, yeah, you definitely can do a lot of things. But first, we need to introduce ourselves to the trees." Gerinching smiled at Kumang. "Come, we'd better start."

The male shifters watched the two female shifters walk away towards the forest around the house.

"If this place doesn't have more than four *pintu kayau*, we've got them covered," Pungga broke the silence.

Laja hesitated. "I am not familiar with the landscape, I don't know …"

"Can we ask someone who does?" Pungga suggested.

Laja looked over to the wooden house. "I suppose Bata would know." He made a decision in an instant. "I'll see if I can ask her. The two of you wait here."

LAJA'S DOOR OF WAR

Mystical Forest, the Land

Laja sat on a fat tree trunk that arched over the river. He braced his body by placing both his hands on the trunk. His legs dangled down to the water below. Waiting for the *antu raya* to come at some unknown time left him with nothing to do. His mind soon wandered.

According to Bata's description, the house had three points of entry. The first one was located upstream, whereby visitors would have to cross a river to get to the house. Since he was a *bunsu ai*, he volunteered to guard the *pintu kayau*. The second *pintu kayau* was located downstream, whereby visitors had to climb up a steep hill to reach the house. Pungga, being a *bunsu tanah*, offered to guard the *pintu kayau*. The last *pintu kayau* was located behind the house, whereby visitors would have to pass dense bushes to enter the path to the house. Sampurai was willing to guard the *pintu kayau*.

Because there were only three *pintu kayau* to guard, and all points of entry had already had a warrior to guard, they let Mayas choose which *pintu kayau* he wanted to be at. It was to Laja's relief that he chose to be where Sampurai was at. Among the three Panggau warriors, Mayas was most comfortable with Sampurai, having spent the longest time with him on the land. Not that Laja had anything against Mayas, but with the ape not speaking to anyone, he could not imagine he had to work with Mayas to chase the *antu raya* away. How could they coordinate what they wanted to do when communication was non-existence? Sampurai, on the other hand, seemed to be able to tell what Mayas was thinking of. Laja seriously doubted the accuracy of Sampurai's guess since he knew for a fact that Sampurai was not a mind reader. However, a guess was much better than the zero understanding he would face if he had to deal with Mayas.

Sugie, also as expected, did not want to guard a *pintu kayau*. He chose to stay with Kumang and Gerinching while they were 'redressing' Inik Tuai's house with the surrounding forest. Laja did not know what made Sampurai think that an unflanged orangutan like Sugie, a creature of the land, could guard a *pintu kayau* by himself. Sampurai should not have assumed that just because the orangutan was a male, he could fight well. Not every male was cut out to be a warrior. A male orangutan was unflanged, precisely because he did not have good fighting skills. What made Sampurai think Sugie was any different? But Sampurai was always like that. He simplified things, ignoring how small details could create fundamental differences.

They did not need to persuade Bata not to get involved. She insisted that she continue watching over her Mistress while she was healing her patient.

His thoughts were disrupted by the sound of the leaves being tossed aside, followed by a stream of voices. He stood up and climbed the nearest tree to look for a place where he could find out who was coming without being seen.

"I'd say we should still be careful. The magic she put over the forest could not just disappear. This is like she opens her own front door to invite us in. I don't like it. It feels like we are walking straight into her trap," a male voice was heard from behind the trees of the forest.

"Your Uncle Jantan thinks it is because she is using her power to heal someone," another male voice responded. "That means she has no power left to maintain the illusion of the forest."

"I don't mean to disrespect Uncle Jantan, Apai, but I believe he said that because this has always been his wishful thinking. He's been waiting for something like this to happen for centuries. The truth is she has stopped healing patients ever since she killed Rida," a third male voice commented.

"I agree with Bijau, Apai. I mean, if she still practices healing, something like this would have happened a lot sooner than now," a fourth male voice joined the conversation.

"Be that as it may, we should look into this new development. This might be a chance for Jantan to finally find his peace. He needs it. We are his family. Not only that, we are all he has left. We can't let him down in a time like this." The Apai stepped out of the forest to scan the bank of the stream.

"Yes Apai," the children answered almost in unison.

And one by one they appeared in the open for Laja to see.

One of the children said, "Personally, I don't see how she would bring us any danger. She is only a healer after all." He kept his eyes on his father's back.

"She is very good at playing tricks on your mind!" Another child refuted the idea. "That is dangerous enough!"

The young male turned to his brother to defend his opinion. "Yeah, but she has never been hostile to us. She protects herself from us, which is not surprising. Other than that, she never attempts to attack us."

"That's because we never give her a chance! And we should not give her the chance now. That is all I'm saying," the other young male continued arguing with his brother.

The third young male did not join the argument. He went to stand next to his father. "What do you think, Apai? Where should we go from here?"

Their Apai took his time staring at the stream in front of them. Laja wondered why he acted as if the stream could do them harm. He guessed that they must have had too many dealings with Inik Tuai in the past such that they treated everything in front of them as an illusion.

"This is what we'll do," the Apai finally decided. "We will split into two groups to comb this stream. Saiyan, you go downstream with me! The two of you go upstream. Let's see where it will take us."

Laja grimaced to hear their decision. It complicated his task for now he had two different points to watch out. He had to ensure that none of them decided to cross the river at any point. As the four *antu raya* went their separate ways towards two opposite directions, he transformed himself into an eagle and flew up to the sky. That way he could monitor their whereabouts much better.

PUNGGA'S DOOR OF WAR

Mystical Forest, the Land

Pungga stood at the edge of the steep hill with his hands on his hips. He was confident that no creature could pass this terrain. The only way to access Inik Tuai's house from this point of entry was to climb up the vertical hill under his feet. With his power over earth, he could turn the small probability into impossibility.

He scanned his surroundings one more time to ensure that he did not miss any possible entry. He was satisfied to find that there was none. He commended Inik Tuai's choice of site for her house. Even without the presence of Mystical Forest, the house was situated on a difficult terrain to reach. Protecting it was not a challenge at all.

From the corner of his eyes, he caught movements from the foot of the hill. He quickly stepped back to make himself invisible from the creatures down below. Unfortunately, it cost him his vision. He could not see them although he could still hear their voices.

"You shouldn't have come with us, Apai," A male voice was heard.

"I may be old, Son, but I still have the strength to move about," the Apai replied.

"That's not what I meant. You should have gone with Jantan instead of us."

"He is with Layang and his children. It would be too crowded if I went with them. Besides, I thought you need the extra hands."

"You are always welcome to come with us, Apai. I'm just worried about Jantan. I think it would be best if you are by his side in a time like this."

"He will be all right. Especially if we are successful to find the Healer today, he will be more than all right."

"Are you sure?"

"What do you mean? Of course he will be all right. Why won't he be?"

"He has spent most of his adult life trying to get his revenge."

"And he will get it today."

"That is why I am worried."

"I don't know what you are trying to say."

"After he has his revenge, what will he do?"

"Come again?"

"Getting his revenge is the sole purpose of his life. It has been for the last few centuries. When he doesn't need to do it anymore, what will he do with his life?"

"I'm sure he will find something else to do. If he can't figure it out, we will help him. The most important thing is that he will get it today. It will make him happy for a change. He hasn't felt it for centuries."

"Nothing can ease the pain of losing his wife and child, Apai. Killing the Healer will not make the pain go away. It will still be there. It will always be there. If you ask me, I don't think we should help him get his revenge."

"How could you say that?"

"After he kills the Healer, who is he going to blame for their deaths? For the pain of losing them? At least now, he can take comfort in blaming her."

"You are talking as if it was his fault that they died!"

"He was partly to blame."

"Rida died because the Healer refused to help!"

"The poor child died because his parents insisted on having a child they could not have!"

"Every couple longs to have children of their own. There is nothing wrong with that."

"No, I'm not saying that it was wrong for them to wish for a child of their own. But we knew right from the start that Isah was not healthy enough to have a child. Did we not warn Jantan about this? He did not listen. He insisted he want her as his wife. If that was his decision, he should have accepted that their marriage would be childless."

"He never demanded that she gave him a child! She was the one who wanted to have one, so badly that she was willing to get it through an alternative treatment."

"They were not meant to have children, it means the universe did not want them to have children! Taking an alternative treatment by asking a mind trickster for help? I can't believe he agreed to her plan. I understand that he loved his wife, and he wanted to give her whatever she wanted. But as her husband he should've been able to make her come to her senses by telling her that what she wanted was impossible!"

"But it was possible! They had Rida, didn't they?"

"At what cost, Apai? At what cost? It robbed Isah of the small amount of health she had in the first place. Rida was not fully formed when she was born."

"They would have continued living if the Healer had kept her promise."

"She shouldn't have promised them something she could not keep. *That* is her fault."

"For that she deserves to die!"

"The fault was equally divided among the three of them Apai: the Healer, Isah, and Jantan. Isah has paid for it with her life. Now, you want the Healer to pay for it with her life. What's next? Will Jantan pay for it with his life?"

"Don't speak ill of your cousin! What is the matter with you? Oh, I know. Your wife has been feeding you this idea, hasn't she? I knew it! She has never liked Isah. I don't know why."

The son's laugh sounded amused. "If you must know, Apai, my wife did say all these things. Oh, no, don't get it wrong. I am not Jantan. I know how to put a

317

stop to my wife if she starts talking non-sense. But she is absolutely right about this. You know she is right. You just don't want to admit it because in your eyes Jantan can do no wrong. You care for your nephew more than you care for your own children."

"Now, hold it right there! I love all my children. It just happens that Jantan has a very hard life, with my brother passed on to Sebayan so early in life, and his mother...," the Apai let out a big sigh. "I don't need to tell you how that female never fulfilled her responsibilities as a mother. So I give the boy extra compassion. I try to be the father and mother that he never had. I expect my children to give him just that – compassion - by treating their orphan cousin as one of their brothers. Is that too much to ask?"

"I do see him as my brother, Apai. That is the reason I said ..."

"Apai, we've reached a dead end." A third male voice interrupted. "Where do we go now?"

The Apai replied, "Ask your Akik. We'll do what he says."

"Akik?" the third male asked the grandfather.

"Let's see," the Akik responded. "Is it possible to go around this wall?" He answered his own question. "No, I don't think so. I don't see a path leading to either side of the wall. I'd say we try to climb this wall. What do you think?"

The son replied, "I suppose we could ..."

He was interrupted by the sound of a loud bang.

Pungga looked up to the sky to gauge where the sound came from. He saw a fireball explode in the sky. It had to be Sampurai. That meant he had started his confrontation with the *antu raya*.

He heard the creatures below continue their conversation.

"That's Jantan's fire flare," the Akik said.

318

"That's not a distressed flare, Akik," the grandson sounded relief. "Uncle Jantan found something interesting."

The Apai said urgently, "You'd better go to him, Apai. Whatever is happening there, he'll need you to be there for him. Busu, go with your Akik. I stay here with Bana. We'll climb this hill to find a new path."

"Will the two of you be all right?" the Akik sounded unsure.

"We will be all right, Apai. If there's any danger worth mentioning, I'll send a flare of fire to alert you."

Pungga realized immediately that the creatures below were *antu raya api* – the fire reapers. They harvested fire to create lightning. He wondered if Laja and Sampurai were aware of this. He closed his eyes and his jaw tightened as soon as the consequence of this realization sank in.

"All right, you two take care of each other," the Akik bid goodbye.

"You do the same, Apai. Busu, watch out for your Akik."

"Yes, Apai," the son answered obediently.

"Now, Bana, let's figure out how to climb this wall," the Apai instructed his other son.

Pungga narrowed his eyes. He had to make sure that the two creatures down below would never climb up. His original plan to guard the entry point could no longer be used. This was not the time to be defensive. He stepped forward to stand on the edge of the hill. He could see two creatures standing at the foot of the hill. They were too busy discussing the best way to climb the vertical barren wall that they did not see him.

He stomped his foot to the ground. He jumped back quickly as the ground beneath his feet crumbled down fast, forming a landslide that instantly buried the two creatures at the foot of the hill.

He hardened his heart to see what he had done. To lessen his guilt, he told himself that they were not dead yet. They still could survive if someone came in time to dig them up. But for now, he had ensured that they would not go up the hill while he left his *pintu kayau*.

Although he did not know from which *pintu kayau* Jantan sent the flare of fire – Laja's or Sampurai's, he knew exactly where he had to go. They were facing the fire reapers. Sampurai was in trouble.

SAMPURAI'S DOOR OF WAR

"I can't believe you let Mao talk you into guarding a *pintu kayau*." Sampurai walked up and down the narrow path of the forest. "Even you can't resist a pretty face with charming smiles, huh?" He turned around to face Mayas.

As usual, Mayas's face did not move a muscle. He sat on the ground next to a buttressed tree root with his legs crossed and hands placed on his knees. He looked straight ahead to some distance place inside the forest, completely ignoring Sampurai.

"Don't get me wrong," Sampurai continued pacing. "I don't mind guarding this *pintu kayau* with you. I just think that we're wasting our time here. I mean, we are warriors, you and I! We fight battles. That's what we do. We don't scare other creatures away. The whole arrangement is ridiculous!" He threw both hands in the air.

As Sampurai made a turn to face Mayas, the ape blinked and shifted his eyes fleetingly to him. He winced. "I know! I know! It was my idea to come here in the first place. And I was right, wasn't I? They need our help. I only have a problem with how they choose to deal with this *antu raya* family. If it were up to me, I'd ... what is it?" He was suddenly on guard as Mayas blinked again and shifted his eyes to a point beyond Sampurai's left shoulder.

"They're here?" Sampurai turned his back on Mayas with his hand on the handle of his *parang*. He stared at the dark path in front of him, anticipating the enemies to appear. He made a loud click of the tongue when he remembered that he was not supposed to attack the incoming creatures. He was only allowed to chase them away. He let go the handle of his *parang* with great reluctance. He rolled his eyes. This task was so degrading.

He was still feeling sore for not being able to fight a battle when four figures appeared at the end of the dark path. He quickly transformed himself into his true *gerasi* form. His body height shot up to be as tall as the trees of the forest and his body emitted fire from his stinking toes to a pair of sharp horns on top of his head. As soon as they came closer he raised his arms high and roared as loud as he could to scare the four creatures in front of him. He expected them to flee in fright.

They did not.

Apart from being astonished to see a moving tree trunk engulfed in a blaze of fire, they did not show any sign of fear at all. The astonishment on their face turned into a look of interest, and shifted to glee within an intake of breath. Without a word, all of them withdrew their swords and pointed them at him.

Sampurai let excitement get the better of him. Surely he had the right to fight back if his opponents meant to hurt him. He let out a war cry and charged forward at full speed towards them.

He did not get far.

Two of the *antu raya* ran to his sides - one to his left and one to his right - while the other two stayed in front of him. The tips of their pointed swords drew out the fire from his body. Instantly he felt that he was being pulled to three different directions: front, left, and right. He could not move forward, nor could he shift his body to the sides. There was only one way he could get himself free.

"Jantan, cover his back. I'll replace you there!" one of the *antu raya* in front of him shouted.

The *antu raya* on his right moved swiftly to his back, while the one in front of him took his place without taking their swords from him. Their movements were fluent as if they had rehearsed them a million times before this.

Sampurai struggled to free himself. The more he tried to pull away from the ropes of fire, the more he was being pulled towards four different directions. It was not the pain of being torn apart that started the panic attack in him. It was the knowledge that he was slowing losing his power. The ropes of fire were not cast on him to keep him in check. The *antu raya* were harvesting fire from his shape-shifter's power, thus, sucking life out of him. He roared angrily to himself for not realizing from the start that these *antu raya* was *antu raya api* whose source of power was fire.

He fell down to the ground like a lifeless tree when they finally pulled out their swords. He had never felt so weak. He did not think he was injured or anything like that. The pain of being pulled apart was gone the moment the ropes of fire were released from his body. However, he did not have any energy left to even move his little finger.

He heard a whooshing sound being sent to the sky and one of the *antu raya* said, "Don't waste fire, Jantan. We need our swords fully charge to face the Healer."

A male, who Sampurai guessed was Jantan, laughed. "We have more than enough source of lightning. This creature is filled with endless source of fire."

Sampurai could hear footsteps coming towards him. They stopped abruptly to show a pair of feet to his limited vision. "What kind of creature is he? I have never heard of his kind. Do you think he is the Healer's pet?" a female voice was heard.

"I don't mind having him as my pet. It would be great to be able to harvest fire whenever I want. Can we bring him home and keep him, Apai?" From a different side, another male made a request.

"I don't know, Son. He's awfully big," the Apai expressed his objection.

"There are four of us. We can drag him together," the son refuse to give in.

"I suppose we could," the Apai relented. "But first, we need to settle our business with the Healer. And I don't want to drag him here and there with us."

"Oh, I know! We could tie him up to a tree and leave him here for now. When we're done with the Healer, we'll come back and bring him home. How about that?" the son sounded excited.

"Tie him up with what?" the female *antu raya* asked.

"Use your head, Beragai. We are in the forest. I'm sure we can find creeping tendrils somewhere nearby," the son sounded irritated.

"We came here to find the Healer," Jantan protested.

"We have waited several centuries to find the Healer. We can wait a little longer. We can't let go of the chance to keep a fire blazing pet. Please, Uncle Jantan, this is an opportunity of a lifetime," the son pleaded.

Jantan grumbled under his breath. "How do you know for sure he won't break free while we're away?"

"Look at him! He can't even move now. We have completely drained the fire out of him."

Sampurai could hear footsteps coming fast from his behind. He gritted his teeth as a foot was jammed on to his shoulder. "See? I told you he can't move!" the son exclaimed.

"Help us find something to tie him up, Jantan. The sooner one of us finds it, the sooner we can continue looking for the Healer," the Apai said.

Jantan relented. "Fine! Let's look for something to tie him up. Hurry!"

Sampurai closed his eyes as soon as he could no longer hear any footsteps around him. He was alone on the floor bed of the forest. This was his chance. He wished against all odds that he could move his body to get away from there. He let out a silent scream of frustration when he failed. He never felt so powerless in his life. He'd rather die than becoming someone's pet!

He opened his eyes in alarm when he heard and felt a big thud next to his face. His eyes grew bigger due to excitement when he saw Mayas' face. 'Get me out of here' was a silent plea he sent to the orangutan.

In response, the orangutan showed him his fists. Then, he started to knock them together in a fast rhythm. Sampurai wanted to cry out his relief because he recognized that sound. It was the sound of rocks being knocked together. He knew what it meant.

In no time, a spark of fire was lit. Mayas hosted it on a pile of dried leaves. He kept it burning right in front of Sampurai's face.

Sampurai closed his eyes. He inhaled the smoke greedily because his life depended on it. He opened his eyes again when he felt Mayas's hand on his head. He caught the ape's dreamy eyes and blinked his eyes to signal his agreement. He knew what Mayas wanted him to do.

He closed his eyes one more time and focused all his efforts to inhale the smoke from the fire in front of him. The fire was too small to give him his original power back, but it should be enough to help him get away from there.

"Eh? Where did the fire come from? Landak! You had better come here. Quick! Look at this. He still can make fire!" Beragai's voice reappeared.

When Sampurai opened his eyes, he saw a female coming towards him. He did not know if he had gathered enough shape-shifter power in him, nevertheless, he knew he had very limited time to escape. Thus, he transformed himself into a human form.

The female let out an exclamation of surprise to see his transformation and moved backwards in haste.

Sampurai scrambled to get up, but his body weight was too heavy for his depleted power. He slipped to the ground and stayed there. He stared at the female anxiously, calculating what she would do to him and how he could protect himself from her when he was unable to move.

Fortunately for him, the female only gaped at him, completely mesmerized. She seemed to be more interested in inspecting his appearance than doing something to him.

Then, a male came into the scene. "What happened, Beragai? Why did you scream?" He followed her gaze, and he gawked at the naked body on the forest ground. "Where did he come from? What is he doing here?"

"That's your pet, Landak," Beragai said in awe. "He changed form."

"What?" Landak exclaimed. His gaze went to Sampurai once more. He pulled her behind him. "This is not right. It's the Healer playing tricks on our mind. That creature is not real."

"We harvested fire from him. Our weapons are fully charged. He must be real!" She disagreed.

"There is only one way to find out if he is real or not." He withdrew his sword. "Stay back!" he instructed her.

"Landak, don't get too near!" She grabbed his arm.

But Landak was not to be deterred. He wrenched his arm from her and took a few steps forward before he pointed his sword at Sampurai.

Sampurai lay on the forest ground, powerless to move. He knew what was coming. Every fiber of his *gerasi* survival instinct vibrated out of control, screaming the message that his life was in mortal danger, as if he did not know it. They were urging him to get out of there. They did not want to understand that he could not. He cursed his *mensia* body that refused to do his will. He had spent all his energy to transform himself into a human. He had none left to flee the scene.

The prospect of going to Sebayan did not scare him. He was a warrior. Every time he stepped into a battle, going to Sebayan was always one of the possibilities of the outcome. He had learned to live with the risk. What he could not accept was that it happened when he could not lift a muscle to defend himself. He always believed that when his time came, he would go as an aftermath of the greatest battle the world had ever witnessed - a battle like no other that every warrior on the land, above, beyond, and under talked about with envy until the end of time. Certainly not like this! Not here! He shouted the silent screams in his head. Not now!

He gritted his teeth and grudgingly prepared himself for the inevitability. He did not have time to close his eyes when he felt a gush of wind passed by and a hairy arm was wound around his waist. The next thing he knew, he was slung over a hairy shoulder at the same time as he flew upward in a swing movement. He could hear the blast of lightning hit the ground and the scream of a female down below. He realized that he missed the lightning strike in a fraction of breath. Some earth debris from the explosion hit his body on the way up. Luckily, they were the last assault he needed to bear.

Within a few intakes of breath, the rustled of trees and the chattered of animals were the only sounds he heard as Mayas swung effortlessly from tree to tree in order to take him away from the fire reapers.

KUMANG'S POINT OF ENTRY

Mystical Forest, the Land

Kumang looked up to the thin canopy of the forest trees above her head. Gerinching had successfully persuaded the trees nearby to branch out further so that their arms would meet. Because they reached out to each other, they formed a thicker layer that covered the ground from direct exposure to the sky. She hoped it was enough to lessen the *antu raya*'s ability to harvest lightning from the wet clouds. Her hands voluntarily went to touch a pair of hairpins she placed above her ears to clip her silky long hair. Each hairpin's tip was made of metal while the base of it was made of wood. They were her choice of weapon to fight the *antu raya*. She had fought a battle with them before. She knew what kind of weapon she needed. Yes, she was ready to face them now.

She directed her eyes to Sugie, who was sitting next to her legs. "We have given our best efforts to put them into a disadvantage, let's hope we can persuade them to leave without a fight breaking out in this forest." She cast her eyes around. "The trees have been so kind to help us."

She turned her head to the forest in front of her. "It is them, I guess." She smiled ruefully to Sugie. "I don't suppose Jang knows how to chase them away without sending them to Sebayan. It's not his style to use threats. He always does what he says."

She heard a male's voice saying, "We've reached another junction, Apai. Which one should we take?"

Kumang straightened her body posture. "Here they come," she muttered to herself.

Then, a different excited male voice sounded, "Look! I can see a roof of a house on the left path. That must be it! Let's go! Hurry!"

Kumang heard frantic footsteps approaching. She took her position right in the middle of the path while Sugie faithfully stationed himself next to her legs.

The first male who came into sight stopped abruptly when he saw her standing in the middle of the path. He was soon followed by two other males and a female. All of them had to stop because she blocked their path.

The male at the very front frowned at her. "Who are you? What are you doing here?" He scrutinized Kumang from top to bottom, most probably wondering what kind of creature she was since he could not detect her just like she could not detect him and his companions. He completely ignored Sugie.

Kumang smiled. "I should ask you the same question. Who are you? What are you doing here?"

He returned her smile rather reluctantly. "I am here to look for the Healer." He pointed at the rooftop behind her.

"You can't find her there." Kumang kept her smile. "I suggest that you leave."

His smile disappeared. "I should be the one who suggests that you leave. This has nothing to do with you. Don't get yourself involved."

"I am not getting myself involved in anything." Kumang's tone was still very friendly. "And you can't ask me to leave. I came here first. This was not your home when I came here, so I am entitled to claim it as mine if I wish. So once again, you can't ask me to leave. I, on the other hand, have the right to ask you to leave."

The older male at the back, touched the arm of the male in front. He said softly, "Jantan, she is right. Let's go. There's another path on the right that we can check."

Jantan pushed the hand away. He pointed at the roof in sight. "I can feel the presence of *antu raya* somewhere nearby. I know you can, too. She is here! And I am telling you, she is in that house!"

Kumang said in all honesty, "No, you are wrong. I built that roof. I can assure you that it doesn't host an *antu raya* under it."

The male's face turned red. "Look here … I don't know who…"

The only female in the group stepped forward. "Miss, I don't know who you are, but you look like you are a kind-hearted creature. Just hear me out. My name is Beragai. This is my uncle, Jantan." She touched the shoulder of the male standing in front. "We are trying to settle some family matters. That is all. Please let us do this."

Kumang's eyes widened. "Family matters?" She was worried all of a sudden. What did the young female mean?

Jantan's jaw tightened to see her face. "So, you do know her. Where is she? She is inside the house, isn't she?" he flicked his chin to the rooftop behind her.

"She is not in there. And you can't see her right now," Kumang said slowly. Half of her mind was still trying to process the meaning of the young female's statements. Did she mean that they came to settle her family matters which included the source of their animosity towards Inik Tuai? Or …

Jantan did not give her the opportunity to ponder further. "She's healing someone, isn't she?" he pressed on. "Oh, I should know. Her Mystical Forest disappeared for one reason and one reason only. She is using her power to heal someone. I ask you one more time: is she inside that house right now?"

Kumang had to ask, "Why are you looking for the Healer? Are you here to hurt her?"

"She hurt *me*!" Jantan shouted. He took one step forward while he withdrew his sword. "Let me go to her. Or I swear I'll …"

"Jantan, don't start an unnecessary fight with a creature we don't know," the older male said under his breath.

Unfortunately, Jantan was beyond reasoning. He pointed his sword at Kumang and sent out a blaze of lightning.

Kumang did not move away to avoid it. She undid her hairpins, expanded the metal parts and sucked the lightning inside them.

Jantan and his companions took a few steps back because of what she had done.

"As you can see, your lightning does not work on me. I suggest that you leave." Kumang extended her hand to indicate the direction from where they came.

Jantan's eyes narrowed. "I won't leave now that I know she is here."

329

"You can't see her without getting through me. And trust me, you can't get through me." Kumang's smile was the opposite of her threatening words.

"I don't need to get through you to see her, do I?" Jantan snorted. He moved his arm in a big circle.

Kumang raised her weapons, getting ready to receive more lightning strikes. However, none of Jantan's lightning strikes was directed at her. They went upward, grazing the top of the trees. The forest's canopy was instantly on fire. And because the trees were so close to each other, the fire went wild in an intake of breath.

"No! What are you doing to the trees?" Kumang shouted.

She realized at once that these *antu raya* were not the same kind of *antu raya* she had fought before. The ones she was fighting now were the fire reapers. She did not anticipate this, and therefore, she was not prepared for this kind of fight. Nevertheless, she was in the middle of a fight, so she had to improvise fast. Because her first priority was to save the innocent trees, she pointed her weapons up in the air and sucked the air around as much as she could. The fire became smaller in an instant.

Jantan sent more lightning strikes to the forest that went into a blaze of fire.

"Stop burning the trees!" Kumang screamed angrily. "What have they done wrong to deserve your assault?"

She became too preoccupied with trying to control the forest fire that she did not see the older *antu raya* pulled Jantan aside. She did not hear the four of them whispering to each other, pointing at the forest fire. She only noticed them when they were already at the junction. Clearly, they were heading towards the other path where Indai Tuai's house was actually located.

"Hey! Where do you think you are going?" Kumang called out to them. She made a move to stop them from going further, but she had to duck down as the four of them sent their lightning strikes towards her.

Kumang exclaimed in agony as their lightning burnt more forest. Now she had to make a choice between staying there to put out the forest fire around her and going after the *antu raya* before they reached Indai Tuai's house. Difficult as it was to ignore the groaning pain of the trees, Lulong's life was more important

330

to save.

She left the burning forest to enter the other path. She halted abruptly to see the scenery in front of her. The four *antu raya* were fighting Sugie. Her surprise was not stemmed from the thought that an orangutan like Sugie could fight four *antu raya*. It was from how Sugie deflected their lightning strikes. Orangutans were physical beings on the land. They were animals. Animals did not have the power to control lightning. Kumang's eyes widened when Sugie lifted the ground to form a round wall around the *antu raya*, trapping them inside. Did Sugie just do that? Or was it some other creature? She quickly detected her surroundings. No, there was no other shape-shifter nearby.

Sugie noticed her presence. "Don't worry, I can handle them. Go and put out the forest fire," he shouted at her.

Kumang ignored his instruction. She went to him instead. "What are you doing here, fighting with them?"

"They knew that the rooftop was only a decoy because you did not care that it was burnt down. That's why they came here. Don't worry. I'll stop them from going into the house. Go!"

"How did you do that?" She pointed at the earth wall.

"Mao, this is not the time to question ..."

A blast of lightning was heard from behind the wall as it crumbled to the ground.

"Go, Mao. Save the trees. I won't let them get to the house. I promise," Sugie pushed her aside. He punched the ground with his fists and a new wall was erected around the *antu raya*.

"I am not leaving until I know how it is possible that an orangutan like you have the power to do that?" She pointed at the new wall.

"Oh, for heaven's sake, Mao!" In a blink of an eye Keling stood in front of her. "Are you happy now? Go!"

Kumang's jaw dropped. "How could you ...? I did not detect you at all just now, but now I can. I don't understand ..."

331

When another blast was heard from behind the wall, Keling grabbed Kumang's shoulders and turned her around forcefully. "Look at the forest over there! It's burning out of control. Go and put it out before it spreads here. My explanation can wait."

Kumang had to agree with him. The forest fire was getting out of control. She ran to the junction, forcing her way through the herds of animals that were running to every direction they could possibly go.

It was not the herds that stopped her from moving forward. It was the presence of two young *antu raya*. The moment they saw her, they withdrew their swords. Kumang knew she was about to face a new battle. However, before it could start, an eagle cry was heard from above. She looked up to see it coming down to them. It landed next to her as Laja of Panggau Libau.

Using the dumbfounded reaction of the *antu raya* when they saw a man suddenly materialize out of thin air, Kumang asked Laja, "You have your water pouch with you, don't you?"

"Huh?" Laja gave her a quick glance as he withdrew his *parang nyabor*. Any *bunsu ai* whose source of power was water never went anywhere without bringing water with him. "Of course I do. Why?"

"I need you to put out the forest fire over there."

"But …"

"Please Gat, the fire has to stop before it spreads over here and burn Inik Tuai's house. And then, come back here as soon as you can."

Laja gave one last look at the young and shaken *antu raya* who now had got a grip of themselves before he nodded at Kumang. And once again, he disappeared out of sight.

This time the *antu raya* took shorter time to recover from their shock. Kumang tightened her grip on her weapons as lighting came out of the two swords pointed at her. In no time, the burning forest was filled with deafening boom of lightning strikes.

THE CONFRONTATION

"Stop fighting! I am here!"

Although Kumang could not see who came to disrupt the battle, she recognized the voice of Inik Tuai. She could not stop her fight because she did not know if her opponents would stop sending lighting strikes to her.

What happened next was that Kumang heard Keling shout, "Inik, don't come near! Stay away from the battlefield! You will get hurt."

That was when she decided to end her battle. The next time the two young *antu raya* sent more lightning strikes, she used her weapons to suck the lightning out of their swords. That was not the only thing she did, because of the force she used, their swords were taken out of their hands. The swords did a somersault in the air before they came down straight to stab the earth.

Kumang pointed her weapons at the disarmed young *antu raya* to warn them, "It ends here! No more fighting!"

Then, she ran to Keling. She saw that Inik Tuai ignored Keling for she continued entering his battlefield with Bata walking a few steps behind her.

As they came right into his battle path, Keling stopped using his power although he did not take his eyes off his opponents. He did not even acknowledge Kumang's arrival next to him.

Curiously, he was not the only one who stopped the fight. The *antu raya* also withdrew their swords. That left Inik Tuai and Bata standing in the middle of the battlefield. They stood facing the four *antu raya*, who were soon joined by the two young *antu raya* who had fought Kumang. The older *antu raya* pulled them back to stand behind him.

Inik Tuai stood with perfect poise. "I am here. This is what you want, isn't it, Jantan?"

Jantan's eyes narrowed. "Is it really you? Or are you doing one of your mind tricks to make me believe that you have the courage to face me."

"What would I gain from doing it?"

"I don't know. You've been avoiding me for centuries. Why do you want to face me now?"

"I avoided you because I don't want you to kill your own mother."

Kumang held Keling's arm unconsciously upon hearing the admission. She could feel his hand over hers in an instant.

"Don't you dare call yourself my mother! You are none of that!" Jantan spit to the ground.

"I am sorry I neglected you throughout your childhood, Jantan."

"Because you think that healing other creatures' lives is more important than taking care of your own child."

"I am a *manang*, Jantan. Healing creatures is my responsibility – given to me by the higher order of this world."

"Then you shouldn't have had a child that you didn't want to take care!"

"It was my mistake. I admit it. I was a fool with too big of a pride. I wanted to have everything. I thought I could have it all, a loving husband, an adorable child, and sick patients to heal. Sometimes life does not allow you to have it all. I could not be at two places at the same time. I couldn't nurse you while I was healing patients. I had to choose which one I wanted to do."

"Oh, you don't need to explain it to me. I know that strangers' lives are always more important to you than your own bloodline."

By then, an old male and a young male *antu raya* arrived at the scene. The old male positioned himself next to Jantan, while the young male stayed behind with the other two young *antu raya*.

"If I had ignored my patients to nurse you, they would have died. If I had ignored you to heal my patients, nobody would have died. You had your father. I am deeply sorry that you felt abandoned. I was hoping that your father loved you enough to cover for my absence."

"How could you push the blame to him? It was not his fault that I hate my own mother. He was not the one who wronged me!"

"That's not what I meant ..."

"And I'm not talking about my motherless childhood. Do you think I would complain about such trivial matter? I am talking about Rida, my daughter – your granddaughter! Your own bloodline! You chose to heal some other pathetic creature instead of saving Rida's life."

"I've told you then, and I am telling you again now. I can't heal two patients at the same time. After I finish healing a patient, I don't have extra energy to heal another one right away. It will take a few days for my healing power to come back. I am sorry Rida could not wait a few days."

"Sorry? Is that all you can say to me? You're sorry that you put priority on someone else's child over mine? Why could you not help Rida first? Then, you helped the other child!"

"I could not have saved the life of the other child if I had helped Rida first."

"Rida died because you chose to look away when she needed you!" Jantan shouted at the top of his lungs.

"Rida was not meant to survive, Jantan. I am sorry I gave you a false hope from the day she was born. It was another one of my faults. I should have let her pass on to Sebayan that day. Instead, I ..."

"You liked to add more pain to our suffering. You pushed my wife to the brink of despair."

Kumang's attention was shifted to a movement next to Keling. When she saw it was only Laja, who had come back from putting out forest fire, she gave her attention back to the scene in front of her.

335

"I thought … You see, when you came to me, asking if I could help Isah conceive, I was ecstatic that I was given a chance to do what I can do best for you and your family. I thought I was given a chance to redeem myself. I know I was not much of a wife. I'm a lousy mother. Healing is the only thing I am good at. So I wanted to use my skills to do something that meant so much to you. After Rida was born with very little chance of surviving, I still hoped that if I saved her life, you could find it in your heart to forgive me for not being there as your mother."

"Then why didn't you?" Jantan did not seem to know how to stop shouting at his mother.

"The more I attended to Rida, the more I found out that she was beyond healing. You know what happened. In the beginning I only needed to use my healing power on her once in a moon cycle. Soon, it was not enough. I had to do it twice in a cycle. Then, the frequency kept on increasing until I could not use my healing power on anyone else but her."

"You said you wanted to redeem yourself, to be a good mother for me, a good grandmother for Rida. Why couldn't you dedicate yourself to keep Rida alive? Tell me why? I'll tell you why. Because you never meant it when you said you wanted to redeem yourself!"

"A child was brought to me, Jantan. He desperately needed my help. I am a *manang*, it is my responsibility to heal! I could not turn him away."

"Stop saying that! Don't you know how hypocrite you sound? If you truly have the spirit of a *manang*, you would have saved Rida's life!"

"I could not save Rida's life. I have tried my best."

"You did not try enough! You abandoned her just the way you abandoned me!"

"I admitted that I did all the things you accused me of. I own all my mistakes. That is why I am here."

Jantan was persistently suspicious of her motive. "What kind of tricks are you playing at now? I don't believe you are willing to surrender your life to me now after you've done everything you could to keep it away from me for centuries."

"My life is not yours to take anymore, Jantan. You can't kill me now. I am dying."

"Inik!" Kumang exclaimed. She rushed forward to Inik Tuai's side. "Is this true?"

Inik Tuai patted her hand. "Your sister is all right now. I have removed the cursed memory. She is safe."

"How come you are the one who is dying?" Kumang was concerned.

"Silly girl, I had to search which memory to take out, so naturally I have seen the memory. The curse has been transferred to me now."

"Curse? What curse?" The oldest of the *antu raya* interrupted.

Inik Tuai smiled at him. "The curse from Bhiku Bunsu Petara, Ligam. She sent these creatures ..." she waved her hands to indicate the shape-shifters standing behind her, "to find me, hoping that I would heal the curse that one of them received from her. She was right. I could not turn away a patient who came to me for help."

Inik Tuai shifted her gaze to Jantan. "She is doing it for your wife, Isah. Do you see it now, Jantan? You don't need to kill your mother anymore. She is as good as dead. Isah's and Rida's deaths have been avenged. Go home."

"No, I don't believe you!" Jantan shook his head in denial. "You just want to deny me my vengeance."

"Is she telling the truth?" Ligam threw the question to Keling. "Is there a curse from Bunsu Petara?"

"She is telling the truth," Keling admitted.

"Why should I believe you?" Jantan challenged him.

"Jantan, if you insist that the only way you can feel better is to blast that lightning of yours at me, then do it," Inik Tuai said calmly.

"Mistress!" Bata voiced out her protest for the first time ever since the conversation began.

Inik Tuai turned to her. "Now, I don't want you to lift a hand to him for what he is about to do," she said sternly. She extended her warning to the shape-shifters behind Bata. "And the same thing goes to all of you."

"But Inik …" Kumang tried to reason with her.

"It is all right, Kumang. I am a dead creature. He can't kill a creature that is already dead. No matter what he will do to me, he is free from the consequences of killing his own mother. Mother Nature cannot hold him to that offense."

She turned around to Jantan. She took a few steps closer to him and nodded. "Do what you think you must do, Son."

It was probably the use of the word 'son' that incensed Jantan even more. "If you think you can trick me into forgiving you for everything you've done to ruin my life, you're wrong!" He raised his sword and pointed it at Inik Tuai's chest.

Ligam held Jantan's wrist to stop him. "Jantan, she is right. You don't need to do this. If she is under a curse, let her spend the remaining of her days tortured by it, slowly and painfully. It is a much greater punishment."

Jantan turned to his uncle. "No! I have waited for centuries for this day to come. Don't tell me to let this opportunity go!"

Inik Tuai addressed her brother-in-law. "Let him do what he feels is right, Ligam. I owe him this much. Let him go."

Ligam reluctantly let go off Jantan's hand.

Without anybody stopping him now, Jantan let out a loud war cry and lurched forward to Inik Tuai.

"Don't …" Kumang started, but Keling got hold of her and pulled her backwards with him.

"Let him, Mao. He needs to do this to move on," he whispered in her ears.

Kumang closed her eyes and hid her face in Keling's arms. She could not bear to witness what was about to happen. However, Bata's stifled scream prompted her to open her eyes. She saw how Jantan's sword had gone half-way through Inik Tuai's chest. And because he did not let go of his sword, he stood a breath away from his mother.

"Forgive me for every wrong I have done to you, Son," Inik Tuai said breathlessly.

Jantan gritted his teeth, but he could not take his eyes off his mother's.

"Have a good life from now on, free yourself from hatred." Inik Tuai clasped her hands over Jantan's and pulled it to her body causing the blade of the sword to go all the way in, right to the handle. She reached out her right arm to hug her son.

Nobody except Jantan knew what prompted him to recoil from Inik Tuai's touch. He took his sword with him to flee the scene in an intake of breath. He did not see how much damaged he had done to his mother.

It was Bata who rushed to catch the falling body of Inik Tuai before it hit the ground.

The rest of the *antu raya* looked at each other in awkward silence until Ligam signaled them to leave. Soon, all of them disappeared from sight without even bidding goodbye.

Keling, Laja, and Kumang gathered hurriedly around Bata, who was sitting on the ground with the semi-unconscious Inik Tuai in her lap.

"It's all right, it's all right, no need to panic." Bata's voice belied her own words. "It's just a flesh wound. I can heal it. No problem. It's just that she is losing too much blood too fast. I need to get her home as soon as possible."

Keling got down on one knee if front of her. "I can get her home faster than the wind," he offered.

"Please." Bata's eyes were filled with tears.

"Tell me what to do as soon as I get her there," Keling asked.

"Find Endu Gerinching, she knows what to do to stop the bleeding. I will be there as soon as I can to do the rest. Now, go! GO!"

Keling lifted Inik Tuai from Bata's lap and disappeared from sight.

HEALING THE WOUNDS

Keling had opened the door of Inik Tuai's house before Kumang, Laja, and Bata reached the house. He went out to meet them half way.

"How is Mistress?" Bata was all anxious.

"Endu Jie is taking care of her the best that she can. She needs your help," Keling told her.

"I know, I know. I'm coming," Bata ran faster and left them behind.

"How is Lulong?" was the first question Laja asked.

Keling answered him promptly, "She is all right. The procedure went smoothly, that was what Bata told Endu Jie. There should not be any complication afterwards. She is still sleeping now, resting." He travelled back to the house with Kumang and Laja.

"Is she absolutely sure that there won't be any complication afterwards?" Kumang could not forget what happened after Bata had healed Lulong.

"I don't know," Keling replied. "If you want to be sure, we can stay here for a few days to monitor her progress."

"I think we should." Kumang liked the idea.

"We might as well stay. Endu Jie said that she has asked Bata if she could help with the curse upon *mensia*," Keling added.

"Did she?" Kumang was surprised that Gerinching thought about it while she did not.

"It sounds like Bata and Endu Jie get along very well. Anyway, they talked about Inik Bunsu's curse on *mensia*. Bata said she might be able to come up with some kind of potion for those *mensia*. It will take a few days to get it ready. So, we can

340

stay here for a while until Lulong is fully healed and Bata finishes preparing the potion."

"That sounds like a good plan. We can pass the potion to Endu Rikok afterwards. She knows what to do with it. If she doesn't, I'm sure her *mensia* friend does," Kumang extended the plan.

They stopped in front of the house door, which was opened abruptly by Gerinching.

"Hi, Bata told me all of you are out here." She smiled at them. Her amusement faded when she saw Keling. She seemed baffled to find him there. And his presence reminded her of those she had expected to see. She looked around. "Where is Sampurai? And Pungga, Mayas, and Sugie?" Her eyes roamed their surroundings once more. "Are they all right?"

Kumang tilted her head to the right to indicate Keling. "This is Sugie. As you can see for yourself, he is all right."

"Eh?" Gerinching's jaw dropped. "How is it possible that you are Sugie?"

"*Batu pengerabun,*" Keling explained to her.

Gerinching's eyes widened. "Oh, the invisible rock? Did Sampurai lend it to you? No wonder we could not detect your *petara* power all this while. But why did you need the charmed rock to disguise yourself as an orangutan?"

Her innocent question switched the atmosphere into a chilling mode all of ae sudden.

Laja cleared his throat. "I want to see how Lulong is doing. Could you take me to her?" he asked Gerinching.

Gerinching was sensitive to Laja's cue. "Oh! Yes, sure! Of course." She stepped aside to let him in. "Come in, I'll take you to her." She closed the door a little bit too firmly behind her.

Kumang and Keling were left standing outside, looking at each other.

"Are you not going to say anything to explain yourself?" Kumang finally asked

341

when Keling kept quiet.

"I believe I have given you an explanation. As I recall, you told me to stop saying 'I'm sorry' over and over again." He heaved. "I don't know what you want me to say now."

"You know I'm not talking about that," Kumang hissed. "I want to know the answer to Endu Jie's question: why did you use *batu pengerabun* to disguise yourself as an orangutan?"

"I thought the answer to that question is obvious. I want to be by your side, but you told me that the sight of me gave you pain. You said you wanted to forget all about me. I respect your wish. I looked for a way so that I could always be there for you without you having to feel any pain. I remembered Jang's *batu pengerabun*. I asked him to lend it to me. I have been using it ever since."

"No wonder he looked like he had something to hide from me when I saw him in his den in Pelagus. Hah! I suppose he has known all along that Sugie is actually you in disguise. You told him your plan," Kumang did not like the thought that she had been tricked.

Keling shrugged. "I don't know if he knows that Sugie is me."

"Oh, sure he knows. Everything he said about you indicated that he knows." Kumang felt worse that Sampurai had known something that she had not.

"I never tell him. If he knows, then, I don't know how. I suppose if you ask him, he will say that his *gerasi* instinct told him."

Kumang had to suppress a smile even when she did not feel like smiling. Yeah, she knew how Sampurai always put forward his gerasi *instinct* as the justification for all his unexplainable behaviors.

"Ah, you smile. Does that mean I am forgiven?" Keling's mouth twitched.

"Forgiven for what?"

"Following you around." Keling's hope was guarded.

Kumang appeared to consider. "Tell me something. Now that I know you are Sugie, you can't pretend you are him anymore. If I tell you to go away, you will do as I say, but you will find a way to be around me, won't you?"

"Yes."

"What if I take the charmed rock away from you so that you can't use the rock to disguise yourself around me without being detected as a *petara*?"

Keling's eyebrows rose. "How are you going to do that? I won't give it to you."

Kumang took a step closer. "I *can* take it away from you, Keling."

Keling stood his ground. "I know you can, Kumang. It doesn't matter. I'll find some other means to be with you without you knowing I'm nearby."

"What other means?"

He frowned. "I'm not going to tell you."

"In that case, I'll ..." Kumang paused. "Wait, you started following me as Sugie when I met Lium and Che by Mentarang River."

"Yes."

"And every time I was on the land, you assumed Sugie's form?"

"Yes."

"So it was you who chased the clouds away when Lulu and I were in the longboat travelling towards the *mensia*'s village."

"Ah! That wasn't me. I was somewhere nearby. I saw the two of you in the longboat, but I did not do anything. I know you can get rid of rain any time of the day. I thought you did it."

"No, I did not. If I did not and you did not, who did?"

"I don't know."

"Hmm...that is curious."

Keling let silence fill the air for a while before he asked, "Any more questions?"

"Yes, I ...eh ... When I went to look for Inik Bhiku Bunsu Petara in the second layer of the sky, you did not follow me."

"I did."

"You can't go there as Sugie! He is a creature of the land. He can't go up to the sky."

"*Batu pengerabun* allows me to be anything I want. I don't have to be Sugie at all times."

Kumang was curious. "Who were you then? There was no other creature with us, or following us …not that I am aware of."

Keling only smiled at her.

"So? Who were you?"

"It's not who. It's what."

"I don't understand."

"I turned into air. It was easy to follow you around in the sky as air."

"Air? You can turn into air?"

"Naturally, as I said, the charmed rock allows me to be anything I want – dead or living things. Jang turned into air once. I stole the idea from him."

"Really?" Kumang needed more time to digest what the invisible rock could do. Then, she remembered something. "Oh, was it you who stopped the carpenter's wall from falling on my head? I felt a gush of wind passing by."

"It was me." Keling bowed slightly.

She was actually quite impressed. "I wonder …" She bit her lip when she remembered. "Were you also inside Inik Bunsu's longhouse?"

"Yes."

She swallowed. "You heard my conversation with Pungga." Her voice was a whisper.

His face did not change. "Yes."

"That means you know about my decision to leave everyone behind after Lulu has fully recovered, and she is safe in Gelong."

"Yes."

Kumang let a lengthy pause fill the air before she said, "You will let me do it, Keling of Panggau Libau."

"That is not going to happen."

"You can't stop me from going away!"

"No, I cannot and I will not stop you." He took a step closer. "But you can't get rid of me, Kumang of Panggau Libau. You'd better learn to live with the fact."

Kumang shook her head in confusion. "Didn't you listen to what I said to Pungga?"

"I said I did."

"Then, why can't you let me go? My life is cursed."

"Oh, please, what makes you think you are the only creature with a cursed life? I have to carry a much worse curse than you." He adjusted his demeanor to appear solemn. "I know that by insisting on being around you, I bring my cursed life into your life, too. I thought you knew what you got yourself into when you agreed to marry a creature like me. Correction, to be fair, you probably did not realize how much curse I carried with me before you married me. Anyhow, it's too late to change your mind. I won't let you change your mind. You might think it's not fair, but I don't care. You are stuck with me for the rest of your life. And that's that."

"How could you still want me to be around you, knowing that I am the cause of the deaths of your wife and child?"

"Ah, that's where you are wrong. They did not die because of what you did. They died because of what I did."

"What did you do?"

"Do you remember when Jang killed Si Ganti of Bukit Bangkai? I sent him to the moon to stay with Inik Andan until we could find a solution to the mess he was in."

Kumang nodded. "Inik Andan agreed to help with a condition."

"That I agreed to her request. There would be a day when I was required to be at two places at one time to save the lives of my family. She asked me to promise that I would choose to save Jang and forsake the other."

"I remember. You were worried it would be Endu Rikok's life you had to forsake."

"I truly believed it was her life that Inik Andan was talking about at the time. I was wrong. That was not the choice I had to make. So when that unfortunate day came, I went to save Jang. I left my wife and my unborn child behind. They died in my absence."

"I am sorry."

"I am not." His voice was void of any emotion.

"Come again?" That was not a statement she expected from him.

"I am relieved they died that day."

Kumang could only stare at him in shock.

"Yes, you heard me right. I am glad it was them. I am happy it was not your life I had to forsake, or Indai's, or Wai's, or Endu's. I would not know how I could go on living if in order to save Jang I had to sacrifice one of you. I would not know how I could live with myself if I had to sacrifice Jang to save one of you. That is the reason I am glad the lives that I lost were the lives of some *mensia* I just got to know."

"You don't mean that." Kumang did not believe him. What he had said was awful.

"I do. From the bottom of my heart, I do." His laugh sounded more like a cry. "This is the kind of creature you have as a husband, Kumang. A creature who married a woman out of pity because she was the one who nursed him back from the brink of death. A creature who gave the woman a child and then abandoned them when they needed him the most. A creature who was glad that they sacrificed their lives so that those he truly cared about could live." He diverted his eyes away from hers.

And once again, Kumang saw the deep despair in him that she often observed after he had come back home from his battle with Apai Ribai. Ever since she found out about what had happened to his *mensia* wife and child, she thought he suffered because he had loved them so much that he could not bear the pain of losing them. She was wrong. He was broken inside for feeling grateful that they were the ones who ended up dead to fulfill a promise he had made.

She did not know what to say or what to do other than staring at him. She could not imagine what it felt like to be him.

"This is the kind of life I have, Kumang. I did not ask for my life to be like this, but this is the one given to me. Oh, I'm not blaming anyone for the decisions that I've made in the past. Like in this case, I chose to save Jang. I gave my word to Inik Andan on my own free will. Nobody forced me to choose him. But why did I have to be in a situation where I had to choose who lived and who died? That was not supposed to be my choice to make. The choice was forced upon me anyway. I tried to make the best decisions upon the worse choices given to me. No matter what I had decided, it would have been the wrong choice."

"Nobody blames you," Kumang finally said something. She bit her lip. That was not true. She blamed him. She blamed him when she should have eased his pain. She should have been one of his pillars of support, but she was more engrossed in her own insecurity over her childless state rather than lessening his burden.

"Nobody needs to blame me. I still have my conscience." Keling's voice was full of turmoil. "Sometimes I think that is exactly what life wants, for me to lose it. It kept hitting me with incidents that tore my soul apart. I feel like I am fighting a losing battle."

Kumang decided right there that it was time she stopped feeling sorry for herself. "We will not let it win, will we? You are right. This is the life given to me – to us. It doesn't always make sense. We don't always like how it turns out. Who am I kidding? I hate some of the things I have to face. But we still have a say in it, by making a decision that …" she grimaced, "… is more bearable to carry forward."

Keling took her hands in his. "That's why I can't let you go. I'm sorry I drag you into my wretched life, but you promised you would be a part of it by agreeing to marry me. You can't back out now. I can't let you. I won't let you. I need you to keep my conscience alive. I know it is very selfish of me to even ask you to share this kind of life, and heavens know I have tried to keep you out of it as much as possible…"

"But I don't want you to keep me out of it. That is our problem, Watt. You are trying so hard to keep me out from where I have always wanted to be."

"I'm afraid you will hate me if I let you enter my life entirely -- to know what I have done, to hear all the horrific decisions that I have made."

Kumang shook his hands. "This is no longer your life, nor mine. This is our life. We are supposed to share it, the good and the bad. But you keep making me feel that you don't want to share yours with me."

"Excuse me, may I remind you that you were the one who did not want to share your cursed life with me."

She could continue arguing with him on that subject, but she decided to let it go for now. "Let's make a deal. If you are willing to share my cursed life, I'll share yours."

"Deal!" Keling pulled her into his embrace. When he finally put a distance between them so that he could gaze into her eyes, he smiled. "Does this mean you are not leaving Panggau Libau?"

"I …"

A loud cough was heard in the background. They let go of each other the moment their eyes found Pungga standing nearby.

"Dom! Good to see you're all right," Keling greeted him. Pungga's face alarmed him in an instant. "What is the matter? Something happened?"

"Jang is …"

"Did something happen to him?" Keling walked over to Pungga. "Tsk! Of course, why didn't I think of it! They are *antu raya api*. What did they do to him?"

"He is not wounded, don't worry," Pungga quickly calmed him down. "But he is …"

"Dom!" Laja called out from the opened door. "I was wondering who was coming."

"Where is he?" Keling asked Pungga.

"Mayas is with him. He wants to take Jang back to our den in Pelagus, but first …"

"Why does Mayas need to take him? Is Jang wounded?" Laja left the door to approach Pungga.

Pungga had to repeat his reassurance. "He is not wounded. It's just that the *antu raya* harvested his shape-shifter power. He is completely helpless now. He doesn't even have the energy to stand up."

"Bring him here. We've got a *manang* who can nurse him back to health," Kumang suggested.

"I told him that. He refused. He insisted that he's not wounded. He doesn't want a *manang*," Pungga explained.

"So why are you here? Oh, you want to tell us not to worry about him?" Kumang asked.

"Jang asked me to fetch Endu G. He doesn't want to leave her behind."

"Tsk! She is safer here with us than with him when he is wounded like that. What was he thinking?" Laja argued.

"He is not wounded!" was the unison response he got.

Laja chuckled. "All right! All right! He is not wounded." He asked Keling, "Now what do we do?"

"Go inside and fetch Endu Jie, Dom. I'll go with the two of you to send him back to your den," Keling instructed Pungga.

Laja stepped aside to let Pungga pass by.

"I suppose you want to stay here with Lulong until she is fully healed?" Keling asked Laja, who had turned half-way to follow Pungga.

Laja was taken aback by the question. He froze on the spot as he grappled to

349

find words to say.

"I would feel much better to know that you stay here with Mao and Lulong while Dom and I take care of Jang." Keling helped him make up his mind.

"All right." Laja nodded. He hesitated further before he walked towards the house.

Kumang waited until Laja went inside. "You could have been more delicate in asking him the question," she chided Keling. "I can tell that he was embarrassed."

"Oh, come now, Igat and I don't need to beat about the bush. Did he not come here solely for her? Am I wrong to conclude that he wants to stay here until he knows for sure that she is all right? I would if I were him. Wouldn't it be heartless of me to take him away from the very reason he came here in the first place?"

Kumang stared hard at the closed door. "To tell you the truth, I don't know what is really going on between the two of them." She had always thought that Lulong preferred Sampurai to Laja. However, having seen how Lulong behaved towards Laja in Inik Tuai's house, she was not so sure anymore.

Keling patted her cheek affectionately. "I suggest you stay here with them to get to the bottom of it."

She smiled at him. "Give *batu pengerabun* back to Jang. You don't need it to hide from me anymore."

Keling laughed softly. "Oh, I don't know. I might keep it, just in case you change your mind."

"I won't change my mind." Kumang reassured him. "I'll wait for you here. Now, go to him. Return his precious charmed rock to him. Then, come back to me as soon as you can."

Keling looked past her as the door was opened one more time. "Are you ready to go now, Dom? Endu? All right, let's go." He returned his attention to Kumang one last time. "I'll be back before you have the chance to miss me."

THE POTION FOR THE CURSE

Ezra scanned the forest around him. "Are you sure it is safe to talk here?" His eyes stopped at the longhouse up on the hill.

"It is safe," Adam assured him.

"You told me over the phone that you've got something to tell me?" Ezra shifted his eyes from Adam to Imah. "I hope you're not here to say you won't help me because you lost the *pua* I gave you."

"We have found a way to help your family from the reoccurring nightmares." Adam offered a bottle full of liquid to him.

Ezra inspected the bottle with Jack Daniel's label on it. "I take it that this is not an ordinary *tuak*?" he commented on the yellowish substance inside.

"The content of the bottle is not our rice wine. It is a potion brewed by the best *manang* we know who is specialized in this kind of problem," Imah explained.

Ezra took another look at the content of the bottle. "What do they need to do? Drink it? How much?"

"A small glass will do. Each of them only needs to drink it once. I think I need to mention that it may not work," Imah warned him.

Ezra widened his eyes. "You're giving me a medicine that might not work?"

"Nobody, not even the best of our *manang*, has control over someone's mind. It has never been designed that way from the beginning of time. We have our own free will. We choose to remember what we want to remember."

"I don't quite follow what you're trying to tell me."

"The curse works on the premise that the design contains a secret of the universe that we, mere mortals, are not allowed to know. As long as the people

351

who have seen the *pua* are willing to forget about what they've seen in the *pua kumbu*, the potion will work just fine."

"You mean they need to forget the day Daniel took them to the preview of the exhibition?" Ezra asked for clarification.

"Not necessarily the whole day. They just need to forget about the design of the *pua kumbu*," Imah clarified.

Ezra seemed to ponder on the possibility. "I don't think that will be a problem."

"I don't think so, too." Imah's smile was filled with confidence. "I don't mean to belittle your family, but I don't think they understand what they have seen in the cursed *pua kumbu*. As far as they are concerned, they saw a beautiful pattern, and nothing more. I am quite confident that all of them will be all right after they drink the potion."

"That's good." Ezra was relief. "And the *pua kumbu*?" he asked.

"It is in a safe place. Nobody will see it now." Imah gauged his expression. "Why? Do you want it back?"

"Nope, I am more than sure that I don't want to see it, or hear about it for as long as I live." Ezra was very sure.

"Now then, if that is the case, our deal is done." Imah smiled at Ezra.

"Done? No way. What about my father? You promised me you would get him out of his coma in return of me giving you the cursed *pua kumbu*."

Imah exchanged looks with Adam.

"Ezra, we can't do anything about your father," Adam broke the news.

"You said you can bring his soul back from ... what is it you call that place? ... oh, I don't care where it is... you said you can return his soul to his body!" Ezra insisted.

"Your father had an accident. He is in a coma because of his physical injuries. His condition was not caused by spiritual creatures. His soul is not in their hands. We can't get it back from them if they don't have it in the first place,"

Adam tried to reason with him.

"So what do I do to wake him now?" Ezra wailed.

"I'm sorry we really can't help." Adam touched his shoulder. "Your best chance is the doctors in the hospital."

"They can't do anything for him. He's been there for years without being able to move a muscle. I don't know if he is still here with us or not."

"Maybe it is time you consider letting him go to the next life," Imah said gently.

Upon Ezra's glare she continued, "I know it is a cruel thing for me to say, but you need to face the truth. If the doctors said they can't help him anymore ..."

"No, I can't accept it. I won't accept it. The doctors may not know how to help now, but modern medicine makes a new breakthrough every day. One day they will find a way to wake him. I will wait. I can afford to wait."

"I hope you'll get your wish one day." Adam sounded sincere.

"For now, try to find comfort in having the rest of your family safe and sound by your side. Give the potion to them as soon as possible," Imah added.

Ezra tightened his hold on the bottle.

Imah gave him a comforting smile. "Tomorrow is another day. Who knows what it will bring. It may offer us something that today cannot."

EPILOGUE

THE BLOOD MOON

THE CHAMBAIS

Kuching, the Land

"Where is my camera?" Elle turned the cushions of the sofa upside down. "Come on, where is it when I need it the most? I put it here. I only have a few seconds to capture the eclipse, and it decides to go missing on me now," she complained.

"Why don't you use your phone? It's the same thing." Standing under the door frame of their mansion, Ezra tried to pacify his sister.

"It's not the same thing. This is a super blue blood moon, Ezra. This is a lunar eclipse which occurs at the second full moon in a month. On top of that, it is the nearest the moon can be to the earth. How rare is this! The last time it happened was 150 years ago. You can't capture a rare phenomenon like this with a camera phone. My camera has special lenses and … oh, what do you know about photography," Elle continued grumbling. She straightened her posture to scream at the kitchen, "Minaaaaaahhhhh!!! Where is my camera bag? Find it and bring it to me. HURRY!!!" She ran to the middle of the vast garden and started to aim her phone at the moon.

Ezra walked towards his mother, Elsa, who was sitting on a couch in the big veranda of their mansion. He sat next to her. "She spent a fortune to buy that phone, and she said the camera is not good enough. She will ask you for more money to buy a more sophisticated phone after this."

Elsa smiled at her daughter, who was busy pacing the garden, looking for the perfect angle to take pictures of the moon. "It is all right. We have her back. That is all that matters, isn't it?"

Ezra patted his mother's hand. "I am glad I have you and Elle back, Mom." He leaned over to her. "You don't have any trace of your nightmares, do you?"

She shook her head firmly. "I have none of them. I don't even remember what they were about or even how it felt. I only remember that I used to have nightmares. Elle told me the same thing. According to Thea, she and Daniel's family have lost the nightmares too."

"But not Daniel?"

"Daniel..." Elsa hesitated. "He had another dream the other night. He said it was a different kind of dream. He could actually remember what it was about."

"Oh? What was it about?"

"He said he met a beautiful woman who warned him not to approach any of the weavers of Skrang to buy sacred *pua kumbu* from them and then sell them to the highest bidders or else ... something along that line."

Ezra frowned. "Will he listen to the warning?"

"Because of a dream? Daniel? You know what he is like! Thea said he woke up feeling frightened in the middle of the night. But as soon as daylight broke, he completely forgot about his fear. Thea is worried that he is not fully recovered from his nightmares."

"Things certainly did not turn out well for him lately." Ezra took a sip of the wine from the glass he held in his hand.

Elsa poured more wine inside her glass. "Are you talking about his last exhibition? Oh well, it was unfortunate that he lost the master piece at the last minute like that. But they had other collections that were equally beautiful. I'd say it went quite well. The turn up was good. People were impressed with the arts. The newspapers wrote good reviews. The result of the auction was also quite decent. I admit that it might have been better had the master piece been there. "

"That is not his biggest lost. I heard the weaver also died, that means he lost his primary source of getting master pieces for his exhibition."

"It is a pity that she died. She was still very young. They said she was completely heartbroken over the loss of her husband and his grandmother within a span of weeks." Elsa took her time to enjoy her wine before she continued, "I don't want to sound heartless, but as far as the exhibition is concerned, finding a new Master Weaver should not be a problem. I'm sure Skrang have more than enough Master Weavers who can replace her."

"I'm not so sure about that, Mom. I heard that there were rumors circling around the longhouses in Skrang that the series of death in Lubok Sawo longhouse was because they have angered the spirits by selling the sacred *pua kumbu*. I don't think many dare to repeat the same mistake, at least for the time being. Ah, you know these people. They are still superstitious deep inside although they don't want to admit it."

"They will come to their senses soon enough. In the meantime, I am worried about Daniel's health."

"My friends have already warned me that the medicine works differently for each of you. Everyone's body is different. They even said that they were not sure it would work at all with any of you. But look at you now." Ezra's eyes roamed his mother's face. He squished her hand. "I'm glad it worked out perfectly for you and Elle."

Elsa smiled at him before she aimed her eyes to the sky. "I wish your Daddy was here with us to see the eclipse." Her eyes went misty. "Or to be here to share every little thing of our life. I miss him so much."

"So do I, Mom." Ezra pulled his hand away from her.

"Can't they do something for him?"

"They?" Ezra shifted his eyes to her face. How he dreaded to see the hope he found there.

"Your friends, who gave you the medicine to cure us of those dreadful nightmares, can't they do something for your Daddy?"

"Daddy's case is different, Mom," he said evasively.

"I know. Still, can't they do something for him?"

"They said they will see what they can do. It may take some time for them to figure out what to do. And it may not work."

356

"But *can* they do something for him? They can try, can't they? Didn't they tell you that the medicine might not work for us? But it did. It fully healed me, Elle and Thea. Whatever they have in mind might work for your Daddy, even if his chances are slim."

"I thought you don't believe what Daddy believes, Mom." He tried to put her off.

"I don't. But if they can bring him back to us, how can I say no to them? I'll do anything to have him back. I am willing to …" Elsa hesitated, "… ignore the differences in our beliefs for once. Money is not a problem, have you told them that?"

"I have, Mom, I have." He did not want to tell her what Adam had told him - that they could not do anything for his father. Imah even had suggested that the best thing for them to do was to let his father go to the next life.

He inhaled deep before he faced her again. "What are the odds that we can see a super moon, a blue moon, and a blood moon in one appearance? But here we are, witnessing it." He spread his arm to the sky. "I don't see why Daddy can't come out of his coma even if his chance is a billion to one." He patted her hand fondly. "You leave it to me. I'll make sure they keep trying until they find a way to bring Daddy back to us."

TANSANG KENYALANG LONGHOUSE

The Second Layer of the Sky

"It has begun." Singalang Burong stared at the blood moon. His hands braced against the window's frame.

"But they are so not ready for this!" Ketupong, his eldest son-in-law, fretted from behind him.

"Does it matter if they are ready or not? It is happening," Embuas, another son-in-law, stated firmly.

"Should we give them a warning, Apai?" Pangkas, another son-in-law, asked for advice from the nearby window.

"We have warned them for centuries that it is coming. What did they do to our warnings? They ignored us. They totally ignored us. They turned their backs on us. There is nothing more we can do for them." Kelabu Papau, another son-in-law, shrugged.

Singalang Burong caressed his long eyebrow. "I regretfully have to agree with you, Pau. There is nothing we can do for them." He turned around to his guest. "I am very sorry that we have ignored your presence, Niram. Let's have a seat. Come," he extended his hand to usher his guest to the center of the *ruai*. "Now, what can I do for you?"

Raja Niram sat with his legs crossed on the floor of the *ruai* to face his hosts. He stated the reason for his visit in his usual grim face, "I am afraid I came here only to bring you more bad news, Lang."

As long as Singalang Burong could recall, Raja Niram never brought good news. After all, what good news could the Lord of the Underworld give? He smiled indulgently, nevertheless. "Oh? You mean in addition to the appearance of the blood moon? Has something bad happened?"

Raja Niram nodded. "Sebayan experienced a break-in." He gritted his teeth when he admitted the atrocity that had happened under his watch.

The *ruai* of Tansang Kenyalang was instantly filled with murmurs.

"Who wanted to break into Sebayan? Do you mean that they voluntarily sent themselves there without you having fetched them? Just accept them and keep them there. I thought you reserve a special space for these lost souls," Nendak, a resident of Tansang Kenyalang, pointed out.

Raja Niram frowned at Nendak's obvious mistake. "That was not what happened in this case. We have received that kind of souls on regular basis. That is not a problem at all. We know what to do with them. No, this was something totally different. A soul entered Sebayan without using the usual route. And it did not come to stay."

"What did it want?" Singalang Burong was curious.

Raja Niram clasped his hands into fists. "It wanted to take a soul from Sebayan and brought it back to the land of the living." He paused before he added gravely, "Unfortunately, it succeeded."

"In other words, you have a breach of security in Sebayan. That's the bad news you came all the way to tell me?" Singalang Burong still could not guess why Raja Niram came to see him to report this incident. Raja Niram held full authority over Sebayan. He did not need to report to Singalang Burong about a glitch of security that happened there.

"That is not the bad news."

"Then, what is?"

"After we realized what had happened, we recounted every soul in Sebayan to find out who was missing, and this is when the bad news came from..."

"Let me guess, you lost more souls than just the one intended to be snatched out of Sebayan?" Singalang Burong asked with a twinkle in his eyes. The incident must have created a big dent in Raja Niram's ego.

"Yes, we lost a few souls." The admission came with great reluctant.

'A few', eh? Singalang Burong peered from below his thick eyebrows. Knowing Raja Niram well, he would not be surprised if the number was actually higher than what could be classified as 'a few'. He put his elbows on his knees. "So now you have a number of fugitives in the realms of the living." He stroked his long white beard. "Hmmm... I can see how it is a problem. Are you here to ask for our help to rally them back to Sebayan as soon as possible? Let's see, I suppose we can arrange ..."

"I haven't told you the bad news."

"Oh? There's more to it?"

"You see, one of the souls that we found missing is ..." Raja Niram swallowed hard.

Singalang Burong's hand stopped stroking his beard. "Yes, Niram? Whose soul is it?"

"Nising." Raja Niram bent his head in defeat. "I am sorry, Lang. I really did not see it coming. Unfortunately, there it is now. We've lost Nising to the realms of the living."

There was an instant hush in the *ruai* of Tansang Kenyalang, following Raja Niram's revelation.

Singalang Burong straightened his back. His eyes involuntarily went to the blood moon outside the window.

This was going to be an apocalypse of an epic proportion.

THE HEALER AND BATA

"Stop staring at the moon, Bata." The Healer placed her hand on Bata's shoulder. "It won't change color no matter how hard you will it."

Bata shifted her sitting position to give more space for the Healer to sit next to her. "Are you all right, Mistress?" she asked carefully.

"I'm fine, Bata. You have more than enough *manang* skills to heal a flesh wound like this." The Healer touched her wound gently.

Bata bit her lip before she continued, "I was asking about how you are feeling, considering what just happened between you and your son."

The Healer winced as if her wound suddenly gave her a piecing pain. "I wish I could make him forgive me, but I suppose my trespasses were too great according to him. If only he could just let go of his anger and find a way to start a new life so that he can be happy again, I would be more than grateful to Mother Nature. Sadly, there are some things we cannot change no matter how much we wish it, Bata, like the blood moon over there." She pointed to the sky.

Bata turned to her Mistress. "Wouldn't it be great if we could?"

The Healer smiled. "Take comfort in the fact that we have done all we could when it comes to this coming apocalypse."

"But Nuing did not survive! Our efforts went in vain. You sacrificed the life of your own granddaughter for nothing!"

"Oh, he did survive, Bata. I have no doubt about it."

"But she said ... they both said they didn't know anyone called Nuing in Panggau Libau. How can you say that he survived?"

"I went inside her head, Bata. I saw all her memories. And they are full of him. I suspect that is the real reason she was so adamant that she did not want to use the charm of the Queen of Water Spirit. She did not want to lose those memories."

361

"Does that mean … she lied? Both of them lied to us?"

"No, they really don't know anyone called Nuing." The Healer smiled at Bata's incomprehensive stare. "He is using a different name now."

Bata's face lit up. "I see. They gave him a new name."

"The best way to start a new life is to give him a new identity, so that he could grow up to be someone new, free from his past and all the dreadful hopes they imposed on him."

"That is true. Hmmm … Si Gundi was very resourceful." Bata asked with curiosity, "How is Nuing now? Has he changed much?"

"I must say that he still has that boyish charm about him that made you fell for him in the first place, Bata."

Bata grinned sheepishly. "But he really was the most adorable little boy I have ever met. The way he smiled at me simply melted my heart. Are you saying that he still looks like that?"

"Ah, he is no longer the innocent chubby boy we knew then. He is all grown up now. Life has toughened him up. He looks different."

"Then, how did you recognize him?"

Now it was the Healer's turn to look for the blood moon. She stared at it in silence for quite a while until Bata thought she would not get an answer to her question. When the answer was given, it came in a mere whisper:

"He looks exactly like his father."

LIUM

The blood moon had come! It could only mean one thing. The apocalypse was approaching soon.

He did not have much time. He had to work faster to eliminate all the potential boys who would destroy the world.

Only five boys remained out of the original seven. He knew who they were. The fastest course of action was to exterminate the boy from Panggau Libau. He knew where and how to find him.

He grimaced as soon as he remembered his promise to Pungga that he would spare the boy from Panggau Libau for last. As much as he wanted to go after him at once, a promise was a promise. He never went back on his word.

Lulong's description regarding the apocalypse only served to confuse him. It did not fit into the information he had already known. He put so much effort to know what was woven in the *pua kumbu*. It turned out to be a waste of time.

His eyes narrowed at the thought that Lulong might have lied to him. But why would she have done it? He had given her a lengthy explanation about the danger this boy posed to their world. He was convinced that she fully understood him. Was she trying to protect someone? Who? The boy from Panggau Libau? It was so obvious to him that she was shaken to the core when she saw the design on the *pua*. Did she recognize something, or – to be precise - someone, that she did not expect to see there? Still, why would she want to protect a boy who could destroy them? She should be glad that he, Lium, was willing to risk his life to save them from this boy. No, she could not have lied to him. It did not make sense at all if she had.

He shook his head to discard the thought of the useless *pua kumbu*. He'd better focus his efforts on his original plans. He would hunt the boys one by one. Now, who was next in his list?

He was in a better position to do it now. His stunt to stop Sampurai and Pungga from fighting the crocodiles of Batang Lupar was made known to Simalungun, who now treated him with respect. Simalungun had the biggest crocodile army in the water sheds of the land. He could use them to hunt the rest of the boys. It was worth losing Cherurai after all.

He fixed his eyes to the blood moon again. He could stop the apocalypse from happening. He could save this world.

RIBAI

Ribai stared at the blood moon from the edge of a cliff. The sign of an apocalypse - the end of an era – had appeared. He thought of his father and his obsession about saving the world from the boy who would destroy it. He wondered if his father had been with him at the moment, would he have been happy to know that his prediction was right all along.

But then again, it could be just an end to a much smaller era. The era of the crocodile kingdom that he inherited from his father perhaps? His jaw tightened. His father was a much bigger figure than he was, he acknowledged without bitterness. Ever since his father was fatally wounded and, thus, was not able to perform his duty as the King of Baya, he – Ribai – had stepped up to fill the vacant role.

Not every crocodile from all the water tributaries accepted his new reign, especially those who thought they were more senior in rank than he. Simalungun, in particular, who ruled over the biggest population of crocodiles in the water sheds of the land, had shown signs that he believed he was more suited for the role than Ribai.

The random reports he had been getting from Lium about Simalungun's activities indicated that he was preparing for something big although Lium could not say what it was. Without solid evidence, he could not raid Simalungun's territory. It would mean starting an unnecessary war, asking brothers to fight against brothers. That would be wrong. On the other hand, if he waited until he had something concrete about Simalungun's plan, it could be too late for him to save his father's kingdom.

Ribai massaged the back of his neck. He really wished his father had been there with him. This issue would not have started in the first place.

He was too preoccupied with his troubles that he did not hear the frantic footsteps approaching him. Nevertheless, Guang's pitchy voice managed to penetrate his deep thoughts.

"My King ..." Guang had to stop talking to inhale more breath. He panted heavily as the result of running uphill.

365

Ribai closed his eyes in irritation. Had he not told them that he did not want to be disturbed at this moment? Why couldn't they obey him on a simple command like this? Did he not possess enough authority to have his order followed? Guang would have never dared to even think of disobeying his Apai. No wonder Simalungun thought that he was a soft target.

"My King ..." Guang tried again.

"Did I not tell you that I do not want to be disturbed?" He turned around to bark at Guang, who retreated a few steps back upon receiving his fierce glare.

"But ... but ... my King, you said ..."

"What did I say? I said do not disturb me! Which part of my instruction that you do not understand?"

Guang gulped to see Ribai's face turn as red as the moon. "Unless ..., my King, you said 'unless' ..."

Ribai frowned. Had Simalungun come to raid his territory? He could not have! Lium would have given him a warning. Had Lium betrayed him? "Unless what, Guang? Speak up!"

"It's the King of Baya ... I mean ... your father, my King."

Ribai was instantly on his feet. "What happened to my father?" He started running down the hill with Guang tailing him closely. "Has his condition gone worse?"

"He opened his eyes," Guang said breathlessly. He nodded vigorously at Ribai, who stopped running to gape at him as if he had heard him wrong.

"Yes, my King. Your father has regained consciousness."

KELING AND KUMANG

Keling and Kumang stood hand in hand in front of two mounds of earth.

"Are you all right?" Kumang used her free hand to caress his arm.

"Not really, but I have hope I will be one day." Keling smiled ruefully at her.

Kumang got down on her knees in front of the graves. She adjusted the positioning of the flowers Keling placed on top of the bigger mound. "Thank you for taking care of him when I was not here to do that for him. Rest in peace, Wai. Don't you worry about him. I will take good care of him from now on," she mouthed the words to the silent grave.

She stood up and went closer to Keling. "Are you sure the cursed *pua* is safe here with them?" she whispered in his ear.

Keling nodded. "Nobody will find it. The curse of the Weaver Goddess ends here," he whispered back to her.

"I am perfectly content that Lulong is fully healed. She has never shown any signs of disturbed memory or something similar to that since the day Inik Tuai extracted the cursed memory. The curse of Inik Bhiku Bunsu Petara has truly ended." Kumang looked up to the sky to find the moon. "Unfortunately, it doesn't stop the apocalypse from coming, does it? It is really coming. What Tenang wove in her *pua kumbu* will come true. There is a boy out there who is going to destroy our world."

Keling scowled. "I don't think it can be avoided now. The universe never lies to us. Yes, I'm afraid the end of an era is upon us."

"It might not be a bad idea," Kumang tried to find something cheerful to say. She continued with an explanation to answer Keling's silent question, "Every time an era finishes, a new era will start. That is how it has always been since the world began." She smiled at him. "Then, we can start a new life."

He smiled back at her. "I'd like that idea."

Kumang noticed how he forced himself to smile. He was too bogged down with worry to smile. She wondered why. The safety of the world had never been her husband's concern.

"What is it, Watt? What is troubling you?" she asked softly. It could not be the apocalypse.

He turned away from her.

"Is there something you did not tell me? You promised me that you would share your life with me." The ache in her heart came back.

When he turned to her again, she knew that was exactly what it was: another secret. She groaned silently. Not again. What was it now? Another wife? Another child? How much more of these could she bear?

"No, no, it's not what you think," he hurriedly said upon seeing her devastated face. "It has nothing to do with us. None whatsoever. It's ..." Once again words failed him.

"What is it?" If it was not about them, then there was only one other thing that concerned him: the safety of his family members. Who was it this time? Which sibling?

"When I went to confront Apai Ribai for killing Apai ..." He gulped.

"Yes?" she prompted because he stopped.

"I asked him ... I demanded that he explain himself for what he had done. I forced him to tell me why brothers had to kill each other."

"Did he explain?" Kumang's mind went to the day she confronted Lium by Kayan River. She remembered what Ribai told her. She bit her lip. She was not going to hear something good.

"He said it was because Panggau Libau was harboring the boy who will destroy the world. Apai had known about it and concealed it from the rest of us. Apai Ribai asked Apai to exterminate the boy. And Apai refused."

"Of course he refused! He had to! It would have been wrong of him to punish a boy who had done nothing to hurt our world."

"Apai Ribai believed the boy had to be stopped before he had the chance to destroy our world," Keling continued. "For the sake of so many millions lives in our world, losing one innocent life was justified. But Apai refused to sacrifice the boy. Apai Ribai wanted to tell the rest of us what he had learned about the boy and let us decide what to do. Apai forbade him to tell anyone in Panggau Libau. Because Apai Ribai insisted on telling everyone in Panggau Libau about what he knew, they fought until one of them died. Apai Sabit supported Apai Ribai. Apai Laja agreed with Apai. They, too, fought until one of them died."

Kumang recalled Tenang's description of the cursed *pua kumbu*. "Did he tell you who he thought the boy is?" She believed she could guess.

The troubled look he gave her confirmed her suspicion. She did not want to force him to say something he did not want to accept as the truth. She took his hands in hers. "Apai Ribai is wrong! You know that, don't you? Your Apai did the right thing by protecting an innocent boy."

"Of course Apai Ribai is wrong. But if he could come up with that conclusion based on bits and pieces of random information, he can't be the only one. There are many others in Panggau Libau who knew what he knew. What if they also think like him? What if they start to demand…"

Kumang put her hand on his mouth. She did not have the heart to let him say it. "Stop. Don't start making wild assumptions. We can spend a lifetime coming up with new ones and found out that we worry over nothing in the end."

"It is a possibility that I have to be prepared for," he argued.

She agreed with him. She did not see how it could be avoided. She knew what it would mean to Panggau Libau and its residents. She stared at his handsome but troubled face. How could she leave him to face this alone? "We will deal with it when the time comes, when it actually comes, but not before."

He could crack a smile now. "We? Are you coming home with me?"

"Yes, I am." She had to find the courage to stay with him, no matter how painful it was going to be. "Have you told anyone about this?"

He shook his head.

"You really ought to change this habit of keeping things to yourself."

"I can't tell Indai what Apai Ribai said to me. It would break her heart to irreparable pieces. I meant to tell you everything that went on during and after my battle with Apai Ribai. But somehow we got to talk about the story of how my life was after I was wounded." His eyes went to the graves. "Then you …"

369

She was so hurt by his admission that he had a wife and a child on the land that she had not given him the chance to tell her anything else. She felt so guilty that she had left him to carry this heavy burden alone.

"Promise me that you will never leave me again. I can't get through this alone. I need you to stand by me through this," he pleaded. "I know I am asking too much from you, but I just can't ..."

"I will stand by you through it all. We will face this together," she solemnly promised.

He pulled her into his embrace. He stared at the blood moon with heavy heart. The day would come soon when he also had to face the choices that his late Apai had faced. His late Apai had made his choice and paid for it with his life.

"Hey!" Kumang placed her hand on his cheek. "We will survive this. All of us will survive this. No more innocent life needs to be sacrificed." Her gaze went to the graves.

Keling's eyes followed hers. "No, no more innocent life needs to be sacrificed." He forced himself to smile at her before he looked at the moon again. He knew what his choice would be when the time came. He knew it without a shadow of doubt. He would stand by it. He tightened his hold on Kumang. No more innocent life needed to be sacrificed, he vowed, no matter what it would cost him. He closed his eyes. He knew just how much his decision would cost him.

"We will ride this storm together, Watt. As long as we have each other, we will get through this." He heard Kumang whispered in his ear.

He opened his eyes to look at the blood moon one more time. In the end, all that mattered to him was that he had done all he could for those he loved. He did not care much about what would happen to him as the result. As long as he could keep them safe, he would not ask for anything more from this life.

ABOUT THE AUTHOR

Oktavia Nurtjahja first went to Borneo Island in 2001 to work in Sarawak where she got to know the people of the land and the rainforest. She met and married Keling, who introduced her to the world of Iban tradition, mythology, and legends. She is now a stay-at-home mom, known by many as *Indai* Sampurai, or mother of Sampurai.

She writes the backstage stories of her books in her blog - *The Return of Panggau Warriors* (www.tropaws.wordpress.com)

Other books of the Series:

When Lightning Strikes

Land of the Giants

Crocodile Tears

The Quest for the Petara

Made in the USA
Middletown, DE
30 December 2021

57355314R00205